INVISIBLE STREETS

ALSO BY TOBY BALL

Scorch City
The Vaults

INVISIBLE STREETS

A THRILLER

TOBY BALL

WITHDRAWN

THE OVERLOOK PRESS
NEW YORK, NY

This edition first published in hardcover in the United States in 2014 by
The Overlook Press, Peter Mayer Publishers, Inc.

141 Wooster Street
New York, NY 10012
www.overlookpress.com

For bulk and special sales, please contact sales@overlookny.com,
or write us at the address above.

Copyright © 2014 by Toby Ball

Cataloging-in-Publication Data is available from the Library of Congress

Book design and type formatting by Bernard Schleifer
Map illustration by Anthony Morais
Manufactured in the United States of America
ISBN: 978-1-4683-0902-7

FIRST EDITION
1 3 5 7 9 10 8 6 4 2

For my sister, Susanna Kahn, and Julia, Jackson, and Peter

Invisible Streets

1

A ROW OF COPS KEPT THE SKITTISH CROWD AWAY FROM A GROUP OF CITY officials who had descended on this gray neighborhood to mark the first step in its demolition. This wasn't Phil Dorman's first such event, but he could never get used to the anger. At the front of the crowd a compact man with a trim white beard and some sort of uniform shouted in a language Dorman was having trouble identifying. Ukrainian? Others in the crowd yelled as well. The cops, submerged in riot helmets and gas masks, shifted nervously from foot to foot, batons held behind their backs, looking vaguely like huge insects.

Dorman looked over at Nathan Canada, the commissioner of Parks and Transportation, who was chatting with a couple of his deputies and with the foreman in charge of the imminent demolition of the condemned building behind them. Canada was not physically imposing—about average height, narrow-shouldered, paunchy—but there was something of the lion at the watering hole about him, and people watched him with a wary eye. Dorman respected that, the man's mere presence putting everyone on edge.

He looked past Canada to the condemned building. Probably not a bad place to live, he thought. He'd picked it for this event because the empty lot next door offered a good sight line from the press area, a safe distance away. It had been a bitch to get everyone out of there— they'd had to bring the police in for the final few holdouts. The last guy turned out to be a hoarder—his little apartment stuffed with newspapers, magazines, pieces of mail, books, shit. He was taken straight to City Mental Hospital.

Dorman liked the beige stonework along the top of the building, the way it stood out sharply against the clear afternoon sky. He turned back to the press that had gathered on this side of the cordon, though still several yards from the officials. Photographers chatted with reporters, a couple of guys with movie cameras set up

their tripods. One of the movie guys seemed to be filming the protestors. Dorman recognized him—thin guy, longish hair—thought
he'd probably seen him filming at other demolitions. Maybe an explosives freak.

Canada had given a brief press conference earlier, answered some
questions, posed for some photos, ignored the noise of the mob behind the hacks.

Art Deyna from the *News-Gazette* strolled over with his usual
smirk. "Nice crowd you got here."

Dorman looked past the cordons. There were a lot of people;
maybe a couple hundred. He hated these events, but Canada insisted.
*Do it quietly and people think you're hiding something. Do it with a
fucking celebration and people will eat it up with a goddamn fork.*
Sounded good in theory, but these people didn't have forks—they had
pitchforks.

"Another group of satisfied citizens." He didn't need to bullshit
Deyna. The *News-Gazette* was on-board.

Deyna winked. "You guys make friends everywhere you go."

They both turned to see a uniform walking their way. He stopped
about ten feet short of them, looking inscrutably at Dorman.

"Excuse us," Dorman said.

"Consider yourself excused." Deyna walked back toward the
press huddle.

The uniform stepped forward. "News for you, Mr. Dorman."

Dorman glanced to make sure that Deyna was out of earshot. He
saw the tension in the cop's face—*was it the news or the crowd?*
"Okay."

"The site over on Kaiser, the dynamite trailer was hit last night."

Dorman sighed. Theft was a constant problem at the sites, made
worse by the knowledge that the department would be buying back
the same supplies next week from some dealer four or five times removed from the initial theft. "How much?"

"The whole thing."

"The whole thing?" That was a hell of a lot of explosives—a huge
haul.

"That's the report."

"Okay, thanks." Dorman noticed activity around the mayor. He dismissed the cop with a nod.

The detonator that would bring down the building sat on a small table positioned so that the cameras could catch the magical moment when Canada depressed the plunger. Canada said something to the foreman. People started to take their places. Dorman ambled over to meet Canada at the table.

"Everything okay?" Dorman asked. He wasn't going to mention the stolen explosives right now.

"Let's get this moving. I've got no desire to spend the whole fucking day here."

Dorman checked the press clutch, raised his arm with his thumb up. The photographers readied their cameras.

"Any time, sir."

Canada glanced at the press, nodded to himself, pushed the plunger down fast. Dorman looked to the building as the charges went off and watched it implode, dust billowing outward and up. There'd been a time, not too long ago, when this sight would have provoked in him a measure of awe. But in the two years he'd worked for Canada, he'd seen so many that the whole thing now seemed almost commonplace—another day at the office.

Dorman watched Canada shake hands with the foreman so the photographers could get a shot with the demolition-cloud in the background. Something was bothering Dorman, and it took him a moment to realize it was the sound. Usually a building implosion like this was met with a strange, awed silence. But now he heard the pitch of the crowd noise turn angrier, more aggressive. The police line took a step back and pulled their truncheons. A man came forward, tall and wiry, a bushy mustache almost covering his sneer as he entered the fray. A cop swung at his knees, brought him down hard. The man curled up, protecting his head with his arms. A second cop landed a couple of shots to his back.

Dust from the collapsing building reached the scene like the wispy edges of a fog. Dorman took Canada's arm. "We need to get you out of here."

He followed his boss's eyes to the photographers shooting the increasingly agitated crowd. A handful of men broke through the barricade to be confronted by police truncheons.

Canada shook his head in disgust, but allowed Dorman to guide him to the waiting Lincoln. He paused before ducking inside.

"You'll see to the press coverage?"

"I'll take care of it, sir."

Canada stooped into the car as something hard hit the hood. Dorman saw a half-brick drop to the sidewalk. He slammed the door shut and pounded on the roof. The car pulled away. A bottle shattered in the street behind it.

Other City officials ran to their cars, dodging rocks, bricks, bottles. Dorman protected his head with his forearm as he made his way to the police sergeant in charge. Cops were swinging their truncheons wildly in self-defense as more protestors broke through the cordon. People lay in the street, bleeding. Two men kicked at the ribs of a fallen cop, before being swarmed under by uniforms. The crowd behind the cordon howled in protest. Women held handkerchiefs up to their mouths to filter the dust. The police line pushed people back away from the street.

The sergeant turned. "We need to disperse these sons of bitches." It wasn't a question, but he looked to Dorman for confirmation.

Dorman nodded.

The sergeant yelled through a bullhorn for the crowd to disperse, doing it by the book. The scene continued to deteriorate. Dorman dodged a bottle. He scanned the crowd for familiar faces, habitual protestors, but the chaos made any kind of systematic survey impossible.

He heard empty thuds behind him. Tear gas canisters rolled into the street, gas spreading, mixing with the dust in the air. The crowd went silent and still, registering this new situation. Then, as if alerted by an unseen cue, confusion began anew as the protesters retreated in panic. A uniform shoved a gas mask into Dorman's hands. It smelled musty inside, but it was better than the gas that was creeping their way.

It took no more than a minute for the crowd to flee, leaving only the injured to be shoved roughly into waiting paddy wagons. The calm allowed Dorman to think, his breathing loud in the mask. He needed to call Lieutenant Zwieg, get someone on the explosives heist.

He looked back to the building, reduced to a pile of rubble, the dust from its collapse dissipating. In the distance, he heard police sirens, but wasn't sure if they were headed his way.

2

THAT NIGHT, FRANK FRINGS LEANED BACK IN A FOLDING CHAIR, SMOKING a reefer, watching a black-and-white film silently projected on the wall of a narrow basement theater. The cameraman must have been shooting out a window or from a roof, probably thirty feet up or so. The scene: a sidewalk packed with people, most of them moving from the right and passing under the camera, then continuing off to the left. The camera stayed stationary as people—dozens, hundreds—passed below. Suddenly, without apparent catalyst, the shot racked in to focus on a woman walking in the crowd and stayed with her. There was nothing that particularly stood out about this woman; she was professionally dressed, carried a handbag, was probably in her thirties, attractive, but not unusually so. She was clearly unaware of being filmed. The camera stayed with her as she walked directly below, and followed her down the sidewalk. The shot ended and jumped abruptly to a new scene. It took a moment for Frings to figure out what was going on: the cameraman was now on the street, trailing the woman, maybe ten yards behind her. Pedestrians glanced quizzically at the camera as they walked past.

Noise from the Cafe Adaggio upstairs filtered down into the tiny makeshift theater: footsteps, dozens of muted conversations, the muffled clink of silverware and dishes. In the theater, three dozen folding chairs, all filled, were arranged in nine rows of four. Sitting in a wheelchair next to Frings was his former editor at the *Gazette*, Panos Dimitropoulos. The projector's light traveled through a long cone of smoke; the dank smell of the place was not quite masked by the scent of cigarettes and marijuana. The occasional sound of scuttling rats could be heard from the front. The movie itself was silent, the ambient noise from above and outside providing the soundtrack, along with occasional coughs and whispered comments from the audience.

Frings leaned over to Panos. "How'd you hear about this movie?" he whispered.

"Rappaport," Panos wheezed. Rappaport had been the art critic at the old *Gazette*.

"This seems a little avant-garde for you, chief."

Panos glared dolefully back. "This is not a joke, Frank. You pay attention, the moment is coming up."

Frings nodded, wondering what could happen in this strange little movie that would be so important to Panos. Panos had not been forthcoming, insisting that it was absolutely necessary for Frings to actually *see* the film and that, no, he couldn't tell Frings *why*, that Frings would need to see it for himself, with his own eyes. Telling him would apparently ruin the moment.

Frings turned his attention back to the screen, the camera continuing to follow the woman through several jump cuts—one extended, maybe to change film. The woman turned onto a side street, leaving the teeming sidewalk behind. The cameraman paused, presumably to maintain his cover, then followed, keeping his distance so that the woman wouldn't notice him. She was farther away now, standing on a stoop. The camera zoomed in and the image went grainy as she fingered through a set of keys before finding the right one, unlocked the door, and disappeared from the street. The camera hovered on the street, now empty, for close to a full minute, nothing happening until a young couple holding hands turned onto the block from the opposite end. At this, the screen went black for a few seconds, and then a new scene began.

Panos tapped Frings's hand. "This is the one."

The camera focused on a girl—not the woman from the prior scene—tall, skinny, and . . . well . . . distinctive looking, Frings thought—an oval face with big, surprised eyes. College age, probably. She was like a painting in her slim dress, straight hair brushing her high shoulders. The camera lingered on her, providing time for the audience to read the sign she held in her hands: *When the people are subjected to pervasive deception, popular will ceases to have meaning*. Behind the girl, far enough to be out of focus, a group of young men smoked cigarettes, holding something by their sides—pistols?—and watching the camera.

Frings considered the aphorism on the sign for a moment—the ideology was familiar, though not the actual words. He had a feeling that he knew where they might have picked up the saying, but Panos interrupted this train of thought. The old man gripped his arm with an unsteady hand.

"Here it is, Frank."

The focus of the camera changed so that the girl was now blurred and the men behind her sharper, though the distance left their features indistinct.

"Look."

Frings strained to pick up what Panos wanted him to see. The four men casually dropped their cigarettes and bent to pick up some rocks. The camera zoomed closer as they hurled their rocks over the girl and at the camera. The camera kept steady despite the incoming rocks, the men's faces now in closer focus and, though not exactly sharp, at least giving an idea of their features.

Frings focused on one of the four: black hair, his eyes and mouth dark patches on his blurred face. "Panos?"

"You see him?" Panos whispered.

The young man was skinny, his white shirt hanging from his shoulders, and Frings might not have recognized him if he hadn't been looking for . . . something.

"Is that Sol?"

"Yes. Yes!"

Sol Elia—Panos's grandson, his daughter's child, whom he hadn't seen in more than two years.

The men hurled more rocks at the camera as the girl stood impassively. The shot pulled back out, bringing the girl into focus again, blurring the men who continued to throw rocks. The girl, Frings thought, was very beautiful in her own sort of way. He'd somehow missed that before. The scene ended. Darkness. Jump to a Negro section of town at night easing by, presumably shot from a car window, people on the sidewalk mostly oblivious, but some giving wary looks.

Panos grabbed Frings's arm. "You saw him, Frank? You saw Sol?"

"Yes, Panos."

Panos sighed heavily. "You need to find him for me."

As soon as they'd arranged this meeting, Frings knew that Panos would ask something of him, and knew that he would accept. Panos had supported Frings's work at the *Gazette* for decades before the old man's health finally confined him to the wheelchair, sapped him of the strength necessary to withstand the daily stress of the newspaper. The bartering of small favors was a constant in Frings's life—with police, criminals, politicians, businessmen. But this was something different. This was friendship, and Frings would do anything Panos asked. Panos had earned that and Panos knew it.

"Okay."

Panos didn't immediately reply. Frings turned to see the old man's shoulders shaking as he quietly wept. "His parents are gone, Frank. His grandmother's gone. It's just me and him, and I haven't heard from him in over two years. His friends said they hadn't heard from him. I thought he was dead, Frank. But now, maybe, I face the possibility that he wanted to be done with me; that his friends lied to me so that I wouldn't find him. Why would he hide from me, Frank?"

Frings put his hand on Panos's shoulder. "We don't know anything, Panos. We don't know when this film was made. We don't know what Sol was doing"—he corrected himself—"*is* doing. It could be a lot of things. Don't assume the worst."

THE FILM ENDED WITHOUT CREDITS. THE LIGHTS CAME ON, CHASING THE rats back to their hiding places and making visible the smoke-stained walls, the yellowed linoleum floor. The crowd, a collection of aging bohemians, college kids, and a couple of younger men who, to Frings's eye, seemed in the clutches of some dementia, stood and stretched and filed up the stairs to street level. Frings found his cane where he'd leaned it against Panos's wheelchair and walked to the back of the room, his knee throbbing and stiff from sitting. He knocked on the door to the projection room. After a few moments, a balding young man in a wool sweater opened the door.

"Can I help you, friend?" His voice was raspy, ravaged by cigarette smoke.

"Yeah, look, can I ask you a couple questions about the film?"

The guy shrugged. "Shoot."

"Let's start with who made it."

"The director? Andy Macheda."

Frings shook his head a little, not recognizing the name. "When was it shot, do you know?"

"Depends on the part. Some of it, let's see . . . 1960 was the first, I think, you know, two years ago, maybe more. Other parts, could have been last month, last week."

"Last week?"

"He brings in new parts, takes out old ones."

"Macheda does?"

"Sure. It's a living film, you know. It changes. This one, it's called *Film 12*, and next time he adds something it'll be *Film 13*."

Frings sighed. It was never easy. "So the part with the ginks throwing rocks at the camera . . ."

The guy closed one eye and raised the other eyebrow: some kind of thinking expression. "Year and a half, maybe two. Something like that. It's hard to keep track of sometimes, you know? From the first version to now . . ." He let the thought drift.

Frings waited.

The guy was looking at him intently. "Do I know you?"

"I don't think so. My name's Frank Frings."

The guy's eyes widened. "Shit. Yeah, I thought I'd seen you before. What brings you here? You . . . you heard of my cinema?" It seemed as if the answer would mean something to him.

Frings nodded—a lie. "Thought I'd have a look. Hey . . ."

"Lane."

"Lane. You have splicing equipment back there?"

Lane narrowed his eyes. "Sure. I need it for when Andy comes in with a new piece, or when the film breaks. Why?"

PASSING CARS, WET WITH RAIN, GLISTENED UNDER THE STREET LIGHTS when Frings and Panos emerged into the autumn night. Frings carried, secured in an envelope in his pocket, a celluloid frame with the four rock-throwing men's faces as clearly focused as they could find. The projection room had been something of a nightmare: cans of film stacked against the walls beneath decades-old black-and-white smut photos, tiny scuttling sounds coming from the corner, Frings trying not to imagine hundreds of cockroaches crawling over each other. In the close quarters, he had felt Lane's mania—the unease with interaction, the anxiety of admitting someone into *his place*. But Lane had cut the frame for him. Only, he'd explained, because it was for Frank Frings. Andy would be cool about it, he'd said.

Frings had asked, "Where do I find him?"

Lane—was that his first or last name?—had shrugged. "I don't know. He seems to shoot everywhere."

"Where does he live? Do you have an address for him?"

Lane had shrugged again. Frings had nodded. He could see why Andy Macheda might not be all that eager for an odd gink like Lane to be able to track him down.

Frings had thanked Lane and backed out, the smoky air of the makeshift theater comparatively fresh after the heat and stink of the projection room.

Outside in the rain, Panos slumped in his wheelchair, exhausted from ascending the stairs, even with Frings essentially carrying his weight—a difficult task in its own right, given his age and crippled knee. Frings held an umbrella over them as they waited for a cab.

"You'll find that boy, Frank?" Panos seemed to be fading, his voice faltering.

"Yes, Panos. I'll find him."

Panos nodded and closed his eyes. Frings stared down the street, trying to spot a cab amid the creeping flow of nighttime traffic.

3

THE MORNING SUN FAILED TO WARM DETECTIVE TORSTEN GRIP AS HE leaned against a chain-link fence and watched construction workers file into the work site, a dozen floors of finished office building exterior topped by another twenty-some floors of steel skeleton. They were an eclectic, diverse group, culled from the City's endless ethnic enclaves—second- and third-generation immigrants from Eastern and Southern Europe, Negroes from over on the East Side, newly-arrived Asians and, as was always the case on the high-rises, Iroquois from around the northern border.

Grip eyed the men as they walked through a crude turnstile lodged in the fence. He was trying, in theory, to identify union organizers who'd begun to infiltrate these construction crews. The unions weren't illegal, but the mayor's office had asked the force to be a presence at the sites, to maybe intimidate the organizers without actually making arrests. Grip had a healthy hatred of unions and, especially, the communists he was certain ran rampant within them, but, even so, this was a bullshit assignment: standing around, each morning a new site, looking threatening. There were more effective ways of handling the unions—ways that didn't involve wearing a badge. He liked, though, the wary looks of the workers as they filed past him. He was, at the very least, being noticed. Although only five foot nine in shoes, his shoulders and chest seemed nearly as wide, and no one mistook his pug's face for that of a soft man.

He had to get through this wasted hour every morning before hitting the streets for the real detective work. He complained about the kinds of cases he drew lately—his days in Homicide were a thing of the past—but he liked the job regardless, knew that he was good at it. Crime needed to be fought, criminals caught. He did more than his part.

Grip watched the men walk out on the beams, three hundred feet above him. Crazy. He'd been up once, never leaving the platform by the lift. The Indian guys up there had told him not to look up—that was how you lost your balance, following the clouds. He'd taken their word for it, but didn't look down either—just straight ahead, which was bad enough.

Grip was surprised to see Lieutenant Zwieg walk in behind a couple of Italian welders. Grip watched him survey the site, catch sight of Grip, and walk over.

"Sir?"

Zwieg nodded at him. "Detective." Zwieg was a big man, easily eight inches taller than Grip, but he'd lost his physical edge and gotten fat, though his hands still held menace. "Scaring the Reds this morning?"

Grip didn't say anything. He wasn't much for small talk, especially not with an asshole like Zwieg.

Zwieg gave him a half-lidded glare, not happy to get no response. "I've got something for you, Detective. Something that we need to keep under wraps. Get you off this duty."

"Sure."

"The Kaiser Street site, the night before last, the explosives trailer was emptied."

"Emptied?"

Zwieg nodded.

Grip scratched his temple, thinking. A full trailer of explosives was a big heist, much bigger than the usual haul of construction materials or light equipment. "Leads? Suspicions?"

"Hard to know. Sounds like a truck from Standard Ironworks, or . . . I don't know, I can't keep these fucking companies straight. A truck making a late delivery interrupted them, probably kept them from grabbing the little bit of dynamite that they left behind. You'd think maybe Kollectiv 61, but they didn't leave any of their usual words of wisdom. Maybe they didn't get around to it because of the delivery truck. Who knows? So, you're really starting from scratch, here. Two things, though. This needs to be discreet, Tor. We're keeping it out of the rags, using a little muscle with a couple of them, as I hear it. So practice your usual subtlety."

"Right." Zwieg was joking.

"And you report straight to me. We're keeping the number of people in on this to a minimum." Zwieg paused for a moment. "Even Kraatjes."

Grip kept his expression neutral, but this was strange. Kraatjes was the police commissioner, and while he wasn't personally aware of every ongoing investigation—there was too much crime in the City for that—Grip had never heard anyone suggest that the brass be kept *intentionally* in the dark.

Zwieg seemed to read Grip's hesitation. "We're not exactly sure where he stands," Zwieg said in a hushed, conspiratorial tone.

"I get it," Grip said, not really getting it at all, but uncomfortable with the direction the discussion was taking. He changed the subject. "You say it was a night heist? You talked with the security guys?"

"Strangest thing, Detective, none of them showed up last night."

This actually *was* unusual. The way these thefts usually worked, the security guys needed to be there to keep the gates open and let the perps in. They would simply deny everything later, and the company that employed them, Consolidated Industries, never pressed charges. Easier to eat the losses than constantly investigate and recruit new guards, who'd all be coming from the same tainted pool, anyway. Price of business.

This haul, though, was on a much different scale than what Grip normally saw.

"You got their addresses, sir?"

Zwieg smiled. "That I do, Detective Grip. That I do."

4

FRINGS SAT IN THE HEARING ROOM OF A HULKING ASYLUM THAT HAD once been called All Souls' but was renamed, in a moment of inspiration, City Mental Hospital. He was one of an audience of about a dozen—half reporters and half, apparently, family of the man sitting at a narrow wooden table, his wrists and ankles shackled. The family wore shabby clothes and exhausted expressions.

The light in the room was at once harsh and dim, the only natural illumination filtered through a row of high windows fogged with decades of grime and pollution. Two bare bulbs behind heavy wire mesh gave everything a sickly sheen. The man in shackles had the pallor of the long-incarcerated. His body was swollen from lack of exercise. His head had been shaved. Frings had seen his eyes when he'd been led into the room, and they'd been empty—unseeing, uncomprehending. The wall clock had a hum that rose in volume and pitch until the minute hand ticked over one spot, at which point the hum started low and soft again, a miniature detonation once a minute.

Next to the man in shackles sat a public defender—one of a legion of City lawyers who lacked the imagination and competence to hold down a job at a firm. These lawyers instead attempted to carve out a living through a large volume of clients on the City's dime, none of whom received much in the way of actual representation. Also present was a senior City Attorney, dressed in a suit that probably cost what the other lawyer made for a couple months' work; a board of three psychologists with imperious eyes; and the judge, a forbidding man named Asplundh.

The defense lawyer looked profoundly uncomfortable, and Frings couldn't blame him. The man in shackles, Andre LaValle, had, four years prior, assassinated the chief of police by stabbing him in the chest with a hunting knife. He'd stuck the blade in four times before anyone could pull him off. The trial caused a media storm and LaValle had been deemed not guilty by reason of insanity. It had been hard to argue with the accuracy of the verdict: LaValle had been, for the most part, uncommunicative in court, and when he spoke it was clear that he was entirely unaware of his circumstances, or of the fact that the trial had consequences for him. He'd apparently been hearing a different question in his mind, repeatedly answering "5842 Vilnius Street," his address, a residential block in a neighborhood known as South River. This had been his dull-eyed answer to every question. Initially, commentators had accused him of fakery, but soon even the most cynical among them conceded that LaValle was truly incompetent. *Crazy.*

According to the decision, LaValle would be given a hearing every three years to determine his mental state. A rumor had since circulated that there existed a legal loophole that—while unlikely in the extreme—could result in his unconditional release upon a finding of mental competence. Nobody wanted that—not the prosecutor, not the police, not even LaValle's own lawyer, who was better off banking his supposed work on LaValle's behalf indefinitely. This was the first of the mandated hearings and Frings, who had offered newspaper commentary on LaValle's trial, was there to chronicle this next step.

The prosecutor, sitting in his chair, tried to engage LaValle. "Mr.

LaValle, do you acknowledge belonging to a group known as the People's Union in the years 1958 and 1959?"

From where he sat, Frings couldn't see LaValle's eyes, but the faces of the doctors and the judge indicated that there had not been much of a response.

"Can you describe for me, Mr. LaValle, the goals or intentions of the People's Union?"

Again nothing. One of the doctors cleared his throat, and a few people in the audience shifted in their seats.

"Okay. Let me put it to you this way. Would you describe the People's Union as an anarchist organization?"

The lawyer didn't bother to object. Frings knew that this question was meant to bait LaValle into communication—or not—but the subtext of the question, that belonging to an anarchist organization was somehow an indication of guilt, annoyed him.

In fact, the People's Union had been pacifists. Their horror at LaValle's actions had led, eventually, to their quiet dissolution. Graffiti from a group called Kollectiv 61 had appeared months later at the scene of vandal attacks on building projects. The common wisdom— then as now—was that Kollectiv 61 had been formed by the more aggressive members of the People's Union—the ones more predisposed to action—and in the years since, the attacks had grown progressively more destructive.

The reporter next to Frings, an old hand from the *Trib*, whispered into Frings's ear. "I got a source here says they took him off his medication for this show, see what happened. Cold turkey."

Frings nodded. They'd want him nearly catatonic for the hearing.

He'd seen this prosecutor before, preening in the courtroom in front of the jurors. Now, without the need for an act, he simply read questions from a legal pad without any verbal histrionics.

"Were you aware, Mr. LaValle, that while the People's Union was critical—some would say harshly critical—of the City's governance and law enforcement, that they, in fact, publicly and repeatedly renounced your violent actions?"

LaValle sat motionless. Frings rubbed his neck. There was no story here. Nothing today was going to change LaValle's status. Frings absently spun his pencil around his index finger, wondering what LaValle was like when medicated—if he communicated then. The press had been barred by court order from seeing him, Judge Asplundh uneager to give the man a soapbox.

The questioning continued like this for another ten minutes until it had been established to everyone's satisfaction that they wouldn't get anything from the unresponsive LaValle and, in an anticlimax, the audience slowly drifted out of the hearing room. An older woman with her head bent and tears dropping to the floor—Frings assumed this was LaValle's mother—was escorted by a younger man who resembled the LaValle of four years ago, before his incarceration and mania had transformed him. Frings stashed his reporter's pad in the inside pocket of his jacket, folded the morning's *News-Gazette* under his arm, and followed the crowd out.

In the claustrophobic foyer, a boy whom Frings recognized as an assistant from the *News-Gazette* office stood waiting, an envelope in his hand.

"Mr. Frings?" The words echoed off the walls, seemed almost amplified, and the boy looked mortified.

Frings flashed a quick smile to reassure him. "Yes?"

"This is for you." He handed Frings an envelope. "I'm supposed to make sure that you got this before you left."

Frings thanked him and put the envelope in his trouser pocket. For reasons that he didn't reflect on, he didn't want to open it in here, this place of madness and despair.

The enormous square in front of the hospital was empty, as if the usual indigents—the ones who gathered in the City's unclaimed spaces—as if even they found the proximity to so much insanity a deterrent. Frings paused, feeling the warmth of the autumn sun on this cool, breezy afternoon, and opened the envelope. Inside was a note in the hand of his editor at the *News-Gazette*.

It read, simply: MY OFFICE. 11:30. H.L.

5

FRINGS HAD A SMALL OFFICE ON THE THIRD FLOOR OF THE *NEWS* BUILDING, a twelve-story box of steel and glass on the edge of Capitol Heights. When the *News* had taken over Frings's old paper, the *Gazette*, and become the *News-Gazette*, he'd been given this office, supposedly a gesture of respect for his status as the best known journalist in the City. This, like so much else about the *News-Gazette*, was bullshit. He'd been deposited in this office, two floors down from the news room, to get some distance between him and the young reporters. He'd heard rumors to the effect that the brass had made it clear to the younger reporters: associating with Frings was a bad career move. The *News-Gazette* wasn't the *Gazette*, wasn't a leftist rag. Management had wanted Frings under their thumb, so they'd kept him on, but he was isolated. He wrote a weekly "dissenting view" column, and he wasn't sure that anyone would care—or even notice—if he just stopped coming to work.

His office was sparse—desk, two chairs, window overlooking the street. He'd hung a map of the City on the wall to his right, and behind him a propaganda poster of Lenin reading beneficently to young socialist children, just to screw with the suits. A mysterious duct ran along the ceiling, in through one wall and out another. It was quiet now, but he often heard the hollow rush of air—he had no idea where it came from or where it went.

He dropped the notebook that he'd taken to the hearing on his desk, kept the front section of the newspaper. The front-page articles had put him in a foul mood. He stopped in the bathroom on the way to the elevator, his footsteps echoing hollowly on the yellow tiled floor. Let Littbarski wait a few minutes.

FRINGS SMILED AT THE EDITOR'S SECRETARY, A GORGEOUS CREATURE named Lois, and was rewarded with a smile in return.

"They're waiting for you."

They?

Frings found Littbarski, a small gink with sad, bowed shoulders, smoking a cigarette, reading the previous evening's edition of the *Sun*. He looked up at Frings and reflexively pasted back the trim mustache that ran along the upper lip of his tight face.

Across the desk from Littbarski sat Art Deyna, who had started as a junior reporter at the *Gazette* before it was acquired by the *News*. Under a new, more conservative regime, Deyna had risen to become the paper's golden-boy reporter. He was in his late thirties, though he looked barely out of his teens—slender, hairless jaw, delicate face. Even more surprising was the presence of Michael Endicott, the chairman of the *News-Gazette* board, his position one of a small number of concessions the *Gazette* had been granted during the merger. He was ten years Frings's junior, a wealthy man with a wealthy man's paunch, though still handsome. He wore expensive glasses and his straight hair was slicked and parted on the side.

Frings wondered why Endicott and Deyna were here. Endicott was an ally, Deyna definitely an adversary. Regardless, he would now have an audience to witness the objections he'd been harboring since reading the morning's paper before LaValle's hearing.

He dropped the front section on Littbarsi's desk. "What the hell is this on our front page today?

"Frank," Littbarski said in a warning tone.

Frings read from the paper in his hand. "'An unruly mob in the sway of professional provocateurs turned violent during a ceremony celebrating the next step in the construction of the Crosstown Expressway.'—Professional provocateurs? Do we have any evidence of that?—'Police responded to crowd incitement with remarkable restraint before the situation became too dangerous and the agitators were dispersed with tear gas.' Did we let Canada write the goddamn article for us? I didn't see his name on the byline."

Deyna was out of his chair, face crimson.

"Jesus, Art, sit down," Littbarski snapped. "You too, Frank. You weren't there, Art was. His reporting is solid."

"Give me the name of a professional provocateur, Art. Just one. It sounds like a great story."

Frings looked to Endicott, who watching this scene unfold with seeming indifference, then back to Deyna.

Littbarski banged his fist on the table. "This paper is not run to please you, Frank. This isn't the fucking *Gazette* anymore where every business owner is in league with the Devil and every goddamn radical with a picture of Mao in his wallet is a hero. Things are different now, Frank. You know that. Jesus."

Deyna was trying to stare down Frings. Frings ignored him.

Endicott spoke. "Frank, we didn't call you up here to get your opinion on the front-page stories, though, to be honest, I share your concern to a degree." He looked at Littbarski with false benevolence. "We got an interesting leak this morning."

"*I* got an interesting leak this morning." Deyna settled back in his chair.

Littbarski jumped in, trying to regain control of the meeting. "Credit where it's due, Art. Anyway, Frank, Art's got a source in the Force who gave him some information with the *assurance* that we won't publish until we get his—the source's—okay."

"Who's the source?" Frings asked.

Deyna shook his head in disgust.

"You know that's not how we do things here."

"Given his track record—"

"His track record is excellent, Frank. You don't have blemishes on your record? Glass houses and all that. Okay?"

Frings nodded.

"Art's source tells us that two nights ago a significant quantity of dynamite was stolen from one of the Crosstown demolition sites."

"How significant?"

"He didn't specify," Deyna said. "But he was clear that it was very big."

Frings shrugged, looked to Endicott. "Okay. I assume they're keeping it quiet, don't want the bad publicity for the New City Project, don't want people panicking."

Endicott gave a barely perceptible nod.

Frings turned to Littbarski. "So, what are we going to do?"

"Get a jump on the story. Have things in place for when we *can* run it."

This all made sense, but Frings still wasn't sure why he was here. "What am I missing?"

"Kollectiv 61," Deyna said in the tone of a man gleefully relating bad news.

"Is that something you know or is it a guess?"

Littbarski stepped in again. "What we've been told, Frank, is that they left one of their little aphorisms."

Deyna looked at his notebook. "The creation of capital is not the highest goal of civilization."

Frings nodded. Stolen explosives, the New City Project, radical aphorisms delivered via spray paint—all Kollectiv 61 hallmarks. When Kollectiv 61 had first appeared, they'd been vandals, starting small—sand in the gas tanks of construction vehicles, torched lumber stocks—before moving on to more ambitious subterfuge, mostly explosives stolen from construction sites. They'd blown up on-site trailers, construction supplies, and equipment, though never when anyone was present. Property damage without fatalities. And always, painted somewhere nearby, a signature. The first one: "As technology progresses, freedom regresses."

"Okay," Frings said.

Endicott said, "You're here because we're hoping that you might receive another message."

"They don't get in touch with me very often."

"We're aware of that. But at the moment it's our best hope."

In the past, Kollectiv 61 had communicated with the press by sending letters to Frings—words cut from the *News-Gazette*, pasted to paper. Frings, they'd explained, was an inspiration. His book, *Alienation and the Modern City,* a full-blooded philosophical critique of Nathan Canada and the New City Project was, they claimed, one of the touchstones of their movement. They had taken his ideas and created something different, something destructive.

"I'll let you know if I do."

Endicott nodded.

"Is there something else?"

"Art is on the story. If you hear anything . . ." Littbarski stopped there, looking for Frings's reaction.

"I'm not going to hear anything."

Littbarski seemed to contemplate saying something else, glanced at Endicott, decided against it.

NILES, FROM THE PHOTO DEPARTMENT ONE FLIGHT UP, DELIVERED THE blowups of Macheda's film frame to Frings's desk. He fanned them out, five in all. The first was an enlargement of the whole frame, the four men looking at the camera; all young, maybe college, maybe a little older, the image crisp but too far away to discern much. Then four close-ups of the individual faces, the definition completely lost in the magnification, the features barely more than dark patches on white faces. He could just make out Sol Elia with his dark hair and dark eyes, his expression too blurred to read, but all the more unsettling for it. *A crude mask.* The other three were the same—probably just clear enough if you knew who you were looking for, otherwise it was just a sense, a description you could give in a few words: blond, square jaw, close-set eyes.

"Sorry, Frank, that's the best I could do."

"That's great, Niles. I appreciate it."

Frings watched him retreat down the hall and wondered if the prints would be of any use.

6

DORMAN STRODE THROUGH THE CITY COUNCIL GALLERY TO THE PRESS section, where a small clutch of rumpled men were engaged in muted conversations, while the councilors shuffled papers and muttered to one another behind their long, curved table. The chamber had been recently renovated at great expense, the detailed molding painted metallic gold, lush against the powder-blue walls. A bronzed sculpture of a riverboat hung gleaming from the center of the domed ceiling.

Who had actually financed the renovation was the topic of some speculation—Dorman had once asked Canada about it, receiving a dismissive grunt in reply.

At some point in the past, the City Hall beat had come to be seen as a backwater, a dead end for ambitious young reporters. So the men that were there, day in and day out, were jaded vets whose ambitions had long since been frustrated.

"Good morning, fellas," Dorman said brightly.

A couple of the reporters muttered "good morning," but most just nodded or frowned.

"You've got my number if you need to follow up later."

The only response came from an older guy named E. W. Lambert—the skin of his face stretched and buckled, like an old pudding. "Something going to happen today that we're going to need to follow up on?"

Dorman shrugged. "I have no idea. Just wanted to let you know that, as always, I am at your service."

This earned him a general rolling of eyes. Dorman gave them a quick wink and walked back the way he had come, to find a spot at the back of the room from which to watch the proceedings.

PUBLIC QUESTIONS HAD JUST ENDED. TO THE LEFT OF THE COUNCIL, propped on two easels, was the seemingly ubiquitous map of the New City Project, a huge area of gray surrounding a central core that was checkered in a variety of colors, and, cutting through the whole map, the dark blue line of the as yet uncompleted Crosstown Expressway. The entire plan in shorthand: transform the center of the City into a single, powerful, enormous business district using tax incentives, at the expense of who knew how much current and future City tax revenue; and build a modern network of multi-lane highways—most notably the Crosstown—to link the new, wealthy suburbs with the City center, bypassing the outer neighborhoods entirely.

Dorman knew he hadn't missed anything during public comments—only the continued drumbeat of citizens opposing the New City Project. Nobody ever spoke *for* it in public comments. No one needed to. The whole thing was a fait accompli, the work on the City Center already well along and the Crosstown construction in its early, but irreversibly destructive, stages. Some neighborhoods were being razed to make room for the new highway, while others found themselves suddenly slated for a future in its permanent shadow.

The New City Project had for months been consigned to the margins of Council debate. There was not, in truth, much to be discussed. Business was on the side of the project; the councilors—nearly all of them—were either bought and paid for or intimidated into cooperation. This corruption was an open secret, but one that seemed to go unremarked upon except by old radicals such as Frank Frings, who, Dorman thought, should realize they were wasting their time.

DORMAN WATCHED AS THE UNHEROIC FIGURE OF NATHAN CANADA SHUFfled to the witness table, carrying a folder in one hand, a cup of water in the other. The councilors followed his progress, and their anxiety was palpable, even from where Dorman sat. Canada took his seat, opened his file, and sorted through the papers it contained. For all the notice he paid to his surroundings, he could have been alone in his office.

This was a Canada tactic, impugning people's importance by ignoring them. Dorman had experienced this any number of times, beginning the day he'd interviewed for his current job. Being ignored had not bothered Dorman then—he hadn't been particularly interested in the position, to be honest. But, once they did start talking, something about Canada had intrigued him. His approach seemed different than what Dorman was used to in the military—less direct.

"They've told you the salary?" Canada had asked at one point.

"Yes, sir."

"And it is acceptable?"

"It's more than adequate."

"More than adequate." Canada chuckled, a response that Dorman later came to associate with calculation. "You know, I spent a great deal of time settling on a number. The person in this job, Mr. Dorman, will be offered myriad financial enticements by people who will want their desires given a sympathetic hearing by my office. Do you understand what I'm talking about?"

"It sounds like you're talking about bribes."

"Exactly! Bribes. I can't hire anyone from the City—it's impossible to be sure where loyalties lie. But someone from outside the City—you, for instance, or someone else—your loyalty would be to the project, unless someone else *bought* your loyalty."

Canada paused, and while Dorman wanted to jump in to assure him that he was predisposed not to accept bribes, he knew it would sound empty, so he stayed quiet.

"Which brings me back to your salary," Canada continued. "The trick was to make it generous enough that you could live well with the money you make. But it also had to be low enough so that the position would not be attractive to someone whose ambition is simply to make a great deal of money. That kind of person, in my experience, is prone to accept extra income wherever he finds it—regardless of need—and will put money ahead of goals, such as those of the New City Project."

Canada paused again and leaned back slightly, which Dorman took to mean that he was finished.

"The salary is more than adequate," Dorman said. And it had proven to be more than adequate. He was not the type of person who wanted a lot of *things*. He lived comfortably, was able to afford to do the things he wanted to do. More than a dozen times people had approached him with bribes, and he had always sent them away. After a while, he'd earned a reputation as incorruptible. Canada's instincts had again been correct.

DORMAN WATCHED WITHOUT MUCH INTEREST AS CANADA DELIVERED HIS report in a bored monotone, rarely looking up from the paper he read from. To anyone paying attention, it was clear where power lay in the chambers. When he was finished, Councilor Eva Wise, representing a collection of Negro neighborhoods on the City's East Side, announced that she had some questions. She thanked Canada for appearing and hurried through the rest of the niceties. Something about her tone, though, left the gallery with little doubt that this would be more than a pro forma exercise.

Dorman knew this was coming. He'd received a tip from an assistant on the councilor's staff, to whom he paid a modest monthly stipend in exchange for exactly this kind of information.

"Mr. Canada, I have a young man on my staff recently graduated from City College with a degree in accounting, and I think—I believe that you will join me in this belief—that his example does credit to City College and makes an argument for the College's continued *prioritization* in our budget." She paused, picking up a sheet of paper. "He spent a couple of days last week going through the budget figures that your office provided, which, to be honest, seem to be intentionally obscure. His conclusion, Mr. Canada, is that the Crosstown is well overbudget at this stage and is on track to be possibly as much as $30 million over budget when all is said and done. My memory is not what it once was, but I don't recall having heard anything from your office about this."

Canada had a tone that he used for responding to the Council's questions, as if he was responding to a somewhat dim but insistent child. "I'm not sure, Councilor Wise, that this report *does* deepen my regard for City College, or at least its accounting department. Parks and Transportation accountants have been extremely thorough, and while there have been minor cost overruns, they will be absorbed in later stages of construction."

Councilor Wise frowned. "Do you not think that this type of information would be important for the Council to know?"

Dorman had prepared Canada for this.

"My understanding is that the Council does not concern itself with the details of departmental budgets."

"I beg your pardon?"

"I notice that there are unspecified discretionary accounts in the Infrastructure and Utilities budgets, and a similar account in the Health budget, and this is without even getting into the Police Department's black budget."

Dorman smiled. His boss was a master of this kind of thing.

"What is your point, Commissioner?"

"My point," Canada said, his voice remaining calm as he fixed the councilor with a glare, "is that if the Council is interested in auditing governmental departments, I believe there are more bountiful hunting grounds than my budget, and I question why the Councilor would ignore those in order to prioritize mine. I wonder if there is a reason beyond the promotion of," here his voice was heavy with sarcasm, "'good government' in her targeting of my department. I wonder if there is not an ulterior—"

The Council Chair banged his gavel. Councilor Wise attempted to talk over Canada as he continued his harangue.

Dorman stood, nodded to the cop at the door, and walked out.

• • •

FROM THE KOLLECTIV 61 MANIFESTO, *Prometheus*, FALL 1961

8. Comfort is the Mortar of our Prison: Historically, totalitarian governments have resorted to the use of threats, violence, and material poverty in order to maintain a subservient populace. In the last half-century, however, we have seen an evolution in the means of population control. The substantial increase in the technology of modern comfort has resulted in a society that accepts, if it even notices, the totalitarian instincts of its government, as long as a certain level of domestic comfort is maintained. People are unlikely to actively oppose government action that doesn't directly affect their day-to-day lives if those day-to-day lives are experienced at a reasonable level of comfort and the people have an expectation that they will remain so. IN ORDER TO ENCOURAGE RESISTANCE TO TOTALITARIAN ACTIONS BY A GOVERNMENT, MATERIAL COMFORT MUST BE EITHER UNDERMINED OR SHOWN TO BE ILLUSORY. THE USE OF VIOLENCE TO UPSET THE SENSE OF COMFORT IS NOT PREFERABLE FOR ACHIEVING THIS AIM, BUT MAY BE THE ONLY WAY THIS CAN BE ACCOMPLISHED BY A SMALL NUMBER OF PEOPLE.

7

ART BOUTIQUES HAD BEEN SPRINGING UP AROUND THE CITY LATELY, FILLING
the gap between the high-end galleries, which made their millions off
of the glossy works of big-name artists, and the run-down store-front
operations, which charged artists fees to hang their work and collected
a healthy commission on anything sold. In a neighborhood that was
both newly fashionable and still occasionally dangerous, one of the
new breed, a small renovated bank building, was opening an exhibition of three young artists.

Frings sipped a gin and tonic in a room that had once been a bank
vault, but which now displayed a series of doctored photographs
taken by a young artist named Wendy Otis. The room was maybe
three-quarters full, mostly younger people—college-aged or a little
older—as well as some heemies wearing clothes that had once been
expensive, but were now threadbare or just tired.

Frings was standing with Al Rappaport, who had been with the
paper when Panos was still editor. When the merger was arranged,
Rappaport, like a number of others, had retired rather than toil under
Littbarski and the rest of the new regime.

"I've been seeing a lot of that little shit, Art Deyna, on the front
page recently."

"Littbarski's decided that he's his golden boy," Frings said, mildly.

"Right. Like you were with Panos."

Frings let that go. Rappaport had never been able to hold his
drink.

"And you," Rappaport continued, "I read your column every
week. You're staying on the Crosstown and the New City Project and
I admire that. A voice in the wilderness—but you were never too
caught up with having to win."

"No," Frings said, looking for a way to escape. He saw his friend
Ben Linsky, a poet, deep in conversation with Wendy Otis. Linsky was
as close to a celebrity as existed in this scene. He was mostly known
as a poet, but he also edited *Prometheus*, the Tech's official literary

magazine, whose content and criticism set the tone for the City's art scene. His approval or disapproval would be crucial to Wendy's success—or failure.

Frings tried to catch Linsky's eye, without success.

"I don't know how you stomach it, Frank, with little Art Deyna getting the headlines and you . . ." It seemed, then, to dawn on Rappaport that he might be making an ass of himself and, to Frings's alarm, he plucked another drink from a passing tray.

"Enough about work," Rappaport continued. "How have *you* been, Frank? Who's gracing your arm these days? You always seem to have a bird. I was never sure how you did it, to be honest. The actresses, the singers, the socialites. But I guess I don't need to tell you. At *our* age, though," he paused and gave Frings what might have been a sly smile, "it must be difficult keeping up with the younger women of today."

"There's no one at the moment, Al," Frings said, becoming exasperated. "What brings *you* here tonight? I'd have thought this was a little too . . . cutting-edge for your taste. It's not as if you have to file a review."

Rappaport smiled. "Yes, that's right. But Wendy there, she's been friends with my Elizabeth—the overseas one—since grade school. Another daughter, almost. I'm very proud of her. I wouldn't miss her first show for anything. Sometimes you have to be a proud parent—or what have you—and leave the critic's lens at home, for once. What do you think of her work?"

Wendy's photographs were of urban and rural scenes blown up to poster size. She'd taken white paint and carefully traced over all of the man-made items in the various photos, leaving negative space anywhere humans had altered the visual landscape. In a photograph shot from a city rooftop, for instance, the antennae and power lines had been painted out, drawing attention to the shapes that people never noticed in the course of their lives. In a photo of a ranch, somewhere in the Southwest, Otis had whited out a split-rail fence, creating a strange, depthless, ladder-like space in the foreground of the photo.

"They're provocative," Frings said, hoping to leave it at that. He saw, to his relief, that Linsky and Wendy Otis had finished their conversation. Wendy was headed in their direction, clearly distressed, her eyes on Rappaport.

"I WAS PROBABLY TOO BLUNT WITH HER," LINSKY SAID, AND INHALED deeply from a joint he was sharing with Frings in the alley behind the gallery. It was dark, the only light from a bare bulb above the gallery's back door. Jazz music and the sound of voices leaked through the crack in the door where they'd propped it open.

"She was near tears, Ben." Linsky was a little older than most of the gallery crowd, in his late twenties. He was actually a very kind man, but Frings didn't like the spirit of his critiques. Linsky shared his opinion without giving a second thought to the effect his words would have. This had been one of those times.

"I need to learn to be more circumspect."

"They look up to you."

Linsky grimaced. "I know. And you know me Frank, I want everyone to be happy. But, as I told her, what she's got up on those walls, that's not art. It's pointing out something on a photograph. There's no art there. It's an essay. Art needs to comment on its own medium. Without that, it's nothing."

"I'm not sure everyone agrees with that assessment."

Linsky exhaled a cloud of pungent smoke and smiled. "Those people, they would be wrong."

"Ben, listen, I've got a question."

Linsky raised his eyebrows.

"You heard anything from Kollectiv 61 recently?"

Prometheus had run what purported to be Kollectiv 61's manifesto two years before, and there was a general feeling that Linsky was in occasional contact with members of the group.

"Rumors of my interaction with them are greatly exaggerated," he said, grinning broadly.

"Is that your way of saying you haven't?"

"It is, indeed," Linsky said, and took another drag.

8

FRINGS HADN'T BEEN ON THE TECH CAMPUS FOR YEARS AND FOUND, ON this cold, clear afternoon, that his memory of it as an anachronism still held. In the midst of the no-man's-land between Praeger's Hill and the Hollows—a dense patch marked by grinding poverty and routine violence—there was the Tech: a gated patch of sixteenth-century England, dropped intact into the City. Inside the walls, the setting was nearly rural: wide, green quads; perfectly manicured trees; handsome stone buildings meant to evoke Cambridge; well-groomed kids in sweaters, slacks, skirts, and penny loafers—all of this in a place where the City could be forgotten, if not for the car noise and, at night, the gunshots (infrequent) and police sirens (far more frequent).

But there was something else here, too, something new: a threat to the ideal picture that the Tech tried to present to the outside world. Frings thought he could see it in the faces of some of the students he passed: a look whose nature he couldn't quite glean, but which seemed to hint at a knowledge, an understanding, that had caused them to fall into cynicism, anger, even despair.

He passed the admissions building, where a group of students—unshaven men, women wearing wool caps—stood outside holding signs and passing out papers. Frings took one as he walked past. It was a call to admit more Negro students and hire more Negro professors. The signs were blunter: TECH ADMINISTRATION = JIM CROW, TRUE INTEGRATION TODAY. The Tech had always been very white—Negro and immigrant kids went to City College. Frings agreed with the kids' sentiments, but wondered what results, if any, these efforts would bring.

Frings walked stiffly, the temperature binding his knee in a dull ache. He asked a group of well-bundled co-eds where he could find the film department, and was pointed to a newer building, its unweathered bricks just visible above the dorms surrounding the quad.

• • •

THE DEPARTMENT WAS TUCKED INTO A SMALL SUITE OF OFFICES ON THE fourth floor of the Truffant Liberal Arts Building. A male student with thick glasses sat behind a desk in the middle of the foyer, reading a pamphlet of some kind.

"Anyone in?" Frings asked.

The kid glanced up from his tract, face pinched dramatically in annoyance at the interruption. "Ballard," the kid said, nodding to the only open door and returning quickly to his reading.

Frings poked his head into the open office. A skinny gink, probably Frings's age—on the good side of sixty—balding hair cut very short above a narrow face, was bent over his desk, reading something he held very close to his eyes.

"Doctor Ballard?"

The man looked up, startled.

"Sorry to interrupt your reading. I'm Frank Frings. I was wondering if you had a moment."

Ballard sat up in his seat. "Frings . . ." He thought about the name for a moment. "The reporter?"

Frings nodded.

Ballard frowned, gestured to a chair on the opposite side of his desk. His cramped office had room for little more than his desk, a couple of chairs, and shelves full of books. Frings had to lift a pile of books off the chair and place them on the floor. The top one was titled, *The Reflective Lens: Civilization and the New French Cinema*.

Ballard had wire-framed glasses on now, rubbing his hand along his scalp as if slicking back the hair that he'd once had.

"Dr. Ballard—"

"Eben."

"Okay. I'm Frank. Eben, I'm trying to track down a guy named Andy Macheda, might have been a student here."

Ballard leaned his head back and made a low humming sound, smacking his lips manically. Embarrassed by the odd tic, Frings glanced past him and out the window, which looked onto a parking lot. Ballard returned his attention to Frings. "Macheda, right, I remember him. Only here for a year or so—at least in this department. Brash fellow, as I remember him. Macheda, yes, it didn't work out for him here.

Film is funny, Mr. . . . Frank, film is funny because it is new, there isn't a history dating back centuries like painting or sculpture or even literature. Anyone of any ambition who comes into this department feels they are going to change the way films are made or the way they are experienced. Some are naive, some are genuinely exciting, some, like Andrew, find themselves on an unpromising tangent.

"He wrote a paper—this is why I remember him now—a paper to explain a film project that he had done: terribly disorganized, meaningless—the film, that is. The paper reflected some sort of formula that he'd come up with—that technical proficiency was somehow equivalent to science and science was equated with the creation of the Bomb and therefore technique was immoral. He dressed it up, but that is the essential argument." Ballard paused to let the audacity of the notion set in. "I showed it around the department. It had decidedly few admirers. The paper, though, was more memorable than those terrible films, or Andrew himself, for that matter."

"So he must have considered himself a radical."

"Oh god, yes. Him. Others. Craft is not immoral, Frank. Narrative does not inherently pervert truth. Telling a coherent story is not the moral equivalent of the Bomb. It's preposterous."

Frings got the point, trying to bring Ballard back to Macheda. "Andy Macheda, Eben, he was here when?"

"Three, four years ago. Something like that. He didn't stay long. I don't know if the other faculty might have some other memories of him beyond that paper. I'm sure he felt constrained here, that he was being judged to a standard he didn't agree with, but just because it's film doesn't mean that there are no rules, that anything goes."

"I saw a film of his."

Ballard's eyebrows rose.

"It was called *Film 12*. I was told that he comes into the cinema every once in a while and makes changes, taking out parts, adding others. After he makes the edits, he changes the title to, say, *Film 13*."

Ballard shook his head. "Foolishness."

Frings opened his briefcase and took out the five photos taken from the film still. He handed them to Ballard. "Do you know any of these people?"

Ballard removed his glasses and brought the photos close, so that they were almost touching his nose. He studied each in turn, concentrating.

"They're not very clear."

"I apologize for that."

"I can't say that I recognize any of them, though it could just be the poor quality of the images. Are these from a film still?"

"Yes."

"Well," he said priggishly, "I can't make out enough to say anything about them."

Frings put the photos away.

"I'm trying to run down Andy Macheda. Do you have any thoughts about where I might find him?"

"I can't imagine he's still in school—he was here years ago—but I think I may have heard that he's sometimes with Will Ebanks at that house of his. In fact, that doesn't surprise me. I can see a certain affinity between them. Ebanks has something of a *following* here," Ballard said with undisguised distaste. "Have you heard of him?"

Ebanks was, in fact, a friend of Frings's.

Ballard began to shuffle papers around on his desk, so Frings thanked him for his help and made his way back to the campus gates, where he could hail a cab. At the curb he looked across the street at the narrow stretch of housing associated with the Tech; maybe three blocks in length, it provided a buffer between the campus and the City beyond. Will Ebanks's house was in this neighborhood.

Frings was thinking about the strange scene that Ebanks had created at the house, when a cab finally pulled to the curb.

9

THE STREET WHERE THE THREE GUARDS FROM THE CROSSTOWN LIVED was unusually narrow, more like an alley. Grip wondered who the hell had designed this stretch; figured it must have predated automobiles because, although it had a center line, there was no way two cars could pass. As if it weren't cramped enough, parked cars and vending stalls straddled the curbs on both sides. But there wasn't any road traffic moving through anyway, just a delivery truck parked in the middle of the block, no driver in sight.

Everything in the neighborhood was close and loud and smelled unusual—not bad, exactly—just foreign. Grip found himself literally pushing through the crowd. Where the hell had all these people come from? The vending stalls seemed to be doing a good business in food, clothing, tattered books, a huge variety of things. Negotiations were carried out in rapid Bulgarian, of which Grip didn't understand a word.

He found some room to move on the edge of the sidewalk, brushing up against the faded walls of apartment buildings. Down the block he arrived at the address that he wanted, a narrow brick building, blue door with peeling paint. Looking up, he saw four floors, probably two apartments per floor. One buzzer for the whole building. He pushed it.

He heard the sound of someone fiddling with the chain, then the slide of a bolt. The door opened the crack that the chain allowed. The woman inside was very young, maybe even in her teens.

Grip spoke slowly. "I'm looking for George Petrov. Is he here?"

"Petrov?" She seemed uncertain.

"Yes. Petrov. Is he here?"

She shook her head.

"What about Zanev?"

She shook her head again. She seemed to be concentrating. Probably trying to decipher his accent.

He thought about pulling his badge, decided not to—probably spook her. "How about Malakov? Is he here?"

She shook her head again. "You wait." The door closed.

Grip waited. Four children stood in a group just a few feet down the sidewalk from him, checking him out. His suit, he realized, set him apart here. He winked at the kids and they scattered. In the distance he could hear sirens. The door opened against the chain again. This time the woman was older, probably the first one's mother.

"You look for Zanev?" Her English was heavily accented, difficult to understand.

"Do you know where he is?"

She made a fist, shook it, and then mimed a throw.

"What? Dice?"

"Dice," she said, remembering.

"Where?"

"Klimchuk's."

Dorman wasn't sure he'd heard the name right, but she repeated it—Klimchuk's. She pointed to her right. "Down street. Klimchuk's."

"Right, Klimchuk's."

Before she could close the door on him, he asked, "Is Zanev's wife here?"

"Wife?" she asked, puzzled.

"Yes," Grip said a little louder. "Zanev's wife."

"Zanev have no wife."

"Petrov?"

"Petrov also have no wife. Malakov, also. No wifes."

Grip was about to thank her when she closed the door and slid the bolt in place.

GRIP FOUND THE WINDOWLESS BAR TWO BLOCKS AWAY. THE CROWD WAS thinner down here, no stalls, no banter—the vitality gone, replaced with gray drear. The building looked as if it had once been some kind of storage facility, which had been converted fairly recently: the blue painted KLIMCHUK'S above the entrance was still bright. Grip tried the door. Locked. He could hear people inside. He knocked. The door opened to a huge man, fat, several days' stubble.

"Can I help you?" The guy blocked the view inside, gun bulge under his jacket.

"Can I come in?"

"I don't know you, chief."

Grip flashed his badge, watched the big man take it in, think over his position. He made Grip wait a long moment before stepping aside.

The place smelled like cigar smoke and boiled meat. Thirty or so tables were spread around the featureless room—craps, cards, half of the tables open and busy. Definitely illegal. Men only, excepting a dozen prostitutes in shabby cocktail dresses hanging around the long bar. Grip headed in that direction, smiling at the girls, giving off a cop vibe that kept them away. The bartender raised his eyebrows at Grip, who ordered a beer. When the bartender returned, Grip dropped a five on the bar.

"I'm looking for Zanev, Malakov, or Petrov. You seen them?"

"You a cop?"

"What tipped you off?" He followed the bartender's glare to the big doorman who scowled back at them.

"Why you want to know?"

"Just some questions, see if they know some things. I went by their job site but they weren't there. So here I am. No big deal. But a place like this . . . why not just help me out, get me on my way."

The bartender thought this over. A jukebox was blaring unusual music—the notes crashing into each other in a kind of whirling madness—a lot of accordion. Grip pulled on his beer, looked at it, threw it past the bartender into the line of booze bottles, where it shattered. Grip could feel the room's attention shift to him.

The bartender's eyes narrowed. He was angry, not intimidated, but understood that he needed to get Grip out of there. "Petrov was here with Zanev, playing craps. Malakov came later, pulled them off the table. They left together."

"When was that?"

"Two hours ago. Something like that."

"You know where they went?"

"How would I know that?"

Grip shrugged. "Look, those guys come back, can you give them something for me?"

The bartender raised his eyebrows. Grip dropped another five on the bar along with a business card. The bartender picked up the card, looked from it to Grip.

"Look, Ivan, you really want to make a stink about this, make me bring in backup, put you on the police map? You want the beat cops showing up every week, knocking on your door?"

"My name's not Ivan."

"The hell it's not," Grip said. "All of you're named Ivan."

The bartender scowled, pocketed the card, dropped the five in the tip jar, and moved off to another customer. Grip turned his back and leaned against the bar. The collective attention in the room returned to the tables, and Grip watched the adrenaline-fueled action from a distance. A prostitute—young, skinny, slightly cross-eyed—approached him.

She touched his arm. "I know you from somewhere?"

Grip shook his head. "I'm a cop."

"Buy me a drink?"

Grip wasn't sure what to make of this—stupidity or moxie? He pulled yet another five from his billfold, handed it to the girl.

"Have a drink. I've got to go." He walked out past the fat man at the door, patted him on the stomach, emerging onto the street wondering where the hell the three security guards had gone to.

10

THE RESTAURANT OF THE HOTEL LEOPOLD II WAS SITUATED ON THE TOP floor, taking advantage of its location on the crest of Capitol Heights. From the window where Frings sat, you could see more than half of the City. Skyscrapers rose in the downtown to the west, and the residential neighborhoods and smaller business districts filtered into the northern blocks, which had begun to be slashed to make way for the Crosstown, running relentlessly, neighborhood after neighborhood, toward downtown. Once you began to think about it, the New City Project's footprints were everywhere: the Riverside Expressway, hugging the contours of the river; a narrow concrete band separating the City from the water now that cargo no longer came up on barges; the Garibaldi Bridge over the northwest bend in the river, connecting the City to the northern suburbs, cutting commuting time to a quarter of its previous duration.

The restaurant was maybe two-thirds full, the ambience not quite what it was at night when the lighting was dim and the full spread of the City lights dazzled. Now, apart from the view, the place was just a fancy restaurant with tuxedoed waiters, fine linens on red tablecloths, expensive wine on the tables. Businessmen discussed deals; high-priced lawyers consulted with their wealthy clients; gangsters shooting for respectability tried to look comfortable among the real elite. There was more power in this room, Frings thought, than in all of City Hall. A jazz trio played softly in one corner. He washed down a solitary lunch with a glass of water, thinking about Sol Elia, Panos's troubled grandson.

EIGHT YEARS AGO, FRINGS HAD BEEN IN PANOS'S OFFICE WHEN THE CALL had been patched through from the police. *Urgent.* Frings had read the grave lines of his editor's face and stood to leave, but Panos held out a hand as he listened to the other end of the line. This was before the merger, and Panos's office stank of stale cigar smoke and leather-bound books decaying on the dusty shelves. Frings watched Panos's eyes—surprise, realization, then, slowly, profound dismay.

His grandson, Sol, had come home to find Panos's daughter Iliana and her husband Tom shot to death in the living room of their apartment in a high-rent neighborhood in upper Capitol Heights.

The investigation was frenzied. Tom was a public figure, a successful and dashing city attorney who seemed destined for a judgeship and, perhaps, even bigger things. Iliana was, in addition to being Panos's daughter, a frequent subject of the society pages in the lower-brow City newspapers—the *News* among them.

The early investigation focused on possible enemies of Tom's. He'd put plenty of people behind bars, stirred up trouble in the ethnic gangs that had been gaining traction in some neighborhoods. The tip line rang off the hook, plenty of people trying to settle scores by pointing a finger at this person or that, but nothing came of any of the leads. Everyone seemed to have an alibi, and the ones that didn't had no connection to either of the Ilias. The investigation stalled.

But Torsten Grip had interviewed the son, Sol, a couple of times early on and come away with a bad feeling. Something indefinable was wrong there, he'd told Frings, who'd contacted Grip on Panos's behalf. Grip brought the boy back in and ran through his story again. Sol had been four blocks away that afternoon at a friend's house, hanging out, listening to records. No, the friend's parents hadn't been home. The friends vouched for him, but it was a thin alibi. No problem getting lowlife friends like Sol's to lie to the heat.

Panos tried to intervene, using Frings to set up a meeting with Detective Grip. Panos made the case for his grandson's strange attitude and unseemly friends. His father's first priority was his career. He barely interacted with his son. His mother, Panos was ashamed to say, was a preening narcissist (his words). Was it any wonder the boy was finding his own way? But even as he was saying it, Panos could see how Grip was taking this. Alienated kid, resents—maybe hates—parents, scores a gun from his hoodlum friends and . . .

Grip stayed after Sol, but never could get far enough, couldn't get the big break. The gun never turned up. Sol's friends couldn't be shaken off their stories. Sol got used to Grip's "interviews," staring dolefully at him and eventually becoming unresponsive. Panos's lawyer alleged harassment, and Panos threatened to use the *Gazette* to make public Grip's seeming obsession with Sol. So eventually Grip had to give it up, move on to other cases. Panos went crazy trying to help the kid, getting him to move into his apartment, sending him to the Tech, protecting him in any way he could from the suspicion that followed him around. Watching it play out, Frings wondered if maybe Panos thought that Sol *had* done it, and by somehow steering his grandson straight, Panos could undo it. Which was why his disappearance had come as such a blow to the old man. Sol had turned away from his one ally, the one person who loved him. Now Panos had a new purchase on Sol, albeit in a film that might be as much as two years old.

The waiter came with the check. Frings wondered why Sol had stayed clear of Panos, if reconnecting them was a good idea. And he wondered, as he had since the day of the murders, whether Sol was a killer.

11

HIS COLLAR UP AGAINST AN ICY WIND, GRIP WALKED PAST A SMALL FERRIS wheel, maybe thirty feet high, the entire contraption gone to rust. A fairground in miniature: a tiny roller coaster with gently sloping rails; little booths, the signs mostly bleached away but still discernable: "five shots for five cents," over a deteriorating shed whose contents were long gone. Grip felt the eyes of animals staring at him from the dark gaps—a sign of years of abandonment. His shoes were soaked through, yellow-brown puddles standing in every depression in the sandy dirt. He heard a whistle and stopped, tried in the sickly orange light to get a fix on the direction. He heard it again and looked toward a shack. Above the boarded-up service window hung a COTTON CANDY sign, now missing both T's and the N and D from CANDY.

The side door was gone, and Grip stepped through the opening into semi-darkness, the place smelling of wet dirt and mold. Leaning against the far wall was runty Nicky Patridis, the stub of a cigarette dangling from his lower lip, smoke wafting damply to the ceiling.

"The fuck you find these places?" Grip mumbled.

"Jesus, Grip, you're always complaining. Don't worry, what I've got, it's gonna be worth it."

"That right?"

"Sure. You got a fag for me?" Nicky had the hard, wiry physique and tense eyes of people who lived on the City's margins, surviving from meal to meal, cigarette to cigarette. Grip shook a pack and offered it to Nicky, who took a cigarette and lit it off his stub. The two men were roughly the same height, but Grip probably had sixty pounds of muscle on him.

"You going to make me smoke alone?"

Grip shook his head. "I don't plan on sticking around that long."

Nicky shrugged.

"Okay, Nicky. What the fuck am I here for?"

Nicky took a long drag, held it in his lungs and then blew it at the ceiling. "What I heard is: someone hit one of the construction sites, made off with explosives. Lots of them."

Grip raised his eyebrows, noncommittal, though not surprised that the word was out so quickly.

"I know this ain't news to you. Something like that? The cops are on it early."

"You're a fucking genius. What've you got?"

"What I *got* is a cousin, works as a floater for the Project security crews. You know they all work for Consolidated, right? They have some guys, like my cousin, they send to different places, fill holes if someone gets fired or sick or whatever. So anyway, my cousin, he says he was on the site last night, working with some Russians or something. Said they see a panel truck pull up to the gate, hit the horn a couple times and suddenly one of the Russians gives my cousin a twenty to go for a walk, have a cigarette. He pisses off, right? But he finds a place where he can get a look at what's going on 'cause he knows I'm on the payroll occasionally and thinks he might get in on it, too. Two guys, he says, not big. They empty the whole fucking trailer. Took the whole thing."

Nicky was taking his time, and it was getting on Grip's nerves. "There a point to this?"

"Look, there's a way this shit goes. You know that. Nobody sits on any of the construction heists, least of all explosives. It's got to go through a lot of hands before it's clean to sell back to the project. That's how it works. So, something this big, people are waiting for the dynamite to get in the pipeline. But it hasn't shown up."

"It's only been a couple days." But Grip knew Nicky was right. Something was off.

"Come on, detective. You'd sit on a haul of dynamite that'd take down a couple of buildings? This shit's done fast, there's people need to get it depending on where you nicked it from. If it don't turn up, people start getting worried. Like now."

Grip could see where this was going, but he strung Nicky along, wanting to hear his reasoning. "New operator?"

Nicky leaned back against a ragged wall, took a drag. "You'd have to be stupid as hell. Like I said, it's all set up, the whole process. Go through it, take your cut, repeat. It's easy. Why fuck with a good thing?"

"You going to tell me?"

They looked at each other. Nicky blew a smoke ring. It wobbled upward.

"Any time, Nicky."

Nicky shook his head as if he couldn't believe Grip was so fucking dense. "You been listening? From where I sit, it don't look like the guys nicked this dynamite plan on selling it back."

"Right," Grip said, as though this was obvious. "They're going to use it."

Nicky seemed a little deflated by this response. Grip decided to have a cigarette after all. Nicky cleared his throat as Grip fished one out. He pulled another. The little bastard could probably use it. Grip lit his own cigarette with his lighter. Nicky pocketed his extra, smirking.

"Kollectiv 61," Grip said, exhaling smoke as he spoke.

Nicky showed his palms. "You said that, not me."

Grip sighed, fished out his wallet. Outside, a crow was making a racket. Grip wanted to get out of there. He handed Nicky a twenty.

"That's it? Come on, man, this is good information; gets you started on the right foot."

"You think I'm stupid, Nicky? You think I haven't figured Kollectiv 61? You get twenty now, 'cause you've probably saved me some headache. This leads to anything, you'll get what it's worth. I've never screwed you, Nicky. That's why you called me."

Nicky gave a half-smile. "Yeah, I guess that's right."

12

WILL EBANKS LIVED IN A GRAND HOUSE A COUPLE BLOCKS FROM THE Tech campus. He was a member of one of the City's aristocratic families, going back four generations to Brewer Ebanks, who'd owned the riverfront docks and warehouses and possibly a few mayors, as well. While the family's power had faded, the Ebanks name still held the cachet of what passed in the City for noble birth.

The house had once been the residence of a City elder named Heyteveldt, who'd funded the construction of the first Tech buildings. Ebanks had bought it a few years back from Heyteveldt's great-grandson, or maybe it was the great-great-grandson, Frings couldn't remember which. A wide front porch sprawled before ornate oak double doors, the available space cluttered by all matter of wood and rattan chairs. The house was painted a sky blue with yellow trim, and the two low towers that rose a story above the house on each side were a bright red. It was a strange looking place. A plaque next to the door read INSTITUTE FOR CONSCIOUSNESS EXPLORATION.

Frings rapped on the door with his cane, like something from a movie, which was why he did it—to amuse himself. He stood back from the door and waited, watching the pedestrians—mostly Tech professors and their families. He knew that Ebanks wasn't popular with his neighbors because of the unusual people he attracted, the parties, the strange goings-on at all times of day and night.

The door opened to a small gink, probably college aged, wearing a frayed green wool sweater.

"Who're you?"

"Frank Frings. Is Will around?"

"You have an appointment?"

An appointment? "No, we're friends." Technically true, he thought, though they hadn't seen much of each other over the past decade as Ebanks had pursued his stormy academic career—and now the drugs.

The man in the green sweater thought about this for a moment, a funny grin on his face. "Come on in. I'll see if he's available."

Frings followed him in, a little annoyed that this kid presumed to play gatekeeper. The grand foyer reeked of marijuana and incense. A group of college students sat on couches, talking and passing a pipe. Behind them, flanking a set of double doors, a twin staircase wound up to a balcony behind which, Frings knew, were Ebanks's living quarters. The man in the green sweater gestured Frings to a sofa beneath a print of Dali's *Last Supper*, then climbed the stairs.

Frings took in the room, surrealist prints on the wall, statues of animal-headed Hindu gods perched on pedestals, chairs upholstered in mismatched paisley fabric. The college kids gave him a cursory look and then proceeded to ignore him, talking about people whose names he didn't recognize. From beyond the double doors, Frings could hear more people talking, a guitar being strummed. There was something indefinably *off* here. Frings considered it, trying to isolate the cause, but thought that maybe it wasn't any one thing, so much as a more fundamental dissonance, like an instrument being played in a different time signature from the rest of the band.

Green Sweater came back, an aloof expression firmly in place, and told Frings that Ebanks was waiting for him. Frings struggled up the stairs, one step at a time, his knee stubbornly refusing to bend.

He found Ebanks sprawled across an upholstered chair, smoking a cigarette, talking to a younger man—blond hair down to his collar, thick mustache—sitting in an identical chair and arranged in a nearly identical posture of relaxation. Ebanks saw Frings in the doorway and gave a broad, sincere smile.

"Frank!" He stood, tall and poised, his body slim like a college kid's. He was handsome in a patrician way, with sparkling blue eyes and tousled brown hair. He gave Frings a hug that Frings, surprised, reciprocated. This, Frings thought, was a little unusual, even for a free spirit like Ebanks.

"Will, you got a minute maybe we could talk alone? Then I'll let you get back to whatever it is you're doing."

Ebanks raised his eyebrows. "Sure." He turned to the younger man in the chairs. "You mind, Blaine? Maybe get us some coffee from downstairs."

The young guy rose—barrel-chested but not fat—not seeming to mind at all. He nodded to Frings as he walked out. Frings was reminded somehow of a cowboy in a cigarette ad.

"We were talking about this amazing experience that we had yesterday," Ebanks explained. "Debriefing really, research reporting."

The young guy pulled the door shut behind him. Persian rugs covered the floor and two of the floor-to-ceiling windows had been paned in stained glass, lending the room an unnatural light—at once heightened and subdued.

"What kind of experience?" Frings asked, because Ebanks seemed to want him to be interested.

"Oh, LSD. Have you tried it, Frank? Lysergic acid diethylamide? I actually don't believe you have or I would know." His eyes were alive and bright. "But you should, you really should. It's . . . it's hard to explain what it is, but I guarantee you won't look at things the same way again. It opens up the spiritual world. It opens it all the way up, shows the connections between things, Frank. Very heavy. You realize that you don't see the half of it, not even a tenth."

Frings nodded. He'd heard about LSD, knew that Ebanks was an enthusiast, and that he'd been kicked off the faculty at the Tech because of it, though Frings didn't know the details. The drug held a vague interest for him, the way certain kinds of exotica sometimes did, but he had no desire to actually try it—his time for that kind of experimentation had long since passed.

"I hate to do this, Will, because I'd rather chat, catch up a little. But I'm working on something right now that you might be able to help with. I was wondering if you could take a look at a few pictures, see if you can identify the people."

He could see Ebanks's disappointment that he wasn't more interested in the drug.

"Sure Frank, you bet. What's up?"

"You know a guy, Andy Macheda? Film guy?"

"Yeah, I know Andy. He shows up here every once in a while."

"You know anything about the film he shows over at that little basement theater on the edge of the Heights? Film something-or-other."

"I saw it, actually, back when it was *Film 8*, I think, or something like that. He's got some ideas about a living film or some such, keeps changing it, he says, reflecting the moment or some shit like that. Weird hombre." Ebanks had always possessed an offhand charisma, a knack for putting people at ease. Something about him now seemed beyond that, a kind of magnanimity that made itself felt just in his presence.

"These photos, they're enlargements of a still from that film." He pulled them from his jacket pocket and handed Ebanks one of the prints.

Ebanks squinted at it, shrugged. "I don't know. Maybe, but I don't think so. It's really blurry."

"I know." Frings handed him the one of Sol Elia, Panos's grandson.

Ebanks shook his head. "You know, maybe. There are so many people come through here, Frank."

"Okay. How about this one?"

"No." Ebanks shook his head, smiling. "Really, Frank, what do you expect?"

Frings didn't know, but handed the picture of the fourth man to Ebanks.

"Yeah, not sure about him, either."

Frings took the photos back. He assessed his friend, the gleaming eyes, the eager face, but despite his enormous charm, something was not quite in sync, like he'd felt downstairs.

"You know where I can track down Macheda?"

"I can find out for you. But . . . what's up, Frank? What's with the questions?"

"The second guy I showed you is a kid named Sol Elia. He's Panos's grandson and he's been missing for a while."

"Is that the kid . . .?"

"That's him. Give me a buzz when you find out about Macheda, okay?"

Ebanks frowned, tilting his head back a little. The posture bothered Frings for some reason.

"Sure, Frank," Ebanks said, sounding distracted, as if he was thinking something over.

13

GRIP'S USUAL BAR DIDN'T HAVE AN OFFICIAL NAME BUT WAS KNOWN AS Crippen's, after the original owner, now deceased. Crippen's occupied the basement of a building that had housed a number of businesses, at the moment a tobacconist who sold pornography out of a grim room in the back. In the months immediately following the tobacconist's opening, the sidewalk in front had become a meeting spot for a group of seedy porn enthusiasts. The patrons at Crippen's weren't the type to ignore the sudden influx of perverts onto their block, and there followed a number of incidents where a group of drunks would emerge to chase off the pervs and hand out a beating to anyone unlucky enough to be caught. Yet they came back, stubbornly, pathetically. Grip eventually took the matter into his own hands, paying a visit to the owner, a near-blind old man named Krebs, who still had the arms and hands of a brawler, the type of guy who'd understand the realities of power. *You want the morals squad paying you a visit every fucking day? No? Then keep the perverts off the block.* The old guy got it, and the problem went away, the pervs doing their shopping and then making sure to get the hell out of there, if they wanted the store to be around when they came back.

Grip found Crippen's peopled with its usual collection of old-timers drinking whisky at the bar and some off-duty cops shooting the shit. He didn't go there for the atmosphere—linoleum floors, Bakelite tables with mismatched chairs, a bar made out of rickety, piece-of-shit maple. The place didn't even bother to keep the lights down to hide the seediness—it was lit up bright, though this was mostly for the benefit of the old-timers reading *Freedom's Call*, the weekly far-right rag, or the sports scores and obits in one of the dailies. Crippen's was a gathering spot for a certain brand of committed anti-communist: men—because there were never any women—for whom the Red Conspiracy occupied a position of primary importance in their lives. The rantings of radio hosts blared from the back, the intensity of their bile monotonous.

Raising two fingers to the bartender, Grip walked over to a table where a former cop named Ed Wayne drank beer with a younger guy Grip recognized from the Force, a clean cut, blond kid named Albertsson.

Grip shook hands with the two men, Albertsson's grip hard, trying to prove something. Wayne's hand lay in Grip's, soft and damp, like an eel.

"How're things, Ed?"

Wayne shrugged. In truth, it was hard to imagine how things could be good for Wayne. A half-dozen years ago he'd been a cop—not a model cop, though effective in his own way—but then something had happened to him, some kind of rapid physical decline. He'd lost all of his hair, right down to the eyebrows, and his chin seemed to have dissolved, his head tapering into his neck. He'd never been thin, but loose fat now hung sickeningly over his belt.

He'd been booted off the force several years back for conducting interview room interrogations that were bloody, even by the Force's loose standards, and then, less than a year later, lost his wife to a divorce and a restraining order. Since then, he'd more or less fallen off the mental cliff, too. But, somehow, he managed to remain in the center of things. If something happened in the City's tight, vocal world of ultra-conservative patriots, he knew about it—was often responsible for it. He had a considerable number of friends still on the Force, and he worked as a bagman for various people, including a multi-millionaire named Gerald Svinblad. A significant amount of the vandalism and violence against radicals could be traced back to Wayne or the cadre of young, impressionable men who followed him around in search of ideological guidance.

Today he wore a porkpie hat on his bald head and tinted glasses, which had the odd effect of making him look like he was in costume.

"I was talking to Albertsson here about the olden days."

Grip glanced at Albertsson and was struck by how young he seemed, his expression credulous as he listened to one of the most shameless exaggerators and liars that Grip knew, which was saying something. This was what bothered Grip about the right-wingers that hung around Crippen's—their diagnosis and goals were spot-on, but their self-aggrandizement and conspiracy-mongering rendered the whole effort less serious.

"Great," Grip said without enthusiasm.

"You did some damage in your day," Albertsson said admiringly, trying to suppress a country accent.

In his day?

Wayne leaned in over the table, his breath rank with alcohol. "Tor, here," he said to Albertsson, "is a fucking patriot, a real fucking American. He will kick the shit out of any stinking commie you point to. But he doesn't have the fucking brain, you hear? He doesn't *see* things too well. He's a soldier, Tor is, not a general." Wayne leaned back in his chair and laughed, drunk off his ass.

Grip eyed him from behind his tilted beer bottle. Wayne—the bully turned into a goddamn demon by whatever it was that had happened to him, transforming him from an asshole into something else, something even less pleasant—something that Grip didn't really understand.

"You seem happy about something."

"Happy?"

Maybe happy wasn't the word. It was more like Wayne's approximation of happiness—energy, concentration, a particularly focused meanness.

"You've got something in your head."

Wayne grinned, showing his strange little teeth. "I always have something in my head, Tor."

"Something new."

"Since you mention it"—Wayne said, with a sly glance at Albertsson—"I've been doing a little research, talking to some people about the New City Project. I've found out *things*. Did you know that Nathan Canada's given name is Toporov? He changed it to Canada back in the thirties. He's Russian."

"He's not fucking Russian, Ed. You ever heard the guy speak? He went to the Tech, grew up in the City. All that shit was proved wrong half a decade ago—pretty much when it first came out."

Wayne laughed in disgust. "Proved by who? Someone you trust? The Riverside Expressway, you ever look at the back of the road signs? Codes. Letters. Numbers."

Grip looked to Albertsson, who was taking this in with great interest.

"Okay, Ed, what do they mean?"

Wayne shrugged. "Fucked if I know. Still looking. But Zwieg—you know him."

Grip nodded. He certainly did.

"Zwieg says he saw a memo that went through Canada's office, said that these codes were directions for foreign troops when they roll in. The Riverside, the Crosstown—they're being built to allow troops to enter the City more efficiently. Did you know the elevated sections are designed to hold the weight of a battalion of Russian T-54s? And the top of the Municipal Tower, the observatory—they're wiring it up. It's going to be the command center for the whole fucking thing. Right upstairs from Canada's office. The electricians show up at night in unmarked vans. I know guys at the site who've seen them."

"Huh, that's really interesting," Grip said without enthusiasm. More bullshit from Wayne, who was even edgier than usual. The New City Project brought it out in the lunatics of all persuasions—Kollectiv 61 on one side, the *Freedom's Call* crowd on the other.

Grip stayed busy with his beer, ignoring Wayne for the most part, watching the old men at the bar—World War I vets, most of them—and wondering if this was how it would end for them: drinking every day in this dingy bar, talking shit about things they'd never act on. Grip lit a cigarette. Wayne was seeking his input on something, but Grip hadn't been paying attention and waved it away with a flick of the wrist.

Albertsson got up to use the bathroom, leaving Grip alone with Wayne. Wayne's eyes were watery with drink, his head cocked slightly back, stretching his pale jowls.

"Anything interesting lately, Ed?" Grip didn't think that the Crippen's crowd was involved in the dynamite theft, but Wayne would know for sure.

"You're a sly one, Tor. Casting the line. If I were to say yes, that word is there's a missing stash of TNT, would that count as a big one?"

"You got any thoughts on who might have it?"

"None of ours. I'd know. But you've figured that out, right? I think you've figured it all out. Our friends in the Kollectiv 61, right? But the problem you have is: who the fuck is the Kollectiv 61? *Who are they?*"

Grip frowned, acknowledging the accuracy of Wayne's thoughts.

Wayne took a shot of whisky, wincing as it went down. "Where to look? Where to look?" he mused.

"You have a thought or you just like hearing yourself talk?"

Wayne laughed, cynical and phlegmy. "Right, Tor, down to business."

"Before your friend gets back."

Wayne raised the mound above his right eye where an eyebrow had once been. "Not trusting the new blood? Okay. Ben Linsky. If it was me, that's where I'd start.

The name was familiar. "The poet?"

"The *faggot* poet."

Grip nodded, remembering now that *Prometheus* had run Kollectiv 61's manifesto a year back or so. The Force had looked into it, tried to figure out if there was a more solid link between Linsky and the group, but had come up empty. Zwieg, Grip thought, might have been on that case.

They sat without speaking for a minute, Grip listening to Wayne mouth-breathing, remembering that there was something wrong with his nose, that he couldn't breathe out of it for some reason. Albertsson came out of the restroom, tucking his shirt into his khakis, looking, to Grip's surprise, fairly sober. He sat back down in his seat, forearms on the table.

"What'd I miss?" he asked, grinning.

14

DORMAN HAD A REGULAR TABLE AT THE ARES CLUB, A SEMICIRCULAR booth around a half-moon glass-top in a dark corner of the dark room. The house band played their usual languid jazz, backing a woman who sang in Portuguese, her voice weightless. From where he sat the band was hard to make out beneath the red spotlights and the haze of smoke. He sat alone, some papers on the table, his briefcase on the bench beside him. His martini glass was empty.

He leafed through a report on the upcoming destruction of the neighborhood surrounding St. Stanislaw's church—who would handle the demolition, the waste removal, the infrastructure improvements, and so on. In each of these contracts, extra funds had been allocated, though they would never make it to the contractor. This was the grease, the money that ensured that everything ran smoothly. It wasn't even a matter of keeping two ledgers. The contractors simply invoiced for more than they needed and didn't complain when they only got their actual price. Not complicated. The hardest thing about it was keeping Canada far enough removed from these deals that he couldn't be implicated. Canada was always worried about this distance. He needed it both for (obvious) legal reasons, but also to avoid having the petty corruption used as leverage against him.

Dorman was always protecting Canada, had been for more than two years since he'd taken the job as Canada's right-hand man, straight out of the Navy. Dorman had come out of the service with a big reputation, and Canada had brought him in to interview based on what he'd heard from people who'd met him. Canada had pitched him—*you will be an integral part of the most important urban plan-*

ning project in a century. We need someone uncorrupted in this position—someone incorruptible.

But why him?

Canada had leaned back in his chair, laced his fingers over his fleshy middle. "There are plenty of untouchables out there, Mr. Dorman, but few who know how to persuade and fewer still who have both these qualities and are willing to play the hard game, as well."

So Canada had hired him—the man who could not be corrupted—dropped him into a sea of corruption and told him to navigate without getting wet.

A THIN BLONDE SHEATHED IN A BLACK COCKTAIL DRESS APPROACHED WITH a bottle of wine and two glasses. Dorman sat back, took in her big, heavy-lidded eyes, her cupid's-bow mouth, her slender legs.

"Care for a 1923?" She spoke with an accent, something Eastern European. Dorman had never asked her where she was from, exactly, and she'd never offered.

"Sure." He watched as she put the glasses down, uncorked the bottle with unhurried grace. She poured wine into the two glasses and slid in next to him, crossing her legs so that her foot barely brushed his thigh. His mouth went dry.

"Still working?" She sipped her wine. He knew her as Anastasia, though he was sure this was not her real name. The only women inside the club were employees, and they all used fake names. It was a house rule.

"I could work all day and all night. I just need a reason to stop."

"Like me?"

Dorman nodded and took a sip. Anastasia nearly always came to sit with him when he was here, maybe four or five nights a week. A couple of times in the past another girl had come because Anastasia was out, but the club liked to pair each member with the same girl every visit, build a certain kind of relationship—a mix of discretion and ambiguity.

"You are tired," Anastasia said, her lips shining as candlelight reflected off the sheen of the wine.

"It's been a long day."

It was always a long day. She waited, running her finger around the rim of the glass. She was patient; she would listen when he was ready to talk. Discretion is what they sold at the Ares, billed as a place for men to unburden themselves of their secrets to women who would keep them.

But Dorman couldn't make the leap. "Complications at work."

WHAT HE DIDN'T TELL HER:

Before lunch, Canada called him into his office, Dorman noting the dozen or so cigarettes already lying crushed in the ashtray. Canada sat still in his chair, looking over his reading glasses at Dorman, lit cigarette in one hand, the fingers of the other drumming on his desk. He knew. No point in trying to finesse it.

"I wanted to wait, try to get some information."

Canada snorted, pissed off. "More information," he said quietly.

"Before I told you, Mr. Canada."

Canada took a deep breath, responded in a voice tight with anger. "You think I'm willing to fucking wait to hear that a trailer full of dynamite was stolen? You think I want to hear it from that goddamn spic . . . Jorge, what the hell was his name . . . Goddamn it. It doesn't matter. What matters is I get this goddamned call about a fucking explosives robbery, and I'm caught with my shriveled cock in my hand."

Dorman waited, knowing there was more.

"While you've been doing whatever the fuck it is you've been doing, I've been working your goddamn job for you, and it hasn't been pretty. I had to call that fuckwit Ving, ask him to send over Zwieg. *Ask him*, for the love of Christ. Ving doesn't even know what the fuck's going on, but I tell him, send the stupid Neanderthal over. Zwieg comes in here and I have to explain to him in minute goddamn detail the method by which I will castrate him if there is a leak. *I* don't deal with shitheads like Zwieg. That's why I have you."

Canada took a moment to settle, bring his volume back down to conversational.

"Take care of the press. Figure out what they've got. If you need to bargain, give them something—the cash that priest down in Little Lisbon paid to those Turks to let the Crosstown run through *their* backyard. That's history at this point, no harm."

Having ridden out Canada's temper, Dorman nodded, flashed the boss his cocky half-grin, the one that seemed to inspire confidence. He was good at his job. He'd take care of the problems.

"COMPLICATIONS," SHE ECHOED, HER VOICE BETRAYING NOTHING.

HE DIDN'T TELL HER ABOUT HIS VISIT EARLIER THAT EVENING TO THE steamy basement of St. Stanislaw's Orthodox Church, the pipes from the boiler radiating heat in the close quarters, clanging as air bubbles forced their way through the ancient system. The men waiting around the table wore ties despite the stifling temperature, their sleeves rolled up. They mopped their brows with handkerchiefs.

The leader of the neighborhood delegation was Peter Trochowski, a stocky man, white hair ringing his bald crown, a red drinker's nose.

"Mr. Dorman—"

"Call me Phil, Mr. Trochowski," Dorman was alone, as he liked to be when he had to do this kind of work. He wasn't in any physical danger. No one would cross Nathan Canada.

Trochowski's collar was dark with sweat. "You have to understand that the Crosstown will destroy our neighborhood, the biggest Polish neighborhood in the City. This will be a tragedy, a wrong that cannot be corrected later."

Dorman nodded, half-listening. He'd heard it before—again and again. He gave the same answers that he always gave: "*We are well aware of the enormous impact that the Crosstown will have on your community, etc., etc. We will make every effort to help relocate both people and businesses, and so on.*" Christ, it was hot in there.

The old man reacted the way they often did—with desperation. "This cannot happen in America."

This part was never his favorite, but it was important. People needed to understand that their narrow interests couldn't take precedence over the good of the City.

"Actually, Mr. Trochowski, in America we *can* take your neighborhood from you if it is in the best interest of the state, which, I'm afraid, this is." He saw the loathing in their glares, felt it as an almost physical sensation.

He said, "I need you to understand that if we don't build the Crosstown, the New City Project will not be completed, and if it is not completed every expert agrees that the City will die. Commerce will leave the City and the City will die and with it, your neighborhood."

Trochowski, his face bright red and shedding sweat, wasn't convinced. They never were at first.

"Let me explain it another way, Mr. Trochowski. Your neighborhood is already gone. The decision has been made. It's too late to change that. We've made this situation plain with communities before, and we will make it plain to communities in the future. You can cooperate with us, and we will do our best to help you during this time of change. You can also cause problems, like the incident that you no doubt read about in yesterday's paper, and in that case we will be less . . . predisposed toward your community's welfare." He kept his voice even. You had to be calm, keep it from getting personal, but never retreat for even a second. You could not give any hint that there was room for negotiation, because there wasn't. It was a done deal. This way was better for everyone.

He showed them the case with the money, watched the effect that the stacks of bills had on the men's faces.

Trochowski leaned forward over the table, sweat dropping onto the top bills. "We cannot be bought."

"We're not trying to buy you, sir. We don't *need* to buy you. We're trying to help you. That's all we can do now."

Trochowski stood and slammed the case shut. Sometimes they started by refusing the money. They usually came around.

It was a fool's errand trying to explain to people that while he—Dorman—understood their distress and the devastating effect that the Crosstown would have on their lives, not building the Crosstown would have a different but no less devastating outcome for them as the City crumbled around them. Most didn't understand, and if they did, they couldn't see why it had to be *their* neighborhood and not the one to the east or to the west. These were decisions made through a calculus of money and influence. He didn't want to know the details, only to have to keep them from people. The details weren't his problem.

As he emerged from the old church onto the steps leading down to the sidewalk, he'd heard a whistle and followed the sound across the street, up to the roof of a four-story apartment building. A crude dummy fashioned from pillows hung from a noose dangling from the roof. Even from that distance, Dorman was able to read "Canada" written on the sign attached to the dummy's chest.

NEAR TWO IN THE MORNING, TIRED AND DRUNK, DORMAN GATHERED his papers, another night passed without being able to confide to Anastasia.

He knew that people here took the girls home sometimes, but he had never done that with her. He wasn't sure that he wanted to risk somehow queering their limited relationship. But he felt the tightening in his chest as he stood and she walked with him to the door, her hand on his arm. They paused at the threshold. He looked in her eyes, but she was unreadable.

15

GRIP KNEW THAT HE CAME WITH AN AURA, THAT ALL COPS WHOSE partners were killed in the line of duty had one. It was the kind of thing that set him subtly apart—just a bit on the margins—despite the number of friends he had on the Force and the far greater number who respected or feared him. It was a complicated weight to carry around, the Burden of the Dead Partner. Every cop that knew about Morphy—and who didn't know Morphy, if only by reputation?—felt a number of things at once: the horror, of course—this was every cop's nightmare—pity for the guilt he had to live with, and anger that he hadn't been able to somehow rescue his partner, suspicion that maybe he wasn't a cop that you wanted watching your back. This final reaction, the doubt about his capabilities, was the one that festered in Grip, brought out the rage in him and with it, sometimes, recklessness. He'd been put on admin leave for three months after Morphy's death. When he returned, they'd partnered him with a detective sent over from Violent Crimes, an old hand who would keep an eye on him, offer counsel when necessary. Grip rode it out with the new partner, not as bad as it could have been because this new guy was nothing like the old. But that ended, too, and Grip was allowed to work solo, an arrangement that seemed a relief to everyone.

Now he stood with two uniforms across the street from a shabby little joint called Cafe ?, where the Tech heemies drank coffee and smoked and spewed their Marxist bullshit. One of the uniforms, a mug named Schillaci who Grip barely knew, spit onto the sidewalk and spoke out of the side of his mouth. "You talk to Lieutenant Boyer?"

"What about him?" Grip scowled, chewed on his lip. He should have been in the cafe already—would have been, if these two shitbirds hadn't seen him on the street and come over to see what he was up to.

Schillaci shrugged, "This is his neighborhood, thought you might have run what you're doing by him."

The fiefdoms. Since the last chief had been assassinated and Kraatjes took his place, the Force had shattered into dozens of little domains—sergeants, lieutenants, captains, all carving out territory. Things had become complicated, cops suddenly required to get permission from other cops to conduct business in their neighborhoods. This permission was sometimes withheld. Guns were drawn on occasion, though no one had been fool enough to actually pull the trigger.

And during all this, not a move from Kraatjes, holed up on the top floor of headquarters, doing god-only-knew-what, pushing black budgets through the Council. Most cops had thought that he'd gone into hiding, was ignoring the street, but he'd proved them wrong. A couple of lieutenants had made a move on him, a power grab, tried to frame him up with a cache of cocaine supposedly purchased with black-budget funds. Kraatjes had sussed it out, though, caught them moving the drugs at night, the press on hand to report the whole thing. A month later, they'd been in the pen—forty-five to life.

No one had underestimated Kraatjes after that.

GRIP TURNED TO SCHILLACI, HIS RIGHT SHOULDER NOW CATCHING A LITTLE rain. "What *am* I doing, officer?"

Schillaci spit again, chin down, eyes up in their sockets to see Grip. "You haven't said, but it's got to be something, right? You're not out here in the rain, enjoying the view. All I'm saying is, have you run it past Boyer?"

Grip frowned at Schillaci, leaned back against the wall. He'd be damned if he was going to clear anything with Chet fucking Boyer. He turned to the other officer, a younger guy, the tough look on the kid's face taking some concentration.

"What about you? You watching Boyer's turf, too? Going to make sure I don't shit in his yard?"

The kid hesitated, and Schillaci saved him. "Come on, Detective, you know how it is now. This is Boyer's neighborhood, you've got to work it through him."

"Tell you what. Why don't you go find Boyer, tell him to fuck himself, and if he has a problem with that, have him take it up with Zwieg."

"Zwieg?" Schillaci was suddenly less sure of himself. "What's Zwieg running here?"

"You're so interested, why don't you go ask him?"

Schillaci took this in with a look of pained uncertainty. Grip finished his cigarette and tossed it into the street. "What's it going to be?"

The kid was looking at his feet, abdicating. Schillaci held what was left of his cigarette between his thumb and middle finger and with his index finger flicked it into the street.

"Make it quick."

GRIP TURNED UP THE COLLAR OF HIS JACKET AND WALKED ACROSS THE street, holding his hand out to stop a truck that was creeping along, the driver trying to make out addresses. Grip could feel the tension in his shoulders, his temper straining against his control. Fucking cops acting like gangsters protecting their turf. Their job was tough enough without piling on more bullshit.

He paused under the awning of Cafe ?, patted his gun, palmed his badge. Satisfied he was ready, he opened the door and eased into the smoky room, only five or six tables in addition to four that had been pushed together to his right. His entrance drew looks. He knew he stood out—suit, age, build. He walked over to the gathered tables, showed his badge, watched all the gazes gravitate to a chubby little guy, a few days' stubble, old corduroys, ancient sweater.

"Can we help you, sir?" The guy's voice was strong, confident. *We.* "You Ben Linsky?"

He didn't respond, but his eyes didn't deny it.

Grip eyed a leather satchel leaning against Linsky's chair. "Mr. Linsky, if you would get out of your chair and walk to the end of the table."

Linsky seemed of two minds, but got up and walked slowly to the end of the table. The others stayed in their chairs, looking uncomfortable, though not especially threatened.

Grip lifted the satchel.

"Hey, man." Linsky took a step forward.

Grip looked up, eyes wide. "Get the fuck back." He saw the effect that these growled words had on the others, their eyes suddenly on the tables before them.

"You've got no right to—"

Grip looked at Linsky, giving him some credit for not folding. "Shut up." He unlatched the closure and flipped back the flap.

"You don't—"

"I don't what?" Grip said, glaring, starting to enjoy this. "I don't what?" He went back to the satchel, fingering through the mess of papers. An inside pocket bulged. Grip fished into it with a finger, hooked out a small linen pouch. He sniffed it, looking at Linsky while he did. Linsky was pale, trembling with fear or rage.

With two fingers Grip opened the little pouch and removed a small bud of marijuana, holding it theatrically up to the light.

"This your bag?" he asked Ben.

Linsky nodded, jaw set.

Grip smiled. "I'm afraid that I'm going to have to bring it in as evidence."

"Can I at least get my papers, my work? You can keep the bag and the weed."

Grip pursed his lips and shook his head. "That's not how it works. You want any of it back, come down to the station in a couple of days. We'll have it processed by then. Maybe you can get your papers back."

Linsky chewed on his lower lip thoughtfully. The kids around the table started to get their courage back, at least enough to look up and watch the drama.

"Why are you doing this?" Linsky asked. Grip could see that he was truly bewildered.

He gave Linsky a harsh look and turned to go.

"What's your name, detective?" Linsky's voice was stronger this time, surprising Grip a little.

He turned. "Grip."

Linsky nodded, an expression on his face that discomfited him, as if Grip had just lost some skirmish in a battle he hadn't realized was being contested. Grip's street sense picked up a shift in the balance of power.

He left the cafe, scowling at Schillaci and his partner, trying to fight the feeling that he'd somehow made the wrong move.

16

GRIP DRANK HIS BEER AND WHISKY AT A CORNER TABLE IN CRIPPEN'S, the bottle sweating onto a napkin by his right hand, the contents of Ben's satchel spread before him. Grip had told Oswald behind the bar that he wanted some peace, and Oswald had pulled the three other chairs away from Grip's table. From behind the bar came the high, tinny sound of a radio talker ranting hysterically.

Grip had gone through the papers systematically, some of them held together with paper clips, some typed, some handwritten, and discovered that a good number of them weren't actually Ben Linsky's writing. There were short stories and poems by other people, which

Grip skimmed, looking for evidence of Kollectiv 61, or, failing that, seditious or Marxist tendencies. But most of it was too fucking weird to make sense of, the rest simply tedious. Little comments were written in an exacting hand, the letters straight and compact. Grip read a few. Notes, presumably Ben's, along the lines of "too much" or "where is the truth here?" Not much of interest. The authors of this shit weren't any kind of threat to anyone.

He noticed that there was nothing of any length written in what he thought was Linsky's handwriting. He switched out an empty for a full beer and picked up the next paper-clipped collection, typewritten, and with comments in Ben's handwriting. He considered the possibility that Ben had typed and then commented on the text. For the most part, the pages seemed to be arranged by date. The first page read:

9.2

R. Drake, J. Olin, M. Gudmundsdottir, X. McAllister over for evening reading. Drake reads story about the flooding of a rural town by a new dam. Union-sympathetic. Olin reads from letter to his mother describing eccentricities of various hobos. Gudmundsdottir and McAllister both read poems, both becoming more abstract with words. Conviction diffused by non-linear word deployment.

Lovers?.

9.3

S. Dermott is using words like atoms in Los Alamos, smashing them against each other at high speed and sifting through the rubble that is left.

!!!

J. Eastgate describes trolls ingesting Tech-morsels in her classes! To what end? To what end?

9.6

S. Dermott and J. Eastgate on "drift" with WE hangers-on. Return Nirvana-like. I read to them from Pacific and they listen with beatific grins.

"Drift" n. nirvana? grins? LSD?.

9.7

Vasquez paid, I'm fairly sure)

At ?, saw G. Ambrosini, R. Vaszquez, L. Infantine, and R. Palmer speaking over coffee and a map. They appear as shades, neither seeing those around them nor being seen in the sense that they are real.

Grip set the sheet down, rubbed his eyes. What the hell was all this? Linsky—if Grip's assumption about the typewriting was correct—seemed to be keeping a record of the activities of various people, though his brief reports seemed to Grip either incomprehensible, irrelevant, or both. They seemed, in fact, to be the type of records he would expect to be kept by the kind of person who would also write the ludicrous stories that were in Linsky's satchel. But who the hell would *want* something like this, find it at all useful? Was it for Linsky's own benefit? That didn't seem right. But then who were they for?

He picked up a shot of whisky that the bartender had brought over, unbidden, and sniffed, trying to chase the smell of sweat and stale beer that seemed to always hang about the place. He threw back the shot, chased it with a tug on his beer.

He thought about a next step. Why were these particular people included in the report? Because they were Linsky's friends? Could be. From what Grip could gather, they seemed—at least some of them— to be writers or poets or students. Did this make them less suspicious, or more? And for that matter, what about Linsky himself? Did this document make *him* seem less or more suspicious? Also, did this have anything to do with Kollectiv 61? That was the trouble, of course. Nobody—not the Force, not the press—had been able to actually identify a single member of the group. So Linsky was the best connection available, circumstantial though that connection was. There must be some use for the document, Grip thought, some way to pressure Linsky with it. But nothing came immediately to mind.

Grip could sense a clock ticking, knew how urgent this must feel to Zwieg and Canada's people. He was sure that they'd concluded from the sheer scale of the heist, even without Nicky Patridis's confirmation, that the explosives were outside the usual black-market supply chain, that they were most likely in the hands of people who intended to *use* them. In truth, half the force should be on this case, ripping the goddamn City apart. But the facts of the robbery made that too dangerous. A large police effort would provoke scrutiny and that would be dangerous for the New City Project. More dangerous, probably, than the explosives themselves.

He was feeling the effects of the alcohol. And the anger welled up in him as he thought about these radicals, whether or not they were in Kollectiv 61. He hated their ideology, their idea that you had to tear society down to rebuild it. This case, he realized, had assumed a greater dimension—this was good versus evil, order versus chaos. Grip's body felt charged, ready to act.

17

"WE MAKE A PITIFUL COUPLE, YOU AND ME," PANOS SAID, AS FRINGS pushed his wheelchair along a sidewalk on the Tech campus. Frings's cane lay across Panos's blanketed lap.

"Old and decrepit," Frings said cheerfully. "When did that happen?"

Panos made a noise between a laugh and a cough. Leaves were blowing across the grassy quad to their left; high clouds moved briskly across the sky. The bell in the campus clock tower tolled once for 11:30, and students began to emerge from classroom buildings, buttoning coats against the wind. They made way on the walk for the two older men. In some ways, Frings wished that he could be part of this environment, offer some kind of direction to these kids, guide their energy and ideology. But this was an irrational urge, he knew—though some of these students no doubt knew him from his writings, his moment was past. He was catapulting shots from the periphery—and there was a new generation that would have to storm the bastions.

Some of this new generation stood in a small group, bundled against the cold—the same group he'd seen before his visit to the film department. They'd positioned themselves in front of the entrance to the administration building, holding signs that read END ACADEMIC SEGREGATION. As he tended to do when apprehensive, Panos talked incessantly as Frings pushed his chair along the campus walkway.

"Frank, how many times is it that I have asked you to put aside one of your crusades? In our thirty years together, how many times?"

Frings shrugged, then, realizing that Panos couldn't have seen the gesture, said, "I can't think of any."

"That is, as well, my memory. So, please, do me the favor of considering what I now tell you. The New City Project—let it go."

This surprised Frings. It was no secret that Panos supported the project, but even when they differed, it was unusual for Panos to pressure him on issues of ideology. Unsure how to respond, Frings stayed quiet.

"I have sympathy for what you write," Panos continued, "you know that. But we need the Project. Our City is old. The country has moved on, and we have stayed the same. On our present course, business will leave the City and then what will we have? Frank, I ask you to look clearly at this, without your politics."

"You're just making the same arguments that Littbarski and everyone else makes, Panos. You really think the choice is so stark? Either we accept the New City Project exactly as it is or face a derelict city? I don't believe you really think that."

"I believe that we can either do *something* or let the City, as you say, become derelict. So yes, these are the choices. And, at this date, the New City Project is our only something. If you looked around, you would agree. I wish there was another way, but sometimes the other side has the facts. I don't have arguments that are new, but I hoped that coming from me, who has always supported you. . ."

Frings looked at the back of Panos's bowed head, his shrunken back. He had been physically defeated by age and disease, and it seemed to Frings that he'd also been worn down by the arguments of the City's elite, as though it took more energy than the old man had to defend his own philosophy. This thought tempered Frings's annoyance.

"You know where I stand," Frings said, softly.

"I do. That is why I tell you this, so that maybe you give it more thought."

"Okay," Frings said—not because he would, but out of friendship and pity for an old man for whom he was now the closest thing to family.

THE ADMINISTRATION BUILDING HAD BEEN CONSTRUCTED WITHOUT ANY architectural ambition save for an arching clock tower. For the first decade of the Tech's existence—the 1850s—this had been the school's only building, where two-dozen young men were educated for the purpose of supporting the new web of railway tracks spreading like fissures on fracturing pond-ice.

Frings helped Panos in his ponderous ascent of the first few steps, until two students emerged to help him up the final half-dozen and through the front door. Frings followed, pulling Panos's wheelchair with him. They were met in the hallway by the Tech's president, a soft-looking man named Estes Milledge—basset-hound eyes, reading glasses hanging from a chain around his neck, gray wisps of hair encircling his skull.

"Panos," he said fondly, stepping forward to shake hands. Frings introduced himself, and though they'd met before, Milledge didn't seem to remember him—maybe the man only had eyes for potential donors.

Milledge motioned to an open door to his right. "I had Records bring Sol's file here, so that you could look at it in privacy. I know you understand that you can't take anything from his file with you."

Frings sensed a transaction occurring between the two older men, a calling in of debts that might stretch back over decades. He followed Milledge into a meeting room dominated by a long, walnut table surrounded by high-backed cherry-wood chairs. The walls were floor-to-ceiling, glass-encased bookshelves save for the far wall, where a grand window, tall with a semi-circular top, looked out at an ancient oak tree shedding leaves in the wind.

"You like this room?" Milledge said to Frings. "It is one of my favorites. People have been looking out at that tree since the Tech was founded. It gives a sense of the history of this place."

Frings nodded in perfunctory agreement. Milledge moved a chair to allow Panos to wheel up to the table.

"Here they are, Panos, two folders' worth."

Panos's eyes were grim. A moment passed.

"I'll leave you to look through them. You'll call me if you need anything?"

Another pause, Panos still eyeing the files. Frings gave a discreet nod and Milledge smiled, possibly with relief. He closed the door behind him.

Panos had been through the files four years before, when Sol had initially disappeared, and Frings wasn't sure that a second look was going to be fruitful, but the old man had insisted, so here they were. Above them they could hear the squeak of floorboards under feet.

"How do you want to do this Panos, split them up?"

Panos shook his head. "No, Frank. You look at them with fresh eyes and pass them to me when you are done."

Frings took the first folder, the edges worn from frequent handling. He wondered if this was because of Sol's disappearance—or maybe they'd been keeping an eye on him all along, given the suspicions that followed him around.

The first folder held his academic file. He perused four semesters' worth of decent marks, 3.2 grade point. The class selection seemed unfocused: Psych, Philosophy, History, Calculus, Philosophy, English Lit, Sociology, Biology, History, History, Philosophy, Religion, Psych, Art History, Sociology, Composition.

"You know what he was going to major in?"

Panos shook his head. "I don't think *he* knew."

Frings flipped past these grade reports to several memos. He skimmed the first few. Apparently, his professors had been asked to keep a special eye on him and report their observations to the administration. He could understand the concern. It would be unusual, if not unprecedented, for the Tech to have among its student body a boy whom many people thought had gotten away with killing his parents.

The first three evaluations were not revealing: Sol didn't participate in class unless called upon, his work was of decent quality but not exceptional, he didn't seem to be a threat to himself or others. The fourth was from a philosophy teacher who seemed mildly concerned about Sol's interpretations of some of the readings that they'd had in class, though he admitted that Sol was far from the only student to be intrigued by these ideas, and without the context of his parents' murders, he probably wouldn't have been troubled. Someone had written in the margins, "Covering himself in case something happens."

He skimmed another bland note, and then a final one, from his English professor, who'd noted that it was "interesting" that he had written his final paper on Raskolnikov, even though *Crime and Punishment* had not been an assigned text. The professor went on to say that he thought it possible that Sol had written the paper with a certain irony, playing on people's perceptions of him. A practical joke of sorts.

Frings slid the papers over to Panos and opened the second, similarly worn, folder. This folder was very thin, a three-page ledger of payments received and paid. Panos had covered Sol's tuition and room and board with monthly payments. There were also eleven payments to Sol, ranging from five to twenty dollars. The name of the fund from which the payments were drawn was blank. The only identifying information was an account number: 1TP0281.

"Panos, do you know what the school was paying Sol for?"

Panos looked over, his eyes suddenly light. "Payments *to* Sol?"

"That's right, eleven payments totaling a little over $150."

"When was this?"

Frings went back to the ledger. "Looks like the second semester of his freshman year through his whole sophomore year."

Panos cocked his head, and Frings saw his eyes narrow slightly, taking in this new information.

18

GRIP LEANED AGAINST A SIDE WALL OF THE POLICE STATION, SMOKING with a small group of anti-communist cops who hunched over their cigarettes, shooting the shit. He was still trying to get a purchase on the papers he'd found in Ben Linsky's satchel and, more importantly, figure out what, if anything, they had to do with either the stolen explosives or Kollectiv 61. Or, if he was lucky, both.

Two detectives dominated the conversation, bitching about the Tech's notorious refusal to allow City cops on campus.

"The thing is, they've got no fucking sense inside those gates, letting those kids protest and intimidate the administration. They let us in, that'd end in a hurry. You can't give these fucking kids any room."

"Bust a few heemie heads."

Grip tossed his cigarette butt, watched it fall to the ground and smoke listlessly. "You really want that campus shit to fall to us?"

The detective smirked. "You know what I think? I think a couple days of the heavy stuff, it ain't a problem anymore. Those kids aren't tough—a bunch of rich pussies."

Grip snorted. "Maybe. Kids, though, the cops come down on them, they suddenly get it in their heads they're something special. You see it on the street, no reason why it's different for the Tech kids. Let the campus cops deal with them. If it doesn't leak out into the City, who gives a shit?"

The conversation halted as the cops thought this over. A cold wind rounded the corner into the alley, leaves spinning, crazy, jittery.

"Any of you guys run across a guy named Ben Linsky?"

A uniform laughed. "What? The poof? You need a date, Tor, I can fix you up with my cousin Geoff."

"Fuck you. You know this guy?"

"Sure. I ran into him a couple of times. Zwieg had us do a sweep of some queer bars one night. I remember him because he kind of did the negotiating during the bust, trying to keep us from hauling everyone in, throwing them in the tank. I asked another guy, who's that, and he says Ben Linsky, some kind of poet. A fag poet. Go figure."

"That it?"

"I see his name around, always pinko shit. And he had something to do with Kollectiv 61."

"That's right," another cop joined in. "That's how I know that name."

Grip ignored this and asked the first cop, "You know him well enough to have an opinion on whether he might be *in* Kollectiv 61?"

"Shit, Tor, that's what you're doing now, chasing down kids with spray paint?"

Grip shook his head. He was about to protest that Kollectiv 61 was a hell of a lot more than spray paint, but this would only earn him more shit. "Yeah, exactly." Sarcastic.

"Well," the uniform said, his heavy lips pinched in thought, "I don't see him being the destructive type. He's more of a heemie—smoke some grass, talk about Negroes."

"Okay, I can see that," Grip said without conviction, stepping on his cigarette butt, putting it out of its misery.

IN THE STATION LOBBY, GRIP FOUND A UNIFORM NAMED SUAREZ WHO had done some grunt work for him occasionally. He called the guy over.

"You got time to do something for me?"

"Sure, detective." Suarez had been born in the City, but spoke with the trace of a Mexican accent, like everyone else in his neighborhood.

"I need you to track down a security guard, works Crosstown sites for Consolidated Industries. He's a floater, doesn't have an assigned site, just fills in where he's needed. Last name's Patridis." Grip was hoping that Nicky Patridis's cousin—the one who'd witnessed the explosives heist—was on his father's side. If they didn't share a last name, he'd be impossible to find without getting the full name from Nicky, which Grip did not want to do.

"Got it?"

Suarez winked. "Sure thing, detective."

INSIDE THE STATION, GRIP TOOK THE STAIRS UP TO THE THIRD FLOOR, figuring he'd stop by his desk, see what had accumulated while he'd been out. A hallway ran the length of the third floor, doors on each side, white linoleum bouncing the light from the ceiling tubes right back up again. As he walked by, one of the three elevators in the middle of the hall opened and Deputy Chief Ving—tall, thin, a flattened nose ruining his gray good looks—gestured to Grip. Somebody must have tipped him when Grip had walked in the building.

"Detective."

Grip wondered again how a guy with a soft voice like that could turn on the authority out in the street. Some guys climbed the ladder and a slow process took hold, after a while the guy would lose his fitness, his street sense; he became more and more like a manager in a business and less like a cop. Not Ving, though. As far as Grip could tell, Ving hadn't lost a thing.

"Sir."

"Let's talk."

Grip tensed. "Okay."

"Upstairs."

Shit.

Grip made a move for the elevator, but Ving nodded down the hall to the stairs. They walked shoulder to shoulder in silence, nodding to a uniform as he hustled past from the lavatory.

Grip followed Ving up four flights of stairs, wondered why they hadn't taken the elevator and came up with only one answer: the elevators had cameras. What the hell did that mean?

They reached the seventh floor and Ving wasn't even breathing hard, while Grip's chest pounded from the exertion and apprehension. Why wouldn't Ving want to be seen with Grip on camera?

Ving led the way down a carpeted hallway, their footsteps silent after the echoing stairwell. Ving's office was small, a nice view out toward the Theater District and, beyond that, the Hollows.

"Have a seat, Detective."

The voice was calm, but Grip knew that whatever was coming couldn't be good. He sat in a high-backed maroon leather chair. Ving's desk was no larger than Grip's own—but neat, no papers to be seen, a photo frame turned away from Grip. Room decor was typical cop: map of the City, photo of the president, three framed certificates, flag in the corner.

"I'm told you rousted Ben Linsky yesterday."

Grip became more confused. *Ben Linsky?* Why the big secret about *him*? "Sure. Just gave him a warning, possession of a controlled substance."

Ving nodded as if this was completely reasonable. "That's fine. I'm also told that you confiscated Mr. Linsky's bag."

"I did, yes," Grip said slowly.

"I need you to return that bag to Mr. Linsky." Ving opened his drawer, retrieved a small piece of paper and a pen, and wrote while Grip watched. "This is Mr. Linsky's address," Ving said. "You will return the bag and all its contents to Mr. Linsky. After that, you will not contact him again. Am I clear?"

Grip, startled beyond words, nodded dumbly.

"Say it, please."

"You're clear."

Ving nodded. "Thank you, Detective Grip. I appreciate your prompt compliance."

"You running some kind of operation with Linsky?"

Ving stared at him. Grip nodded, realized that the meeting had ended, stood to go.

"Two things," Ving said, pulling a folder from the top drawer of his desk. "First, everything that has been said here stays in this room."

"Okay."

Ving was leafing through papers in the file folder now, reaching absently for the glasses in his breast pocket. "And take the stairs."

19

THIS MORNING, FRINGS RODE IN UNEASY SILENCE IN THE BACK OF A black Lincoln next to Nathan Canada, who was chain-smoking Camels. Frings did not like Canada. Not only was Canada the man behind the New City Project, but he was also, if not corrupt himself, tolerant of the corruption that kept the project on track. Frings further suspected that Canada was responsible for an incident years ago that had left a man dead and him with a bullet in his knee. No proof, of course, but strong suspicions.

Canada, in turn, hated Frings for his high-profile opposition to the project. Canada, in Frings's experience, made no distinction between the personal and the professional. He harbored personal animus toward anyone who worked against him.

The Lincoln came upon a high chain-link fence, the gate padlocked, huge yellow signs—WORK ZONE KEEP OUT—hung at close enough intervals to show that the owners meant business. Before them, on the far side of the fence, loomed the Carl S. Patterson Municipal Tower, or, as it was usually called, the Municipal Tower, or just the Tower.

When Frings had first heard of the concept for the Tower, it had seemed like the height of folly: two buildings—one on each side of the Crosstown—supporting a larger building, twenty-five floors from the ground, that spanned the Crosstown and tapered, pyramid-like, as it rose another twenty-five floors. Atop the structure, a spire rose a hundred feet into the air, ringed at its peak by a circular observation deck. And yet, here it was, the exterior completed, though the interior wasn't yet ready for occupancy. In his column, Frings had dubbed it "The Colossus of Roads."

Two cops stood at the gate. One approached the driver's window. The driver, a city employee paid to chauffeur Canada around, rolled down his window.

"I've got Mr. Canada and a guest to take a look at the site."

The cop, eager to be seen asserting his authority, nodded at the other uniform to unlock the gate. Frings saw the driver give the cop a tight nod as he pulled past.

They'd had these meetings before, tense affairs where Canada made his case while Frings listened, valuing, if nothing else, the insight he received into Canada's thinking. Frings wasn't sure if Canada expected to sway Frings's opinions through the sheer force of his personality, or if he just liked keeping up a connection with Frings, staying in his head.

They drove down a gravel road to the front entrance of the northern tower. The driver stopped, the car idling. Canada took a last drag and ground the butt into the ashtray slotted into the door. "We'll be a few minutes."

Outside they were confronted with a cutting wind, and the two men hustled as best they could through the door. It was warmer inside, but not as warm as Frings would have expected. Men in construction helmets and work clothes moved about, increasing their pace and sense of purpose when they saw Canada.

"We're installing the electrical wiring, the heating system, that kind of thing, in the lower towers," Canada rasped, lighting a new cigarette. "The upper building isn't as far along."

A workman strode over to them, carrying two hard hats. "Hello, Mr. Canada. You and your friend should wear these while you're inside." He handed a hard hat to each.

Frings put his on and watched Canada do the same. Canada's helmet seemed too big. He would have looked ridiculous, but the seriousness of his demeanor, his determination not to concede the embarrassment of his appearance, made him seem sinister.

"Thank you, Mr. DiIulio. I'm taking my guest to the observation deck."

"I'll let them know to clear out, sir." With that, DiIulio walked away, speaking into a walkie-talkie.

Canada led Frings to a single elevator set apart from the larger bank of elevators further down the hall. There was only one button inside, labeled "12," and Canada pushed it. He talked as they ascended.

"Not that you've ever written about it in one of your columns, but this building is the product of the type of arrangement—government–business partnership—that is the future of the City. As I know you are aware, the City put up 60 percent of the funds needed for construction, and private business contributed the other 40. In return, they will have space in the crown jewel of the New City Project—the best address, proximity to important government agencies that will be headquartered in the other tower, a dedicated exit from the Crosstown directly to the underground garage. This building represents the future of the City, both figuratively and in actuality."

They arrived at the twelfth floor and walked down a narrow corridor.

"The elevator we took was the tourist elevator, which lets out only onto this hall, which leads to the observation deck elevators."

They walked by an empty room. "This will be a souvenir shop. Bring something back to your home in Bumfuck, Wisconsin, to remember your visit to the City by."

The next elevator took them up the center of the spire to the observation deck.

"I had to be talked into this building, Frank. I wasn't sold on it initially. But the Council, they insisted, and, while I have my doubts about their intentions, I believe they were, in this instance, correct. People like boldness. Hell, they like brazenness. That's what this building is."

The elevator doors opened to a narrow lobby that led to the deck. A sign reading NO SMOKING was posted opposite the elevator, and as he walked by it, Canada lit a fresh cigarette from the butt of the one he'd been smoking. He dropped the butt and stepped on it, absently.

The observation deck was a ring—a fifteen-foot-wide circular corridor—the outer wall of which was constructed mostly of thick glass. A walk around the deck afforded an extraordinary 360-degree view of the City, most of it well below the height of the Tower.

"It's spectacular," Frings said, looking east, to where Capitol Heights bled into Praeger's Hill and the suburbs beyond. And gashing through it all, the signs of the Crosstown construction—cranes, rubbled buildings, road sections at various stages of completion.

"It's so close. You must feel like you're this close to winning."

"I'm not close. I've already won."

Frings let that go. "Why are we here, Nathan?"

"Because, I wanted you to see this, Frank. I thought that if you saw it for yourself, you'd realize: it's over. You can harp all you want, but it won't change a fucking thing. You and those Kollectiv 61 shit-fucks—it's time to concede. Use your pull with these people. Tell them to stop. Nothing's going to change. They're just wasting the people's money now."

It was, Frings thought, more or less what Littbarski had told him—not even all that different from what Panos had said. In their minds, the project wasn't just necessary, but a fait accompli. The time for arguments against it were over. Frings subconsciously clenched his jaw, envisioning the Crosstown cutting a swath straight through to the new City Center, imagining the bleak new cityscape.

He thought about the subtext to this meeting—the reason, presumably, why Canada had brought him here in particular. His words hadn't conveyed a threat, because they hadn't needed to. Just by choosing this spot for their rendezvous, Canada was sending a message. It had all happened five years ago, four hundred feet below them, in the Tower's shadow.

• • •

THAT DAY, THE DAY THAT HIS KNEE WAS SHATTERED, HE WAS MEETING A union gink named Laz Wolinak at the spot where the Tower now stood—though at that point construction had barely begun. The plan had been for Frings to meet Wolinak at the on-site foreman's office. He'd found the trailer sitting isolated amid a chaos of broken rock and stacked building materials. Frings saw a cluster of rats swarming on something in a patch of weeds. He climbed the three steps to the trailer door and gave four raps, as Wolinak had told him to.

Wolinak answered, sweating ferociously, cigarette dangling from the corner of his mouth. "Come inside." He practically pulled Frings across the threshold, closing the door quickly. The trailer was dim, claustrophobic, and smelled like an ancient ashtray. Three desks, three file cabinets, and a couple of chairs by the entrance were the extent of the operation, except for the girlie shots taped to the walls. The place hummed with Wolinak's anxiety.

"I didn't get the papers yet," he whispered hoarsely. "I didn't want to have them out if someone else showed up first."

Frings nodded, thinking *just get the papers, I'll take a few photos, we'll get the hell out of here*. Wolinak's nerves were starting to play on his own.

Wolinak walked to one of the file cabinets, keys jangling in his shaking hands. Frings could hear Wolinak's labored breathing as he struggled to get the key in the lock, seeming impossibly tense. He finally managed it and pulled open a drawer. He paused for a moment, then started pawing through the files with increasing alarm.

"Shit."

"What is it?"

Wolinak grunted a reply, slammed the drawer shut, opened the one above it. Again he pawed through the files, again he slammed the drawer shut. Down to the bottom drawer—paw, slam.

Wolinak's face lost all color. "We're fucked."

Frings's pulse began to race. "Where are the files, Laz?"

"Not here. Somebody moved them. We're fucked."

Frings felt the adrenaline. "Okay, calm down, Laz."

"Fuck calm down. We need to get out of here."

"Okay. Okay. We'll go." *What had happened*? Someone must

have known. From outside, he heard the sound of a car approaching the trailer.

Wolinak leaned over and vomited. "Fuck," he said, spitting.

Frings opened the door, hoping irrationally that maybe it was the cops. It wasn't. A black Buick pulled up a dozen feet from the trailer. Three men got out, stockings over their heads, their faces distorted. Frings looked for the license plates, but they'd been removed.

The men approached, big ginks, looking at Frings, guns in their hands. Frings heard Wolinak retching again.

One of the men motioned backward with his head. "Get out here and bring the other one too."

Frings didn't turn, said, "Okay, Laz, we've got to go out." Frings descended the steps cautiously. The men held their guns casually by their sides, but their postures were alert. Frings stepped to the side to let Laz, his chin and shirt wet with bile, step out. The man who'd talked before motioned for them to move away from the door and stand against the wall of the trailer.

The men lined up in front of Frings and Laz, a sense of anticipation now palpable. Frings's breaths were shallow.

The man doing the talking said, "Jesus, Laz, look at you, shit all over you. You really balled this up. You really did." He raised his gun and buried three shots in Laz's chest. Laz collapsed, lifeless. Frings started shaking with panic.

"You, Frings, I'm supposed to give you a message." The gink with the gun brought his aim down a little, put a bullet in Frings's knee. Frings dropped, pain overwhelming him, consciousness ebbing.

"I'm supposed to tell you to stop being an asshole."

Frings curled up into the fetal position, his knee hurting more than he thought anything could hurt, watching the three sets of feet as they walked away. He heard the car start and pull away, crunching over the broken rock and cement. He turned his head so that he could see Wolinak, who'd landed on his chest, his lifeless eyes cast in Frings's direction. In the last moments before he lost consciousness, he wondered if Wolinak had a family; if his decision to help Frings meant that a child—or children—had just lost a father, a wife a husband.

• • •

CANADA WAS STILL WAITING FOR A REPLY. FRINGS TURNED TO HIM. HE registered that Canada, for the first time in Frings's experience, was disconcerted by what he saw.

• • •

FROM *Alienation and the Modern City*
by Francis Frings (1958)

City Planning is, in part, about making predictions in both near and distant terms about all manner of things municipal. In conjunction with statistical analyses, population projections, and geographical maps, the Planners must also attempt to anticipate the mindset of future residents.

In addition to this prognosticative task, the Planners must also attempt to circumscribe the future behavior of residents through planning decisions. It is here, I believe, that the New City Project has gone seriously awry concerning transportation plans, and the effect will be of increasing the aloneness, the alienation, of the very workers the New City Project aims to benefit.

Let us be very clear: with the plans laid out in the New City Project Master Plan, the City has decided that urban travel will be dominated by personal automobiles. This may result from some anticipation of the future desires of commuters, particularly those in sub-urban areas; but it is also—and this is inherent in this infrastructure decision— proscriptive to a vast increase in the number of automobiles on the road and a vast decrease in the use of such modes of transport as buses and trains, where riders are part of a community of commuters.

Picture the City at 8:30 on a weekday morning, a decade hence, and you are confronted with a stream of individual automobiles, most presumably containing a single occupant, heading from the suburbs to the City Center. Commuters are thereby physically segregated from one another, locked in metal boxes where they not only will be unable to interact with one another, but will not even see one another save in passing and through two sheets of glass. How this does not inevitably lead to the alienation of the commuter from both his community of residence and his community of work is beyond my comprehension.

20

BEN LINSKY'S APARTMENT WAS ON THE THIRD FLOOR OF A MODEST building five blocks from the Tech campus and three from Cafe ?, on the edge of a working-class Irish neighborhood called Donegal Town, at the foot of Praeger's Hill. Grip, in a pool of light, leaned against a lamppost on Ben's block, smoking one Camel after another. He carried a tin flask in his pocket and took occasional tugs, feeling the warmth in his chest as the whisky went down, his muscles relaxing into fighting condition.

Grip enjoyed the street flow—the Tech kids moving with nervous energy, knowing that they'd left the campus neighborhood and crossed into territory where their safety was no longer assured. The Irish kids moved furtively too—they were outside the boundaries where their neighborhood laws were observed; not scared, but unsure where they stood, and streetwise enough for Grip's presence to keep them moving until they were out of his orbit.

Ben's satchel lay on the sidewalk by Grip's feet. He took another nip off the flask. *Deputy Chief Ving. Jesus.* Grip had never worked under Ving, but used to see him around, knew his rep as one of those squeaky-clean cops that usually pissed off the rank-and-file who resented feeling tainted by comparison. But he'd been a cop's cop as well, earning respect on the street. Grip actually liked the clean ones, felt his morale lifted by the occasional exception to the corrupt norm. Grip had never taken cash or favors himself, but he knew he didn't carry the rep of a clean cop. Even before Morphy took the bullet he was known as a guy who set his own priorities, pursued his own objectives both on- and off-duty. With Morphy's death, his notoriety solidified until it was cast in iron.

There were maybe—what?—a couple dozen things he'd done that had him mired at the rank of detective, no shot at a promotion. But, really, how bad was his *record*? It was his reputation that was beyond the pale. That, and Morphy.

He knew he couldn't change this about himself: he would never be comfortable with the restraints the badge put on his actions. In Grip's estimation, when you had a chance at justice with a capital *J*, you seized it. The times he'd followed this instinct to action were the ones that got him into trouble, forcing him now to suck up to assholes like Zwieg. Call it indiscipline, call it policing by your gut—whatever it was, it wasn't rewarded.

Ving wasn't an asshole. But he'd more or less disappeared when Kraatjes took over as chief. Grip would see Ving ghosting around headquarters, doing this or that for Kraatjes. But nobody could get a handle on what he was trying to do. Ving had become Kraatjes's man—the chief's conduit to the world—and now he was in Grip's mug about bracing Ben Linsky, which meant that Kraatjes himself wanted Linsky left alone. What did that mean? What the fuck could they be doing with Linsky? Grip might have pegged Linsky as an informant, maybe, but the shit in that letter he'd found? Half of it made no sense and the rest—who met with who? Who was friends with who? Who went to what fucking poetry reading?—what could that possibly be worth to Ving and Kraatjes?

GRIP FOUND HIS MIND WANDERING TO THE STORY HE HAD TOLD SO many times, to Internal Affairs, guys on the force, lawyers, not to mention Morphy's wife, Jane, who had bored through him with her dark brown eyes. He'd gone over it in his head hundreds of times, just like he did now, killing time on the street.

He and Morphy were out to pinch a guy they'd made for the murders of a couple of prostitutes, found strangled in off-the-books hotels carved out of abandoned buildings in the Hollows. The dregs. The guy in question was named Tony Oddo, nicknamed, inevitably, Odd Tony. Oddo worked underground construction, and they'd tracked him down to his current site, a mile-long tunnel where the Crosstown would pass forty feet beneath the tony Capitol Heights neighborhood.

They'd discussed waiting until Oddo's shift was over and grabbing him when he emerged to the street. But this had been a nervous time, and neither of them was comfortable with waiting. So they'd acted.

The foreman gave them a ride down to the shaft level in a makeshift elevator. The guy wasn't too happy to have cops visiting the site but didn't want to piss off the police either, invite scrutiny of some of the men who worked for him. It was noisy as hell on the way down and walking into the tunnel, the volume hit with an almost physical impact. It sounded like something was grinding into the rock—it probably was. The noise was violent and metallic. They couldn't hear each other as they walked down the narrow tunnel. Lights had been rigged along the way, so it was bright, which seemed to somehow amplify the crushing din. Morphy had to duck a little as he walked, the ceiling only six feet high.

They turned a corner to find a group of men twenty yards ahead and, beyond them, extremely bright lights and a shower of sparks. The men wore safety helmets, ear protection, and goggles. Grip followed Morphy on the approach, the men now watching them. Grip stopped ten yards from them, not wanting to be too close to Morphy if things went south. The place was cramped. It would be too easy for them to be overwhelmed in the narrow tunnel.

The sound seemed to fracture Grip's thoughts, as if they weren't strong enough to withstand the onslaught. It made the scene before him all the more unreal. The noises that he would have expected to come from Morphy's footsteps, a human conversation—hell, the sound of his own breathing in his head—nothing was audible. For a moment Grip considered grabbing Morphy, waiting on the street for the shift to end, after all. They could have sent the foreman back down to fetch him. But they both wanted to make this hard on Oddo. They'd seen the corpses. Morphy was not willing to wait.

Grip didn't have a great view. Morphy's broad back dominated the tunnel. He saw Morphy flash his badge and point to one of the men. He could see a shifting of bodies beyond Morphy, then he thought he saw Morphy take a step back. Everything seemed magnified. Maybe it was the noise. Grip took a step forward and realized that Morphy was going for his gun. Grip had his hand on his gun, and as he was pulling it, Morphy's head jerked back. Morphy fell to the ground, his face covered in blood. Grip had his gun up as one of the men brought a pickaxe down on Morphy's chest. Grip fired three times. Two men dropped, leaving at least a half-dozen men standing. More men than Grip had rounds. He turned and ran around the corner of the tunnel toward the entrance. He kept looking over his shoulder, unable to hear any pursuers, but no one was following.

The foreman was waiting with the elevator, and Grip saw the alarm on the man's face as he ran out.

"What—"

"Up," Grip yelled, pointing his thumb desperately up. The foreman hesitated. Grip held his gun to the man's head. "Up."

AS HE WAS THINKING ABOUT THIS, HE SAW A MAN—SHORT AND SOFT LIKE a loaf of rye—ambling down the sidewalk, a small stack of books held under one arm. Linsky didn't see Grip at first. In fact, to Grip's eye, Linsky seemed oblivious to everything. But as he neared, Grip stepped forward and Linsky started, pushing his glasses up on the bridge of his nose with his right thumb.

They stood facing each other for a moment, Grip surprised that Linsky was standing his ground.

"We're done with this," Grip said, dropping Linsky's satchel by his small, battered loafers.

Linsky didn't bend to pick it up, instead holding Grip's eyes. They stared at each other for a few more moments. Grip could not quite believe the balls Linsky had on him. For once, he wasn't sure of his next move.

Linsky's voice, when he finally spoke, was slightly effeminate, but calm and strong. "Don't come my way again."

Grip bit down on his rage. Linsky picked up the satchel with his free hand.

"Detective," he said, nodding, as he walked past Grip toward the door to his building.

21

THE BODIES OF THE MISSING SECURITY GUARDS HAD BEEN DISCOVERED at night, and the police had set up lights at the scene, which were now being powered down as the gray dawn turned to morning. Dorman nodded at the pair of uniforms who stood guard by a barricade that they'd put up to keep the gawkers off the scene. Someone had arranged a curtain of tarps to hide the bodies from the sidewalk.

"It's not pretty back there, sir," warned one of the uniforms, a guy who must have had twenty years on Dorman.

"Three bodies, right?"

The uniform nodded with an expression suggesting that that wasn't the half of it.

On the other side of the curtain, Dorman saw crime-scene guys kneeling around the corpses, which lay on an embankment leading down from a weathered sidewalk to a drainage ditch grown over with weeds. He could see from the angle of their feet that all three bodies were on their stomachs, having fallen forward from the sidewalk.

"Mr. Dorman."

Dorman turned to find Detective Grip, hands in pockets, looking tired.

"Good morning, Detective. You've got this case?"

Grip shook his head. "It goes to Homicide, but I thought I'd have a look as it might be related to . . ."

Grip had the good sense not to mention the stolen explosives. Dorman nodded that he understood what Grip was talking about.

"What happened to them?"

Grip looked over at the bodies. "What, you haven't seen?"

"Not the whole thing." The dew from the grass was working its way through his shoes. His feet stung with the cold.

"Hey, move aside for a second so the big shot can have a look."

The crime scene guys turned to Grip and then stood, backing away.

"Oh, shit." Dorman fought back nausea. The men's heads had

been crushed, their hair wet with blood and other things at which Dorman didn't look closely enough to identify.

"Thanks," Grip yelled to the crime-scene crew, who returned to their work.

"What the hell happened?"

Grip pulled a pack of cigarettes from his coat pocket. "We'll know for sure after the autopsy. They'll probably find fragments of whatever it was those guys were hit with. My guess, baseball bat, maybe a pipe."

"Each guy in the back of the head?"

Grip shrugged. "That's the way it looks."

"How do you pull that off? There must have been three guys, or the other two would have run after the first guy got hit."

"It could work a bunch of ways. Maybe three guys took out the vics all at once. Maybe someone kept a gun on them and they just didn't have it in them to move. Things like this don't always play out in a way that makes much sense when you look at it afterward. There's no way to be sure what happened unless we catch the guys that did it."

Grip took a cigarette and offered one to Dorman, who held up a hand, no.

"You think it has anything to do with the explosives?" Dorman asked.

Grip thought about this for a moment. "Look, the way these guys were killed, it was an execution. No question. I went looking for them a couple of days ago when they'd first disappeared, and they'd been at some kind of underground casino. Maybe it had something to do with that. Who knows?"

"You going to find out?"

Grip sucked on his cigarette. "Not my case. I'll keep in touch with the homicide dicks who pick it up, see what they come up with, if it relates to the explosives."

Dorman was dubious. This didn't fit Grip's rep. "What's your angle, detective?"

"All due respect. . ."

Dorman nodded. He hadn't really expected an answer.

"Why are *you* here?" Grip asked.

Why *was* he here? He hadn't given it any thought. He'd heard that the bodies had been found, and he'd come out.

"I think someone needs to look after the New City Project's stake in this. It's important that if this *does* relate to the thefts that the killers be caught."

"That's my job."

"That's right, of course." Dorman flashed on the case of money at St. Stanislaw's. "You're watching out for the Project," he said, vaguely. "You and me."

22

FRINGS SAT FACING CAFE ?'S GLASS STOREFRONT, MORNING RAIN TURNING the view outside into an impressionist painting—a confusion of colors—giving the reefer a kick in the pants.

"You don't look so good, Ben."

Ben Linsky's hair was unwashed and lank, his eyes bloodshot with exhaustion. His words came fast. "The heat ever get on you, Frank? I mean recently? It's the kind of thing I'd expect from thirty years ago, you know, your time."

Frank winced a bit. "Slow down. What's going on?"

Linsky kept his chin down, eyes on the table, told Frings about his run-ins with Grip. "I've thought about it a lot, Frank. It seems to me that it's got to be political. You see what I mean? What, maybe I smoke some grass. But does that warrant taking my satchel?"

Frings frowned, thinking about how the Force had been used for political ends when he was Linsky's age—mostly rousting Reds and unions. Now the standing assumption seemed to be that the police had moved on, weren't involved in that anymore. But Frings harbored doubts that the police force could ever really be friendly to radicals and, with the decaying central control, wasn't surprised that cops might take the opportunity to intimidate Reds, heemies, and queers.

"Did you catch the cop's name?"

"Grip."

Frings nodded, said, "I know him some. You say he gave you back your bag?"

Linsky nodded.

"So, what aren't you telling me?"

"There's nothing else to it."

Frings shrugged, waited for a moment for Linsky to volunteer something more. He felt sure the poet was holding something back, but when Linsky remained silent, he let it go.

The rain had diminished in force. The window had cleared enough so that Frings could make out shapes through the glass behind Linsky. It was a little hard to tell, but there seemed to be someone standing in the doorway across the street. Or maybe it was just the way the doorway looked with the rain's distortion.

Catching Frings's distraction, Linsky turned in his chair. "What are you looking at?"

"Nothing." Frings returned his attention to Linsky. "Why would Grip have kept this thing?"

"To annoy me, maybe? I don't know, but you can imagine . . ."

Frings nodded, looked beyond Linsky again, but the figure that he'd seen was gone. Probably nothing.

He wondered if there could be a specific reason why Grip would be harassing Linsky and was struck by how soon this followed his having seen Sol on film. Was there anything to this? Sol reappears, and so does the cop who never bought his story. Or was there no connection to speak of? A shot in the dark: "He ask you about Kollectiv 61?"

"This again? Why would he ask me about that?"

From Linsky's reaction, Frings was sure he was being coy.

"Same reason that I did—because of the manifesto you ran in *Prometheus*."

"No, he didn't."

Frings sighed, not convinced that there wasn't more to this, somehow, but conceding that Linsky wasn't going to be forthcoming. "Let's talk about the magazine."

"I think we'll have a good issue. There is some pretty solid writing, both poetry and fiction. Also some film criticism."

"Anything else? Any non-fiction? Any reporting?"

"Not in this one. To be honest, Frank, most people I talk to? They tell me they don't even read those pieces. I've been thinking that we might want to move away from that completely, maybe bring in more photography and art."

"Well, you know how I feel about that, Ben. You've run some important stuff over the years—stories no one else would have published."

"Like the manifesto."

"That's one. But I was thinking of others: the piece on squatters in the Hollows; that hustler's diary you ran last year. Those were great pieces—you can't tell me they were any less valuable than the fiction or the poetry."

Linsky shook his head. "We've got something going here, Frank. This is a real movement, and *Prometheus* is the vehicle. It stands for a certain aesthetic, and I think that gets diluted with the non-fiction. I think we need to narrow the focus, to spotlight the new art emerging from the City."

Frings held his hand up in surrender, not sure that he disagreed with Linsky anyway. And if he did, it certainly wasn't worth the struggle.

23

FRINGS HELD HIS CANE IN ONE HAND AND AN OPEN UMBRELLA IN THE other as he limped toward a lot surrounded by a twelve-foot chain-link fence. A light but steady rain stung the sidewalk, and the damp, along with the cold, had Frings's bad knee throbbing. He was in a gray section of the City, anonymous blocks of low-rise apartments like hundreds of others. A minor adjustment to a pencil line on a map in a back room at City Hall, and these homes would have met the wrecking ball instead of those just to the west, which were giving way for the Crosstown's twelve asphalt lanes. As if troubled by the narrow escape, the buildings here were buttoned up, windows closed and curtained, doors shut, sidewalks empty. Only the occasional cafe was open, and even these seemed to Frings to discourage unfamiliar visitors.

He crossed an empty Buchanan Avenue and walked into the neighborhood that had not been saved. The difference was stark. He limped past a mountain of rubble guarded by fencing and tarps, and then another—both the remains of buildings demolished in the past week or so. Feral dogs had found their way in, sniffing around the piles. Seagulls hovered, screeching. Backhoes stood dormant.

Frings located the next standing building in the line. A small number of workmen, maybe a half-dozen, padded around it in bright yellow rain jackets, laying wires, stringing cordon tape, making preparations for its demolition. About fifteen yards from the building, still within the fence, stood a small canopy, and under it a tall man hunched over a film camera resting on a tripod. He seemed to be setting up a shot of the building, the camera tilted up to catch the top of the façade and the roof.

Frings found the door through the fence and stepped into the construction zone. A worker walked over to him, burly under his coat, several days' growth covering his broad jaw.

"I help you with something?"

Frings shifted his eyes to the man under the canopy, then back to the worker. "My name's Frank Frings. I'm with the *News-Gazette*. I wanted to speak with Mr. Macheda over there."

The worker frowned. "Frings, huh?"

"That's right."

"I got to say I've got a big problem with a lot of what you write."

Frings nodded, keeping the man's eye. "That shouldn't keep me from talking to Mr. Macheda."

"No, I guess not."

Frings waited the man out. Finally, he stepped aside, and Frings hobbled toward the canopy.

Macheda was absorbed in his camerawork and didn't hear Frings approach. Frings waited quietly for a break in his work.

When it came, he said, "Andy Macheda?"

Macheda turned, startled. He studied Frings for a moment, squinting. "Do I know you, man?"

"Frank Frings, *News-Gazette*."

"Oh shit. I thought I recognized you. Wow, what are you doing here?" He wiped his hands on his corduroy trousers, stepped into the rain to shake with Frings. There was an awkward moment as Frings leaned his cane against his leg and switched the umbrella into his left hand so that he could shake with his right.

"Come on in, Mr. Frings."

Frings stepped underneath the canopy, now crowded with the two men and the film camera setup. Macheda, he saw, had a weird energy, his face manically expressive, his words coming in spurts.

"It's an honor to have you here, Mr. Frings. I . . . You're why I'm doing what I'm doing now; why I'm doing this." He spread a hand toward the building before them.

"What exactly *are* you doing?"

"Filming 'progress,' the march toward alienation. My film, it's trying to show visually what you described in your book."

Frings took this in, thinking about *Film 12* and the woman walking alone in the crowd. "I'm flattered," he said carefully.

"Don't be. Please. I'm flattered that you're here." His eyes brightened as he thought of something. "Listen, I don't know if I should ask, man, but it would be great, I mean it would really make this part of the film something else if you could . . . If I could get you to maybe stand in front of the building, you know, on camera, and maybe recite a few lines from your book. I really . . . I hesitate to ask, but it would just be, well, this could be the pivotal moment, you see?"

Frings nodded. He couldn't see any harm, and it might be useful to have Macheda owing him a favor when it came time to ask about Sol Elia. "Do you have a copy of my book here?" Frings asked dubiously.

"Oh, no. Do you need it? I was thinking, maybe that passage about how the commuter is alienated from both his work and home. You know the passage I'm talking about?"

"Sure, but I don't think I can recite it word for word."

"You can't?" Macheda considered this, perplexed. The rain picked up, sounding like buckshot pinging off the canopy. "Maybe you can just talk about it, like an interview."

Frings shrugged. "Okay."

"Yeah, that will be great. You can take your time, take a second if you want to think. I can do jump cuts, break it up a little."

Frings walked out into the rain, holding his umbrella. Macheda wanted Frings to have his cane with him, liked that look. Macheda fiddled with his camera, lowered it to take in Frings and the building behind. Frings felt his pant legs getting wet as he waited.

"Okay, I think we're set. We'll make it short. Maybe just talk about that chapter? Anyway, you know the one?"

"Sure," Frings said.

Macheda extended a microphone on a pole out into the rain to within a couple of feet of Frings. *Film 12* had been silent. Frings wondered if this was a new direction for the next version, or if this was for another film entirely.

"Okay. So, I'm going to roll the camera now. Okay. You're on."

Frings started. "*Many problems of the current trend in urban planning here in the City can be essentially divided into two categories.*"

As he talked, the words came back to him, like reciting music. He felt he could recall the passage almost exactly. "*The first is the conscious arrangement of urban areas by function—such as residential or commercial—or by social class.*"

Frings saw Macheda nodding along, smiling.

"*The second trend is the increasing practice of creating infrastructure and buildings that are constructed to the specifications of* machines, *particularly the automobile, but machines within buildings as well.*"

"*These two categories can themselves be summarized as holding human constructs—social, economic, or physical—in higher regard than humans themselves. We are purposely recreating the City as a place that is literally no longer structured for people.*"

Frings stopped. Macheda shut down the camera.

"Wow, this was really unbelievable you showing up like this. I really, I can't thank you enough. This is really great."

Frings nodded and ducked under the canopy again. "Andy, can I tell you why I'm here?"

This seemed to take him by surprise, as though he thought it entirely within the realm of possibility that this—walking around a demolition site—was the kind of thing that Frings generally did with his time. "Shoot."

"I saw your film at the Underground the other night."

Macheda's eyes widened. "You did? What'd you think?"

"Well—"

"Because it's not really a movie, you know, it's more like a performance I guess. A performance of images. You know, I change the scenes all the time. This must be something like the twelfth or thirteenth version. I lose track. But it's kind of what I'm thinking, like right now. I get rid of this piece or that piece that doesn't seem quite true to me anymore, and then I'll add something that I dig more, like right now, you know? What's true, it changes. It's like jazz musicians. You go see them, it's something different every night, even if they're playing the same songs. But you can dig it every time."

"That's interesting, Andy. And I liked the movie. It really had me thinking," he said, a considerable stretching of the truth. "But there was one scene where there was a girl, a pretty girl, and then behind her were four boys—men, really—and they started throwing rocks at the camera. You know the one?"

Macheda nodded, and for the first time Frings sensed some hesitation.

"I'm interested in one of those men. I've known him since he was young. He's the grandson of a friend."

Macheda nodded again, suddenly less enthusiastic.

"Sol Elia."

"Sol?"

"That's right. You know what he's up to?"

Macheda shrugged, shook his head. "I've only seen him a couple of times since shooting that scene. We weren't friends or anything like that."

"You're sure?"

"Yeah."

Frings couldn't read Macheda. He was nervous about something, but that didn't necessarily mean he was lying. Maybe it was the sudden change in the tenor of their conversation.

"How did you come to pick him for the scene?"

"They were just people around the Tech, students who were willing to spend a couple of hours, had the right political outlook, you know. But they weren't anything special."

"Who's the girl?"

"I don't remember her name."

"Come on, Andy. You're not going to forget her name, a girl that looks like that."

"It was, what, a couple of years ago? I was taking some pretty heavy drugs at the time. I was shooting a lot of footage with a lot of different people. No, I don't remember her name."

"But you remembered Sol's."

"Only because you told me. You tell me her name, I'll probably remember it, too. But not off the top of my head."

Frings knew he was lying, but there wasn't much he could do about it now; just ride out the conversation and go after him again, later, when he had some more information and could probe some more. "How about the other men, you remember any of their names?"

Macheda shook his head. "Like I said before, I didn't see much of any of them after the shoot. They were just people who helped me out, wanted to be in a film."

"Listen, Andy, I'm not a cop. You know where I'm coming from. Hell, you probably know my own book better than I do. Sol's uncle is a close friend of mine, and he just wants to know that Sol's okay; maybe see him, maybe not, but the not knowing is eating at him. He's an old man. Do you get that?"

Macheda nodded, not meeting Frings's eyes.

"It would be great if you could think on that. Maybe you could ask some of your friends if they've heard from Sol or know what he's up to."

"Yeah, sure. Okay."

"I'll come find you and we can talk about it."

At this, Macheda brought his eyes back to Frings's, and they stood like that for a moment, wordless.

24

DORMAN HADN'T BEEN TO THE SVINBLAD INDUSTRIES OFFICES BEFORE, and was fascinated by the furniture in the waiting room. The chairs had upholstered seats with curved backs and tapered arms. The end tables were circular glass tops placed on three-branched pedestals. The receptionist's desk was made of blond wood and chrome, the edges rounded. Behind the desk sat a beautiful young woman, engaged in typing out something that had been written on a yellow legal pad.

The marble floors gleamed.

Dorman decided not to sit. Instead, he looked out the window at the construction taking place some twenty blocks away, in what would be the new City Center. Half-built skeletons reached toward the sky, the tallest ones with blinking lights at their apex. At moments like this, the New City Project's completion seemed inevitable, regardless of his own successes or failures. But this, Canada would have been quick to point out, was a misapprehension. His continued success was still crucial.

A quick double-ring emitted from the phone, and the receptionist picked up the receiver wordlessly. She listened for a moment, then set the receiver down.

"Mr. Svinblad is ready for you," she said and returned to her typing.

Dorman walked past her and opened the heavy oak door.

Svinblad sat behind a huge glass desk shaped something like a kidney. The walls of his corner office were dominated by enormous windows, which afforded an even better view of the new City Center than the waiting room.

"How are you today, Mr. Dorman?"

Dorman returned the greeting and took a seat in one of three identical armless chairs, the seats constructed like *L*'s, set slightly reclined on chrome legs. He adjusted his posture in the chair, but couldn't find a comfortable position.

"My wife had me buy those," Svinblad said. "Danish. You wouldn't believe what they cost."

Dorman felt sure that this was true—this was not a world he understood, nor one he found particularly interesting.

"I saw you at the dinner at the Leopold a few nights ago," Svinblad said. "You know, the one for that jack-off Schermer, the fundraiser for his Council run. I was surprised to see you there, figured it was important enough for Nathan to come himself, but maybe I'm wrong."

Dorman had seen Svinblad as well, but had avoided him, not eager for another round of the condescension and verbal abuse that characterized their interactions.

"My wife was there, too. Have you met my wife, by the way? She's a nice piece of trim. Not like Elaine out there," he said, nodding toward the door to the waiting room, "but she was in her time, and she's still better than 99 percent of the women you'll find in this city. But she says to me, who is that?—and she points to you. And you know what I say?"

Svinblad waited for Dorman to ask him what he said, but Dorman wasn't going to assist in the belittlement that he knew was coming.

"I say, that young man—I take a shit, Nathan Canada sends him to wipe my ass." He paused again, looking at Dorman with a pleased expression. Dorman met his gaze neutrally.

"Nothing to say to that, huh?"

"Not much to say, is there?"

Svinblad grinned nastily. "You're a tough guy, right?"

Dorman stayed quiet.

"War hero, from what Nathan tells me," Svinblad pressed. "You look too young for World War II. What, Korea?"

War hero—this was how Canada liked to refer to Dorman, like he was a Kentucky Derby winner. Himself, he couldn't see all that much heroic in his service.

"Caught the end of Korea. I was in Lebanon."

Svinblad looked him over. "Thing is, you don't look so tough from where I stand. Just because you wore the uniform—"

Dorman stood. He wasn't actually going to do anything, but he was getting tired of Svinblad's bluster. He was gratified to see Svinblad push back in his chair a little, his eyes betraying surprise. Dorman stayed standing for a moment, staring down Svinblad, before sitting again.

"Did Mr. Canada explain why I'm here?"

Svinblad shook his head, keeping his eyes on Dorman.

"The Italians on Luxembourg Avenue, they held out for more money than we anticipated. They'd heard something about how much the Germans got in Pickett East, and they weren't going to give in for anything less, so that's thrown off our budget."

"The Italians wouldn't settle?" Svinblad seemed to have recovered. "Why didn't you just bulldoze their goddamn neighborhood?"

"You don't need me to go through this again with you," Dorman said, catching himself before he added, "Mr. Svinblad." They'd had plenty of similar conversations in the past. It was cheaper to settle with these neighborhoods, even if it involved more money than Mr. Canada felt was justified. Forcing people to abandon their homes and move unwillingly—this was costly, both in terms of money and bad publicity. It was much better to buy them off.

"So, you're coming to me for more money?" Svinblad said it calmly, but the outrage was clear.

"That's right."

"What if I tell you I don't have any more to give? That's going to happen at some point, right? I *do* have limits."

This was undoubtedly true, but what Canada was asking for was a pittance compared to what Svinblad was worth, and there would be a strong return on the investment in the not-too-distant future. Even Svinblad wouldn't dispute that.

"We'd go elsewhere. There are plenty of people who would be happy to get in on the west side of City Center." This was a patchwork of old ethnic neighborhoods that, once the residents were relocated, would be the final piece of the new business district. Canada had arranged for Svinblad to buy this land—blocks that would be worth many millions once they were developed. And he would buy them on very favorable terms, in return for financing the bribery and relocation costs for a number of neighborhoods along the Crosstown. Canada had a number of such agreements with wealthy businessmen in the City—though, to Dorman's knowledge, Svinblad's was the most lucrative.

"Is that your way of playing hardball?"

"I'm telling you what Mr. Canada told me—that there are people waiting in line to throw money at the Crosstown if it means having a shot at those properties. If we reach your limit, it's not a problem. We can go elsewhere. The upshot, though, is that you'll no longer have the exclusive bid. Mr. Canada thought it would be courteous, given your past support, to give you the first opportunity to provide the additional funding we need."

Svinblad fixed him with a venomous glare, but Dorman was essentially immune to the man's anger. Svinblad knew that no matter how many times Canada sent Dorman to extract more money, he would make the money back ten-fold when he had control of the properties. Dorman understood that the man needed to vent—to show the power of his personality—before he'd write yet another check. But that didn't mean that Dorman liked being on the receiving end of Svinblad's insults, or, for that matter, that he had anything but contempt for the man.

Svinblad was up now, a man who in his early fifties was beginning to lose his powerful shoulders and athlete's movements. He still looked strong, but the years were becoming more obvious, the line of his slicked-back hair receding, going gray around the temples. He walked to a window, but kept his eyes on Dorman.

"I like these windows because every once in a while I look over at all that construction and remind myself what it is I'm getting for all this money I'm giving." He shook his head. "How the hell did the Italians find out what the Germans were getting? I thought that wasn't supposed to happen."

Dorman shrugged. In an ideal world, it wouldn't have happened. But it was impossible to stay on top of everyone all of the time—though he tried.

"Subversives," Svinblad spat. "Probably communists, maybe anarchists, but definitely some anti-capitalist subversives. You know, I have a friend, a guy called Ed Wayne, who would be more than happy to put the fear of the Red Blooded Capitalist American God into whoever's behind this. You just let me know."

"Sure," Dorman said, thinking that that was the last thing he'd consider doing.

25

GRIP DROVE AN UNMARKED THROUGH CROWDED STREETS TO KLIMCHUK'S, making sure to avoid the security guards' block with its impassable street. He found a parking spot down in front of a religious bookstore, a few doors down from the bar. Two vagrants squatted against the cement wall, muttering to each other in their native language.

He pounded the door, found the same big man as the other day. Grip smiled at him. The bouncer sighed in resignation.

"You going to let me in?" Behind the big man, it looked as if about a quarter of the tables were in use. This empty, the place seemed smaller than before. The bouncer looked back to the bar. Grip saw the bartender put his towel on the rail, have a word with one of the barflies, and head their way.

"You again?"

"Nice to see you."

The bartender sneered at him. "What do you want?"

"I need a word."

The bartender maintained his belligerent glare.

"Look, Ivan, we can do this now or I can come back in a couple hours with some of my buddies from Vice and take this place down. You want to give me a hard time? You understand?"

The bartender tapped the bouncer on the shoulder, and the bouncer stood aside, uncertain. Grip followed the bartender to the bar.

"Whisky and a beer."

He could see the bartender didn't like this, which improved his mood slightly.

"Go down to the end of the bar, you want to talk."

Grip eyed the barflies, glassy-eyed guys in their sixties and seventies, born in countries that hadn't existed for decades. He'd bet they didn't have fifty words of English among them. But he shrugged and took a stool at the far end of the bar.

"So?"

Grip took a drink from the bottle, looked past it at the bartender.

"Yeah, those three guys I came looking for the other day: Zanev, Malakov, Petrov. You seen them yesterday or today?"

The bartender's eyes narrowed. "No. They haven't been around here."

"See, that's the thing. As far as I know, they haven't been around anywhere."

"That right?" The bartender was good at this, acting unconcerned, but Grip could see the guy thinking hard.

Grip drank again from his bottle, in no hurry. "Any thoughts about where they might be?"

"How the fuck would I know that?"

"I were you, I'd figure out something. This is the last place they were known to be. It's also an underground gambling operation, which makes it a criminal enterprise. You got whores in here. I bet if we grabbed some of these dice and cards, we might find something interesting. What do you think?"

The bartender shook his head at the unfairness of it all.

"What the fuck do you think?" Grip repeated.

"What do you want from me?"

Grip smiled. He'd rattled the guy. "Tell me about these guys."

"I don't know them too well. They're just guys that come here to play cards, throw some dice."

"Why are you fucking with me, Ivan? You think I'm bluffing?"

"I can't give you what I don't have."

"Okay. How about this? You must have known about their credit. Those guys in the hole to anyone?"

The bartender pursed his lips, shook his head. "Not those guys, no. They always had money, made good money at their jobs. They . . ." He hesitated, not certain what he should say to a cop.

"That's better. Look, we know these guys were on the take, we're not worried about that right now. You're telling me they didn't owe money to anyone?"

"No. No." He shook his head vigorously. "You ask anyone in the neighborhood. Those boys, they had problems, maybe it was because they had *too much* money."

"What do you mean by that?"

"Shit. I don't know. I'm just telling you, they didn't have money problems."

"What else? Why would they be missing? Do you think they made a big score, maybe blew town?"

"I got no idea about that. They came in here the other day, there's nothing different. They don't throw money around. They don't place big bets. They don't go with any of the girls. They come in, play some cards, they leave."

"You said last time that Zanev came in and got the other two."

The bartender thought about this. "Yeah, that's right."

"He came in like what? He had something to tell them? He told them something, and they split?"

"I don't know. Maybe."

Grip nodded, thinking. He wasn't sure what else he could get out of this guy. "Any friends, girlfriends, anything like that?"

"Maybe, I don't know. I only see them here. I don't know those things."

"Yeah, alright. Any other cops been here, asking questions about those guys?"

"Once. Two guys. They ask a couple of questions, then leave. Not like you."

Grip snorted a quick laugh. "Okay, Ivan. It took you a while, but you did okay. I gave you my card before, and I know you didn't lose it. You give me a call if think of anything."

The bartender nodded his head, brooding. "And if they show up?"

"Yeah, if they show up, you definitely call me, because then we've got a real problem."

The bartender looked at him, confused.

Grip smiled. "Last time I saw them, they were dead."

26

FRINGS FOUND EBANKS RECLINED ON A PLUSH DIVAN IN A GLASSED-IN porch off the second floor of his house. Smoke rose serenely from a hookah sitting on an oriental carpet. A girl in a sweater and skirt sat with her head back, eyes closed, listening to a record of a raspy French duo harmonizing over strummed guitars. Ebanks rolled his head over, smiling lazily as Frings walked in.

"Fraaaank."

Frings sat down in a leather chair, leaned his cane in the crook made where the arm met the chair back, and looked at the girl.

"Laura," Ebanks called to her in a soothing voice. "Laura."

The girl opened her eyes slowly, registered that Frings was there, smiled and then closed them again, her head falling to rest on the chair back.

"Hashish," Ebanks said, nodding at the hookah. "Help yourself."

Frings frowned and shook his head, though the smell was enticing. He looked to the girl, then back to Ebanks, a question in his eyes.

"She's not paying attention, Frank. She's listening to the music, dreaming her dreams."

Frings shrugged. "What is it?"

"The record? Church music from Martinique. A guy at City College was down there making recordings, slipped me a copy in exchange for some peyote. You dig it?"

"I do."

With some effort, Ebanks propped himself on his elbow, swung his feet to the floor. The afternoon sun was coming in low through the remaining leaves on two large elms, casting faint shadows across the room.

"What brings you here, Frank?"

"You remember I came here the other day, looking for Andy Macheda? I found him, but that's not why I'm back. I'm trying to find Sol Elia—I think I might have mentioned that. I went to the Tech, had a look at his files. It turns out that while he was there he was paid to participate in a study."

Ebanks nodded. "That happens."

"The file didn't have the name of the study, but it listed a fund number and I had them figure out who was paying him."

"Sure, Frank. Who was it?"

"Simon Ledley. I thought maybe you'd have some insight."

Ebanks straightened, as if trying to will himself to clarity. Frings was glad that he hadn't tried the hashish.

"When was this?"

"'59. '60."

"That's an interesting time in the department, Frank."

"The psych department?"

"Si and I were there together, the first years of working with consciousness-altering agents."

"He was experimenting with LSD?"

"LSD, peyote, mescaline, psilocybin, all of the above. He still is, for all I know. It was a strange time. We had these new drugs, and it became a priority in the department. *The* priority for us. That was why I was there, more or less—because I'd been working on it down in Central America. You remember when I was down there?"

Frings nodded. Ebanks had since settled down, but in the years before he'd joined the Tech faculty, he'd been consumed by boredom when he was in the City, leaving whenever he could for whatever remote destination caught his eye. It was during his occasional periods back in the City that he and Frings had been closest. Once he had returned to stay, they had, for whatever reason, grown apart.

Frings knew that Ebanks had trekked through the highlands of Central America, meeting with shamans and traditional healers, convinced that there was something to be learned from their knowledge of the native flora. Before his decision to study hallucinogens under the auspices of the Tech, Ebanks had considered himself a connoisseur of intoxicants—the more exotic, the better.

"Si, he had his students, but he kept it real quiet. He's always been like that, everything secret until he publishes a paper and blows the world away, the motherfucker. So, he was doing what he was doing, and Ralph Landon was working with alcoholics, seeing if psychedelics could help them beat the liquor, but he ended up dying a couple of years ago. Heart attack, I think. And I was doing my own experiments. No one was collaborating. Part of it was that everyone was trying to make breakthroughs on their own. The other part was that we didn't like each other very much."

"And that's what got you in trouble, right?"

Ebanks laughed, his bitterness tangible even through the hash veneer. "You ever watch a bird flying and wonder what he thinks about us, only being able to walk on land? He's got a whole extra dimension on us, Frank, and sometimes I look at that and I feel so goddamn trapped. And LSD is like being that bird, but mentally, spiritually. You don't study birds by watching what they do on the ground, Frank, you have to watch them in the skies. Si, he wanted to use the traditional methods: designing experiments, observing behaviors, talking to people who were actually taking the drug. But he didn't have any personal experience with the stuff. He had no idea what he was working with. I wanted to adapt our methods to the realities of the drugs. I wanted to study the birds *from* the sky, Frank."

"You took the drugs yourself."

"When had I not been taking drugs? Look, I took the drugs, other people took the drugs. The point is that we weren't observing subjects, we were observing ourselves, our own experiences. There was a method, Frank, but it was the kind of method that psychedelic drugs required, not the kind that traditional-minded people like Si used."

"It didn't get out of hand?"

"What got out of hand was the scrutiny I was put under for using innovative techniques to address this new capability."

"Okay."

"You don't know. You can't imagine unless you've experienced it for yourself. Let's try another metaphor. LSD, it's like a continent, the last unexplored place on earth. You can't explore with control groups and samples and models. You have to go yourself, and explore and map and record. That's what Si didn't understand. None of them understood." Ebanks recited all this with a quiet intensity, his pupils huge. Frings couldn't read Ebanks's mood, couldn't tell if he'd shifted almost imperceptibly to anger.

"So Ledley ran you out."

Ebanks pulled his hand slowly down his face, sighing. "He charged me with unsound research methods, endangering students, violating research ethics." He laughed at this last one. "I went in front of the board, and I told them the truth, Frank. I told them what I just told you. These drugs, they are the key to understanding the spirit or the soul or God or whatever you want to call it. To think that you can study it using the same methods that you use with lab rats and drug trials? But if you haven't been there, if you haven't trod that ground, there's no point in trying to explain it because it defies words. That's the challenge of what we were—are—trying to do, explain the unexplainable, quantify the profound."

They sat in silence for a moment, the record needle skipping rhythmically against the label, Ebanks staring at Frings. Frings tried to get a handle on this zealous side of Ebanks, who—naively, it seemed to Frings—was proselytizing for this new drug, LSD.

"I'm meeting with Ledley tomorrow."

Ebanks shook his head slowly. "He won't tell you anything."

"He won't?"

"No. He's the God of his little world. He doesn't do what he doesn't want to do and he won't want to talk to you."

"I guess I'll see."

"I guess you will."

27

PRESIDENT MILLEDGE WAITED AT THE ADMINISTRATION BUILDING, STANDING under the stone arch as Frings approached, carrying an umbrella against the torrent. Even the student protestors had been run off by the rain. Frings caught the unhappy look on Milledge's face, as if he was about to perform some particularly distasteful task.

"Is Panos not coming?" Milledge extended his hand to Frings.

"He's ill."

Milledge nodded. "There's a complication, I'm afraid. Dr. Ledley decided that he preferred to meet with you in the company of an attorney."

Frings phrased his response carefully, trying not to appear as annoyed as he felt. "I'm disappointed that Dr. Ledley considers this meeting antagonistic."

"Oh no,"—Milledge said, hand up to placate—"I don't think that's it at all. We are dealing with sensitive issues here, legal requirements, confidentiality agreements. The attorney will be present to ensure that we are not in breach of these agreements. That would put the Tech in a very difficult position."

Frings pursed his lips, nodded skeptically. Milledge himself didn't seem too sure of his own words.

"We're meeting here," Milledge said, leading Frings inside and out of the rain. Originally, they had planned to meet in the conference room on the ground floor of Ledley's building. Frings wondered why he was being kept away.

Ledley and the lawyer waited in the same room that Frings and Panos had used when they'd examined Sol's files. Ledley sat reading a journal of some sort while his lawyer bided time. As Frings entered the room, the lawyer—an aging, though powerfully built man—stood and extended an enormous hand.

"Rolf Westermann," the lawyer said. "I believe we've met." Westermann was one of the City's top lawyers, with a clientele that included many of the City's most successful men. Their paths had occasionally crossed.

"Yes, we have." Frings didn't bother to compete with the strength of the man's handshake, and Westermann sat down with a look of vague satisfaction. Frings reached out to the sitting Ledley, who looked up from his reading, regarded his hand with little enthusiasm, and shook it limply.

Milledge and Frings sat down opposite Ledley and Westermann—an adversarial arrangement, though with the president on Frings's side.

Ledley wasn't as old as Frings had been expecting—probably in his fifties—but he cut an unusual figure, sitting in a way that indicated a profound lack of physical grace. He wore a threadbare, faded blue sweater over a collared shirt. Westermann was in an expensive suit.

The two pairs of men stared across the table at each other for a moment, the room silent but for the drone of a fan blowing air through the vents cut into the ceiling.

Milledge cleared his throat, nervous. "You received my memo, Simon, with the ledger items?"

Ledley nodded.

"I understand that these payments were most likely incentives paid to Sol Elia for participating in one of your studies. Can you fill me in on the study and the nature of his participation?"

Ledley sat stone-still. Westermann said, "The study in question is subject to confidentiality agreements that prohibit disclosure of the information you are requesting."

Frings glanced over at Milledge, who shifted uncomfortably in his chair.

"How about the name of the study, to start off with?"

Westermann cleared his throat. "The study in question is subject to confidentiality agreements that prohibit disclosure of the information you are requesting."

Frings stared at Ledley. "You can't even tell us the name of the study?"

Ledley closed his eyes and shook his head slowly, radiating arrogance.

Milledge's voice was tight with anger. "Who was the sponsor of this program?"

"The study in question is—"

"We get it," Frings interrupted. He turned to Milledge. "Were you expecting this?"

Milledge looked back at Frings with a mixture of fury, embarrassment, and helplessness. "I was hoping that Simon would be more forthcoming."

Frings turned to Ledley. "You understand that Sol Elia is missing?"

"Oh, really?" he said, eyebrows raised, voice bored. "Missing from whom?"

Frings took a moment to gather himself. "The police will be the next people to visit. They'll bring a warrant to go through your files. You understand that, don't you?"

"On what basis, Mr. Frings? I looked into it when I received the request for this meeting. There is no missing persons case filed for Sol Elia. If there were, I fail to see how privileged files related to my studies would be germane to his whereabouts."

"That's how you want to play this?"

Ledley regarded Frings with meager interest, said nothing. Westermann slid some papers from the table into his briefcase. Milledge sat quietly, looking slightly ill.

28

AT THE DOOR TO THE DOUBLE EAGLE, A PUB LESS THAN A BLOCK FROM St. Stanislaw's church, Dorman was met by two older men, whom he recognized from the previous meeting in the church basement. They reintroduced themselves, shook hands. Inside, the place seemed to be doing a decent business. The tables were full—mostly older people, mumbling to one another, sharing wine and meals. The bar was also packed, though with a younger crowd, all men: workers done for the day, having a drink or three before heading home to their families. Dorman followed the two men to the back, where a door led to a function room of sorts. Trochowski sat at a table for two, the chair opposite him empty, two cups of tea steaming. Three more of the men from St. Stanislaw's were there, sitting at another table off to the side. Everyone looked up as Dorman entered.

"Mr. Dorman." Trochowski stood and beckoned Dorman over. They shook hands and sat. Dorman looked over at the other table where the five men talked quietly, so that they could also hear Dorman's conversation.

"The note you sent indicated that you had a change of heart, Mr. Trochowski."

Trochowski nodded. "Yes, this is right."

"What made you change your mind?" Dorman was sure that the answer was greed. It was easy to turn your back on that kind of money on the spur of the moment. Later, though, as you lay in bed and thought about the amount—how it could change things for you or even for your community—the moralistic objections suddenly seemed less and less convincing as the benefits became more tangible.

"We spoke among ourselves after you left. The road will come through our neighborhood no matter what we do, yes? So, we talk and decide, why not get any good that we can see from this? It is not a fair recompense for our troubles, but it is better than nothing at all."

"I understand. What did you have in mind?"

"The same deal that you offered before, the other night at the church."

Dorman felt his chest contract and sweat form on his upper lip, under his arms. He had to push this a little, see what happened next. "What deal was that?"

"You don't remember the details?"

Dorman saw that Trochowski wanted him to say it, make the offer. "Why don't you tell me what you're thinking."

The old man was stopped by this, unsure how to proceed. Dorman helped him along. "I don't remember any kind of offer being made the other night at the church. If you remember such an offer, remind me." He looked over to the other table where the conversation had stopped and all the attention was centered on Dorman and Trochowski.

Trochowski looked him in the eye, and Dorman saw the hostility. "I cannot believe that you don't remember, Mr. Dorman."

"I can't remember because I didn't make any offer."

Trochowski mulled over his next move. Dorman leaned across the table, grabbed Trochowski's shirt, and ripped it open. He was wearing a wire. Dorman glared at Trochowski—who'd reddened considerably—but said nothing.

The younger men were up now, advancing on Dorman. Dorman made a move for the door, but was cut off by two of the men. He feinted toward the table, then lowered his shoulder and barreled toward the door. He knocked one of the men back hard against the wall. The other one punched him twice in the back of his head and kicked him behind the knees. Dorman turned and swung wildly, missing everything. Behind his assailants he could see Trochowski, red-faced, rebuttoning his shirt. Dorman pulled on the door knob and wrenched the door open as he ducked to take a blow on the shoulder. He stumbled backward into the restaurant, where conversations immediately ceased.

The three younger men followed him out, kicking and punching at him as he scrambled toward the exit, bumping people at their tables in his retreat. He was aware that some of the men at the bar were taking shots at him as he passed and was thankful that no one grabbed him. He stumbled. A kick to the ribs hurt but knocked him back to his feet. He found the front door and shouldered it open, falling into the street. The three men stormed out after him and threw punches as he bent over and protected his head with his arms. He was pushed against a car and bounced off swinging, felt his fist graze someone's face. He could feel blood running down his chin. Someone grabbed his right arm, and he tucked his face into his right shoulder to try to protect himself when he heard the chirp of a siren on the block. His arm was released. One of the men kicked him hard in the shin and Dorman went down onto the sidewalk and lay there, resting and in pain. All he could think was, who the hell had Trochowski wearing a wire?

29

THE TEMPERATURE IN THE SUN WAS PROBABLY TWENTY DEGREES WARMER than in the frigid shade. Grip checked his watch, saw it was eleven, and tossed his cigarette down a sewer grate. He kept an eye on the street for a prowl car. He realized he was pushing his luck by being here, on Lieutenant Boyer's turf, for the second time in so many days. Normally, Grip didn't mind confrontation. But it would be a hell of a lot easier if word didn't get around—especially to Ving—about him being here, across the street from Ben Linsky's building.

Grip wasn't sure about what he was doing. One of his strengths as a cop was his decisiveness. He generally thought things over, debated merits in his head, then acted without second thoughts. In his estimation, he took very few wrong steps, though his mistakes could be big ones. His instincts weren't perfect, but he had a good sense of how much to mull over any decision—and the ability to banish doubts once he was in motion. Today, though, he wasn't sold on his own plan, wasn't sure that he'd go through with it. He had one lead. He needed to make something out of it. He sensed that time was beginning to run short, that whoever had the explosives wouldn't sit on them for long and that Grip seemed to be the only one in pursuit.

This had been his old partner Morphy's method—if an investigation stalled, you had to jumpstart it. They'd done this kind of thing many times, planting evidence—drugs, money, guns—not as an excuse for an arrest, but for the suspects' associates to discover. When it worked, the technique sowed suspicion—where did this money come from? Was someone holding out? Sometimes it was the catalyst that broke a case. He wasn't confident that it would work in this situation, but for the moment, there just wasn't anything else.

Grip had been working at his desk the previous night, typing up a backlog of reports with neither speed nor enthusiasm, when Zwieg had walked in, dominating the room with his sheer size.

"Everybody out, except Detective Grip."

There'd been three other detectives, and they'd hesitated a moment, uncertain. Zwieg hadn't said anything more, hadn't even moved, but his posture, or some energy coming off him, had been enough, and the detectives got up and left without a word. Zwieg took up a spot where he loomed over Grip, casting a shadow.

"I've got some bad news for you," Zwieg said, smiling nastily. "The Bulgarians, we found the killers. A couple of enforcers for a bookie over in the Hollows. We haven't nailed down the details, but it might be related to that middleweight fight at the convention center last month. Rumors have been flying around that Osmond took a dive."

Zwieg seemed fairly pleased to be imparting this information.

"That's great news," Grip said, slowly.

"I thought you'd be more interested."

Grip shrugged. "I'm working a different angle."

Zwieg tilted his head, narrowed his eyes. "Is that right?"

"Yeah. Little Nicky Patridis had something."

"Patridis?"

"Yeah, not sure how much stock to put into it. It's Patridis, after all. But it's better than dead security guards."

Zwieg seemed to think about this for a moment.

"Why don't I let you know if it comes to something," Grip said, suddenly wanting Zwieg out of the room.

"That sounds fine, detective. You do that."

GRIP TROTTED ACROSS THE STREET, HAT LOW, NO PROWL CARS INSIGHT. He looked through the glass door into the small, bare lobby of Linsky's building. No one inside. He pulled his pick kit from his coat pocket and worked two picks in the lock, looking at the column of call buttons with apartment numbers and names next to them. 302: LINSKY. He noticed that the names of Linsky's roommates were not listed.

He felt the lock mechanism, sprang it; fifteen seconds, if that.

Inside, the lobby was carpeted in a grimy shade of green, on the wall a bank of letterboxes below a faded painting of a seaside—colorful umbrellas and high white clouds.

He walked past the elevators and up the dimly lit stairs, keeping his footsteps light. Listening. He paused at the door on the third floor landing, stood still for nearly a full minute. Silence. Eleven a.m. on a Wednesday, not a time for coming and going. He eased the door open, confirmed that the hall was empty, and walked to 302. He knocked quietly, trying not to arouse attention from the other apartments. No answer. He put his ear to the door. Nothing.

The lock to the apartment door was easier than the exterior lock, no more difficult than if he'd actually had the key. He stepped into the apartment, closed the door quietly behind him.

The apartment was centered on the living room, three couches arranged in a *u* around a coffee table made from an old wooden door. Scattered on the coffee table were cheaply printed pamphlets— sheets of paper folded, then stapled along the fold as a kind of binding. Also, scattered marijuana shake and four empty glasses, one tipped on its side.

Tapestries in different earth tones covered the walls; Grip could make out images of a man with an elephant's head sitting cross-legged next to another man wearing some kind of high crown. Four lamps stood on four tables arrayed at the ends of the couches. An overhead light was recessed into the ceiling. Grip took the scene in, certain that there was something about the room that he was missing.

Four doors led off the living room. A doorless entrance led to a small kitchen. Grip started with the biggest bedroom, which he assumed was Linsky's. A mattress lay on a wooden frame that looked as if it had been made by someone who wasn't much of a carpenter. Linsky's bedroom was orderly compared to the living room, a bare writing desk, a small octagonal rug, a closet with clothes neatly folded on shelves. Grip looked through Linsky's desk drawers, found drafts of poems, clay marijuana pipes, and writing supplies. On the top shelf of the closet, a Smith-Corona typewriter. He carefully searched through the folded clothes, checked under the mattress and rug, played a flashlight into the heating vent. Nothing.

He checked the other two bedrooms while he was at it, though these also turned up nothing. They seemed to be occupied by college boys—text books, cigarette papers, posters with revolutionary slogans and socialist supermen doing industrial work. Linsky's walls had been bare.

He finished by checking the bathroom and the kitchen. He sensed the clock ticking. He didn't want to be caught here. From his coat pocket he pulled the memo that he'd kept from Linsky's bag. He unfolded it and laid it on the table among the stapled journals. He stepped back, making sure that it would be hard to miss. Satisfied, he left, locking the door behind him.

30

THE MAÎTRE D' WANTED A WORD THAT NIGHT, ASKING DORMAN IF HE knew a cop who he claimed was harassing his brother-in-law. Dorman didn't, but said he'd look into it, making a note on the back of a receipt. People never understood that he had little authority beyond the pressure he could bring to bear as Mr. Canada's assistant. This wasn't the kind of thing that would impress a beat cop.

Anastasia was already there, two glasses of wine and an open bottle on the table. This was unusual, Anastasia beating him to the booth. She must have seen him come in, secured the wine while he was talking at the door. It made him uneasy, though. She noticed.

"You have a hard day, today?" Her accent was a little too harsh for her voice to be perfect, but it was pitched slightly low with an erotic trace of hoarseness, perhaps from the cigarette she was smoking now, blowing the smoke sideways out of her mouth, her face turned to him.

"You could say that." He picked up the flower vase on the table, trying to make it look subconscious, like he was distracted. He held it up high enough to see that there was no bug on the bottom. This meant nothing, of course. There could be a bug beneath the table, in the leather cushions. He wasn't going to tear the place apart.

"Your face," she said, touching a swollen knot just beneath his right eye, where he'd caught a fist at the Double Eagle.

"That's part of it." He turned his head slightly, and she let her hand trail down his face and settle on his arm.

"Tell me."

He met her eyes. "Let's see, it started, I went to a murder scene."

This didn't seem to startle her. "Who was killed?"

"Security guards."

"Do you know who did it?"

Dorman nodded. "Apparently, they owed some money or fixed a boxing match or something like that."

"What is this to do with you?"

"Nothing, I guess." In truth, he wasn't convinced that their deaths were unconnected to the heist. It was far too much of a coincidence. He was jarred by a sudden wave of distrust, and wasn't sure if it was directed toward her. He floated something false, like he sometimes did, to see if it led to anything over time, if this conversation was truly private. "We think that at least one of them was selling drugs." He regretted it as the words left his mouth—he was essentially accusing her of treachery.

"I know I can trust you," he said.

She looked surprised, as if the statement had come out of nowhere. She cupped her hand around his neck. His skin tingled. "Of course," she said, her husky whisper barely audible above the languor of the band.

"Live with me," he said.

She withdrew her hand, leaned back with a pout. "Phil. You know I can't do that. It is against the rules."

He didn't bother to pursue it. Having said it was enough.

THEY LISTENED TO THE BAND IN SILENCE FOR A WHILE, A CHASTE SPACE between them. Dorman tried to think of the three security guys, laid out on their stomachs, heads caved in from behind. But his mind kept coming back to the bug. Whose bug? Whoever it was, they already knew quite a bit to target him through Trochowski. He massaged the bridge of his nose.

"Phil?"

Dorman knew that Anastasia was uncomfortable when he was so clearly stressed.

She asked, "When you came to the City, what did you know of this New City Project?"

"Not much."

"But you come and you work for Nathan Canada, yes?"

Dorman nodded.

"So, how do you know you are on the right side?"

"What do you mean?" He didn't like the defensiveness in his voice.

"Do you ever wonder if maybe the changes to the City aren't so good?"

"If the City doesn't change, it will die. I've told you that."

"I know, Phil. But you were brought here by your boss, and you knew nothing of the project. How do you know he is correct in his beliefs? How do you feel so sure that you do what you do? When I left my country, that was an easy choice. I look around and see what is happening—the fear, the arrests—everything changed. But here, I don't know. It's not so clear."

"You have to take a side and commit, Anastasia. You have to be-lieve in your side and work for it as hard as you can. I'm not kidding myself—if I were born in Moscow I'd probably be fighting like hell against the Capitalist Menace. Maybe if I'd come to the City under different circumstances, I'd see the New City Project differently. But I didn't. I have to take things that are gray and change them into black and white. If I didn't do that, I'd never act."

Anastasia looked at him with her head cocked. "Is that what they teach you in the Navy?"

"No. That's what I need to get through life."

THE MAÎTRE D' WALKED OVER, HIS EXPRESSION PAINED, THE WAY IT ALWAYS was when he had to disturb a table.

"There's an Arthur Deyna requesting to see you."

Dorman checked his watch. Midnight. Why would Deyna be coming to see him now?

"Okay."

Anastasia looked uncertain.

"A reporter. Give me ten minutes."

Deyna arrived at the table as Anastasia slid out of the booth. He smiled at her, turning to watch her walk away, surprising Dorman, who hadn't thought of Deyna as being much interested in women.

The maître d' hovered.

"Drink?" Dorman asked.

"Scotch."

When they were alone, Dorman said, "It's a little late for business, isn't it?"

"I won't be long."

"Okay."

"Three dead security guards, bats to the back of the head."

"Sure."

"Any thoughts you want to share?"

"Plenty of people are murdered in the City. It sounds like the police have it under control."

"That's it? Any connection with the New City Project? Maybe something connected to site theft? What site were they on?"

Dorman kept his expression blank. "From what I've heard, there's no connection at all. It's a gambling thing. Where are we going with this, Art?"

Dorman thought he could see in the dim light a trace of a knowing smile on Deyna's boyish face.

"Just looking into a story, Phil."

The scotch arrived. Deyna took down half of it.

Dorman smiled coldly. "Is that all?"

Deyna chuckled. "Yeah, for tonight. No promises about tomorrow. Hey, what the hell happened to your face?"

Unconsciously, Dorman touched the lump under his eye. "Nicked myself shaving," he said, flatly.

"Of course. That's exactly what it looks like." Deyna finished his scotch and winked. "Nice seeing you tonight. I'll be in touch."

They shook hands.

DORMAN WATCHED DEYNA WALK TOWARD THE DOOR. ANASTASIA emerged from somewhere and their paths crossed. Deyna said something and she stopped. Deyna leaned into her, whispering something in her ear, looking right at Dorman. Anastasia nodded, not smiling. Dorman went cold.

31

DORMAN WALKED THROUGH THE DRIVING RAIN IN THE EARLY MORNING, the streetlights still on, their sharp glare reflected in the wet street. There was no one on the sidewalks and the roads were clear, save for a handful of delivery trucks. He felt a kind of grim enjoyment at the near emptiness as he strode over puddles, his shoes quickly becoming soaked. He'd grabbed four hours of restless sleep before deciding he had no more stomach for the nightmares. He took a shower, the hot water making the swelling around his eye ache. In the mirror he saw that the area had turned dark blue and yellow. He headed to work.

The overnight guards were still on their shift, looking bored as hell, when he arrived at City Hall. He nodded to them, took in the empty foyer. If the foyer was crowded, which it generally was during working hours, you couldn't really see the mural that ran along all four walls. It was an odd piece of work, tracing the history of democracy from its origins in Greece—balding, bearded old men in togas instructing younger men sitting on the steps of a Greek temple—through the signing of the Magna Carta, the American Revolution, the Civil War, and so on. All of these tableaus were framed by clouds, which in turn were littered with cherubs, some of whom seemed to be blowing on horns. It was pretty weird—far too weird not to distract from the point that the artist had tried to make.

He took the stairs up to the second floor, saw his door open, and found a maid cleaning his office. She was startled by his presence and bolted upright, a stocky young woman, hair wrapped in a white scarf.

Dorman smiled at her. She looked frightened, as if he might chastise or punish her for being in his office; or maybe it was just the sight of his swollen face. He shook out his umbrella in the hallway, hung it and his rain jacket on the hooks attached to the back of his door. She watched him do this. He thought she might feel trapped if he stood in the doorway, so he took a step out, made an exaggerated gesture encouraging her to leave. She picked up her rag and a bottle filled with yellow liquid and edged past him, keeping her suspicious eyes on him. He watched her broad frame as she walked away, her weight shifting heavily with each step.

He smoothed out his hair with his hands and returned to his office, shutting the door behind him.

HE SAT IN HIS CHAIR, LOOKING AT HIS HANDS CLASPED ON HIS DESK. A pile of papers awaiting his attention was stacked neatly on the right corner, next to a pen box and desk lamp. He was in the grip of a strange mood, a kind of paralysis. He was stuck in a mental loop: contemplating the implications of Trochowski wearing a wire, unable to get beyond the fact that there *were* implications, thinking that these implications—whatever they were—could not possibly be good. He didn't want to see anyone, address any problems—he needed to *think*.

He heard people walking in the corridor beyond his door, arriving for work. He glanced at the clock. Nine a.m. He'd been there for two hours, hadn't even touched a paper, done any work at all. Canada would have arrived sometime in the past hour. Dorman knew he'd be reading through memos, leafing through the morning's newspapers, barking out notes for his secretary to take down, observations or things to do. He needed to speak with Canada, but it was so much easier to sit in his office. Avoiding. Procrastinating.

A knock on his door. He waited for a second, wondered if the person would go away. Another knock.

"Who is it?"

"Fleming, from Procurement."

"Come back later.

"When would that be, sir?"

"An hour."

"An hour, then."

Dorman listened to the footsteps recede down the hall. This interlude had jostled him from his stupor. He picked up the phone, called over to Canada's secretary, asked if the old man could meet with him.

CANADA WAS READING THROUGH A STAPLED REPORT OF SOME SORT, PEERing through half-lens glasses. He didn't look up when Dorman closed the door behind him, nor when he took the green leather chair on the other side of the desk. Dorman waited. Still, Canada didn't look up. Dorman shifted in his chair. Mr. Canada peered over his glasses, not moving his head.

"Lost your goddamn voice?"

"Sir?"

"What do you want, Mr. Dorman?" There was something troubling about the tone of Canada's voice.

He'd come to this meeting intending to tell Canada about the incident with Trochowski and the wire, but suddenly decided that he didn't want to.

He hadn't suddenly lost his trust in Canada—nothing so dramatic—but he couldn't help but think that if his trust *were* misplaced, if he'd somehow miscalculated, then there'd be consequences.

He decided on another topic of conversation. "I saw Gerald Svinblad yesterday. He was a little testy. We may start butting up against the limits of what he's willing to give."

"Of course he's going to act like he's reaching his limit. He has no reason not to. Is that what you came here to tell me?"

"I know that he'd put on a show of reluctance, sir. What I'm saying is that I deal with this kind of thing every day, and I've developed a sense for these things, and my sense is that Svinblad is serious."

Canada nodded and appeared to give it more thought. "What, in your opinion, should we do about it?"

"I think we should do what we always do—let him know who's running this show."

Canada nodded thoughtfully. "That's the most important thing, keeping the pecking order straight. Maybe I should contact him myself."

Dorman didn't say anything. Canada didn't expect or want him to weigh in on this.

Canada looked across the desk with one of his unreadable expressions. "Are you sure this is why you came to talk to me?"

Dorman nodded.

Canada squinted at him. "What the fuck happened to your face."

32

A DECADE AGO, IN AN EFFORT TO DRAW TOURISTS, THE CITY HAD INVESTED in a narrow municipal park that traced the curving arc of the river. The hope was that the park would be the first revitalizing step in this deserted riverfront—that the blocks bordering the park would be given over to apartments for the wealthy who would enjoy the river view and the shaded path. The park had barely opened when Canada had arranged for the construction of the Riverside Expressway, an early phase of the New City Project. Instead of a quiet street and wide promenade separating the park from the river, there now ran an eight-lane highway. The apartment buildings never materialized—the City had, as usual, undermined itself.

Walking the path now, Frings reflected that anyone with a sense of the City's history could have foreseen the inevitable next step—the annexation of the park by drug dealers and prostitutes working for menacing pimps. During the day, a walk could be pleasant if you ignored the indigents sleeping in the bushes and didn't get caught around a remote bend by the gangs of teenagers who seemed to roam around at all times of the day and night.

Frings walked with Ebanks, who seemed a different person today, more engaged, his personality not so diluted. Frings had suggested meeting somewhere other than the house, hoping that a different environment would animate Ebanks. It seemed to have done so, though Frings wasn't entirely sure that the change of scenery was the reason.

The clang of the pile drivers upriver was just audible over the din of the traffic, just out of sight, on the other side of the high, landscaped shrubs.

Ebanks listened without interrupting, walking with his hands clasped behind his back, his head tilted slightly forward, as Frings recounted his visit with Ledley. When he was done, they walked several yards in silence.

"That motherfucker," Ebanks said with surprising venom. "That fucking perverted son of a bitch."

Frings kept walking.

"Get a warrant and take him down. The motherfucker deserves it."

"I'm going to try," Frings said cautiously, "but it's not easy. I've got to arrange something with the police, convince them both that Sol Elia is a missing person and that Ledley's files are relevant to the case. It doesn't seem very likely."

Ebanks shook his head, and Frings could see his jaw working. Ebanks's neck was red.

"Will, can you tell me what you know about Ledley's work in the years that we're talking about—'58, '59? Do you know *anything*?"

"I don't, Frank, I really don't. Understand, we weren't colleagues. We were opponents, competitors. There was only so much money, so much journal space for this kind of work, and he and I were both after those things.

"What I *can* tell you is that we had different research methods. You know about mine. They got me fired. Ledley stuck to what he knew, experiments, observation of subjects; but what exactly he did, I have no idea. It was all kept behind closed doors."

"But he did experiments? On people?"

They were walking again. "Yes. Students, I think. Maybe others."

"And he would have paid students for taking part."

"Sure, especially if it took place over time, if he needed them to keep coming back. He needed to give them a reason."

Frings thought about this for a moment. "Would these experiments be . . . potentially harmful to the students? Could there be negative effects?"

Ebanks shrugged. "Sure, there *could*. Listen, you can't understand this stuff unless you've taken it. You can't understand where I'm coming from, what the potential is. It's impossible to explain because there is no frame of reference. All I can give you is analogies. It's like seeing the world in black and white and suddenly it's in color. It is like being confined inside your body and suddenly having your soul released, incorporeal."

"So it's powerful enough that it could be harmful if used incorrectly?"

"God, yes. But why would someone would want to do that when you have so much beautiful potential?" His face darkened. "But Ledley, Ledley would be the guy. He's blind to beauty. He wouldn't see it if it slapped him in the face. LSD shows you how false the way we humans order our world is. Ledley is committed to that order. I don't know how the hell he would deal with that contradiction."

They continued their walk, the leaves forming intricate latticed patterns of shadows on the path. Frings was troubled by what he was hearing—and seeing—from Ebanks. In the past couple of years, the only time he'd seen Ebanks had been when Ebanks was either intoxicated on powerful drugs or recovering from using them. Without the chemicals, there was something different about him, some mix, Frings thought, of anger and arrogance. Frings wasn't surprised that Ebanks would be upset with Ledley, a rival who'd bested him, even gotten him fired. But the intensity of the rage on display was hard to square with the man he'd known for years, whose personality had been bound up in his aristocratic calm.

"I need another way in, Will."

They walked some more, Ebanks thinking.

"He had a research assistant for a while, a grad student. He's over at City College now. I'm trying to think of his name."

"He would have worked with Ledley on his LSD project?"

"The timing is right, but I don't know for sure. Ledley kept things tight. But so did I, I guess. What was his name? A weird little guy, though of course you had to be weird to last working with Ledley."

They heard footsteps behind them and their conversation stopped as a group of boys, probably in their early teens, came upon them, surrounding them, looking them over, projecting aggression.

Ebanks stiffened, his face reddening. "Get the fuck out of here before I kill all of you," he growled.

The kids froze. Frings stopped. The hairs on his neck bristled.

"Get the fuck away," Ebanks screamed with unrestrained ferocity. "I will *kill* you."

The boys looked at each other, but found no confidence and began moving away, keeping their swagger to save face.

Frings looked to Ebanks, who was heaving in breaths. "What the hell was that, Will?"

Ebanks nodded absently, humming something to himself, oblivious to Frings's question.

"Toth," he said, smiling triumphantly. "Leonard Toth. City College."

• • •

Excerpt from *True Revolution*, a pamphlet by William Ebanks

Now let us turn to how Spiritual Insight will lead to True Revolution. When we speak of revolutions, real revolutions, we are speaking mainly of oppressed people, often formerly colonized people, who take up arms

against their oppressors in a violent
attempt to overthrow the existing government and replace it with a new one, presumably more responsive to the wishes of the
people or at least the revolutionaries.
These revolutions are important and should
be supported by people who believe that
freedom does not truly exist without freedom from oppression for ALL people.

But this is not True Revolution. Why not?
Because these revolutions merely replace
one hierarchical structure with another.
This new structure may be more JUST than
the last. It may, in fact, be The Most Just
Structure that one can have. But it is
still a Structure. There are still people
who rule and people who are ruled, even if
this relationship is no longer that of
oppressor and oppressed. After the blood-
shed and the destruction, what has changed?
The leaders. Perhaps the nature of the
government and its attitude toward the
governed. Is this True Revolution?

Any revolution, any struggle for that
matter, is doomed to failure because the
Roles in Society are not changed, the
people who perform those roles are. We have
already seen how humans play Roles in their
lives, Roles that are in large part
assigned at birth, then perhaps modified
through the assertion of particular talents
or ambitions, and follow us to our graves.
By taking these roles we accept that we are
shedding our Identities to become a TYPE
and are therefore become alienated from our
True Nature. If we look at society as an

amalgamation and ordering of these Roles,
you will see that only through the destruction of these Roles will meaningful change
be brought to any society.

   This is how Spiritual Insight with the
aid of the new door-opening drugs will lead
us to True Revolution. Spiritual Insight, by
allowing a person to commune with his or her
Identity and therefore his or her True Nature, allows, no, FORCES the shedding of the
Roles accumulated over the person's life-
time. We have already discussed this. Now,
imagine this on a societal level, masses of
people achieving Spiritual Insight, casting
off the Roles that they have been assigned
and reordering society based on the needs of
people's Identities. This is True Revolution, a true overturning of existing society
and the creation of a new form that allows
people to achieve actual fulfillment and
HAPPINESS, conditions denied when Identity
is subjugated to Role.

33

GRIP HAD LINSKY'S PLACE STAKED OUT FROM THE WINDOW OF A COLLEGE
pub called the Ale House, which occupied the ground floor of an
apartment building. He'd got the names of Linsky's two roommates
when he'd planted the memo and looked them up in a Tech year-
book in one of the administration offices, while an aging secretary
kept a nervous eye on him. Norman Lane and Oliver White.
Heemies, of course, and, though a head-and-shoulders shot wasn't
the best thing in the world to go by, the route from campus to Linsky's place passed by this window, and he thought he'd be able to

ID them. The problem would come if Linsky walked by first. Everything depended on one of the roommates finding the letter.

Grip drank slowly, just fast enough to keep the beer from getting warm at the bottom. Time passed. He found himself on his fourth with his bladder rioting. He couldn't risk leaving his spot, though, on the chance that Linsky or one of the roommates walked by while he was gone. Jesus, but he was uncomfortable.

Minutes later he gave in, sticking his head out the front door to see if anyone likely was coming down the street, and seeing no one, hurrying back to the restroom. When he returned, someone was sitting in the other chair at his table, boyish face turned up to chat with the young waitress. Art Deyna.

Grip sat down, tipped his glass to the girl for another beer, and, pointedly ignoring Deyna, glanced out the window to the empty sidewalk.

"Afternoon, Detective." Deyna wore a knowing grin he must have practiced in front of a fucking mirror.

Grip pursed his lips, gave Deyna a steady look.

Deyna cocked his head, voice friendly. "I didn't expect to find you in this kind of establishment. It's a long way from Crippen's."

"You didn't expect to find me, what the fuck are you sitting at my table for?"

"Happy coincidence."

The waitress returned with their drinks. Deyna looked to be drinking whisky on the rocks. Grip took down half his beer and looked outside again. A group of students, the right basic look, walked down the sidewalk toward them.

"What brings you to the Tech, Detective? This isn't your turf."

"What brings *you* here?"

Deyna smiled. "I thought I might look in on your friend Ben Linsky."

Grip kept his face blank, took another long pull on his beer, but his guard was up. The students were almost by the window now. Grip thought he might recognize one of the boys—sandy-haired kid, long face—among them. As they passed by he became more certain, felt the tension ease in his shoulders.

"Detective?"

Grip turned back to Deyna.

"You didn't answer my question."

Now that Linsky's roommate had passed, he was no longer trapped at this table.

"Fuck you." Grip got up.

Deyna laughed. "You really screwed yourself when that partner of yours got himself killed. Am I right? I don't know if you've got the quality for the upper ranks, but surely you could have made sergeant by now." He shook his head in wonder. "But you two were crazy and it caught up with you. You had everyone scared of you—or were they just scared of Morphy? That makes more sense, because once his luck ran out, you turned into a goddamn puppet for shitheads like who-ever's got you doing this. Who is it, Zwieg?"

Grip stared down at Deyna, breathing slowly, willing himself to maintain his calm. If there was truth in what Deyna said, there was also Grip's understanding that he needed to restrain himself, not let his anger take over.

"You know what I think you're doing?" Deyna taunted. "I think you're staking out Ben Linsky's place. Actually, I know you are. But I ask myself, why?"

Grip fished into his wallet and dropped a five on the table.

"And I'm not exactly sure, but I think I might have a guess. Do you want to hear it?"

Grip replaced his wallet in his back pocket.

"It has to do with some missing equipment from one of the Crosstown sites. I'm right about that, aren't I? You know, it sounds crazy. It really does. But you start putting together the pieces and you can come up with a connection between Linsky and Kollectiv 61, and if you think that Kollectiv 61 took the explosives—I'm not sure if that means that it's *likely*, but it is definitely *possible*. I was thinking I might pay a quick visit to our friend Ben Linsky and see what he thinks. That just might be where the story is."

Grip walked out into the street, lightheaded. Deyna's mocking laughter cut off as the door closed behind him. How the hell did Deyna know so much about what he was up to?

34

DORMAN ARRIVED AT THE STATION AFTER THE SHIFT HAD CHANGED AND Zwieg was already gone. A cop in the squad room recommended The Shield as a likely place to find him, so Dorman walked the two blocks to a dark bar on the first floor of a towering office building. The place was full of off-duty cops, loud conversations, games of darts in the far corner, testosterone in neutral. Dorman eased his way through the crowd. From his time in the Navy, he knew how to move with the cop swagger. He fit in.

Zwieg was at a table with four younger guys. One of them, a guy with black-framed glasses and a wispy mustache, was telling a story that had his three buddies smiling and Zwieg looking bored. Dorman caught Zwieg's eye, watched him say something to the table before coming his way.

"Mr. Dorman, you here to buy me a drink?"

"I could do that." Dorman saw Zwieg checking out his swollen eye, but didn't offer an explanation.

The place was nice, Dorman thought, a lot of shiny wood, brass, hanging lights with heavy colored-glass shades. The line of liquor bottles behind the bartender was impressive. He let Zwieg carve a spot at the bar. Zwieg ordered them drinks without asking Dorman for a preference, then put out a hand for cash. Dorman gave him a five and got nothing back.

Whisky shots. Zwieg nodded at him, and they both tipped them back. Dorman hadn't intended on drinking, but the alcohol felt good going down. And anyway, it was necessary, he told himself, to start off on the right foot with Zwieg.

"So, now that you've bought me my drink, are you going to take me home like a common slut?"

Dorman nodded toward a corner. "Let's talk over there."

This seemed fine to Zwieg, and they walked to a spot against the wall in the far corner, on the far side of a line of three pool tables. Dorman didn't normally size cops up. The advantage that he could exploit wasn't physical, though he felt he could take a lot of guys. But even though he was out of shape, Zwieg was still too damn big, a tough bastard.

"Okay, Dorman, you've got five minutes."

Dorman waited a moment, not letting Zwieg rush him. There was an issue of power here—there was no official hierarchy to sort out the relationship between the two men. He wouldn't be bullied.

"Who was on the three security guards killed the other day?"

"I've got a couple of my guys on it—younger guys. It wasn't a complicated case."

"Wasn't?"

"No."

"You found who did it?"

"A couple of tough guys, working for a book down in the Hollows."

"You sure about this?"

Zwieg shifted a little, and their size differential became even more apparent.

"Because," Dorman continued, "it seems like a hell of a coincidence after the site they were guarding got hit with a major heist."

Zwieg glared at him.

"That seems like an angle," Dorman said.

"You telling me my job?"

"I'm saying it looks like a big coincidence."

"Oh, shit. Are you a cop now? On top of everything else? Look, you've got some weight 'cause you work for Canada. But this is outside your jurisdiction, okay? This has nothing to do with the Crosstown, nothing to do with the New City Project, nothing to do with you or Canada. We investigated; we identified the culprits; we apprehended them. We are not going to fuck around with a triple homicide, no matter what you want to believe. Stay the fuck out of it. Last thing we need is some asshole with a clipboard sticking his nose where it don't belong. You stick to your business and let the grown-ups do the police work. You get me?"

They stood for a moment like that, staring each other down, before Zwieg shouldered past Dorman, leaving him staring murderously at the wall.

35

DORMAN ARRIVED AT THE CROSSTOWN SITE ON IDAHO AVENUE AS THE police cruisers pulled out, leaving yellow tape around the blackened husk of a foreman's trailer. Work went on as usual, cranes lifting girders high into the air where workers stood in wait on perilously narrow beams. Trucks came and went, the place bustled. The guard at the gate recognized Dorman, waved him in, and radioed to the foreman, a guy Dorman knew named Insua.

"He's on his way," the guard said.

Dorman nodded his thanks. He scanned the streets surrounding the site, looking from a distance to see if he could make out any occupied cars or people waiting around on the sidewalk, possibly watching. He came up empty. He turned his attention back to the building site and saw Insua coming his way—a big guy, dark skinned, a beard under his flattened nose, his construction hat pulled low. He carried a second hat that he handed to Dorman.

"Mr. Dorman." He had a deep voice still tinged with some kind of accent.

Dorman followed him to the bombed-out trailer.

"Nothing much to see here," Insua said, gesturing broadly. "The police took pictures, bagged some paper, maybe dynamite wrapper."

"Definitely dynamite?"

"Oh, yeah."

Dorman nodded to himself. It might be Kaiser Street dynamite, or it might not. There had been plenty of other, smaller, dynamite thefts. He wondered if there was any way of determining from which site the dynamite had originated. Maybe that was something he could mention to Mr. Canada to put in front of the Consolidated Industry guys. Put some kind of marker for each site, help trace where the stolen dynamite ended up. Dorman could hear the objection already—how would that help anything? How would we be any better off with that knowledge?

"They left graffiti?" he asked.

Insua led Dorman to an adjacent trailer. The usual black spray paint: "Freedom and Technology are negatively proportional."

"The police got photos?"

"Sure."

"Okay. Paint it over."

While Insua found someone to take care of the graffiti, Dorman walked around the base of the building, rising nearly sixty stories above him.

Insua returned. "What else can I do for you, Mr. Dorman?"

Dorman looked skyward. "Let's go up."

THEY TOOK A LIFT ABOUT TWO-THIRDS OF THE WAY UP TO A WOODEN platform, forty stories above the street. They stepped off, Dorman eyeing a couple of guys in hard hats sharing a thermos. They saw Dorman and stood. Dorman shook his head.

"Go ahead."

The men looked to Insua, who nodded, and they resumed their drinking.

"Let's walk out a bit." Dorman nodded toward a girder probably three feet wide and three hundred feet above the ground.

"You sure?" Insua looked concerned. "We can send these guys out there."

Dorman didn't respond, but stepped off the platform onto the girder and began to walk. It was breezy up here, the lower wisps of clouds blowing by his legs. He liked being out on the beam, everything laid out below him. Out in the Pacific he'd swum in water a mile deep, but five thousand feet was no different than fifteen—if you swim, you don't drown. Up here it was the same, four feet or four hundred: keep your balance and no problems.

He saw a couple dozen workers up here, mostly Indian, he knew, from up north. For whatever reason, these Indians didn't seem troubled by the heights, a fact that held endless fascination for Canada. "Fucking redskins, crawl all over those frames like it was nothing. Wonder what it is. Must be something in the genes." Dorman had asked Insua about this once, Insua saying he didn't know what it was, but that they worked hard and made much better money than they would on the reservation.

The wind made enough of a racket that Dorman couldn't hear Insua walking behind him. He stopped, turned slowly around, rotating his feet ninety degrees twice so that his balance was never in question. He hazarded a glance down. It was so far to the ground that it almost seemed unreal, impossible to imagine actually falling. How long would it take to hit?

"What are we doing up here, Mr. Dorman?"

"Anyone ever talked to you about wearing a wire?"

Insua squinted at him, not getting it.

"A wire. Like a recording microphone, so that they can tape your conversations."

Insua shook his head, genuinely confused. Dorman nodded; he hadn't thought so.

He got to the point. "So nothing was missing from the site today, just the damage?"

Insua nodded.

"Do you ever . . . Okay, you have to trust me on this. I just need to know, do you ever know beforehand when your site is going to get hit by thieves? I'm not trying to get you into trouble. I just need to know exactly how these things work."

The question seemed to startle Insua. "How would I know?"

Dorman grimaced in frustration. He couldn't tell if Insua was being honest or cautious. "Do you ever wonder why we never catch these guys? It seems like we could post guards, right, and catch at least some of them. Doesn't that make sense?"

Insua seemed to grow more uncomfortable. "Sure. I guess."

"Do you have any thoughts about why that might be the case?"

Insua looked at Dorman helplessly. Dorman rubbed his face with both hands. Had he really expected Insua to be forthcoming? Did he think Insua trusted him to that degree?

"Okay. Sorry. Never mind. Let's go back down."

36

THE POUNDING OF THE PILE DRIVERS WAS RELENTLESS IN THIS BLOCK OF the Hollows, the river only seven or eight blocks to the north. Grip rolled down Pristina Road, the old row houses transformed into makeshift apartments. It wasn't raining, but the air was saturated and things were still getting wet. The usual sidewalk traffic—winos, prostitutes, and others living on the City's margins—was nowhere to be found. Grip had an address.

Not many people who lived here owned cars, and the curbs were mostly empty—the street traffic seemed to consist of delivery trucks and jitneys. The street numbers were not entirely logical: some buildings seemed to be numbered according to whatever numbers had been around to nail above the doors. But Grip could figure out the general direction, at least, and he kept on, passing alleys strewn with garbage, men sleeping under rigged shelters. A thin dog trotted past, wary eyes on Grip. Grip brushed his hand across the lump in his jacket made by the butt of his gun, found some reassurance in its form.

He found the building he was looking for, and pulled to the curb. The place was a three-story walkup, cigarette butts littering the base of the steps. He pulled his gun and carried it close to his hip. At the top of the stoop he took a look at the door—wood with a frosted glass window at eye level—and gave it a trial push with his shoulder. It didn't feel too sturdy. He stepped back and rammed his shoulder into the door. It buckled. He stepped back again and the second effort flattened it onto the foyer inside.

Pistol extended, Grip entered a living room littered with beer bottles and dirty dishes. A balding, unshaven man looked up from where he lay on a couch, his eyes unfocused.

Grip looked down on him. "Where's Nicky?"

"I don't know, baby. I'm sleeping."

Grip could see through an open door into an empty kitchen and more squalor. He walked quietly up the stairs, keeping his footfalls light, not for reasons of stealth, but so that he could hear any motion above him. All that he heard, though, was the metronomic pounding from the river.

Four doors off the hall, one cracked. Grip looked in to find the shared bathroom. He walked to each door in turn, listening but hearing nothing from inside. Without hesitating, he kicked down the first door and stepped into a room with a bare mattress set in the middle of the floor. Empty. He moved faster now, aware that kicking in doors would arouse anyone in these rooms, no matter what their chemical state.

He kicked down the next door and recoiled in time to avoid the baseball bat that slammed into the door frame, making a dent in the soft wood. Grip sighted his gun on Nicky Patridis's forehead.

"Shit, Detective, I didn't realize—"

"Shut up, drop the bat, and sit down on that bed." Grip nodded to a mattress pushed into a corner. Nicky was wearing boxer shorts and a sleeveless undershirt, exposing his spindly legs and arms. His hair was pushed up on one side, and his eyes were still puffy from sleep. He retreated to his mattress.

"You know what I found out, Nicky?"

Nicky stared at Grip, equally dazed and scared. "How the fuck would I know?"

"I had a guy try to track down your cousin, the security guard. Funny thing: the guy doesn't exist."

Nicky's voice was up an octave. "He's on my mother's side, different last name."

Grip shook his head. "They don't have floaters at Consolidated Industries, Nicky. It was all bullshit."

Nicky's eyes got wide. "Oh, shit."

"That's right, Nicky. Oh shit." Maybe a dozen cockroaches scuttled around the perimeter of the room. Grip bit down on his anger, pointed the gun at a group of roaches but didn't pull the trigger.

"Who put you up to it?"

"What?" Nicky's hands were shaking.

"Don't fuck with me, Nicky. Who—" Grip was stopped midsentence by the sound of footsteps coming in the front door. They stayed frozen like that for a moment. From below, someone called out, "Detective Grip." Grip recognized Zwieg's voice.

He heard footsteps advance up the stairs, and hazarded a peek out the door. Zwieg was in the hallway, walking unhurriedly in Grip's direction. Grip ducked back into the room, confused.

Zwieg stepped into the room and took in the situation. Grip kept his gun on Patridis, but understood that his control of the situation had slipped.

"Put the gun down, detective," Zwieg said in a tone of disgust.

Grip lowered his gun. Zwieg's presence made it unnecessary, anyway.

"Nicky," Zwieg said. "Screw."

"Hold on a sec—" Grip protested.

Zwieg turned on him, "Shut up, Tor." He looked at Patridis, again. "You deaf, Nicky? Get the fuck out of here."

Patridis looked nervously from Zwieg to Grip and then hustled out the door. Grip noticed that he didn't even bother to put on his shoes.

They waited in silence, giving Nicky time to get down the stairs. Grip tried to keep his anger under control.

"Detective—" Zwieg started.

"What the fuck is going on? That little asshole lied to me. He fed me false information."

"Don't take that tone with me, Tor."

"I didn't realize that we were in the practice of letting our snitches get away with lying to us."

"Shut up and listen to me. Nicky might have lied to you in the details, but his information is good."

"What does that mean?"

"It means you are to proceed as if his information was accurate."

"With all due respect, Lieutenant, I'm not sure that makes sense."

"Are you being insubordinate, detective?"

"No, but I don't see how pursuing a—"

"No, you don't see. But that's what you'll do."

Grip stared at Zwieg. There was a professional hierarchy between them, but also a personal power relationship, and in that one Grip did not feel inferior. They were already way beyond normal police protocol. He thought they had entered into another realm altogether, one in which he didn't have to respect Zwieg's authority.

"We'll see."

Zwieg snorted a laugh. "Is that right, Tor?" He reached beneath his jacket and Grip flinched. "Don't get excited. I'm just reaching for an envelope."

Grip watched Zwieg pull a white envelope from his pocket. "What's that?"

"This is my insurance that I can count on you to continue your investigation."

Grip laughed. "Is that right?"

Zwieg handed the envelope to Grip. "Take a look, Tor, then see if you're still laughing."

The envelope wasn't sealed, and he pulled out three photographs. He stole a glance at Zwieg who smiled smugly.

The first photo was of a type familiar to Grip, a surveillance shot taken with a telephoto lens. In it, Grip and his former partner Morphy, were approaching a small house on a city block. Grip could see the address. He began to sweat.

The second photo had been taken just a few moments later, and in it Morphy leaned back against the front of the house next to the door while Grip hunched over the doorknob, picking the lock. The final shot had them leaving the house.

As Grip stared at Zwieg, he couldn't conceal his shock. "You knew about this all along? You've had these the whole time?"

"I have, Tor. I kept my mouth shut before, knowing that a day like today might come. We were staking out that house, Tor. We knew that's where some of the People's Union people were meeting. When they came to me, during the investigation, to ask if we'd seen anything, I said we hadn't, that whoever it was that got in must have slipped in the back somehow. I respected the code, Tor. That's why you and Morphy—god rest his soul—were never caught."

"But now . . ."

Zwieg mimicked hurt feelings. "Tor, I'll still respect the code, as long as you do your part."

"Continue the investigation?"

"Continue the investigation," Zwieg affirmed. "When you've completed it, I'll give you the photos. Don't worry about Patridis—just because he lied doesn't mean he's wrong about the big picture. You've done good work. Don't let one lying snitch get you off track."

Grip wasn't sure that he believed him, but Zwieg wasn't leaving him a choice.

37

THE CAMPUS OF CITY COLLEGE COULD EASILY HAVE BEEN MISTAKEN FOR a working-class neighborhood whose best days were fifty years past. Even on bright days, the buildings were weather-worn and dour. Today, with everything gray and damp, the place radiated gloom. The students here didn't carry themselves with the confidence of the elect like the kids at the Tech: they were the children of immigrants, working people, Negroes. They walked to class among derelicts, shatteringly loud road work, groups of hoodlums who almost blended in.

Frings walked from his cab to a twelve-story building. A guard stood by the door, staring down the students as they walked past him into the lobby. Frings nodded as he passed, but received no reply. A queue had formed in front of a bank of four elevators. The one on the far left arrived and disgorged a dozen kids. The queue for the elevator parted to let Frings on first, a deference that he found a little disconcerting, but he stepped into the elevator and leaned in a corner, giving his cane-arm a rest.

He'd been surprised that morning to receive a call at the office from Ebanks, who had sounded distracted over the phone. Ebanks said that he realized he wasn't going to be able to talk Frings into trying LSD, but he wondered if Frings might want to see how some people he knew were using it in interesting and—in his words—revolutionary ways. He seemed to think that his friends would be enthusiastic to have Frings present. They were apparently concerned about the New City Project as well, and the LSD experience, Ebanks explained, was some kind of reaction to the transformation of the

City. Though it was a strange offer, Frings was intrigued enough to accept.

First, though, he needed to talk with Leonard Toth.

PSYCHOLOGY, LIKE MOST OF THE CASH-STRAPPED DEPARTMENTS AT CITY College, was populated mostly by adjunct faculty who taught a class or two a semester, but had offices and practices elsewhere. Closed doors ran along both sides of the empty corridor. Most of the students had stayed in the elevator for higher floors. The echoes of his footsteps preceded him down the hall.

He found the door with a plate bearing Toth's name. He knocked.

The voice from inside was tentative. "Who is it?"

"My name's Frank Frings."

A moment passed. "Come in."

Frings opened the door on a bare office, beige tiled floors, bare off-white walls, a metal desk in front of a dirty window, and behind it a small man with short, curly, brown hair, wearing a white oxford cloth shirt and a blue and yellow diagonally striped tie. The man's eyes darted behind round glasses—from Frings to past his shoulder and back again.

"Close the door."

Frings stepped in and closed the door behind him. He didn't see a chair, so he leaned against the wall, taking the weight off his bad leg.

Toth was looking out his filthy window to the street. "You come here alone?" he asked, his back to Frings.

Frings was surprised by the question. "Yes, of course." He looked over the files on Toth's desk, but everything had been turned face down.

Toth turned away from the window, sniffed, sat down in his chair. "I recognize you."

Frings nodded, not sure what to say.

"Newspaper man. What brings you here?"

"Simon Ledley."

"Ah, shit."

"Why do you say that?"

Toth's eyes were wide, as if he had spotted something fascinating and potentially dangerous. "It can't be anything good, can it, you coming to see me about Dr. Ledley all these years later?"

Frings put his hand out in what he hoped was a calming gesture. "It's nothing that should trouble you. I'm just trying to track down someone who took part in one of the projects you ran with Ledley at the Tech."

This didn't seem to reassure him. "That I ran with Ledley? I didn't *run* anything. I took orders."

"Okay," Frings said. "I get it. But I'm still looking for someone."

"Who?"

"Sol Elia."

Toth sighed. "I haven't been in touch with him since the project ended."

"Which project?"

"You need to ask Dr. Ledley about that."

"He's been . . . reluctant to talk."

Toth laughed without much humor. "I bet he has. I can't talk either. I signed assurances."

Frings nodded, smiling. "I know. This is just between the two of us. I'm just trying to find Sol, that's all. There's no reason for anyone to be the wiser."

"You're a newspaper reporter. Your job is to get it out there."

"Not on this one. I'm just looking for Sol. A favor for a friend."

Toth shook his head. "I can't tell you about the project, and I have no idea where Sol Elia is."

"Listen, I understand your reluctance; I honestly do. But as far as I can tell, you're the only one who can help me. And I'm not leaving without some information."

Toth was breathing deeply. "Or what?"

Frings sighed. He preferred not to have to resort to coercion, but Toth seemed set on being uncooperative, and Frings thought he'd be susceptible to pressure. "Or I start digging into what you're doing here, what you did at the Tech. You want that kind of scrutiny, Lenny? Are you clean?"

"Shit." Toth stared at his desk. "Fuck. Okay, look, I can't tell you much, I signed assurances, they'll find out. But I can tell you who was involved, who the subjects were. But you didn't get those names from me, right? It didn't come from me. Shit."

Frings pulled a reporter's pad and pen from his jacket pocket. Toth was clearly terrified about divulging these names, which didn't necessarily surprise Frings, though the intensity of Toth's fear did. Frings wondered if he was prone to this kind of all-consuming panic, or if there really was something to be afraid of.

Toth had his head in his hands.

Frings tossed the notebook on the desk.

"No. No way am I putting this down in my writing. There's a limit."

"Okay. Okay. No problem." He picked up the pad. "Go ahead, I'll take notes."

Toth closed his eyes, exhaled loudly. "Okay, there were twelve of them."

38

DORMAN CARRIED HIS BRIEFCASE DOWN THE STEPS INSIDE CITY HALL, nodding now and then to a face he recognized. The great lobby seemed to encourage hushed conversation, but even the low voices echoed along with footsteps to create a hollow sound.

He shot a quick smile at a man he thought he recognized, sitting on one of the waiting benches and reading the *News-Gazette*. He acknowledged the guards at the door with a quick see-you-fellows-later and then walked into the brisk outdoors. He turned to see if he should hold the door, but no one was coming. But he did see that the man with the newspaper had stood up and was now walking in his direction. The man was Dorman's height, wearing a heavy tweed coat and a wool cap. Dorman let go of the door and descended the granite steps quickly, his eye on a cab that was just now depositing a young man in an Army uniform and a well-dressed young woman. He raised his hand for the hack to wait, but stopped briefly on the sidewalk to look behind him. The man was almost to the bottom step and moving purposefully toward him.

Dorman waved the hack away and the cab darted out into traffic. Dorman now recognized the man—a guy named Stanley Reuther, another neighborhood leader, this one at the western edge of the Heights, part of the area that had been promised to Gerald Svinblad.

"Hiya, Phil," Reuther said. Reuther was a bit older than Dorman, which made him a hell of a lot younger than most of the neighborhood activists that Dorman dealt with. He was aggressive too, though Dorman wasn't convinced that he was as smart as he was energetic.

Dorman extended his hand and Reuther shook it. No harm in starting things on a friendly foot. "What brings you here, Stan?"

"Thought maybe we could talk. You got a few minutes?"

Dorman resisted checking his watch. "Sure."

"Why don't we go for a walk?"

Dorman detected a hint of self-satisfaction in Reuther's tone and he was suddenly on his guard. "Why not."

Reuther had a slouching posture, which made it seem as if his feet were well out ahead of his body when he walked. This was just one of many things about him that Dorman found mildly annoying.

"So, I thought you'd—"

"You're not wearing a wire, are you Stan?"

Reuther looked so taken aback by the suggestion that Dorman decided that he didn't need to pat him down.

"Well, let's see," Reuther said, unnerved. "I was going to . . . well, let you know that I've had a meeting with people from Pickett East and Pickett West, Monkton Heights, and also the Italians on Luxembourg Avenue."

Dorman's mind began racing. These four neighborhoods, along with Corsican Square, where Reuther lived, were the final neighborhoods in the footprint of the planned City Center. Dorman had been working on agreements with each of these communities separately for months. He had people on the payroll in each neighborhood, people who were supposed to let him know if something like a group meeting ever took place. He rubbed the back of his neck to ease his annoyance.

"I see that I have your attention," Reuther said, feeling smug again. "We realized that while each of our pieces are important, the New City Project is really dependent on *all of us* accepting terms to leave our neighborhoods. We realized that our interests were similar as regarding the process, so we got together to compare notes, as it were. It was a very interesting meeting, I must say."

Dorman was sure it was.

"We were quite surprised," Reuther continued, "at the variation in the terms that are being offered. We spent quite some time trying to determine the criteria by which you, for instance, are offering Pickett East nearly twice as much as you are the Italians. We couldn't figure out how you came to that calculation—whether it was based on population, property values, square footage, or what. Nothing seemed to account for the differential. So, as a group, we are going to approach Nathan Canada with a proposal to restart negotiations, but with us as a conglomeration of neighborhoods instead of separately. I'm coming to you beforehand as something of a courtesy, because we have dealt with you for a number of months and will now be bypassing you to negotiate directly with Nathan Canada, and I felt it only fair that you were given some kind of forewarning."

Dorman kept his eyes on his shoes as they walked. He knew that if he looked at Reuther at that moment and saw what had to be a look of triumph on his face, he might not be able to keep his anger in check. They continued in silence for a few moments.

The break in the conversation eventually got to be too long for Reuther. "Phil?"

"Just a moment," Dorman said. He saw an alleyway a dozen yards ahead and focused on it. When they were at the entrance, he grabbed Reuther hard by the arm and hustled him twenty feet into the alley. A few pedestrians watched this happen as they walked by, but no one stopped or said anything. Both of them were dressed professionally. Surely nothing untoward would happen.

Dorman backed Reuther against a brick wall and stood close enough that he had nowhere to move. "How fucking stupid are you? Do you know what you're doing?"

Reuther's eyes were wide in confusion and fright. Dorman could imagine how he looked to Reuther—the anger and the black eye would make the potential for violence seem greater than it was.

"You want to know what criteria I use to figure out what to pay the different neighborhoods? Do you? It's called: whatever I think I have to pay to get the fucking job done. You know what the other factor is? It's how much money I have to work with.

"Do you know what a zero-sum game is, Stanley? It's a situation where there's a set amount of things—let's say dollars—and there are several people who want some of that thing. Every time that one of those people gets a dollar more, someone else gets a dollar less. Do you understand how that works?"

Reuther seemed to think it was a rhetorical question, but Dorman waited until he nodded.

"So this is my situation. I have a certain amount of money that I can use to settle with the five neighborhoods. There's no more money that's going to be coming. I've divided it all out. Now, I divided it up so that every neighborhood felt good about their deal."

That wasn't quite right. Nobody actually felt *good* about their deal. He'd made offers that could plausibly be accepted, given that they had no other real choice.

"Now what you're doing is this: you're taking that same amount of money, and you want to renegotiate how you split it up. And that's fine. I am perfectly happy to deliver it all in a bunch of canvas bags and you guys can split it up among yourselves. But you cannot fucking stay. One way or the other, we will be taking those neighborhoods. Do you understand?

"I had this thing worked out so that each neighborhood walked away with a deal that it could live with and now you, with this meeting of yours, have screwed it up. Now the neighborhoods that are getting less money are going to be dissatisfied with their take. And I don't blame them, to be honest. I was the one who screwed them, so that the other neighborhoods could get more. And now that these screwed neighborhoods want a fair deal, where is the money going to come from? The neighborhoods that I looked out for in the negotiations. Neighborhoods such as yours, Stanley.

"And, just so I'm clear, all those neighborhoods *will* be cleaned out and there *will not* be any more money allocated to your compensation. You are more than welcome to bring all of this to Mr. Canada's attention. But I think you are aware of his reputation when it comes to negotiations. He has asked me to handle the negotiations because he appreciates that I can be reasonable. He also knows himself well enough to understand that in these types of negotiations he is constitutionally unable to be reasonable. So, again, I am perfectly happy for you to take this up with him. My fear is that *all* of you come away the worse for it, instead of just *some* of you."

He pulled back from Reuther, who was sweating heavily from his brow. He felt like driving his fist into Reuther's gut, but this instinct, he knew, was more about the pressure coming at him from so many angles than it was about Reuther, who was the least of his worries. He was, in fact, barely a worry at all.

39

GRIP DROVE AIMLESSLY, THINKING. HIS ADRENALINE WAS JACKED, HIS anxiety threatened to overwhelm him, but his hands were steady at the wheel, his feet relaxed on the pedals. His mind, though, was all over the place.

Something was fucked up, terribly fucked up. Grip ran through what he knew. Nicky Patridis—a career loser, snitch, nobody—had lied to his face, told him that his cousin had seen the explosives heist, had pointed him toward Kollectiv 61, and now Zwieg was protecting him.

Why had Zwieg put Patridis up to this? Why hadn't he simply told Grip to look into Kollectiv 61 to begin with? He could have flashed the photos then if necessary. Instead, he'd gotten Patridis involved. The thing Grip kept coming back to was this: Zwieg had had him look into Kollectiv 61 because he didn't want to do it himself. It was too dangerous—so dangerous that Zwieg had kept himself at a distance. He'd used Patridis to point Grip in the right direction, and he hadn't shown his hand—or a part of it, anyway—until the whole thing seemed in jeopardy. Grip tried to piece it together: Kollectiv 61

meant Linsky, and the thought of Linsky brought him back to Ving—
the top cop's unlikely arrangement with the queer poet. But how was
it all connected?

Early afternoon at Crippen's saw a couple of older drunks
already leaning hard against the bar. The radio in the back room
blared the usual anti-communist station through a hail of static.
Only one table was occupied—Ed Wayne, looking like he'd been
pulled from the grave, drinking a whisky on the rocks, reading the
latest *Freedom's Call*. He wore a porkpie hat and a shirt with a loud
tropical print, unbuttoned a bit to show the pale flesh of his formless
chest. Grip waited for the bartender—himself drunk—to pour him
a beer. The old-timers nodded at Grip, then returned to their desul-
tory conversation.

Wayne continued to read, sucking on his teeth, as Grip sat down.
The chair wobbled slightly side to side. Grip read the back of Wayne's
newspaper, saw a headline about communists in the State Department, knew exactly how the article would unfold. The papers seemed
to print the same articles every week with only the slightest of varia-
tions. But Wayne, he knew, would read them all, using them as fuel
for his hate. Grip hated Reds too, but not with the same kind of all-
consuming intensity. The anger seemed to be literally rotting Wayne's
body. A guy who came in here sometimes, some kind of professor,
had said that Wayne was like Dorian Gray, but in reverse. Grip didn't
know what he was talking about, but found the book and, after getting over his surprise that Dorian was a guy, caught the prof's meaning. It seemed like the hate worked on Wayne like a disease.

Wayne put down his newspaper. "You know, Tor, that they're
making the roofs of the new downtown skyscrapers big enough to
land three two-prop helicopters?"

Grip shook his head. "That right?"

"Yeah, that's fucking right. Know why?"

"So they can land three whatever-it-is on the roof?""

Wayne spat an ugly laugh. "Funny, Tor. *Troop transports*. Dropping troops right into the heart of the City. The Municipal Tower, it's

for air traffic control. It's all being laid out in front of us. That's the goddamned genius of it."

"You're on this again?"

Wayne smiled, showing Grip his diseased teeth. "Damn right." He looked at Grip's beer. "What, you're not on duty, Tor?"

Grip shrugged. He was, technically, on duty, but he needed some time to figure out his next move. The investigation hadn't really changed—only his reason for pursuing it. He needed to sort it out, though. Who could he trust? What, now, were the right questions to ask? Zwieg had him trapped—he couldn't *not* investigate—but he knew that this was trouble.

"What's the problem?" Wayne's tone was more mocking than sympathetic.

"No problem."

Wayne laughed in disgust.

Grip said, "What fucking tragedy happened that has you so happy?"

Wayne smiled. "I'm just thinking about things."

"What things?"

"You know me, Tor. Plans. Making things happen."

Grip rolled his eyes. Since he'd left the Force, Wayne had planned, ruminated, schemed, but never acted. He was always on the verge of the Big Event, but nothing ever came of it. "You going to tell me about it?"

"I don't think so, Tor. I'm not sure that I trust your commitment to do what is necessary. I think if you knew, you'd try to stop me somehow."

"Okay, fine." Grip drank half of what was left of his beer. He'd ordered the beer to get his bearings, but chatting with Ed Wayne was just making things worse.

Wayne was still at it. "But when it happens, it will be big. Everyone will know."

"Sure they will, Ed." Grip drank the rest of his beer and stood. "I'll keep my eye on the front page."

Outside, someone had dropped a newspaper, the wind scattering it in the street. A prowl car rolled past. Grip made eye contact with the cop riding shotgun, felt the first twinge of panic tighten his chest.

40

EBANKS'S FRIENDS HAD TURNED OUT TO BE COLLEGE KIDS, TWO GUYS AND a beautiful young woman. Frings met them where construction of the new City Center was furthest along—a half-dozen square blocks of building either completed or mostly so, surrounded by skyscrapers in various stages of construction. Occasionally visible between the buildings—or through the skeletal upper floors of those in early construction—was the Municipal Tower, at once bizarre and ominous. The two guys—introduced as Sebastian and Augie—stood close to each other. They wore sunglasses and were looking around, moving their heads at what Frings decided was LSD speed, as if they were just waking up and hearing their names called from everywhere at once.

The woman, whose name was Joss, was tall and wore a wool cap over her shoulder-length auburn hair. She was very excited to meet Frings, going so far as to give him a hug. Augie and Sebastian smiled at him, but seemed too far inside their own thoughts to really understand who he was. Joss seemed familiar to Frings, though he couldn't put his finger on why.

She had a map. She explained to Frings that they were about to undertake the *drift*, which involved two people dosed up on LSD or something like it, while a third, in this case Joss, followed them, taking notes on their impressions of the surroundings. This was part of a project, she said, to canvas the whole City in this way, to determine which places were "human-friendly" and which were not. The end result would be a "drift map," a kind of drug-facilitated psychological map of the City.

"This place," Sebastian said, looking around at the new high-rises, the massive glass windows of their upper floors reflecting the ball of the sun. "I don't like the buildings, man. They're like giant boxes, like match boxes that you open up and insert people in and just close them back up again until someone opens them again. It's like people storage. Or more like an oven where you close the door and all the stuff happens and when you open it back up everything is done. Like an oven."

"I see that," Augie said. "You're right. I don't like it."

Joss stepped forward. "Can you explain that?"

"It's . . . the buildings, they're containers, that's all. You store people there while they work—people and machines. That's what happens . . ." He seemed to lose his thought.

Augie nodded. Frings saw his eyes wide behind the dark lenses. Joss made a note of what Sebastian had said.

"Cross this street off?" she asked.

"Oh, yeah." Augie replied. "Definitely."

With a pencil, she blacked out the block on her map.

"This is what you do, get a positive or negative response and mark it on the map?"

"That's part of it," Joss replied. "There's also the notes that we add. I'd love to show you the map sometime."

"I'd like to see it," Frings said, noncommittally.

To the other man, Joss asked, "Okay. Where to?"

Augie and Sebastian stood in the middle of the sidewalk, turning in circles, looking up at the buildings, at the different directions they could head in. Pedestrians passing on the sidewalk didn't seem quite sure what to make of it, the two guys with their strange behavior and Frings and Joss so obviously observing them.

Finally, Augie nodded further up the block. "Up there and then let's go left, get off this street."

Sebastian nodded. "Yeah, man. Let's get the fuck off this street."

Frings and Joss followed them from several paces behind, not interfering with their somewhat addled wandering.

"You look familiar, Joss. Do I know you from somewhere? Or your parents, maybe?" He couldn't bring himself to say "your grandparents," though that might have given him his best shot at an answer.

"I don't know. My dad is Bruce Parmeneter. Do you know him?"

Frings knew *of* Parmeneter, a surgeon and—Frings thought—a teacher at the Tech medical school. But he'd never actually met Parmeneter, not that he could recall.

"I guess not." He changed he subject. "So, have you ever done what they're doing?" He motioned up the block, where Sebastian and Augie were fully absorbed by a department store's display window.

Joss stopped walking, so as not to get too close. "Sure. I've done it a few times. That's the fun part."

"What happens?"

"When you're on the drift? You know, you're kind of prepared, so you know what you're trying to do, and it kind of focuses you. That's a little strange, when you think about it, that you get focused so you can drift." She thought about this for a moment. "Usually, with the drug, your mind can be all over the place. But, on the drift, you're really paying attention—and I know this sounds flaky or dumb—but you pay attention to the vibe of the place. The drug really helps you pick up on that. It lets you see how sterile so much of the City is."

"Can't you pick up on that just by looking around without the drugs?"

Joss cocked her head slightly in thought. "That's an interesting idea. I guess you could a little. But with the drug—it's like instead of reading sheet music, you're actually hearing the song."

Frings nodded. Nobody seemed to be able to describe the LSD experience except in metaphors.

He saw a man with wild, disheveled hair, and several days' growth on his jaw stride over to where Sebastian and Augie were now looking around aimlessly. The man wore a heavy pea coat and walked with his hands stuffed down in the pockets.

He began to yell at Augie and Sebastian. "You think you can just stand in the sidewalk, looking around? You think they *allow* you to examine the block for any sign of life? They won't let you. They will find out who you are, and you'll find that your soul has been wrung."

"Oh, boy," Joss sighed. She walked toward the men. Frings followed, thinking that, between them, Augie and Sebastian were as confused as any people he'd ever seen.

• • •

From "Invisible Streets: Using Pharmacology to Reveal Urban Micro-Identities
AUTHOR UNKNOWN

. . .the chemical acts as a deobscurant, removing the identity from the self, allowing for an unmediated perceptual event, revealing the object as what it is, not the programized category assigned it by the identity."

Thus we come to the second pillar of our project, Ebanks's conception of man's mediated perception and the use of certain pharmaceuticals to unmediate. Expanding on Heidegger's model of the interlocution of the self in perception, Ebanks constructs a system whereby in perceiving things, the self is conscious of its own identity, a culturally constructed lens which distorts the true nature of the things being perceived. It is in the creation of identity—a process utterly unreflected-upon by most men—that modernism is, in a way previously impossible, able to inculcate the essential docility and acceptance of capitalistic values. As Marcuse writes, "Rationality is being transformed from a critical force into one of adjustment and compliance. Autonomy of reason loses its meaning in the same measure as the thoughts, feelings, and actions of men are shaped by the technical requirements . . . Reason has found its resting place in the system of standardized control, production, and consumption."

To bring this to our current, local situation, I have shown that advances in technology necessitate dramatic accommodating societal changes that, in some cases, are more affecting of society than are the products of the technology. At our moment in history, technology has reached a stage so advanced that it is endowed with values and characteristics previously reserved for men and, conversely, men have been reduced to material goods—commoditized. Or, put another way, where technology once served man, man now serves technology. As Marcuse notes above, society has, without perceiving its acquiescence, accepted and internalized this shift into the collective identity, and societal judgments are therefore seen through this prism. This has resulted, in our City, in the New City Project, the urban, physical manifestation of the inversion of the relative valuation of technology and man, with capitalism as the fulcrum.

In proposing The Drift as a means of perceiving the effects of the partial destruction of the organically evolved City and its replacement with an engineered urban scheme with the creation of capital through the elevation of technology over man as its core, I acknowledge the problems inherent in perceiving the physical world when wearing—as I have earlier described it—the lens of the identity of the self, skewed as it is by the internalization of societally proscribed values. As discussed earlier, Ebanks has described the efficacy of a certain class of pharmaceutical substances, most notably lysergic acid diethylamide (LSD) in suppressing the obscuring influence of the self's identity, freeing the self to perceive without mediation. Unconstrained by the influence of society's relative valuation of man and technology, the individual engaging in The Drift, is capable of perceiving and understanding the physical environment as it pertains to the welfare and happiness of man, as distinct from the creation of capital . . .

41

FRINGS MET PANOS AT THE RESTAURANT IN THE HOTEL LEOPOLD II. THE dinner hour was in full swing, but Panos had a standing reservation, and was already seated when Frings arrived. As Frings followed the maître d' to Panos's table, he saw Gerald Svinblad sharing a glass of wine with a couple of men in suits whose faces he recognized, but whom he'd never met.

He could see Panos waiting expectantly and knew that the progress report would be disappointing to the old man. There were, as of yet, no answers.

"Do you bring news?" Panos asked, once Frings had sat down and ordered a martini from the waiter. Frings told Panos about the visit to Lenny Toth's office, about Toth's paranoia and reluctance to give Frings any information.

When he was done, Frings took his notebook from his jacket pocket, tore off the page with Toth's twelve names on it, slid it across to Panos. Panos scanned the names.

"So, here is Sol."

"Do you recognize any of the others?"

"No. None of them."

Frings hadn't thought he would. "I've put one of the new reporters on the case—he's tracking them all down."

"Littbarski let you near one of his impressionable young people, maybe catch a bad case of socialism?"

"He's in a good mood because he thinks Deyna is going to break a big story. Stolen explosives."

Panos nodded thoughtfully. "Stolen explosives?"

"That's right. Why?"

Panos frowned. "I wonder, with Littbarski, if maybe there is not something more."

Frings waited, but Panos said nothing else.

"Do you know Gerald Svinblad?" Frings asked.

"Sure, a little. Why do you ask?"

"I think he's coming over to our table."

Panos straightened in his seat the best he could.

"Don't get up gentlemen," Svinblad said as he arrived at the table. "I saw you over here and thought maybe this was a *Gazette* reunion, talk about the days when you were sticking it to the capitalists."

"Hello, Gerry," Panos said warily, and the two men shook hands. "Have you met Frank Frings?"

"Not in the flesh, no." Svinblad didn't offer his hand. "But like everyone else, I've read his work for years. I *feel* as if I know him."

Frings didn't say anything, and a silence settled upon them that Svinblad didn't seem to find uncomfortable.

"Gerry—" Panos began, but Svinblad interrupted him.

"You're not letting go of the Project are you, Frank? It's okay if I call you Frank?"

Again, Frings stayed quiet, looking at Svinblad with scant interest.

Guys like Svinblad thought they could play the bully because they had money, but this didn't work with Frings.

"Normally," Svinblad continued, "I am the first guy to admire someone who says fuck you to everyone, does what they want. But sometimes, you've got to know when you're licked, and, Frank, you're licked. Your whole fucking ideology is licked. The *Gazette* is gone. You'll say that it's merged, but I read the paper and all I see is the *News*. You're the last bit of the *Gazette* left. You're like an infected appendix there, not good for anything—holding on until it's removed. And the Project? Once upon a time, you might have had some weight, made things tougher. But now?" He grunted dismissively.

"Gerry," Panos said, sounding exhausted.

"They never run my letters to the editor," Svinblad said, sarcastically, "so I thought I'd chat with Frank, here, let him know my thoughts man-to-man."

"Well, you've said what you had to say. It was nice seeing you."

Svinblad seemed reluctant to leave.

"Good-bye, Gerry."

Svinblad nodded to Panos, smirked at the still silent Frings, and ambled back to his table.

"I'm sorry for that," Panos said.

"That? That doesn't bother me. I just don't waste my time arguing with people like that. Once you open your mouth, you've lost."

Panos nodded, his attention turned to where Svinblad retook his seat, laughing with his companions.

42

FRINGS TOOK A CAB AT A CRAWL THROUGH THE MORNING STREETS TO Little Lisbon. Rain blew in horizontal sheets. People folded their umbrellas rather than risk having them torn apart by the wind. The cabbie had the radio on; as always, the news was dominated by the rising cost of the New City Project, City Council members affirming its importance, critics raging about corruption and fraud. Frings half-listened in the back, damp from his dash from the front door to the cab.

They pulled up to a small cafe on a side street. No name, just a sign that read COFFEE. The place was packed—younger bohemian types at some tables, aging radicals at others. It was on the dangerous verge of becoming trendy.

He saw his friend Bert Oliva—greasy hair a little too long, unkempt beard, heavy-framed glasses—lounging at a table against the far wall. At any given time, the City had a half dozen or so shoestring weekly newspapers running the ideological gamut. Oliva had edited several of the radical rags and was currently at the helm of *The Eye*, a conspiracy-oriented paper distributed in three languages to factory workers and laborers.

Oliva didn't stand, but shook Frings's hand warmly, his left hand patting the back of Frings's right. He was drinking tea, but mouthed for the waitress to bring Frings a coffee.

"Nice to see you, Frankie."

"It's been a while."

"We're both busy. That's how it is in this life." Oliva had a warm, genuine smile.

The waitress dropped off the coffee, which smelled strong and dark.

When she was gone, Oliva said, "You wanted to talk?"

"About Will Ebanks."

Oliva rolled his eyes. "He's a friend of yours, right?"

"Yeah, but I'm trying to get a better handle on him."

Oliva gave Frings a questioning look.

"He's"—Frings searched for the right words—"sort of fallen off the map with all of his interest in LSD, mescaline, that whole thing. The few times I've seen him, well, if I hadn't heard stories I might have put it down to the normal changes over time. But it sounds like I might not be getting the whole picture."

"You've heard rumors."

Frings nodded.

"And you want to hear mine."

"If that's okay."

"It's a little uncomfortable, to be honest, Frankie. What with him being your friend."

"You're my friend, too. I need to know what's going on with him."

Oliva drew a deep breath, gathered himself. "Okay, the first thing is that I never actually saw or talked to Will when all of this went down. I just wrote about him. I was editing the *Sentinel* at the time. You remember that one, a year and a half or so ago, lasted about fifteen editions?"

"I think I contributed a couple of articles under a pseudonym."

"Major Aaho."

Frings laughed. "That's right."

"Anyway, Ebanks had just gotten fired by the Tech, and he was starting to have those LSD parties at his place. You might remember that the *Sentinel* considered itself a real revolutionary rag, exposing the hypocrisy of a mayor who preaches capitalism and all that free-market shit, but wants the government—in the person of Nathan Canada—to rearrange the way the whole fucking City is laid out—where people can live, where roads can go, all that shit. I guess I don't need to tell you about that.

"At the same time, the papers are making this big deal about Will being some big radical, and he's digging it, playing it up. But he's not a radical; he's just a guy experimenting with drugs, and we thought that we'd point that out. So we did. We compared him to Andre LaValle, the difference between revolutionary action and self-absorption. We were trying to make a delicate point about violence and revolution on the one hand, and spiritual retreat on the other. I didn't think that Ebanks came off that badly, we even played up the spiritual angle, not the drug angle."

"You contrasted him with LaValle?"

Oliva chuckled at the memory of it. "We did. We were being provocative. And it worked—with Ebanks, at least."

He took a sip of tea, pursed his lips before continuing. "The day after it hit the streets, a couple of dudes came to visit me. They weren't all that big, but they were big enough, and they had that look about them that they could probably dish it out, you know? Just angry-looking dudes. So they came into my office, slapped this piece of paper on my desk and said to run it in the next edition of the *Sentinel*. I picked it up and read it through, and it was basically a letter from Ebanks explaining that our article on him was full of lies and conspiracy bullshit. He threw in some "fucks" and called us "cunts," and it was ridiculous—even if I *was* a guy who'd run something some asshole had slapped on my desk, which I'm not.

"So they wouldn't leave. They just fucking sat there in my office, and I'd get up and use the john and come back and they'd be there and they'd just stare at me while I worked, trying to intimidate me. And the pisser is that it basically worked. Not that I stopped doing anything, but it was definitely unnerving. Finally, there was a guy working there who was involved with one of those black nationalist groups—I can't remember which one—and he called on a few of his friends—tough, tough dudes—who came down and threw them out. Those fuckers didn't go easily, though. Kicking and swearing and threatening to come back. But those Negroes were tough as hell, man, and just tossed them out on the sidewalk. I waited for them to come back the next day, the day after that, but they didn't, which was a relief.

"You know what happened next. I don't know how, but they got their hands on a printing press and some newsprint and copied our logo and look and put out their own fucking version of the *Sentinel* the day before we put out our next edition. I still don't know how they pulled that off." He paused for a moment, had another sip of tea. "Anyway, it was a weird rag, a mixture of abusing us, talking about how we were playing at revolution without even understanding what we were fighting against, and then also some stuff that looked like it had been written by Will about how people fundamentally misapprehend the nature of what is real or some bullshit like that and that we all had to take LSD or mushrooms to unlock the secrets, blah, blah, fucking blah."

"That's crazy," Frings said. "Not just what was in it, but going to the trouble of printing a whole edition of the *Sentinel*." Frings shook his head. "And the expense . . ."

"I still don't understand it, man, and I've thought about it a lot."

"You think Will put up the money for it?"

"Will? No, he doesn't have that kind of scratch."

"He doesn't?"

"Not from what I understand."

Frings frowned. He thought Oliva was wrong about that.

"Anyway," Oliva continued, "we went to court and got the remaining copies pulled off the street. But the damage had been done and our advertising and our money guys pulled out and the *Sentinel* was gone in less than a month. Just one of many temporary ventures." Oliva half-smiled, his eyes not quite on Frings.

"You say you never actually saw Will during any of this. Do you think it's possible that he wasn't involved at all? Maybe it was just overzealous friends of his or something."

Oliva shrugged. "I guess it's possible, but I doubt it. If nothing else, though, he had the power to stop it. I have no doubts about that."

This seemed right. "One more thing. Those two men who came to visit you? Was one of them Sol Elia?"

This surprised Oliva. "What, Panos's grandkid?" He shook his head. "No, I would have remembered that. Why, is he mixed up with Will?"

Frings had no idea.

43

FRINGS HAD TASKED A REPORTER NAMED CONROY TO TRACK DOWN THE whereabouts of the people on Toth's list. Conroy was fresh out of the Tech, and like a lot of the young guys at the paper, he was at once awed by Frings, and fearful that management would take a dim view of any association with him. So, while he was thrilled to help, he declined Frings's offer to debrief over a beer at a local bar, instead preferring Frings's office, which seemed more professional and less chummy. Frings understood Conroy's calculation and was just as happy to skip the beer.

Conroy, who had a broad, reddish face, and carried thirty extra pounds, looked nervous as he handed Frings a page of notes.

"Are you okay?" Frings asked. "Go ahead and sit down."

Conroy lowered himself into a chair. "Look at the notes, Mr. Frings. They're, well . . . just take a look at them."

"Call me Frank. We're colleagues." He looked at Conroy's notes.

Sol Elia — ??
Roger Phaneouf — 143 Albemarle — laborer
Edward Sand — suicide
Philip Hammer — ??
Benjamin Diamond — suicide
Lester Finch — 18291 Galilleo — unemployed?
Oswald Mason — suicide
Joseph Millhauser — suicide
Elgin Holland — 1003 Leipzig — bank vice president
Linus Embry — died, July 1962, cause indeterminate
Stephen Sedgewick — ??
Joos Vander Kierkoff — City College Hospital for the Deranged

He stared at the sheet of paper, thinking.

"You're sure about this?" he asked. It was a stupid question, but he felt the need for some confirmation. The information was jarring. He could understand Conroy's nervousness. The information certainly *seemed* wrong.

"I'm sure. The deaths—suicides—I got two sources."

Four suicides and a death. Nearly half of these men were dead, all of them in their twenties. Maybe more than half, depending on what happened to the people that Conroy wasn't able to track down.

There was a click and air rushed through the ducts. Conroy started at the sudden noise.

"What do you think about this list?" Frings asked.

"What do you mean?"

"Well, there's definitely *something* going on. One third of the people in the study commit suicide?"

"Yeah. Hold on, there's more." He pulled a reporter's notebook from his jacket pocket and flipped through a few pages. "Let's see, the one death—Linus Embry. He somehow fell off a roof. Ten stories or something like that. The police couldn't determine whether he jumped, fell, or was pushed, and, frankly, it didn't look like they put themselves out over it. We can probably chalk it up as another suicide."

Frings nodded.

"These others, the survivors"—Conroy continued—"look at them. Laborer. Unemployed. Hospital for the Deranged. Out of twelve people, all graduates of the Tech, only one has anything like what you'd consider a successful career."

"*If* they all graduated. Sol didn't."

Conroy looked chastised.

"Regardless," Frings said, "this is a troubling list, to say the least. I appreciate your work on this."

Time now, he thought, to knock on some doors.

44

THE ALARM SCARED THE HELL OUT OF GRIP, PULLING HIM FROM A REST-less sleep. He banged the clock off and lay back on his pillow, heart pounding, the first hints of sunlight revealing the dark silhouettes of the furniture in his room. He caught his breath, felt with his left hand along the floor by his bed, finding the familiar steel of his gun. He looked toward the door, and at the bureau he'd propped in front of it.

He rolled into a sitting position, stood up, found he'd left his shoes on while he slept. He walked to the window, edged the side of the curtain open, and looked out onto the empty street. He heard the distant rhythmic thud of the pile drivers.

He found a stale loaf of bread in his breadbox, chewed on it as he walked around, filling his flask with bourbon, pulling a heavy overcoat from his closet. The day was getting lighter, color started to appear, details became visible. Feeling a greater sense of urgency, he found his screwdriver and walked to the bathroom. He unscrewed the ceiling vent cover, reached his hand up, located the envelope, and screwed the vent cover back in place. He pulled the stack of tens from the envelope, counted them. Fifty. He put forty of the bills back in the envelope and dropped it in the inside pocket of his coat. The other ten he slid into his wallet.

Standing in front of the bureau, which still blocked the door, he performed a quick check with his hands: gun, flask, masking tape, envelope, wallet, badge, lock pick, hat. He pushed the bureau to the side, waited for a moment, his ear to the door. If someone was waiting for him out there, they wouldn't be so stupid as to make any noise, but it seemed careless not to listen.

Hearing nothing, he pulled his gun, released the safety, and opened the door quickly. The hall was empty.

A HACK DROPPED GRIP TWO BLOCKS FROM BEN LINSKY'S BUILDING, the sun now risen above the buildings, long morning shadows reaching toward him from across the street. He walked, his head down, hands in his pockets. Ahead of him he saw students walking toward campus. Grip was the only one on the block. He crossed over into the shade and paused at the side of Linsky's building to take a long pull from his flask.

The glass door to the lobby was locked, but a middle-aged woman in a faded dress was retrieving mail from a locked box. Grip knocked on the door. The woman turned, saw him, shook her head, went back to the box. Grip pulled his badge, and held it up to the door as he knocked again. This time the woman walked over, studied the badge through the glass, and opened the door for him. He muttered thanks, walked past her to the stairs. He didn't like elevators.

On the third-floor hallway, he pulled the tape from his pocket, tore four squares off, and placed a square over the peepholes in each of the four doors. He stood with his ear at Linsky's door and listened for three minutes, clocking the time on his watch. Nothing. He tried the door, surprised to find it unlocked. He slid in, closed and locked it behind him.

He scanned the room and instantly knew that something was wrong. The air was very still and in it hung a scent, very faint, that had the hairs on his neck alive, his gun out without even thinking about it.

His eyes fell on the lamps, and he wondered how he'd missed them on his previous visit. There were a number of them: on the tables at the ends of each couch; in the bookcase by the door; by the window. If the place was bugged, they'd done a thorough job. If Linsky was complicit, it would have been easy enough to set up—run the bugs off the lamps' power; turn on the lamp and you turn on the bug. His pulse quickened.

He went through the open door to Linsky's bedroom, and it took him a moment to realize what was wrong with the scene, the pillow hiding Linsky's face, his motionless chest. On the wall above the bed, a single word was spray-painted in black—*snitch*. He flashed to the Kollectiv 61 graffiti at the construction sites, then put it out of his mind, focused on what was before him. He walked to the bed, pulled the pillow away to find Linsky's sightless eyes open wide, his lips blue. Grip pulled off a glove and felt Linsky's face with the back of his hand. Cold. He put the glove back on.

The other two bedrooms were empty. He walked back into the living room and grabbed a lamp, unscrewed the lampshade, found the little microphone attached to the bottom of the shade holder, brushing it accidentally with his glove. He put the lamp back down and replaced the shade. He'd touched the bug. They'd have heard him. He walked to the window, but no one was on the street. That, he realized could very well mean that they were listening from inside the building. In which case, he had to move very quickly.

Back in the hallway, he turned Linsky's door-handle lock to its locked position and pulled it shut behind him, then dashed to each door, pulling the tape off the peep holes. He ran to the access door to the stairs, paused, and took his shoes off. He padded down the stairs from the third toward the second floor, gun in one hand, shoes in the other.

He was starting on the next flight when he heard the door open below him. He sprinted, two steps at a time past the third floor hallway and up to the fourth, nearly silent in his stockinged feet. He opened the door, heard the sound of people quickly ascending the stairs, and closed it quietly behind him, mind racing, trying to figure a way out.

45

Papers were stacked neatly on Dorman's desk, awaiting comments, signatures, or objections. A pile of monotonous work, which, while necessary, felt far removed from the crucial tasks facing him. These were the little things that kept the project going, but they meant nothing until Dorman completed the final work: annexing the last neighborhoods for the New City Project. He spent some time going through the top documents, but realized that he was too distracted by the trouble with Svinblad, Reuther, and Trochowski—each man his own kind of problem. He was just going through the motions. This was the kind of thing that could come back to bite him later—even a small decision, if not thought through, could end up a huge distraction—or worse. So he put his pen down, got out of his chair, and turned his attention to the ultimate source of his anxiety.

An enormous map of the City took up nearly half a wall in his office. Though it covered dozens of square miles, stretching out toward the international airport, the focus was the City Center, the commercial district that would save the City. Dorman used the map to track the project's progress—downtown blocks were colored different shades of gray, indicating when they'd been claimed for destruction and rebirth. The effect was that of an encroaching tide, the gray covering in gradations the entire projected area, with the exception of five neighborhoods, coded in different colors: Pickett East in dark blue, Pickett West in green, Monkton Heights in red, Corsican Square in yellow, and the line of Luxembourg Avenue in orange.

When Dorman had arrived, the areas that were now gray had been mostly a patchwork of different colors, each a different neighborhood requiring a negotiated arrangement to acquire their blocks, move their people somewhere else in the City—often into reclaimed blocks of shabby flats in the Hollows.

Dorman's charge had been unambiguous, and evaluation of his work was simple. He had a budget and a geographic area to acquire, and he either succeeded in annexing the neighborhoods for the New

City Project, or he didn't. He'd been remarkably efficient up until now, and the colored neighborhoods of previous maps had turned gray, one after another. But while the tide of gray had taken over more and more of the map, the areas that remained colored—the last hold-out neighborhoods—dominated Dorman's attention.

Which was why Reuther's efforts were such a pain in the ass. Dorman had little doubt that if worst came to worst and a neighborhood or two proved intransigent, Canada would arrange to have the residents forcibly removed. But this would be an unpopular move—even the *News-Gazette* wouldn't be able to support taking people's homes at gunpoint. The extra money from Svinblad was thus a way to mitigate a potential problem—he could use the cash to close a deal with the minimum of trouble. Still, all of this took time and energy, and as he thought about the challenges still to come, Dorman leaned back at the waist, trying to loosen his back muscles, which were hopelessly bound up by stress.

46

AT THE STRIKE OF NINE O'CLOCK, THE FRONT DOOR OF THE PRAEGER'S Hill branch of Century Guaranty and Trust was unlocked by a slight man in an expensive gray suit. Frings shuffled in, his knee stiff. The ceilings were high, with intricate molding along the edges and an expansive chandelier hanging in the center of the room, about two-thirds of the lights in working order.

Frings let half a dozen people pass him in their hurry to queue up at the teller counter. A secretary sat behind a desk that served as the gateway to the bank management offices.

"Hi"—he flashed the Frings smile at the woman, attractive, mid-thirties, no-nonsense eyes—"I'm trying to find Elgin Holland."

The woman looked him over for a moment. "I'll ring him." She punched a succession of buttons. "Yes, Mr. Holland. There's a man here to see you, a mister . . ." She looked up.

"Frings."

"Mr. Frings," she said and waited on the line for a moment.

"Okay." She hung up, shrugged. "Go on back." She pointed to a door behind her.

Holland had the door open and a hand out as Frings approached. They shook, introducing themselves. Holland was a small man, heavy-set in a soft way, balding. His eyes were blue and seemed to jitter slightly.

Frings sat. "Mr. Holland, I don't know if you've heard of me, but I'm a—"

"Newspaper guy. I heard the name and I thought that it couldn't be *that* Mr. Frings, yet here you are. I'm honored that you've come to our modest bank."

Modest was not the word for Holland's office, which, though small, was appointed in leather and oak, an approximation of a study in an English manor house. An oriental carpet covered the space between the desk and the far wall.

"Well, it's not actually the bank that I've come to talk to you about."

"No?" Holland seemed neither surprised nor suspicious. His manner was professional and ingratiating. "What can I help you with?"

Frings noticed the absence of picture frames on his desk, the bare walls, not even a flag or a certificate. "I wanted to talk to you about your time at the Tech."

"What about it?" Holland leaned forward over the desk, his genteel manner now gone, replaced equally by interest and caution.

"Did you know a student named Sol Elia?"

"A student named Sol Elia?" Holland laughed. "He was far from just a student, Mr. Frings, as I'm sure you know. Not very often that you have a kid at the Tech you could describe as 'notorious,' but that's what he was. Did I know him? A little bit. We ran into each other occasionally. The Tech is a big place, but we were the same year."

"Where did you run into each other?"

"Look, you mind if I ask what this is about?" He had the manner down pat, could have been asking about a down payment or an account balance.

"I'm just trying to track down Sol. I'm talking to his friends to see if they can help."

"I wasn't exactly a friend."

"How did you know him then?"

Holland sighed. "We participated in a study together. There were always studies going on at the Tech, and you could earn a little coin by volunteering for this one or that one."

"And which study did you both participate in?"

Holland thought about this for a moment, directing his eyes to the ceiling. "I'm not entirely sure. Maybe a drug trial. I participated in a few. My family wasn't wealthy. Not like most of the kids there."

Frings thought that he was probably being dishonest, rather than vague. "I think it was probably the study you did under Dr. Ledley."

Holland grimaced and scratched his cheek. "I don't think so."

"I'm fairly sure that it was."

Holland leaned back in his seat, clasped his hands over his belly. Sunlight came through a window behind him, forming a yellow trapezoid on the rug.

"Why are you fairly sure?"

"I've got a list of the people involved."

Holland pursed his lips. "How did you get that?"

Frings shook his head.

"That's confidential," Holland protested. "There's no way that information should be available. My privacy . . ."

"I'm the only one who has it. I just want to find out about that project, the one Dr. Ledley was running."

Holland looked suddenly ill. "I'm not interested in talking about it. Even if I was, I signed waivers. I'm not *allowed* to talk about it."

"Do you ever see anyone from the project?"

"How do you mean?"

"Socially?"

"No."

"You know what happened to them?"

"Like I said."

"Okay. Look, there were a dozen of you, right?"

This time, Holland shook his head, not willing to commit one way or the other.

"My list has a dozen. Four of those people committed suicide. An-

other one died, we're not sure how. A couple more are working man-
ual labor. Three are missing. You're the only one we could find who's
got any kind of life. It's a bit of a puzzle."

Frings saw Holland's jaw quiver, sweat bead on his forehead.

"Those guys weren't my friends. We were just recruited for the
same—"

"Recruited?"

Frings waited, but Holland didn't elaborate.

Frings said, "Okay. They weren't your friends. But you see what's
happened to the others? As far as I can tell, all of their lives have
turned to shit. All except yours."

"You think my life has turned out well?" Holland barked. "What
do you know about my life?"

Frings held out his hands in a placating gesture. "I don't know
anything about your life. I'm saying that from where I stand, it looks
like the people involved with this project didn't end up so well. I want
to know why. I want to know if the project might be the reason. Otherwise, it's a huge coincidence. You see?"

Holland leaned forward, his head in his hands. "I'm not saying
anything else."

"Think about it, Mr. Holland."

Holland looked up. "Think about it? That's all I've done for five
years: think about it. You need to leave before I call security."

"Mr.—"

Frings saw Holland feel for the button under his desk. Frings
stood up, adjusted his cane in his hand and prepared to be escorted
out by the two armed guards he saw heading his way.

47

GRIP DREW THREE SLOW BREATHS, WILLING HIS HEART TO SLOW DOWN,
his mind to focus. Four doors on this quiet hallway, one floor above
Linsky's apartment. He moved to the first on the right, put his ear to
the door. Kids' voices. No good. The next door, some kind of humming from inside—not human, mechanical. The seconds were ticking

off in his head. He pulled his pick set, worked the cheap lock, no problem. Pick set back in his pocket, gun back out, shoes in his left hand, he slipped slowly into the apartment, shutting the door behind him with his foot.

Grip squinted at the scene before him. The place was lit by several unshaded lamps with red light bulbs. Two mattresses were kicked against the wall. A bearded guy slept on one, curled up in a ball, rasping slightly with each inhalation. Against the window sat a machine that Grip, after a moment spent adjusting to the strange, red light, identified as a shortwave radio. Wires fanned out from the back like so many tentacles, tacked to the ceiling, the walls—some even snaked out the window. The speaker hummed with soft white noise.

Grip left his shoes by the door, headed to the three doors off the living room, two open and one shut. The two open doors led to a filthy bathroom and what must have been intended as a bedroom, but seemed to function as a storeroom of sorts as well: boxes, books, piles of clothes. The final door was closed. Grip listened but heard nothing. He carefully eased the door open and found another bedroom, this one occupied by a woman sleeping under a sheet, a man next to her. The man sat up slowly, staring at Grip in a daze, hair greasy and lank.

Grip put a finger to his lips, showed the man his gun, though the guy didn't seem to register it. Grip fished for his badge and showed that, too, but, again, to no effect. He tried to catch the guy's eyes, but they seemed locked on something else, something Grip couldn't figure out. Grip looked for a telephone, but didn't see one. The guy seemed too out of it to be a threat, so Grip closed the door again, went to the living room windows.

Past the fire escape, he saw a single prowl car on the street, lights going, two uniforms leaning against it, watching the building. No way they would miss him if he took the fire escape, even to the roof. A sudden noise from the radio startled him. A Woody Woodpecker laugh, a blast of static, then back to the humming. Grip felt light-headed from the panicked rush of blood to his head. *Fuck.*

The guy on the mattress hadn't stirred. Grip walked back into the bedroom. The man from the bed was up now, naked, so thin that Grip figured he could break the guy in half over his knee. The guy was just standing, staring at something in the corner. Grip looked and saw a big-leafed plant of some sort. He turned to the guy, put his gloved hands on the guy's bony shoulders. The guy's collarbone stood out alarmingly.

"Hello? You awake?"

The guy met his eyes. Huge pupils. No one home.

"Can you hear me?" Nothing.

"Listen. I need to stay here for a little bit. I'll just sit in the next room. If someone knocks, I need you to answer the door and just be exactly like you are. You get it?"

The guy looked toward Grip's face without focusing. Grip took him by the shoulders, laid him down on the bed with the girl, who rolled her back to him without waking up.

Grip walked back out into the living room, looked at the mattress and decided to sit on the floor with his back to the wall. He listened to the policemen's footsteps as they searched the floor below, thought about Ben Linsky, about the memo he had left on Linsky's table the other day. He thought about the word spray-painted above Linsky's bed. *Snitch*.

THIS WAS THE SECOND TIME THAT A SUSPECT HAD DIED IN THE MIDDLE of one of his investigations. During the crazed weeks that followed the chief's assassination by Andre LaValle, Grip and Morphy had lost all their restraints. In their off-duty hours, the pair had always made a habit of menacing communists and unionists—often with their fists—but once LaValle was linked to the radical movement, the badge was no longer a deterrent to violence. Even though the mayor and Kraatjes had both ordered the Force to refrain from retaliation, no one listened. It was open season on radicals, heemies, organizers—anyone on that side of the political spectrum—and Grip and Morphy led the way with a concentrated fury.

Paul DeBerg was a twenty-two-year-old kid who'd found his way into the People's Union while at City College. After LaValle's connection with the Union became public knowledge, DeBerg had been the designated spokesman, strongly denouncing LaValle's crime and reiterating the group's non-violent philosophy. But it had been too late. Talk was worth little when one of your people had brutally murdered a public official. Less than a week after LaValle's arrest, DeBerg, like everyone else who could be traced back to the Union, went underground.

Grip had picked up a tip from one of his street grasses that every few days, DeBerg would visit a Union house in the Hollows to pick up books or pamphlets or whatever he needed at the time. Grip and Morphy found the place, and the latter watched the street while the former picked the front-door lock. That moment had been captured in one of the photos that Zwieg had shown him at Patridis's apartment.

He and Morphy waited for nearly three hours in this filthy house, a couple of threadbare couches and boxes full of radical leaflets, tattered books, clothes packed in mothballs. Morphy's pacing became increasingly manic as the time passed. He was huge, a solid six foot five—he intimidated with his very presence, and he did what he wanted. By the time DeBerg walked in on them, Grip almost felt sorry for the guy.

DeBerg didn't even have a chance to register surprise before Morphy had backhanded him across the cheek, putting him on the ground. He'd tried to scramble to his feet, but Morphy grabbed him by the shirt and threw him against a wall. DeBerg put his hands up, his face panicked, asking what it was that they wanted. Morphy hit him with an uppercut just below the ribcage and DeBerg fell back to the ground, gasping for breath.

They'd found a high-backed chair and tied DeBerg to it—both arms, both legs, a rope around the chest and another around the neck to keep his head still. They'd asked him questions, but they weren't really after answers. They were there to scare the hell out of DeBerg— make him wish he'd never heard the words "People's Union."

Grip gave the guy credit—he hung in there. Morphy wasn't giving it everything he had, but DeBerg kept his mouth shut, wouldn't answer any of their questions. If they'd been after anything, it would have been frustrating. As it was, Morphy batted him around, making sure that DeBerg would look as bad as he felt the next day. It would send a message to his friends.

After a half hour or so of this, they decided that they'd done what they came for. They left him tied to the chair, figuring that someone would come looking for him before too long, and the sight of him bound and bloodied would be a good thing for them to see. Morphy gave him a last knuckle-tap before leaving, and that was what had made the difference.

Another of Zwieg's photos had been of them leaving the house. They'd gone by Crippen's for a few drinks that night, then headed home. The next day, they heard that DeBerg had been found dead in the house. He'd lost consciousness and been strangled by the rope around his neck.

The next couple of weeks were nervous ones as they waited for their complicity in DeBerg's death to be discovered. But the days came and went and no connection was made. The stress ate at the two of them, though, and their police work reflected this. They became more reckless. They took chances that they would not have taken in the past. They fed off of each other, ignoring the pleas from friends on the Force to take it easy. They were on edge and found this type of policing cathartic.

Three weeks after Paul DeBerg died, Grip and Morphy went beneath the streets to arrest Tony Oddo and Grip's life was again thrown into a tailspin.

48

RETURNING FROM HIS VISIT WITH ELGIN HOLLAND, FRINGS HEARD HIS name being called as he made his way into the *News-Gazette* building. Half a block away and walking quickly toward him was Fache, a small, fastidious cop and an occasional source. Fache leaked, Frings knew, out of fear as much as anything, wanting someone in the press to be on his side if he ever needed it, which, in his mind, was more than likely.

Frings waited for him, leaning on his cane, wondering what information would compel Fache to meet him *here*, of all places. As Fache approached, Frings could see the expression, both sympathetic and official, that cops wore when they had bad news. Frings's stomach went heavy as he tried to think what this might be.

"Frank."

"What's going on? What are you doing here?"

"I'm sorry, Frank, but I thought you should get a jump on everyone else. You've earned it."

This was another annoying thing about Fache, these little compliments, trying to buy extra favor. "What are you talking about?"

"Ben Linsky, he was murdered."

The information didn't register at first. There was hardly a less likely person in the City to be murdered than Ben Linsky. Who the hell would want to kill him? What would be the point? Yet here was Fache, grim-faced, telling him that this was exactly what had happened. Frings felt his breath go shallow. Ben was so young and was, in a certain way, important—important to the City, to its future.

"Do you know who did it?"

Fache shook his head. "Nothing right now, but we just found the body. Frank, the killer, he wrote the word "snitch" above Linsky's body."

Snitch? This, too, made no sense: first, that Ben Linsky would be a snitch; and second, that he would have information that would be of any interest to the police. Part of Linsky's aura was his anti-establishment values. Frings couldn't imagine what it would take to get Linsky to be a snitch, and nothing in Linsky's life seemed to warrant the police investing much in what he could tell them.

"Do you know why that was written? Is there any chance he *was* a snitch?" Frings suddenly felt very tired.

Fache shook his head. "Again, it's early."

FRINGS WATCHED FACHE WALK AWAY. THERE WERE SO MANY REASONS to grieve for Ben Linsky, but he kept coming back to one. Frings had reached the age where his contemporaries had begun to die. These people died too young, of course, but many of them had lived substantial lives. But Linsky, though he'd certainly accomplished much, far more than most—Linsky had been cheated out of *half his life*.

He gazed down the street, watching the stream of car traffic, the working men walking the sidewalk in their suits, the steel and glass rising above the street, and even higher, the skeletons of the new buildings that seemed to enclose the streets, cut them off from all but a sliver of sky.

49

THE WHISKY FLASK WAS LIGHT IN GRIP'S POCKET—WHATEVER INHIBITIONS he had against violence had slipped cathartically away, leaving him with itchy fists.

For hours he'd waited in that goddamn apartment, with goddamn Woody Woodpecker laughing every fifteen minutes, followed by that goddamn blast of static. He'd heard footsteps in the hall, knocks on doors on the same floor, retreated to the bedroom where the couple had again lain unconscious. The banging came, strong and staccato, followed by cop voices identifying themselves, asking for the door to be opened. Grip pulled his gun and wedged himself into the closet. He heard the guy who'd been sleeping in the living room pad to the door, then voices in a conversation that he, frustratingly, couldn't make out. It seemed to go on for too long. Grip was sure that the guy on the mattress had no idea he was there, but worried that the cops would find the scene in the living room too strange not to investigate. That, or find his shoes, which he now remembered leaving by the door. But nothing happened. He heard the door slam shut and waited for the sounds of multiple footsteps, but, instead, he heard only the squeak of the mattress as the guy lay back down. The tension left Grip's body. He had a rush of delayed panic as he realized that Woody Woodpecker had not laughed while the cops were at the door, and that this fortunate timing had saved him.

He'd waited another couple of hours in the apartment, the guys both sleeping through, the girl emerging once from the bedroom wrapped in a sheet. Her body was thin beneath the linen, but, even in her disheveled stupor, she held for Grip the appeal that women her age held for men of his. She'd looked at him, not seeming very surprised, and then walked slowly back into the bedroom. Grip had watched her through a crack in the bedroom door, half-expecting her to wake her boyfriend. But she'd just crawled back into bed and stared blankly ahead of her.

HE WALKED BLOCK AFTER BLOCK, DRY LEAVES SKITTERING ACROSS THE sidewalk. He kept to the building side of the sidewalk, moving with the pedestrian flow, trying not to stand out. Police cruisers drove by, and Grip fought the instinct to duck or turn, give himself away. He made it to the Tech campus and walked through the gate. He followed the sidewalk away from the street, feeling some safety here, where the police wouldn't happen upon him.

He sensed he was skirting the edge of something vast and dark— a feeling he hadn't had since Morphy's death.

Snitch.

The word seemed to hover before him as he walked, black spray paint on a white wall. The memo he'd planted in the apartment—the wrong play. One of the two roommates had discovered the note, then either killed Linsky or given it to someone who had. He wanted to hit something.

For the most part, he didn't regret the occasional consequences of intimidation or violence—they were outweighed ten-to-one by the advantages, because no matter how out of control things might seem to get, he always had a sense of when to pull back before it went irretrievably wrong. But Linsky's death was a result of his tactics, and it had left him a tangle of nerves, second guesses, and intense regret. This was worse than DeBerg—it felt like an assault on his core as a person, and the hours spent in that fucked up apartment, alone with his thoughts, had him fighting to maintain his calm.

He emerged from the other side of the campus, two blocks from Cafe ?. He paused in an alley and took another long draw from his flask, caught a sensation behind his eyes that felt as if centuries of civilizing restraints were falling away, leaving him only with his instincts. His area of vision narrowed. His adrenaline flowed.

He strode the two blocks quickly, gaining some momentum for

what was about to happen. Speed was going to be key. Speed and force. He needed to be out of there before Schillaci and his partner showed up.

He blew through the door, looking first to the table where he had seen Linsky and his friends. The table was populated again, and he recognized some of the same faces. Still moving, he registered their expressions as they turned to him. They looked tired, distraught, grieving. They also looked high, at least some of them. Grip showed his badge to the place with a sweep of his arm. He approached a kid in a flannel shirt and old khakis, a wispy beard on his face. He grabbed the kid's collar and pulled him up with a jerk, knocking the chair a couple of feet onto its back. Grip pushed him up against the wall, saw him try to focus his hopped-up mind on what was happening: should he be scared shitless or not?

Grip put his face right up to the kid's. "Ben Linsky's roommates— where are they?"

The kid stared back at him, too stunned to speak.

"Where do I find Norman Lane and Oliver White?" More urgent this time.

Grip saw motion in his peripheral vision, swung around to a short, soft kid in wired-framed glasses approaching with his hand held tentatively out. Grip used one hand to keep pressure on the kid against the wall, turned to the kid with the glasses.

"I know you're not going to touch me," Grip growled. "Once you touch a cop, there's no turning back."

Glasses blanched, froze. Grip turned back to the kid against the wall. "Where," he yelled in the kid's face.

The kid was shaking, tears starting to flow.

Grip held the kid's eyes, saw that he was too scared to be cagey, pulled him off the wall, and pushed him toward his fallen chair. The kid looked at it, stunned, unsure whether to set it up again.

Grip looked to the table. "Lane and White, where can I find them?"

Faces stared back at him, scared, clueless.

Grip grabbed the table, tipped the assembled glasses and mugs off, the drinks landing in the laps of the people sitting facing the wall.

Empty theatrics, but he thought it would be effective with these kids.

A girl—it figured that it would be a girl who had the guts in this crowd—spoke up, trying unsuccessfully to keep her voice strong. "We haven't seen them today. We thought we would, but we haven't. We're grieving. I'm sure they are as well."

This stopped Grip for a moment. He hadn't thought that something also might have happened to the roommates. The moment quickly passed—there'd only been one body. He scowled at the table and turned to leave.

"You've still got it, Detective, despite your advancing years."

Grip turned to the voice, bristling. Art Deyna leaned against the wall, cocky smirk in place. Grip stalked over to him, moved into Deyna's space, their noses inches apart.

Grip gave Deyna a half-lidded stare. "The fuck you here for?"

Deyna laughed through his nose. "From the sounds of things, the same reason you are. Detective, why don't we sit down and talk this over for a minute."

"Fuck you."

Deyna tutted regretfully. "So hostile. You never seem to quite understand that we're on the same side, the side of the angels."

"I don't know what you're talking about."

"Don't play stupid, detective. We both know the real threats to this city. Let's sit down, talk about Kollectiv 61, Commissioner Kraatjes. Compare notes. Have a seat. I'll buy."

Grip stared at him, feeling exhausted. "You stay out of my way." He shook his head. "Just stay the fuck out of my way."

50

KAPLAN'S WAS AN OLD BAR LOCATED OFF AN ALLEY LESS THAN TWO blocks from the old *Gazette* building. It had been popular with some of the *Gazette* reporters because it wasn't the kind of place you happened upon—it didn't even have a sign out front. You could really talk there, not worry about who was listening. That was the old days. With the *News-Gazette* now twenty blocks east, Frings wondered how old man Kaplan kept the place going. But he did, somehow. The clientele was more depressing these days—older, wearier. Of course, Frings was, too.

He had a cigarette and a reefer going, alternating between the two, the cigarette covering the smell of the dope. Kaplan didn't care, so long as the tobacco stink overwhelmed the marijuana. It was dark, as always, a little natural light seeping through the tinted window cut into the door. The ceiling lights seemed somehow underpowered, the illumination barely penetrating the smoky haze. Small wooden chairs surrounded even smaller wooden tables. The bar was made from the timber of a barge that had sunk in the river within spitting distance of the cargo docks, sometime in the last century.

Frings nursed a pint of beer, thinking about Ben Linsky, trying to make sense of his death. It didn't fit with Frings's understanding of how the City worked, and, after so many years on the beat, there wasn't much that surprised him. He looked down the bar at a couple of old-timers playing cards. The one furthest from Frings laid down his hand and began laughing a toothless laugh as he looked toward Frings, mouth gaping, eyes hard.

FRINGS MADE A CALL FROM THE PHONE AT THE END OF THE BAR, THE OLD-timers moving down a couple of seats to give him room. The line hissed as he was connected to the detectives' room at Headquarters.

A Detective Molloy answered. Frings asked for Grip and was met with a beat of silence, then a curt "hold on." Frings listened to the hiss, a palm covering his other ear against the old men's chatter, the jukebox.

The voice that answered was not Grip's. "Can I help you?"

"I'm trying to reach Detective Grip."

"Who is this, please?"

"Frank Frings. Who is this?"

"Frank, it's Anders Ving."

Frings paused, puzzled. Frings had known Ving for twenty years, regarded him as a competent and honest cop. Frings had been optimistic about the future of the Force when Kraatjes became chief, and the appointment of Ving as deputy chief had only seemed to confirm his initial enthusiasm. Frings was confused, though, by Kraatjes's brief tenure to date, which seemed to be characterized by a certain neglect. Frings hadn't expected that.

"I was trying to reach Torsten Grip," Frings said.

"That's what I understand. What did you need to talk to him about?"

Ving's guardedness struck Frings as strange. "I just need to talk to him. Following up on a story. The usual."

"Frank, I'm sorry, but can you be more specific?"

"A case that he might have been working."

A sigh. "Which case?"

Frings considered his answer. Normally, he wouldn't have worried about divulging this kind of information to a senior cop that he trusted. But with Ving's tone of voice, Ben's death, and Grip's obviously tenuous standing in the police department—he hesitated. Finally, he said, "Ben Linsky."

Ving answered too quickly. "What about him?"

"Look, Anders. Ben asked me about Grip the other day, out of the blue. He thought that I knew him. A couple days later, Ben's murdered."

Another sigh. "What did he want to know about Detective Grip?"

"I'm not saying anything else until you tell me what's going on here."

"Frank, we have a relationship, right? Have you known me to hold back on you before? But I can't talk to you about this. I need to know what Ben Linsky asked you about. It's important."

Frings thought about this. Ving was basically right that he'd always been honest with Frings, didn't play games like so many of the other brass did. But Frings didn't like giving up information like this.

"Frank?"

"He wanted to know if I knew Grip because Grip had been hassling him and he couldn't figure out why." It would earn him a chit he could use later.

Ving didn't reply.

"You still there?"

Even through the phone line, Ving's voice was taut. "Keep this conversation between us, Frank. Someday, it will turn out to be the right move for you, okay? You've got my word on that."

The line went dead, leaving Frings holding the receiver, trying to figure out how to read Ving's last comment: as advice between friends, or a threat.

He hung up, watched the men play out a last hand, and headed for the street.

51

DORMAN RODE THE ELEVATOR UP TO THE RESTAURANT OF THE HOTEL Leopold II with a group of three businessmen who'd been talking in the lobby, but now, with him in the elevator, they'd gone silent, exchanging glances and not quite restraining their smirks over some private joke.

He followed the businessmen from the elevator lobby into the restaurant. The place was nearly full and hummed with conversation. A tuxedoed quartet played jazz quietly in the far corner. The crystal chandeliers glistened in the smoky air. The maître d' seated the businessmen, who were back to their conversation. When he returned, Dorman told him that he was there to see Gerald Svinblad. The maître d's professional manner couldn't hide his confusion.

"Mr. Canada couldn't make it. He sent me."

The maître d' gave Dorman a tight smile and, without a word, led him to Svinblad's table, situated by one of the huge windows overlooking the City. Dorman saw that Svinblad had spotted his approach and, even from several tables away, could see his face redden with anger.

"Mr. Dorman," the maître d' said with a brief nod.

"My expectation," Svinblad said through gritted teeth, "was that Nathan was meeting me tonight."

"Mr. Canada sends his regrets." Dorman sat down and took a sip from the water glass at his setting.

"I'm unclear why your boss thinks that he can take my money and then send you to meet with me, like I'm one of those serfs whose neighborhoods you pave over."

A waiter arrived, sparing Dorman from having to answer. Svinblad ordered them both whisky and sodas.

DORMAN ENDURED A FEW MINUTES OF SVINBLAD'S IRE. HE'D KNOWN this would happen and kept his expression neutral, nodding occasionally in acknowledgment rather than agreement. The waiter returned with the drinks, and they ordered dinner. When the waiter had again departed, Svinblad seemed calmer. He'd apparently decided upon a new goal for the dinner.

He regarded Dorman critically. "Since you're here instead of your boss, let me ask you a question."

"Okay."

"Who else do you work for, besides Nathan?"

"I'm sorry?" Dorman said, warily.

"Who else? Who's giving you a little something every month, helping you buy gifts for your girlfriend, keeping your wardrobe stocked with nice suits?"

"Nobody else."

"Don't screw with me. You're not stupid and you're not a saint, so don't tell me you don't get something here or there."

Dorman began to sweat under his suit. He flashed on Trochowski, wearing a wire in the back of the Double Eagle. Svinblad couldn't be wearing a wire, though, could he? He'd been expecting Canada, not Dorman. Unless Canada had set Dorman up—sent him here to be tested, see if he'd take the bait. But that simply wasn't the way Canada worked. It was paranoid thinking. So, if Svinblad wasn't wearing a wire, he was feeling Dorman out, testing him, inquiring about his willingness to be his man inside Canada's office. Plenty of people were on the take. Dorman himself had just this kind of arrangement with two-dozen people in strategic positions in government and business. He sometimes thought that the City wouldn't function if it weren't for these relationships.

But Canada was a different story. He didn't want to think about what would happen to anyone caught taking bribes in Canada's office.

"I don't have any arrangements."

"Okay, then. What's your price?"

"I don't have a price," Dorman said, wondering if that was really true.

Svinblad laughed disgustedly. "That's precious. I throw fifty thousand on the table right now and ask you to look after my interests with the New City Project and you're going to tell me no?"

"Are you offering me fifty thousand dollars?"

"I am asking you a question. Would you turn down fifty thousand?"

"I would have to give that some thought."

"You'd have to give that some thought."

"That's right."

"Let me continue this hypothetical, if you will. Let's say, for the sake of argument, that I do offer you fifty and you decide to accept it. Now, if something should come up—and I can't think of anything off the top of my head—but if something should come up and my best interests and Nathan Canada's best interests were in opposition, how would you decide whose interests you would give weight to?"

Dorman looked outside, to where the City's lights shone like a galaxy. "That's a lot of ifs, and that's one of those things that I'd have to think over as I considered whatever offer you hypothetically made me."

"You're not inclined to answer my questions, are you?"

"I think I'd be answering a question that you haven't really asked."

Svinblad frowned, but seemed to accept that this was as much as he was going to get out of Dorman for the time being.

52

AT NINE IN THE EVENING, THE EIGHT BLOCKS OF PRUSSIA BOULEVARD
known as the Hard Mile were a confusion of drunks, hookers, hoodlums, and the occasional cop. Grip, half in the bag, exhausted, walked
through the crowd, shoulders squared. The pros wore threadbare
coats over their scant clothes, trying to balance enticement with
warmth. In the artificial light of the street lamps, their painted faces
seemed ghoulish, like distorted masks leering out at Grip from the
crowd.

He made his way past dive bars whose stale beer stink wafted out
into the street and hot sheet hotels that advertised hourly rates on
their grimy windows. He kept his eye out for uniformed beat cops,
adjusting his spot in the crowd to avoid any he saw. Finally, he came
upon the White Rhino Hotel, a dingy place, metal grill on the plate-
glass storefront, a sign advertising rooms for a dollar an hour or five
a night. The girls loitering outside recognized him, a couple making a
go at an enticing smile. Grip kept his head down, pushed through the
entrance and into a lobby that smelled of piss and cigarettes.

A couple of older prostitutes stood in the relative warmth, talking
to two aged perverts whose faces glowed with perspiration. Grip
walked past them to the front desk, guarded by a window of bullet-
proof glass with a money slot cut into the bottom. Ed Wayne sat with
his feet up, his porkpie hat tipped back on his pale, misshapen skull,
reading a true-crime magazine. He had a beer in one hand and a cigarette dangling from his mouth.

Grip knocked on the window, the glass streaked with hand prints
and filth. Wayne looked up, annoyed, then smiled his awful smile as
he saw Grip.

"What brings you to my fine establishment, Tor?"

"I need a room for the night."

Wayne squinted at him. "Here?"

Grip nodded. Wayne shook his head as if it made no sense. Which,
in fact, it didn't.

"You heard anything about me on the street?" Grip asked.

Wayne laughed. "I hear people are looking for you."

"Who from?"

Wayne shrugged. "I don't remember. Maybe Albertsson, my young charge."

"What, that little fuck from the other night?"

"He's a patriot, Tor. Reminds me a little of you back in your frisky days."

Grip scowled at him. "Why don't you find out from your *charge* what they want from me."

"You don't know?"

If the glass weren't there, Grip wondered, would I bust his jaw or just think harder about it? "I'd like to get it clarified."

Wayne snorted a laugh. "I'll talk to him, see what he knows." He wiped his nose on the shoulder of his yellowed shirt.

Grip stared at Wayne, wondering how it had ended up that this crazed freak was his best ally. For the first time in a while he found himself desperately wishing that Larry Morphy was still alive. Morphy wouldn't be giving him shit in a situation like this—laughing and smirking. Morphy would damn well start knocking some people around until he found out what the story was. Then he'd put an end to it. Grip wondered if maybe that was what he should do. But people didn't fear him like they used to fear Morphy. Hell, they didn't fear him the way they feared him ten years ago. There was too much to sort through, and he was too exhausted. In his mind, questions seemed to swirl, unmoored from any connection or logic: Who had killed Linsky? What was Kollectiv 61? Where exactly did Zwieg and Kraatjes fit in, and what did they have to do with Patridis and Linsky? He was overwhelmed, unable to sort his thoughts. He needed a few hours of shut-eye, a clear head.

"Okay, Ed. I need a room. A clean room."

"Hell, Tor. You want a clean room you'll have to find yourself another hotel."

53

LESTER FINCH'S APARTMENT WAS ABOVE A PAWNSHOP, THE STREET number hand-painted in yellow on a black metal door. Frings had taken a cab from the *News-Gazette* building, watching the blocks flow past, people carrying umbrellas or putting their chins to their chests against the steady rain. Frings looked for a buzzer, or some other way to get in touch with people in the apartments upstairs, but the wall around the door was empty. He looked up, rain catching him in the face. He jiggled the doorknob and the door opened slightly. Pulling the door open, Frings saw a thin man, maybe in his fifties, standing in the stairwell, a sleeveless tee shirt revealing well-muscled arms, his hair graying and wild, his eyes red. Too old to be Finch.

Frings folded up his umbrella, excused himself as he walked past the man, and started up the stairs. He glanced behind him to see the man still at the bottom of the stairs, watching him ascend to the dim landing. Two doors led to two apartments, one overlooking the street, the other probably facing an alley. Frings knocked at the door of the rear apartment.

A voice from inside yelled, "Yeah?"

"Mr. Finch?"

"Who wants to know?"

"Frank Frings, from the *News-Gazette.*"

After a pause, the voice said, "What d'you want?"

"A quick chat. A couple of questions."

Another pause was followed by footsteps moving toward the door. The door opened a crack, and Frings saw an eye peering out. The door closed again, and Frings heard the chain lock being undone. The door opened: a wiry gink, dark complexion, stubble, brown hair shaved nearly to the skin, holding a gun.

Frings showed the man his palms, keeping his cane upright with his wrist, but dropping his umbrella. The guy gave him a long look, frowned to himself, lowered the gun.

"It's alright. Come on in." He spoke quickly, as though he only had a limited time to get the words out.

Shaken, Frings picked up the umbrella with unsteady hands, and walked into the tiny apartment, the man pulling the door shut behind them. The thing that hit Frings first were the guns, the sheer number of them. They were propped on nails driven into the wall above the spare, single mattress lying on the floor—at least thirty of them: rifles, pistols, shotguns, the whole range. Frings didn't like guns, especially in the hands of a man who Frings thought was probably unstable. The adrenaline from his fear made him jittery.

"You're Lester Finch?" Frings asked, making sure.

"Les," the man said, nodding to a single kitchen chair pulled up to a chipped Formica table. Frings sat. Finch reclined on his mattress, slouching so that his upper back was propped against the wall. He laid his gun on the bed next to him. Frings felt some of the tension ease.

"You here about the study?"

"Why would you say that?" Frings asked.

"What else would you be here for?"

Frings nodded at him. "You've got a lot of guns."

Finch looked around the room as if confirming what Frings had said. "Yeah, I guess I do. It's a hobby, guns. I like to clean them, take them apart, put them back together."

Rain slammed against Finch's window like radio static. Frings saw dirty dishes sitting in the tiny metal sink, beer bottles on the counter.

"You're right though, Les"—Frings said, his voice almost a parody of calm—"I came here to talk about the study. Ledley's study."

Finch's eyes bore in on Frings. He blinked in spasmodic bursts and then stared. "What d'you know?"

Frings shrugged. "Not very much. That's why I came to see you."

Finch shook his head a couple of times. "Where do you want to start?"

"That's up to you."

Finch stood up from the mattress and walked to the window. "You see a guy on the stairs?"

"I did." Frings's adrenaline spiked again now that Finch was up.

"The guy's there a lot. I ask him if he lives here and he says no. I ask him if he's here looking after me or maybe he wants to kill me and he says maybe. And I ask him, *maybe what? Are you here to look after me or to kill me*, and the guy laughs like there isn't much difference, you know?"

"I know, Les. There's not much difference," Frings said cautiously.

"You know that?" Finch turned away from the window, locked in on Frings, his eyelids fluttering.

Frings frowned, nodded gravely.

"'Cause that's what I found out from Ledley's study, you know? I found out that watching over and killing's two sides of the coin. Killing you inside."

Frings nodded gently. "How did you learn this?"

"Listen, this is how it went. I was a sophomore at the Tech, I got a letter from Dr. Ledley—*the great Dr. Ledley*"—Finch spit the words out—"says ten dollars a session to take part in a psychological study. Ten bucks a session? You bet. So I go and the first four, five times I just take tests, a whole bunch of them. They go on and on, some of them on paper, others with Dr. Ledley or one of his students asking me to do things, put pictures in the right order or repeat numbers back to them in a different order. That was, what, maybe four times. Four or five.

"The first session after that, they give me a pad of paper and a pencil and they say, *write your philosophy of life*. I say, 'What does that mean?' and they say, you know, to do whatever I want. It means whatever I want it to mean. So I wrote about things that I thought were important at the time. Crap things like no nuclear weapons and ending diseases and other stuff like that. People being able to live how they wanted. So I did that and they gave me ten dollars again."

Frings nodded.

"Next time I come back, they put me in a room with like a couch and some magazines and there's some jazz music going, and they ask me to suck on a sugar cube until it dissolves into my mouth, which seemed like kind of a weird thing, but I did it. A half hour later and the whole world starts changing, getting bigger or smaller and anything that moves is leaving like a little trail."

"LSD?"

"Yeah, LSD. I didn't know what it was at the time, but I figured what was going on had to be from the sugar cube, and I asked the man who was there watching, a little guy with glasses, I ask him if this is going to wear off and he smiled and said, yes, of course, so I went with it."

"What did you do?" Frings asked.

"Different things. He wanted me to guess when a minute was up. Like he'd say, 'go,' and then I was supposed to say stop or something when a minute had passed. But I never got it."

"What do you mean?"

"I mean we tried three or four times but I always got distracted, forgot what I was doing. The little guy kept reminding me and then we'd start again."

"Then what?"

"More stuff like that. He'd ask me how far away something was or to throw a ball into a waste basket, see how I did. It was hard, trying to get a hold of that stuff in my mind. Distances, time, all messed up."

Finch sat back down on the mattress, slouching again. He picked up the gun and turned it absently in his hands. Frings wondered if it was loaded.

"Was that it?" Frings asked.

"For that time, yeah. They let me go, and I was still, you know, not all there for hours, just walking around campus, looking at things: people, trees." There was a pause. "But the next time was different."

54

GRIP GRABBED A GYPSY CAB, FLASHED HIS BADGE AT THE GUY, SAID HE'D pay him a ten spot to drive him around for the morning. Plus, Grip wouldn't turn him in for driving an unlicensed taxi. The driver wasn't too happy about this arrangement, but he grudgingly did as he was told.

Grip had him drive to the Tech and then by Ben Linsky's apartment building. Grip saw the lights on in Linsky's apartment, wondered if forensics was still working the place over or whether they'd let the roommates back in. He spotted an unmarked parked illegally at a fire hydrant and, not liking his odds, told the hack to keep moving.

His priority was survival. It was hard to do much digging, and he could barely figure out what was going on. He could no longer tell when he was acting independently, and when he was being manipulated. Like with Linsky—how could anyone predict that Grip would have planted the memo, that it would have gotten into the hands of someone who'd take it as a reason to murder? He couldn't talk to Zwieg—this was now clear—but he wasn't sure that he could talk to Ving, either. The situation was too precarious. He needed to figure out what the hell was going on, first. Then he'd decide what to do.

They drove to Cafe ?, and Grip had the hack pull up to the curb, told him to wait. The cabbie's eyes did a little shift, looking from Grip down the road, then back to Grip.

"Don't be an asshole. I'd find you."

The cabbie sighed with resignation, and Grip went in the front door. The place was half-empty, just a few college-aged heemies spread out among the tables. There was a tangible gloominess to the place, and Grip put it down to Linsky's death. Grip saw the girl from the previous day, textbook open, drinking a coffee, wearing a white blouse and jeans. Now that he thought about it, everyone there was wearing something white. He walked over to her, sat opposite, his elbows on the table.

"How are you this morning?"

She looked at him without any particular expression. She looked exhausted, her eyes sunken and dull.

"I was wondering if maybe you'd run into one of Ben Linsky's roommates since we last talked." He was trying to speak soothingly, but this wasn't exactly a natural register for him.

He watched her eyes switch quickly to a man sitting two tables to his left, then back to him, not sure if it was intentional or a reflex.

"That's one of them?"

She hesitated. What was she thinking about? Whether to give away the kid at the other table? Did she think that she hadn't tipped it with the glance? Or was she thrown off by Grip's manner this morning, so polite after the previous day's harsh intimidation? Grip gave her a moment to think.

"That's Norman Lane over there." She nodded toward the kid. Grip turned to look at him, skinny, hair a little long, hanging down in his eyes. He was staring at a book on the table before him, but his eyes were still, as if he weren't actually reading, just trying not to be noticed.

Grip gave the girl a tired smile and walked over to Norman Lane's table. He dropped his badge on the open book and took a seat. Lane looked at the badge without touching it, pursed his lips, looked up at Grip. Grip saw that the kid's eyes were red, dark patches beneath, his shoulders sagging with exhaustion under a white fisherman's sweater.

"I already told you guys everything I've got."

"That right?"

"Sure. Come on, man. I was in the station for fourteen hours. I've got nothing left.

Grip smiled at him, watched him scan the room. Grip felt eyes on him; didn't give a shit. "How about this? How about I tell you something that you didn't tell the guys at the station? We can talk from there."

The kid said nothing, confused.

"How about I tell you that you found a letter Ben Linsky wrote to the police, a letter that passed on gossip about you and your friends? How's that?"

Lane stared with eyes equally mystified and frightened. "Wait. You—"

Grip spoke softly. "Don't think about lying to me."

Lane shook his head, Grip thinking he was trying to buy some time, figure out what he wanted to say. Grip glanced over at the girl, who was watching them. She looked away immediately.

"Okay, I found it."

Grip nodded.

"But I—"

"You gave it to somebody."

Lane was confused again, nodding. "Yes. . ."

"That makes it easy." Grip didn't make Lane as a murderer. He didn't think that murder had ever crossed this kid's mind—not even in a situation like this. What *would* cross his mind would be to give the letter to someone else who might know what to do about it. "Who did you pass it off to?"

"I don't know if—"

"Don't know? Listen, this isn't some buddy who stole something, maybe got friendly with the wrong girl, and you're covering for him. This is a fucking murder. Someone's going to take the juice for this."

"I know that," Lane said petulantly.

"So you know that you are very goddamn close to being an accessory. Keeping your mouth shut at the station. Jesus. Probably didn't even have a lawyer."

The kid looked sheepish.

Grip softened. "Listen, let me help you, try to keep you out of deeper shit. Tell me anything and everything you know about who you passed that note to. Okay?"

Lane went pale. Grip kept a hard stare on him. The kid had been questioned for hours; he'd be exhausted, mentally spent. The place was silent while Lane thought, just the hiss of rain from outside.

Lane leaned back in his chair, ran his hand through his hair, gave a quick glance at the girl who was now pretending to read her book. He turned his weary attention back to Grip. "Okay. I'll tell you. But the thing is, he didn't do anything to Ben. He was at Will Ebanks's house that night. A bunch of people were."

"Okay, got it. You gave him the note, but he didn't kill Linsky," Grip said calmly, keeping his frustration under control. "Who did you give the note to?"

"To a cat named Andy Macheda."

55

LES FINCH DIDN'T HAVE A REFRIGERATOR, BUT HE KEPT HIS BEER COLD in the tank of his toilet. He asked Frings if he wanted any, and Frings said, "yeah," not because he wanted the beer but because he wanted to make sure that Finch would drink one. Maybe it would slow him down, relax him a little. At any rate, it couldn't hurt.

To Frings's relief, Finch took the two beer cans to his kitchen sink and rinsed them off, toweled them dry. He handed one to Frings.

"The tank water's clean," he said, smiling without embarrassment. "I just figure it's nice to rinse them off for guests."

Frings nodded, the guns on the wall back in his field of vision as Finch returned to the bed. "You were talking about . . ."

"The study, sure. You ever been down in that basement?"

Frings shook his head.

"Down in the psych building, that's where most of the study took place, but they've got a part of it sectioned off with a door, at least they used to. You ever done LSD?"

Frings shook his head.

"The thing with it is that a little bit really changes how you see things. Like you realize how much things aren't set, their size, their color. Even time. It really changes how you look at things. But you take a lot and it's as if the world, this world, isn't even really there. You're somewhere different, a world within our world or without our world or something. You see what exists that we usually can't see ourselves. You feel things, things that are more real, you know, to yourself and to everything else. You don't understand so much, but you can feel what's there. You catching this?"

"It's a lot to take in," Frings said.

Finch nodded, this concession by Frings seeming to validate something for him. "Well, I don't know what to say about this, because I don't remember it mostly, and what I do, I don't know, it's not like the memories I usually have of things. You just can't . . . it's hard to explain." Finch had finished his beer, but his eyes were still frantic, even as he sat almost motionless on the bed.

"Plenty of people have tried to explain it," Frings said, thinking of Ebanks. "Nobody seems to have found the right words."

Frings got a good look at Finch's expression and saw relief—something more profound than simply being reassured during a conversation. Frings wondered about this guy, sitting in his apartment with all of his guns, trying to make sense of an experience without success. Maybe Frings had even given him some peace of mind—no one seemed to be able to make sense of all of it.

"Yeah," Finch said.

"So, what *can* you tell me," Frings asked, quietly.

Finch shook his head. "It mostly happened in this one room, the room with the light. They brought me in there, I was all alone, the drug really working on me, and they had a really bright light pointed right at me and it's too bright, painful. I couldn't see past it, I remember, and I knew there were people on the other side, but I don't, didn't know who they were, what they wanted." He was talking even faster now, hands fidgeting in his lap like he was trying to get something off of them. "There was a guy, though, who spoke from the other side of the light and this is part of what I don't remember exactly except to tell you that he seemed to *know* me. And he just took me apart." Finch stood up and walked to the window, looking down on the street. It was still raining. Finch tapped his finger rapidly against the window pane.

"He asked me questions—don't ask me what, I don't remember, or, I don't know, maybe I'm making myself forget—and I'd answer as best I could, but it's so hard to concentrate on those things when you've taken that much, and then you hear the question and you have to figure out what it is that you're being asked, and what might be an answer and then what is *your* answer, the one you want to give. See? And the whole time the light's just blazing—it's so bright that even if you close your eyes it's still there, and you know that there are people behind the light and you don't know . . . what they want. So I'd answer, or I'd think I answered, and he'd just destroy me, not just what I said, but the whole reason why I came up with that answer, the things I thought about the world, I guess, and how things work. And I don't know how to explain this to you, but when you're on the drug, it's got more impact than you'd think. It undermines you, man. It undermines the most important things you believe, and there's nothing you can do to get perspective. Does this make sense to you? Do you understand?"

Frings nodded, leaning forward in his chair, his mind humming with intensity. "What was the point? Why were they doing this?"

Finch crossed the room to the door, put his ear against it, holding up one finger for a moment of quiet. Satisfied there was nothing to hear, he said, "I don't know. I think about this all the time. *All the time*. But what could it be? What could be the reason for subjecting someone to that kind of hell?"

They sat in silence, Frings giving Finch a moment to compose himself. He was again acutely aware of the guns.

"Did you finish at the Tech? Did you graduate?"

Finch laughed brightly, jarringly. "I failed every class that semester and dropped out. Did you hear what I was just telling you? You don't recover from something like that. You don't come back to where you were, living the life you always had. It makes you realize you don't know anything, don't even know how to think about things. How do you continue?"

Frings thought about Conroy's list: suicides, failures. "Did you know Sol Elia?"

"Sure. He was part of the study, too."

"Did you ever talk with anybody else who was part of the study? You know, compare notes or something like that?"

Finch rubbed his eyes, his posture slumping. "No, Mr. Frings. That was the last thing I wanted to do. I wanted to forget—still want to forget. The only thing that keeps me together is thinking that maybe I'm remembering this wrong, that this is some trick my mind is playing on me. If someone confirmed to me what happened, I . . . I don't know what I'd do."

• • •

FROM *Alienation and the Modern City* by Francis Frings (1958)

Among the insidious consequences of a "major business zone"— or Capital Zone, as it is marketed in the New City Project literature— is how it creates an impossible situation that arises for the types of businesses necessary to serve the needs of the "major businesses." The problems inherent to this arrangement are numerous, and the distance between services and clients, the advantages of large service cor-

porations over small service businesses, and many other, similar, top-ics will be addressed later. But before we examine those in-depth, let's take a look at an example that provides at once a simple and wide-ranging picture of this type of situation.

The economics of restaurants necessitates 1. the ability to serve at least two meals and to have a constant minimal number of patrons during the course of business hours. These factors are a consequence of a constraint—that of square footage on occupancy—and on a de-sired goal—maximizing the number of meals served per day by hav-ing people come and go at a rate that varies but whose peaks are not undermined by economically catastrophic valleys.

Now let's look at the situation for restaurant owners and, by def-inition, the working-class people who are employed by these owners. In the "major business zone," corporate workers show up to work in the morning, generally after having breakfast in their sub-urban home, and leave the office in the evening to have dinner at their home, as well. The vast, vast majority of meals consumed at restaurants by these corporate workers are lunches. Hypothetically, we would expect the distribution of meals purchased to be something like 10 percent breakfasts, 85 percent lunches, and 5 percent dinners. A graph of this distribution would look something like a bell curve with small curls at each end.

It is apparent that the vast majority of restaurants would be re-quired to make nearly all their sales during the lunch hour, which is largely the same among corporations, leading to a "customer surge" between 11:30 and 1:00 and then near silence during the hours out-side of this time. Survival for restaurants in this environment re-quires employing a large number of people for a small number of hours each day to service this "customer surge." The service workers, then, who are paid hourly, are left working 3–4 hour days during the week. The weekend would, of course, constitute another dead time for these restaurants.

Now think about the effect of, say, six theaters in the district. These theaters, with their evening-oriented shows, would provide the restaurants with a dinner clientele and even an after-show drinks crowd. Suddenly, restaurants that competed for the tiny 5 percent of dinner business would have an entirely new population to serve and at a time when the corporate workers were not potential customers. More restaurants would be able to survive. Restaurant workers would work through two meals and thus enough hours to earn enough for a dignified existence. Additionally, the theaters would drive both lunch and dinner crowds on the weekend, providing still further opportunities for service workers.

This is, of course, a simplified model, but consider the effect of multiple-use zones on the fates of restaurant employees and extrapolate that to low-wage service employees in all manner of industries and you will see why a single-use "major business zone" is inherently anti-worker.

56

A CRIME REPORTER AT THE *NEWS-GAZETTE* GAVE FRINGS THE ADDRESS for Crippen's, along with a funny look.

"It's hard to think of a guy and a bar more badly matched."

Frings had smiled, said he'd heard great things about the women there, which had cracked up the reporter.

Now, stepping into the bar, Frings felt the nervous energy. The place was as grim as he'd imagined, but smaller and lit well enough to see the filthy floor, the stained walls. As it was, the customers were nearly as dingy as the room, mostly older ginks—crew cuts and work shirts, fading tattoos, angry eyes. Frings felt those eyes on him as he moved slowly between the tables, his cane tapping on the linoleum floor. From the back room, a storm of static obscured the tinny voice of some radio host on a diatribe that Frings couldn't make out.

A waiter brushed past Frings from behind, and Frings caught his attention. "Ed Wayne here?"

The waiter, another old gink, looked at Frings with something like contempt, and Frings realized that he'd probably been recognized.

"Ed Wayne," he repeated.

The old waiter kept his eyes on Frings, nodded at a corner table. Frings saw specks of white spit in the corners of the man's mouth.

Two men sat at the corner table: a small guy, fit, sitting military-straight, and an odd-looking guy, pale skin, a head that seemed to seep into his body, no neck or chin of note. He wore a terrible wig, red hair that didn't fit at all well on his head, almost comically askew. Frings walked over to the table, the guy with the wig watching him through slitted eyes. At the table he realized, to his unease, that this odd man with the wig was Ed Wayne—something about his eyes or maybe his posture. When had Frings last seen him? Ten years ago? A dozen? Before he'd been kicked off the Force. What the hell had happened to him since then? They'd been on opposite sides of a dispute over a Negro community almost fifteen years ago. Frings had worked to help save it; Wayne had wanted to burn it to the ground.

"Ed Wayne."

"You aren't welcome to sit here." Wayne was leaning back in his chair, a half-grin on his face. His friend, the little guy, was trying, unsuccessfully, to bore a hole through Frings with his stare.

"I'm not here to chat, Ed. I'm looking for Torsten Grip."

Wayne barked a phlegmy laugh. "You and everybody else."

"What does that mean?"

Wayne didn't answer, just fixed him with a smug grin.

"Tell you what, Ed. I'm going to leave a card with you. You run into Grip, you give it to him. He's better off seeing me before he sees anyone else." Frings tossed a card on the table.

Wayne kept his eyes on Frings. "Why don't you get the fuck on out of here while I've still got my pleasant demeanor."

Frings frowned. "I'd love to catch up, Ed, but my knitting circle's about to start. Give that card to Grip if you see him."

Wayne finally looked down at the card. While Frings watched, Wayne picked the card up, put it in the breast pocket of his shirt. "Satisfied?" Wayne turned his head, hacked, and spit a thumb-sized ball of phlegm onto the floor.

57

THE SECURITY GUYS AT THE IDAHO AVENUE SITE WERE ALBANIANS, THREE of whom didn't seem to have any English at all, while the fourth had enough to act as a translator, though an improbably incompetent one. Insua, the foreman, was back tonight after going home for dinner, and his presence vouched for Dorman as far as the Albanians were concerned. As for the people who would come later, they'd been told that Dorman would be here. He wanted to be sure there were no surprises. Things would be complicated enough without them.

It was well below freezing. Dorman held a steaming cup of coffee with both hands as he and Insua waited in tense silence.

Dorman heard a honk at the gate, and the security guards hustled over to open the padlock, pull off the chain. A white panel truck pulled onto the site, stopped by a storage container. Two men got out of the cab, the first talking to the English-speaking Albanian, the second walking over to Dorman and Insua.

"Mr. Dorman."

"That's right." They shook hands.

"We're going to get the truck loaded up, then we'll move out. We're going to have to put a sack over your head. Just precautions."

Dorman wasn't prepared for this and looked to Insua who nodded.

"It's okay, Mr. Dorman. You've got weight here."

"It's for your protection," the driver said.

Sure it was.

The driver joined his partner and the guards as they unloaded building materials—mostly copper pipes—from the supply trailer into the panel truck. The driver kept checking his pocket watch, growling at the men to hurry up, they were running late.

Dorman found the quiet of the site unnerving. The sounds of the men's footsteps on the gravel seemed amplified, their mutterings in Albanian—behind it all, rhythmically, relentlessly, the hammering of the pile drivers on the river.

58

GRIP REALIZED THAT HE WASN'T THINKING CLEARLY. FATIGUE HAD STARTED to dull his mind. He'd caught a couple of hours of sleep at the White Rhino, paying by the hour, not feeling comfortable staying there for long. Too many people had seen him on the street. Better to go where he wasn't known, he thought, where there wasn't anyone around ready to sell him to a cop for ten bucks.

He walked through the empty streets of upper Capitol Heights, the part of the neighborhood that gave the place its name. Nobody knew him here, that was certain, but the stillness of the place left him feeling vulnerable. Any prowl car moving through couldn't miss him. He listened for cars as he walked, spotting places to hide if one seemed to be nearing his block. He felt like he could hear his nerves humming—the neighborhood was so fucking quiet.

He found Frank Frings's townhouse on a block of expensive walkups. He checked his watch—four in the morning. He rang the bell and waited. A light came on in an upstairs window. Light appeared in the three tiny windows high on the front door, followed by the sound of footsteps. The door opened a few inches and then jerked to a stop at the full extension of the security chain. Grip leaned over so that Frings could see his face. The door pulled closed. He heard the sound of the chain being undone, and the door opened wide to Frings standing in a dressing gown and slippers, his short hair sticking up on one side, his eyes swollen from sleep.

"Detective," he murmured.

"You were looking for me?"

"Come in."

Grip stepped inside. Frings closed the door, engaged the deadbolt, reattached the chain. Frings inspected Grip in the light of the hallway.

"You look terrible."

Grip felt terrible. He shrugged.

"You want some coffee?"

"I wouldn't turn it down."

Grip sat at a small kitchen table, watching Frings make coffee in silence. The place was nice, must be worth what Grip made in ten years. Fucking Frank Frings, how'd he do it? Dated those beautiful singers and actresses, made a mint. Watching the guy move around the kitchen, Grip saw that he wasn't all that good-looking. So what was it? And why didn't he have any of it?

When the coffee was ready, Frings joined Grip at the table with two cups.

"So Wayne gave you my message?"

Grip registered the surprise in Frings's voice. "He's an asshole, but he likes to be in the thick of things, likes the conspiracy."

Frings nodded. He looked better now, his eyes clearer. Grip's lids felt heavy. He fought to keep his concentration.

"I tried to reach you at the station. Seemed like they hadn't heard from you for a while—they put me through to Ving."

Grip frowned. That sounded about right—Ving assuming that Grip was AWOL because of Ben Linsky's murder, keeping tabs on who was interested, because Ving was himself interested. "Why were you calling for me?"

"I heard about Ben Linsky being murdered."

"And that made you think of me?"

"A few days ago, I met with Ben Linsky, he mentioned that you were all over him for some reason. So, when he turns up dead, yeah, I'm interested in talking to you."

Grip nodded, it made sense. "So?"

"So why were you interested in Ben Linsky? Why were you asking if he was in Kollectiv 61?"

Grip's head swam. He was reluctant to talk to Frings, whose politics were near the opposite of his—and a journalist to boot. But after days of confusion and conspiracy, he was desperate for an ally, for someone who was fucking *sane*. Frings was an unlikely choice, but they were both concerned over what happened to Ben Linsky, and Frings's word had always seemed good. Still, he wasn't sure. "You know that explosives theft from the Crosstown site on Kaiser? I know your pal Art Deyna's all over it."

"I heard."

"I got a tip that pointed to Kollectiv 61, but it turned out the snitch had been put up to it."

Frings had a funny look on his face. "Who'd you get the tip from?"

"A snitch. Nobody special."

"We got a tip, too. From inside the Force. That's how Art found out."

Grip fought his exhaustion, trying to make sense of this. Somebody in the Force had set him up and leaked the same shit to the press. "You know who?"

Frings shook his head. "Art's pretty happy keeping that a secret."

"You need to find out who."

Frings nodded. That was obvious. But it seemed unlikely that he'd be able to. Hell, he'd kept the identities of some of his sources secret for decades. There was no reason why Deyna couldn't do the same.

His elbows on the table, Grip ground the heels of his hands into his eyes, thought for some reason that this might clear his mind. He wasn't sure how much he was willing to tell Frings, his natural suspicion fighting the urge that he felt to share his thoughts with someone, get them out there.

"What is it?" Frings asked.

Grip looked at Frings, working to keep his eyes open. Trust or not? What did he have to lose?

"What I've been wondering—look, I've been on the Force for twenty-five years, I know how things work. But in the last week, things have been happening that I can't figure. That snitch, who pointed me toward Kollectiv 61? He's a lowlife scumbag, but it turns out he has protection inside the Force, which I think is because they used him to set me up."

"Who's that?"

"Hold on a sec. Next, Ben Linsky, I found out he has protection—or I guess he *had* protection."

"Do you know why?"

"Maybe because he's a snitch?"

"Do you know, or are you asking?"

"I've got reasons to think so."

"Who warned you off him?"

"You talked to him."

"Ving?"

Grip nodded. "And when it's Ving, it's the chief, Kraatjes. All the way to the top."

Frings seemed to think about this. "How about the snitch, who's protecting him?"

"Cop named Zwieg."

"And this guy was *your* snitch, too?"

Grip nodded.

"So, I'm trying to get this straight. Zwieg and Ving, are they working together on something?"

"No way. They don't see eye to eye."

"Okay. So you think Zwieg is protecting your snitch because he set you up? What did he do?"

"He gave me a story—pointed me toward Kollectiv 61 for the Kaiser Street heist."

"Why?"

Grip shook his head. That was the question, and his fatigue was keeping him from thinking it through clearly. "Zwieg wants me to go after Kollectiv 61 for the dynamite. Don't ask me why, or why he did it this way. I don't know." He didn't have the energy to tell Frings about his other suspicion—that Zwieg thought the investigation was too dangerous, which was why he'd shielded himself behind Patridis and Grip.

"Do you need some sleep, detective?"

Grip shook his head again, the motion making him light-headed. He needed to keep moving, take care of things.

Grip let Frings walk him to the door, the floor seeming to list under his feet. Frings paused at the door.

"You know a guy named Andy Macheda?"

Frings narrowed his eyes. "I've met him, why?"

"Know where I can find him?"

"No I don't. He's a tough guy to track down. Why do you want to know about him?"

"No reason," Grip said.

59

DORMAN DIDN'T TRY TO KEEP TRACK OF TURNS OR DISTANCES. HE leaned back in his seat, closed his eyes inside the hood, thought about what he was doing. The feel of this meeting, the precaution of the hood, made it seem more dangerous than it probably was. This was the dark secret of the New City Project—the arrangement that Canada and the board of Consolidated Industries had with the underworld. Controlled theft kept the gangs in money and allowed Canada to hide cost overruns by tallying the losses and keeping the book so that the repurchased stolen materials were recorded as new—purchased at the full rate.

Dorman had been appalled when he'd first heard about the agreement. He'd thought it was a capitulation to the criminal gangs. But Canada had walked him through the books, showed him that this was the only way to make the New City Project work. There will always be corruption, he'd said, and the key is to maintain it on your terms.

HE REALIZED THE RIDE WAS OVER BY THE CHANGE IN THE QUALITY OF the sound as the car entered a warehouse, the noise suddenly more immediate. He heard a metal door slam somewhere behind him.

"I'm going to take off your hood."

Dorman squinted against the light. He heard saws, pounding. The volume increased as the car door was opened, a huge man gently pulling Dorman from the car. His eyes adjusted, and Dorman took in the scene. Stacks of lumber and girders, palettes of tools, bags of concrete, hardware—storage for stolen goods. Beyond the stacks, men sawed down boards, performed some kind of torch-work on steel, packaged rivets, wires, other supplies. Sparks plumed and the sound was deafening.

Dorman watched a man walk toward them, another big guy, ample chest, ampler belly, round face, receding hair.

"Mr. Dorman," he said boisterously. "Nathan Canada's man. The man who makes the Project go. About time we met." The man extended his hand. They shook.

"Mr. . . ."

The man shook his head. "Not necessary for you to know. Call me Jones." The guy spoke with the trace of an accent, as if he'd come over from the old world sometime in his teens.

"Okay."

"You don't mind . . ." Jones mimed spreading his arms and legs. Dorman hesitated, looked at the man questioningly.

"Make sure you don't have a wire."

Dorman sighed and spread. The big man who'd helped him from the car gave him a quick pat-down.

"How do I know *you* don't have a wire?" Dorman asked.

Jones smiled. "Trust."

Dorman snorted a cynical laugh. "Trust."

Jones nodded to his left. "Follow me."

The big man accompanied Dorman and Jones as far as Jones's office door, then stayed outside. Jones shut the door behind them. The office was filthy—oil-smudged papers on clipboards, smoke stains on the ceiling, a pinup calendar nailed to the wall. It was quieter in here, though, a relief.

"So, I hear you're here to talk about Kaiser Street."

Dorman nodded. "The explosives."

"It wasn't us. You know that."

"I'm willing to assume that."

"It would make no sense for us. It upsets the whole process."

This was the reason why Dorman was pretty sure that the usual groups were not involved. They had a great arrangement, as long as they toed the line of the agreement. The explosives broke that agreement, and for not much gain.

"Are you doing anything about it?" Dorman asked.

"What, us?" Jones looked at Dorman as if he was crazy. "That's your job, fella. This is one for the cops."

"No. We can't let the word get out. It would undermine the public confidence in the Project. We need to keep it secret. There are people working on it, but not many."

"Well, that's your business."

Dorman's heart pounded. He was isolated here, didn't know how much he could push. "It's your business, too. The whole agreement is in question."

Jones straightened up in his chair. He spoke quietly. "What is this?"

Dorman leaned his forearms on Jones's desk, meeting his eyes, thinking about how Canada would play it. "This is a fucking crisis. If something happens with that dynamite, whether something gets blown up or the press finds out it's missing, whatever—if either of these things happen, the Crosstown is in jeopardy, the New City Project is in jeopardy, and your arrangement is sure as fuck in jeopardy."

Jones stared back at him behind half-closed lids.

"Look," Dorman continued, "we have a shared stake in this. I need you to do your part, have your people listening on the street. Okay? You're criminals, for god's sake."

Jones's face had become blotchy. "What's your angle on this? Who are you looking at? Heemies?"

"Maybe Kollectiv 61."

Jones frowned. "I guess that's where the smart money is."

Jones stared at his desk, thinking. Dorman listened to the sound from the warehouse, metallic screaming; heavy objects being dropped onto thick concrete.

Jones looked up. "That's not my world, man. We can keep an ear out, but I wouldn't expect anything."

That was probably as good as Dorman could hope for. "Another thing that I've been wondering about."

"Yeah?"

"Those guards, the ones from the Kaiser Street site."

Jones's mouth pursed in concern. "Yeah, I heard that. Nasty business. Baseball bat to the head."

"They lined them up. It was an execution. You know who'd do it that way?"

Jones shook his head. "I've been studying on that and haven't got anywhere. That's like something from the '30s—lawless bullshit. We don't truck with that."

"What about debts? Maybe they were in the hole to someone in the neighborhood."

Jones thought for a second. "Hard to collect when they're dead, you know. Maybe if they were sending a message—but then the word would be out, they'd be taking credit. I don't see it."

"Alright, so that's it?" Dorman asked.

"That's it. I'll keep my ear to the ground, man, but I don't figure I'll hear anything."

Dorman stood to go.

"You know," Jones said, "if you want to get the word on the street, a cat you might want to see is Ed Wayne."

"Okay," Dorman said. He'd heard the name from Gerry Svinblad, and from others, too. The guy provoked strong feelings.

"Catch the guys that did this," Jones said. "Last thing we need is some fool blowing this for all of us."

60

FRINGS WALKED THE CHILLY SIDEWALK PAST THE SPIRALED TURRETS OF THE City's original post office into a neighborhood known as Marrakesh, or just the Kesh. Women wore long black dresses under their coats, burkas on a few, scarves over the hair of the rest. The men were dressed for work, some in suits, some in laborers' garb. The store signs in the Kesh were in Arabic, the street signs printed in both Arabic and English. The cold air carried the smell of food from warmer climates.

He arrived at a block where paper condemnation notices written in English had been tacked to every door. A small group of men huddled around something on the far end of the block. He saw Andy Macheda moving in their midst. He seemed to be assembling something. Frings leaned hard on his cane as he walked until, halfway down the block, he stopped, taking a seat on a bench in front of a shabby market. His knee burned.

Not even ten and already the day seemed exhausting, starting as it had with Grip's visit. Frings hadn't returned to bed and had arrived at work just after dawn. He'd spent the time skimming through the daily newspapers, thinking about Grip and Ledley. He'd had it in mind to visit Ledley that morning, but decided it could wait when Conroy showed up at his office and dropped a sheet of paper covered in his small, neat script.

"This is from the film?"

Conroy settled into the guest seat. "I went last night."

"Okay." Frings read down the list, street names, a park, a few addresses thrown in as well.

"I wrote down the places that I could identify in the film. Blocks, addresses, whatever I could figure out."

Frings nodded. A number of the streets on the list had been demolished, at least in part, to make way for either the City Center or the Crosstown. Others, Frings thought he recognized as areas soon to be razed. Then there were a few that he really couldn't place, couldn't understand how they were related: Vilnius, Oregon, de Gama, Debrecen. Still, he felt sure that he was missing something—something that he should have been able to see.

After the movie, Conroy had chatted with some people who he thought were "in the know"—this was his phrase. From them he'd found out where Macheda would be filming that day. So the visit to Ledley had been postponed, and Frings hopped a cab that dropped him at the edge of the Kesh.

He took a deep breath and pushed himself up from the bench. He walked stiffly over to where Macheda was now trying to line up a shot with a movie camera mounted on a sturdy tripod. The men who had earlier surrounded him had retreated a few yards to give him room to work. Macheda pulled his eye away from the camera eyepiece and saw Frings approaching. Frings thought he saw a quick scowl.

"You're a tough gink to track down."

Macheda shrugged. "People find me. Can I help you with something, Frank?"

"Did you ask around about Sol Elia?"

"Sure. Nobody's seen him."

He was lying. "You're sure?"

Macheda nodded.

"You know, Andy, after I ran into you shooting the other day, I started to wonder how you picked your locations for *Film 13*. I actually wondered enough that I had someone go to the movie last night and keep track of where each scene took place."

Macheda smiled confusedly. "On the level?"

Frings nodded.

Macheda bit the corner of his lip, looking back at Frings. "You must have figured it out, Frank. It's not very complicated. Most of those spots are gone or about to be gone, making way for the fucking Crosstown or the City Center. I'm recording the loss."

"I *did* get it. Most of the locations are like that, but some aren't. What are those?"

Macheda rolled his eyes to the side, a petulant tick. "Some scenes, they aren't about the location. You have to shoot *somewhere*."

Frings nodded. People across the street had stopped to watch this conversation, the two men clearly out of place and drawing a different kind of curiosity than Macheda had with his film equipment. Macheda had, he noticed, sensed this, too.

"Ben Linsky," Frings said, sensing that he didn't have much longer.

Macheda started at the name.

"Did you know him?" Frings pushed.

"Sure."

He saw the same change in Macheda he'd seen the day on the demolition site, a retreat. "You know he was killed."

Macheda nodded. "Everyone knows."

"You have any thoughts about it?"

"Like everyone else, I can't get my head around it—that he's gone, that someone would kill him."

"You can't get your head around that someone would want to murder him?"

Macheda shrugged helplessly.

"Because, Andy, someone *did* murder him, and it seems like it was because they thought he was a snitch. What's your thought about that?"

"I don't think I get you," Macheda said, an edge creeping into his voice.

Frings held his hands forward in conciliation. "I'm not imply-ing anything. I'm just wondering what you think, if you have any idea why someone might think he was a snitch—if he even *was* a snitch."

"I don't know." Macheda looked past Frings, across the street and up.

"Okay."

"Anything else? 'Cause, I've got to get to work, man. The sun crests those roofs and my shot's fucked."

"Fair enough." Frings nodded thoughtfully, then added as if it had suddenly occurred to him, "You wouldn't know of anyone in Kollec-tiv 61 would you? I'm trying to track down someone to talk to."

He lost Macheda with this question, the filmmaker's face going blank. "I don't know anyone in Kollectiv 61, Frank, and fuck you for asking. I'm an artist, for god's sake, not a fucking vandal."

Frings shrugged. "Okay, Andy. I appreciate your time." He hesi-tated. "Listen, Andy, a cop was asking after you."

"Why's that?" Macheda said, without much interest.

"He didn't say, but it's probably along the lines of what I was ask-ing you."

Macheda didn't respond, so Frings walked away, leaving Macheda on the sidewalk with his movie camera and case, the crowd of on-lookers watching motionless from across the street.

61

FRINGS HAD BEEN FORCED TO WALK SEVERAL BLOCKS BEFORE FINDING A cab to take him to the Tech, to drop in on Ledley. The hack steered off the street and down a Tech sidewalk to Bristol Hall, kids glaring as they made way.

Inside, Frings took the stairs to the basement one at a time, leaning hard on the railing. The building was quiet, the scrape of his shoes on the tiled stairs echoing faintly in the stairwell.

The basement hall was barely lit, but he saw a pool of light spilling from an open door and limped over. He tapped on the door with his cane, peered into the room to see Simon Ledley sitting on the edge of his bare desk, straightening his collar with both hands.

"Dr. Ledley." Frings saw Ledley look to Frings's right, then back to Frings.

"Mr. Frings."

Frings stepped halfway into the room before realizing that someone else was there, sitting in the chair against the wall. Frings took the woman in: severe face, a body that was sharp and thin, her hair a little untidy, her cheeks flushed. Her eyes, though, were cold. Frings smiled at her, not expecting much back.

"An unexpected pleasure," Ledley said with forced cordiality. "This is my colleague, Ada Hauptmann."

This time Frings nodded along with his smile. Ada Hauptmann did something with her eyelids that looked almost like a nod, but not quite.

"Ada, I'm sorry, could we have a moment," Ledley said. Ada didn't seem happy about this, but stood and walked past Frings without a word. Ledley smiled weakly and motioned Frings to the seat Ada had just left.

Ledley looked across the desk quizzically. "I confess that I thought we'd completed our business."

"Well, we've found some new and interesting information I wanted to discuss with you."

Ledley sighed and leaned back in his chair. "As I told you last time, I am prohibited from talking about the study involving Sol Elia. I can have my lawyer explain it again."

"That's okay. Let's see where we get. Indulge me. For instance, have you kept up with the people who were in that study? I mean, do you know what they are up to now?"

Ledley looked away for a second, down and to his left, on guard now.

"Because I can tell you," Frings continued. "Three suicides—at least. And five more are leading really marginal existences by the standards of Tech graduates."

"I wasn't aware of that."

"Now that you know . . ."

"It's unfortunate."

"That's it? Unfortunate?"

"You have me at a disadvantage, Mr. Frings. I don't know anything but what you've told me. I'm uncertain how you came to know the names of the subjects of this study. I am, actually, a bit suspicious that you might not know what you think you know."

"I don't think you need to worry about that."

Ledley thought about this for a moment. Frings looked around the room, was surprised to see photos of Ada Hauptmann on the wall, staring coldly out into the world, her face angular and humorless.

"You talked to Toth."

"Who?"

"My former assistant."

Frings shrugged. "I don't discuss who I did or didn't talk to."

Ledley bore in on him with his eyes. Frings gave him a quick smile.

"I don't have anything to say about it."

This time it was Frings who sighed.

Ledley smiled, leaned forward to put his elbows on the desk. His posture seemed friendlier. "Are you familiar with the term 'dyadic study'?"

Frings shook his head.

"This is the way I like to conduct my research or, for that matter, my life. In most studies, there are subjects and there are researchers, and the researcher is a neutral or absent observer. In a dyadic study the researcher and subject are both participants. It is a difficult type of study to conduct because of the researcher's participation and the discipline and nuance necessary to maintain a viable objectivity. Do you see why this would be so?"

"Sure." According to Ebanks, Ledley's methods were too traditional—but none of this sounded very traditional to Frings. Were these dyadic studies common practice, or were Ebanks's methods so radical that Ledley's unorthodoxy seemed normal in comparison?

"In these situations it is also difficult to maintain a distance, a dispassion."

"Okay."

"So, when I say that I don't follow the lives of my previous subjects, it is not because I am callous or dismissive toward them. It is because this is the only way to conduct the kind of research I undertake."

"I understand. But doesn't it bother you when you hear that your study seems to have had a negative effect on the subjects?"

"Why would you assume that it was my study?"

"What else do they have in common? What else could explain a suicide rate like that?"

Ledley's mouth twisted into a kind of half-smile. "I'm not so sure that you can be certain that my study is all they have in common. There may be other factors that would result in the numbers you have given me. It could also be a coincidence or a product of the type of students we recruited for the study."

"What kind of students would those be?"

Ledley smiled, didn't answer.

"What are you trying to get across here, Simon?"

Ledley leaned back in his chair again, his posture showing that in his mind they'd come to the end. "What am I trying to get across? Mr. Frings, you are a journalist and I understand that journalists work with different assumptions and criteria than scientists. But even if your information is correct, you are assigning causality without anything approaching evidence. Do you understand?"

Frings wouldn't let the guy get under his skin. "I do, actually. Thank you." He stood up, his knee straightening painfully. "I expect that we will be talking again soon."

"That"—Ledley said—"will be my pleasure."

FRINGS WALKED TO THE END OF THE HALL, THE TAPPING OF HIS CANE echoing. By Frings's reckoning, the wall cut the hallway roughly in half. A metal door with three keyed locks seemed to provide the only access. Frings grabbed the knob and tried to shake it, but the door didn't budge. He put his ear to it. Nothing.

Turning, he saw Ledley standing in his doorway, watching.

"What's back here?" Frings asked, walking back toward Ledley.

"Labs, meeting rooms. They're not in use anymore."

"Can I take a look at them?"

Ledley smiled ingratiatingly. "I'm afraid I don't have the keys."

Frings smiled back. "Maybe next time."

"Indeed." Ledley nodded a farewell and Frings caught a flicker of something, maybe fear, maybe rage.

62

FOG HAD ROLLED INTO THE CITY LIKE A GENTLE TIDE, FILLING LOW alleys and muffling street sounds. Grip stood by a stoop on a wealthy block on the edge of Little Lisbon. The street lamps glowed in the fog, little suns getting smaller as they receded into the distance. Grip had his gun out. He'd had it out for an hour.

He felt a little better. He'd slept for a few hours in a movie theater showing a matinee double feature. He hadn't lasted past the cartoon trailer, some hysterical pig trying to foil a salivating wolf. An usher had jerked him awake when the lights went up. He'd slunk out, the spider webs in his head clearing with coffee and a couple of fried eggs. He realized he was running out of moves. He had no traction, was no further along than he'd been before Linsky's death. He had to expand his possibilities, and the only way he knew how to do that was to get more information. As he saw it, that meant talking to one of two people: Ving or Zwieg. Neither was an appealing prospect, but, in the end, Ving's authority seemed less daunting than Zwieg's position in all of this—not to mention the blackmail. Which was why he was here, waiting.

He heard footsteps, closer than he was expecting. He raised his gun, waited to hear a footfall on the stoop steps. Moving quickly from behind the stoop, he stuck his gun into Ving's back. Ving stopped, recognized the touch of the end of a barrel.

"Back down the steps," Grip rasped. Even as he did this it seemed unreal, as if he were still going over the plan in his mind. Blood pumped in his ears.

He withdrew the gun, let Ving take two steps down to the sidewalk. Grip nudged him with the gun barrel to the corner beneath the walk-up.

"Turn around."

Ving hesitated, knowing what it might mean if he saw the face of his assailant.

"Don't worry, sir, the shit I'm in won't get any deeper. I just need to talk."

Ving seemed to recognize the voice and turned. "Detective." His voice was uncertain.

He looked exhausted, his eyes deep in their sockets, the foggy light wiping out all color, making him look as if he were projected in black and white.

"Where have you been, Tor?"

Grip shook his head. "I'm asking the questions now."

Ving nodded, his eyes moving from the gun to search Grip's eyes. Grip felt their cold assessment, but he kept eye contact.

"Why were you running Ben Linsky as an informant?"

Ving thought about this for a moment. Grip raised the gun higher, pointing it at Ving's forehead.

Ving kept his eyes on Grip's face. "You're going to tell me you've got nothing to lose."

"Do I?"

Frings could see the uncertainty in Ving's face. "Tor, you can always work something out. Nothing is done."

"That's what I'm trying to do now. Work something out."

"Okay. Why was I running Linsky? To keep tabs on the drug scene."

"That's not what it looked like to me. I saw the note he wrote you. It was all about meetings, associations, people."

"You have any informants that are a pain in the ass, Tor? You have any who think they know better than you what you want?"

"Like Nicky Patridis?"

"Patridis?" Ving seemed genuinely surprised.

Grip didn't want to get into a discussion of Patridis with Ving, so he asked, "Who killed Linsky?"

"I was hoping maybe you knew that. That's not an accusation, Tor. It's just that your sudden interest in him coincided so closely with his murder."

"He wasn't my snitch. I had nothing to do with him until this past week. The way I look at it, whoever took him out, it was probably someone he was informing on or maybe even someone he was informing to."

"What are you implying, Tor?"

"Nothing. Just telling you how I see it."

"I'd think you, of all people, would be aware of the lengths that these radicals would take."

"Right," Grip said, flatly.

"We caught the incident with our bugs. The boys in the room thought that it might have been a . . . sexual episode. Nobody spoke. There were no voices."

"Why are you telling me this?"

"You've got a gun."

Grip thought for a moment. "Who called the *News-Gazette* about the explosives heist and Kollectiv 61?"

"What?"

"Fuck." He didn't like that this question took Ving by surprise. It showed how little Grip understood.

"What do you want, Tor?"

"What do I want? I want to know what the fuck is going on."

"We can figure that out, detective. You put away the gun, we can go to the station, pull in whoever we need to talk to, and get to the bottom of this."

Grip didn't like the way that Ving was making it sound like they were on the same side, that Ving didn't have something to hide.

"I appreciate that, sir. But I don't think that makes sense for me."

"Don't overestimate the difficulty of your situation," Ving said.

But Grip was already walking away, his footsteps nearly silent.

63

FOR THE BETTER PART OF FOUR DECADES, FRINGS HAD REGULARLY DINED out with some of the most beautiful and glamorous women in the City. Being seen in public with Frings was tantamount, in some of the lowbrow rags, to an actress or model or singer having "arrived." Frings had enjoyed his time with nearly all of the women that he'd had any kind of lasting relationship with, but he'd never met one that he wanted to marry. This had been fine with him—it still was. But as he'd grown older, the attraction that he'd held for these women had understandably diminished, and the ones who still sought him out seemed so young to him now that he'd become suspicious of their motives. It no longer felt right. He didn't want to become pathetic in his own eyes. So in recent years, he had occasionally courted women whose age seemed more appropriate for a man of his years, but most of the time—like now—he was alone.

Which is why it was both strange and familiar to be dining with Joss Eastgate in an off-campus restaurant called Bardo's, which she'd suggested. Bardo's was the type of dive where Frings might conceivably dine alone, but certainly not a place he would have taken one of his high-profile paramours. It was small and dim and utterly lacking in elegance. The chairs and tables didn't match; the utensils were stained with rust; the floor was made from unfinished wood. But the food was good, and in the back a woman sang bossa nova tunes accompanied by a man with an acoustic guitar.

They made small talk during dinner, the conversation at one point drifting to Ben Linsky's death. Frings wasn't surprised to hear that Joss knew Ben. Ben, though unambiguously homosexual, did enjoy the company of beautiful women. She'd been among the pool of people that Linsky would often contact to form an audience for a poetry reading or a film screening, or whatever cultural event he was involved in.

Frings also asked her if she knew Andy Macheda, and she'd said that she did, but hadn't elaborated, and Frings got the feeling that she either didn't know him very well, didn't like him, or both. Which was why he didn't ask her about Sol—if Andy had provoked such an ambiguous reaction, he didn't think it would be fruitful to bring up Sol. Anyway, answers to these questions were not the point of the evening.

THEY WALKED THE FOUR BLOCKS FROM BARDO'S TO EBANKS'S HOUSE, Frings leaning heavily on his cane. His was especially aware of his limp as they made their slow progress. His left hand was in his pocket, and she'd put her hand in the crook of his elbow as they walked. Frings felt his years very acutely.

Joss knocked on the front door. Blaine, whom Frings had met in Ebanks's room on his prior visit, let them in, giving Frings a dull stare as they walked past.

Frings had never been in the warren of rooms at the back of Ebanks's house. Joss led him through rooms where people—mostly, Frings thought, Tech students—were smoking reefers and playing guitars, or listening to the hi-fi, or drawing with charcoal. She said hello to a few people as they made their way. Some of the kids seemed to recognize Frings, though no one said anything.

They eventually arrived in a small room toward the back right corner of the house. Joss turned on a floor lamp by the door, and the room was bathed in the soft light that filtered through a heavy lampshade. A card table was set in the middle of the room, with two chairs pulled up on opposite sides.

"We use this room as sort of the headquarters for the Drift," Joss said. "And this is the Drift Map. We've compiled all of the observations made during all of the Drifts onto it."

Frings took a look at the map on the table. Some of the City's prominent buildings were represented by small drawings, parks were depicted with token trees, and so on. The map had been heavily marked. Many streets were blacked out with pen, and some sections of the map—whole neighborhoods in some cases—had been cut out, leaving holes in the paper. Pieces of paper with notes were taped to various spots.

"So, the streets that have been inked out . . ." Frings said.

"We've taken out the places that we've found to be antithetical to the human need for individuality and creativity."

Frings nodded, and as he examined the map more closely, the pattern revealed itself. The Drifters had eliminated entirely neighborhoods that were dominated by large office buildings, and stripped away the City Center, with its new, generic high-rises. Areas that had given way to the Crosstown and the Riverside Expressway—really any part of the New City Project—were also gone. He felt as though he could have created this map himself, following the ideas he'd written about in *Alienation and the Modern City*. It seemed to Frings to be something of an empty exercise.

"I guess," Frings said, "that I don't understand what the point of this is."

"It's evidence. Evidence of what they are doing to the City, transforming it from a place that was built for people into one that is specifically designed for the needs of capital and machines."

Frings nodded. It sounded like she was repeating an explanation she'd rehearsed. He found it depressing, especially because he didn't disagree with her assessment.

"What are you going to do with it when you're finished?"

"Publish it. We were going to put it in *Prometheus*. But now that Ben's . . ." She paused for a moment, and it seemed to Frings that she wasn't sure what euphemism was appropriate for Linsky's murder. "Well, I think maybe you're the person to be in touch with about that right now."

Frings hadn't given the future of *Prometheus* any thought since Linsky's death, though he was sure that he didn't want to take on responsibility for it. He nodded noncommittally. She seemed to find this encouraging and leaned her head back so that her hair fell away from her face, and then tucked it behind her ears. Frings looked for the blocks that he remembered from the list Conroy had made of locations from Macheda's *Film 13*. Most, as would be expected, were not on this map. He found one, though, that had been inked out, and another that had been left untouched. He also noticed that what he had at first registered as a misplaced pen mark or a tiny piece of thread from someone's shirt, was, in fact, a single block marked in red ink. He followed the street with his eye until he found the name: Vilnius Street.

"What's this?" he asked, pointing to the spot.

"Oh, that. That's Vilnius Street. That block, we kind of have an understanding that it's off-limits."

"Do you know why?"

The question seemed to make her uncomfortable. "From what I've heard, there were some bad things that happened on that block. People thought that it might not be a great place to go when you're on LSD."

• • •

Drift Map (Detail)

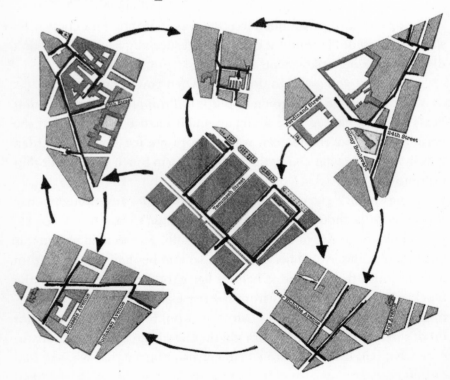

64

FRINGS PATIENTLY SAT THROUGH THE EDITORIAL MEETING. IT WAS A KIND of weekly penance, Frings thought, a discussion of recent events and future plans with an ideological tint that, in most cases, he couldn't agree with. Nobody listened to him, and he couldn't blame them. His suggestions and views were not consistent with the *News-Gazette*'s outlook. Littbarski had long ceased having to tell Frings to save his opinions for his column.

So he sat, listening to the rush of air through the vents, hidden by drop-in ceiling tiles, the mysterious starts and stops. It was pissing rain outside, the ever-shifting complexion of the gray mist providing Frings with a stoned fascination.

He thought about a conversation he'd had earlier that day with Eva Wise, the councilor, walking through Frings's neighborhood, bundled up against a wind that announced the immminent rain. The pedestrians after the morning rush were mostly wealthy women, doing errands or walking to have tea with friends.

"Look around you, Frank. You remember when you were writing that book of yours, how this neighborhood was? You wrote about it: businessmen, artists, bums, shopkeepers, Negroes, whites. What do you see now? Any Negroes? Artists? Poor people of any sort?"

Frings looked around and saw that this she was right. The neighborhood had always been changing, from its earlier days as a rough, racially mixed place, when gangs controlled whole blocks of group flats, and prostitutes plied their trade openly at all hours of the day and night. Over the years, the more intrepid of the almost-wealthy began to buy the old walk-ups, and blocks had been, depending on your viewpoint, won or lost. At some point, maybe ten to twelve years before, some critical mass had been reached—the process had accelerated, with more wealth advancing and more poverty retreating, until Frings saw the neighborhood as it was now.

"Cities change, Frank, not always the way you and I like them to, but they change. There's nothing to be done about it."

"There's a difference between changing and being changed, Eva. You don't have to preserve the City in amber. You have to let it happen. What we're doing now . . . the planning . . ."

"I know, I know. But the die is cast. It's happening. You want to turn back now, waste all that effort and money, spend more to undo it?"

Frings had shaken his head. He liked Eva. There'd been a time, he thought, when they'd shared a political philosophy, a vision of how you could effect change. Now, he felt, she'd compromised on both—even if her arguments remained strong, her positions defensible. But what really bothered him was her assumption that he was no longer as influential as he'd once been, and that this might have been the result of an inflexibility on his part, his ideology not changing with the times. Frings didn't care about the trappings of influence—he never had—but being able to shape the way the City thought about issues? This meant as much to him as anything.

"I've been in a new role," she continued, "one where I have to form policy, not just express my political views. It affects the way you think about things. I don't know if that's good or bad, but it is true. But you, you've continued on as you always have—and I commend you for that. You've become our radical, Frank. The establishment's radical who writes all these things that we would have said thirty years ago. You give us that little thrill of righteous anger."

She was so sharp on everything else that he couldn't help but find her assessment troubling—running, as it did, so counter to his sense of himself. He wondered if he, too, saw some truth in what she said, but decided that he didn't, that her words were mostly intended for herself, to allay her own unease about the compromises she'd made.

BACK IN HIS OFFICE, FRINGS WROTE "VILNIUS STREET" AT THE CENTER of a sheet of yellow legal paper. Andre LaValle had lived on Vilnius Street, and when questioned at his trial did nothing but repeat his address on the 5800 block. That block was marked in red on the Drift map and was considered off-limits. And Andy Macheda, he now realized, had included it as a location in his film. Did it all come back to LaValle?

Andre LaValle of the People's Union assassinates the police chief. This leads to the dissolution of the People's Union and, out of its ashes, the creation of Kollectiv 61. Was this Vilnius Street's significance? Was this why Macheda had included it in his film?

He'd needed to find Macheda again, and this time it would be much harder. After the last encounter, Frings couldn't imagine that Macheda would be eager to talk with him—that he'd be any more forthcoming about LaValle or Vilnius Street than he was about Sol.

And what about Joss's comment that bad things had happened on Vilnius Street? LaValle had murdered the chief far from the block where he'd grown up, so this, at least, couldn't be about him. All of these connections, and yet nothing seemed to cohere. It didn't add up. Still, as he exhaled, he could feel his pulse racing with the familiar predatory excitement: he knew he'd gained a toehold.

Frings took the elevator down to the second floor, riding the three stories with a janitor who'd come back damaged from Guadalcanal— twenty years of flinching, blinking, nerves. Frings told him a joke about a priest and a camel in the desert and left the elevator to the sound of the janitor's wheezy laughter.

WHEN THE NEWS HAD BOUGHT THE GAZETTE, THEY'D MERGED THEIR two archives, two newspapers now for each date since 1941, when the News had come on the scene. A few years ago, when he had some time on his hands, Frings had gone through the dates of a few major events, reading accounts through the two papers' ideological slants. The result had been even less enthusiasm for Littbarski's leadership.

The archives were overseen by a woman named Maude Riordan, as odd as she was efficient, who could seemingly recall the date of anything of note that had happened in the City, though she was oblivious to most other subjects. Rumors about her were pervasive enough that they'd even filtered down to his office. She'd been the mistress of Hastings Bridgewell, the owner of the News back in the '30s and '40s; she'd put her unusual mind to work for Bletchley Park during the War; she was Bridgewell's illegitimate sister; and so on. As far as Frings knew, none of these was remotely true, but their persistence among the *News-Gazette* staff spoke to the intense fascination she provoked within the building.

Frings found Maude Riordan, as he generally did, writing in a black ledger, her handwriting upright and fastidious. He'd snuck a peek at the ledger once when she was back in the newspaper stacks, finding to his pleasure that she was writing in some kind of cipher. He'd have been disappointed, he thought, if this hadn't been the case.

"Hello, Miss Riordan." He gave her a slanted grin, trying to intimate that he didn't consider her part of the wretched community of the newspaper. She was, as always, inscrutable.

"Mr. Frings, yes." Her eyes roamed furiously around her barren desktop.

"I was hoping you could maybe help me with something. I'm working on a story and I keep coming across Vilnius Street. Do you know Vilnius?"

She looked to the ceiling, her thinking tick. "Vilnius Street. Sure. Of course."

"I don't know anything about it, but I'm trying to find out if something happened there, probably around the 5800 block and before 1960. You have any ideas?"

She crooked her index finger, gnawed on the second joint, another sign that she was very focused. "1958. 1958. July or August." She was mumbling to herself, ignoring Frings's presence. "July or August. July. Late July." She took in a deep, sudden breath. "Late July, but the story ran in early August? July 29?" She snapped suddenly back to the present, fixing Frings with a satisfied, somehow unsettling stare. "I think I know. Give me an hour?"

65

WHEN FRINGS RETURNED TO THE NEWSPAPER ARCHIVES AN HOUR AND A half later, Maude Riordan was drinking something that smelled like tea made with kerosene. Frings blinked at the odor.

"Something in your eye, Mr. Frings?" Maude asked, her face not betraying any humor.

Frings smiled weakly at her and took a seat.

She sipped her tea, looking at something over Frings's shoulder like a cat staring out a window. She was going to make Frings ask.

"Miss Riordan, did you turn up anything?"

She puckered her mouth, dabbed her lips with a napkin that she then folded and placed neatly on her desk. "There were a few interesting days at the end of July 1958 on the 5800 block of Vilnius Street." She waited again.

"How so?"

"The article ran in both the *News* and the *Gazette* on August 2, so I'm fairly sure that somebody asked the press to hold off on the story. When the stories did run, they were essentially the same—they were probably taken from a written statement sent out by the Department of Health."

"Department of Health?"

She smiled the way she often did when she was privy to a piece of interesting knowledge. "The 5800 block was quarantined for three days: July 29, 30, and 31. The quarantine was lifted on August 1."

"Quarantined for what reason?" He heard the scuttling of tiny feet in the ducts above them.

She slid him a newspaper folded open to a middle page, an edition of the *News*. "An unspecified virus."

He skimmed the article, finding nothing beyond what she had told him. No mention of the reason for concern about the virus—no one infected, no contaminated water, nothing. The block had been quarantined for three days, the quarantine was over, that was it.

"Not much of a story."

She shook her head.

"And there wasn't any follow up?"

"On that? Would you spend your time on it, Mr. Frings? Would you even remember it three months on?"

Frings frowned, conceding this point. "But you don't seem so convinced about it."

She narrowed her eyes. "I don't?"

"Not from where I stand."

She thought about this for a minute. Frings wondered what she was weighing, whether she was factoring in some assessment she'd made of him.

"It seem right to you, Mr. Frings?"

"How do you mean?"

"Quarantining a block? Ending the quarantine and the problem's gone away? I don't know that I've heard of a block being quarantined in the City. If there was one, I expect there'd have been a good reason, not the kind of thing where they say 'sorry, excuse me, it's over' and that's that. That's what I mean, Mr. Frings."

Frings nodded, thinking along similar lines. "You have any ideas about what was going on?"

She shook her head in frustration. "I poked around some, tried to get the scent"—she demonstrated by inhaling deeply, her whole face scrunching with the action—"but I didn't find anything."

"We'd need more information."

She nodded. "From where I stand."

Frings thanked her.

"I expect"—she said—"that you should feel welcome down here if you find out anything more about this."

"I expect so."

66

THE NIGHT HAD GONE VERY COLD WITH THE SETTING OF THE SUN, AND Frings's knee ached as he made his way home. His fingers were stiff inside his glove where they grabbed the head of his cane. People passed, blowing clouds of steam, shoulders hunched against the chill. He thought about the three days of quarantine on Vilnius Street, kept coming back to the same thing, but it seemed far-fetched. He must, he thought, be missing something.

As he ascended the dozen steps to his door, he felt suddenly old. He wanted a drink and then sleep, to wake up in the morning with a clearer mind, more energy.

He unlocked his door and heard *Le Nozze di Figaro* on the record player wafting in from the living room. He froze, instinct telling him to step outside to the street, find a cop. But whoever was in there had announced his presence, was trying *not* to surprise him. He hesitated, felt both scared, and dumb for feeling scared. The latter overwhelmed the former, and he walked through the short hall and into the living room. Sitting in one of the high-backed upholstered chairs was a young man with his hair cut very short, hooded eyes, clothes that he seemed to have borrowed from someone considerably heavier. On the coffee table lay a gun.

"Sol." He was thinner, exhausted, his hair shorn, but Frings recognized him.

Sol got out of his chair, keeping close to the gun on the table. "Frank." They shook hands. "I've been waiting for a while. You have some great records."

"You like opera?"

Sol nodded.

"How'd you—"

"Is this really what you want to talk about, Frank? Right now?"

Frings nodded, accepting the point. He normally didn't babble— nerves. "I'm getting a drink. You?"

Sol shook his head. Frings fixed himself a whisky on the rocks.

"I heard you were looking for me," Sol said, no malice in his voice.

Frings took a sip. "That's right. Your grandfather's been worried."

Sol sighed. "Papouse. I thought about getting in touch with him a few times, sending a postcard or something. Never got to it."

"Where've you been?"

"Here. The City."

"Doing?"

Sol shook his head.

"Okay, Sol. I've done what I was supposed to do, found you and you seem okay, though you could stand to put on some pounds. Why don't you meet with your grandfather? Have dinner or coffee or something? You owe him that, don't you think? Put his mind at ease?"

"I can't."

"Why not."

"I love him, Frank, but I don't know if I can trust him."

"Trust him to what?"

"Not set me up."

"Sol," Frings said, exasperated. "Set you up for what?"

In Sol's stare Frings could see the manic intensity that he'd possessed even as a little boy, taking in everything with a startling concentration.

"Okay," Frings said. "Can I ask you about something else."

"You can ask." Dubious.

"When you were at the Tech, you volunteered for a study run by Simon Ledley."

Sol's body tensed at this. "I'm not sure I'd call it volunteering."

"Why's that?"

Sol stood, took the gun, walked to the window but didn't look out. "I was asked to participate. Me, several other kids."

"Kids you knew?"

Sol shook his head. "No. A couple I knew a little. Loners, guys that kind of kept to themselves. Like me."

"What was the study, Sol?"

"The study? I don't know. I'm not sure what they were trying to accomplish."

"But what happened? What did it entail?"

"Tests. Lots of tests—written tests—that they paid me to take."

"What kind of tests?"

"Psych tests. Personality tests. IQ tests. Shit like that."

"Okay."

The record reached the end and the needle bounced rhythmically off the center. Sol walked over, turned off the record player, replaced the arm on its stand.

"They had me write, like, a personal statement, a philosophy of life, what I believed in. It took a couple of sessions, and there was an assistant that helped me with it, posed questions, that kind of thing. Prompts, I guess."

"You remember his name?"

Sol shook his head. "Then they started giving me the drug."

"What drug?"

"LSD, I think. Maybe mescaline. They didn't specify. They'd give me the drug and take me into a room and then they'd do things like ask me to tell them when a minute had passed."

"How'd that go?"

He chuckled ruefully. "I'd either forget the question before the minute was up—you know, get distracted by something—or else I'd nail it, right to the second. They'd have me estimate distances or try to throw a ball into a bin, or they'd show me ink stains, ask me what I thought they looked like. Things like that."

"But there was more, right?"

Sol didn't seem to question how Frings knew this. "Sure. That was just the warm up."

"Hold on. Before you go further, these rooms where this project was taking place, were they in Bristol Hall?"

Sol raised his eyebrows. "Yeah, actually, they were."

"Sorry. Go on."

"Why the fuck am I telling you about this?"

"Why not? Why'd you come here?"

"I told you, I heard you were looking for me."

"But you came to see me. Why, Sol?"

Sol was silent, thinking.

"You knew we'd talk about this, right? That's why you came. You didn't come so you could see Panos. So why else?"

Sol paused for a moment, probably gathering his thoughts. "Fuck. Okay. One day they said they were going to have a guy ask me about my philosophy, the one I'd written up for them. So, sure. No problem. But they gave me the drug first, waited until it really kicked in, and this time they'd given me *a lot*. I mean, you can't really tell when you take it, 'cause it's just a sugar cube, but you can definitely tell when it hits you. So," he paused for a moment, trying to remember what he'd been saying. "Right. They took me to this one room that I don't think I'd been in before, and it was weird because it was all pitch dark except for this chair that was in a spotlight. I couldn't see anybody behind the light, but I could hear people whispering back there.

"This one guy, he must have read my paper because he starts asking me questions about it, you know, a couple of basic ones at first—

what did I mean by this, is this what I meant by that—then he starts in on really dissecting it, arguing against what I'd written, the things I believed. And he was good at it, too, really made his case."

Sol paused.

Sol's account tracked with Lester Finch's. This was Ledley's experiment—a systematized routine—giving the subjects the drug and then undermining their sense of self. Frings asked, "What did you think about this? How did you respond?"

Sol cocked his head. "You ever taken LSD or mescaline or anything like that?"

"No."

"Well then it's going to be hard to understand how it felt, because it's so tied into the drug. The setup itself, it was the kind of thing that really fucks with you when you're on the drug. The light, the people that you can't see, the talking that you can kind of hear, and your mind can get really turned wrong by that, it can run away with thoughts. So, it's not a great situation to begin with. But when you add that guy and the hostility, it's like a waking nightmare. This went on for a while, too, man, and it got to the point where it broke me." Sol stared at his hands.

"What happened?"

"I freaked out, couldn't take it. They tried to ask me some questions, I think, but you can't think when you're like that. You're run over by what you imagine."

"Okay," Frings said, "I get it. What happened after that?"

"Nothing. That was it. They just let me go." Sol was rubbing his hands aggressively, his discomfort tangible.

Frings nodded. "Do you know what happened to the other people in the project?"

Sol sighed. "I heard a couple of them killed themselves, I think. I don't know. You know, they must be fucked up. I don't see how they aren't."

Frings nodded. "What was the point of this study? Do you know?"

"Me? How the hell should I know? Do you know? 'Cause it sounds like you know something, and if you know what the point was, I'd really like to hear it. I've been trying to figure that out for a while, now."

"I'm sorry, Sol, I don't. I wish I did. And I wish I could help you. I hope that I can at some point—maybe soon. But you can help me. What did it *seem* like they were trying to accomplish. Do you have *any* idea?"

"To really fuck with people's heads? Listen, Frank, I've read about brainwashing or whatever, but this was worse, this was different. They were destroying people's minds. I don't know, but it had its effect on me, man. I didn't go into the Tech completely together, you know, because of what happened . . . but the study, I haven't been the same since."

"What do you mean?"

"What do I mean? I mean I can't concentrate. I'm hit with these periods, like I'm on the drug even though I haven't taken it. I've read a lot, Frank, trying to figure this out. I've read about madness, about how they thought people were haunted by whatever, and I know what that is. It's like a presence. It doesn't leave. I know the depths that this life can offer."

Frings rubbed both hands over his face to clear his head. Sol was getting agitated. Frings glanced at the gun on the coffee table.

"You know Andy Macheda?"

This seemed to catch Sol by surprise. "No. I mean, I did."

"How about Andre LaValle?"

"LaValle? I knew him a little, back in the People's Union days."

"You were in the People's Union?"

"Sure. A lot of people were, I guess. It's not like you joined or anything. You just kind of participated. But you know that it fell apart."

"And some of those people formed Kollectiv 61."

"Kollectiv 61, huh? You ever met anyone from Kollectiv 61?"

"Can't say that I have."

Sol snorted a laugh. "There's no Kollectiv 61."

"Come on, Sol. The graffiti, the vandalism, the manifesto? It doesn't just appear out of the blue."

"It's bullshit. Look, Frank, Kollectiv 61 is nothing, it's a slogan, a way of making a bunch of pissed-off heemies look like a group. It isn't real."

Frings wasn't sure what to make of this. He was worried that Sol wouldn't continue talking much longer. He seemed to be visibly losing energy. Frings wondered when he'd last eaten.

"Did you know Ben Linsky?"

"Everyone knew Ben Linsky. Did I know him well? No."

"What do you think about what happened to him?"

"That he was murdered?"

"That he was murdered and someone wrote 'snitch' on his wall."

Sol shrugged. "It's too bad, him being murdered. Someone thought he was a snitch, decided to do something about it. I don't know what else to think about it."

"But you don't know who might have done it?"

Sol gave Frings a hard stare. "Frank, I like you. I respect what you've done, and you've inspired a lot of the heemie crowd and all that. But I don't dig the fucking suspicion you're throwing at me."

Frings held Sol's eyes, trying to project calm. "I'm not suspicious of you, Sol. You live in that world and I don't. That's it. I just wonder if you have any thoughts."

"I don't know anything about it, Frank. Sorry." He leaned over and grabbed the pistol. Frings's heart raced.

"Don't worry," Sol said wearily. "I just need to go."

"Listen, Sol, do you want something to eat or a place to sleep? I won't tell Panos, and I won't ask any more questions, but you need to get some rest."

Sol fixed Frings with a long, searching look. "I appreciate it, Frank, but I've got to split."

Frings walked Sol to the door, leaning on his cane, his knee almost impossible to bend.

"You're getting old, Frank," Sol said.

"I am." Frings tried to keep his voice light.

"What do you think of Kollectiv 61?"

"I thought they didn't exist."

"I mean the things that get pinned on Kollectiv 61. It seems like the kind of thing you'd like. Fighting against the New City Project, just like you talk about in your book."

"As long as no one gets hurt, I guess."

"No one gets hurt?" Sol exploded. "How're you going to make any change if no one gets hurt? Is that where you really draw the line, Frank? With everything that's going on, the fucking subjugation of the people, you're worried about a few people getting hurt? I thought you might be more of a revolutionary than that."

They were at the door.

"I think"—Frings said carefully—"that you have to be very careful that what you're doing is worth whatever pain you cause. Some things are, some things aren't. Sometimes the goal is noble but what you're doing isn't . . . efficient."

Sol seemed to think this over.

"How do I get in touch with you?" Frings asked.

"You don't. I'll get in touch with you, or I won't."

Frings spoke softly, trying to make his compassion tangible to Sol. "What's going on Sol? What are you up to?"

Sol looked at him, and Frings was reminded of Sol ten years ago, under suspicion for his parents' murder, giving nothing away, even to the people who were on his side.

"It was good seeing you." And then, as he crossed the threshold, he said, "What am I up to? I'm doing your work, Frank."

67

THE ARES CLUB WAS REALLY ON TONIGHT, MORE PEOPLE THAN USUAL, chairs lined up facing the stage, and a different singer—older, blond, husky voice. Dorman nursed a beer, held his head in his hands, massaged his temples with his thumbs. He didn't like the club when it was like this—when it was different from what he had come to expect. He found himself on edge in the one place where he could ever relax.

This morning, drinking coffee and choking down runny eggs at a diner near his apartment, he'd puzzled over Zwieg's approach to the missing explosives. He did not seem to be expending much effort towards finding them. As far as Dorman could tell, Grip was the only one actively on the case, and even he had said that the murders of the guards were beyond his purview, which seemed . . . well, it seemed a bit half-assed. Dorman understood the advantages in keeping the investigation small, keeping it out of the headlines. But from what he knew of Grip—and it was mostly reputation—it seemed that there were plenty of other men on the Force who would be far less likely to draw attention to themselves.

A woman approached his table, holding a wine bottle in one hand and two glasses by the stems in the other. She was tall and thin-shouldered, dark complected—a narrow face, like a cat's. She smiled at him. "May I accompany you?"

Dorman looked up at her. She was beautiful.

"I usually sit with Anastasia."

The woman smiled apologetically. "I'm afraid she's not at the club this evening."

Dorman closed his eyes. He was almost desperate to see Anastasia, to talk to someone familiar, whom he could trust. He opened his eyes to find the woman still waiting. She raised her eyebrows. He nodded, moving aside, anxiety raging.

THEY FINISHED THE BOTTLE OF WINE. DORMAN WATCHED THE CROWD with drowsy eyes while the woman—her name, she said, was Fatima —leaned against him, her head on his shoulder, her eyes closed.

He felt rooted there, overcome by a kind of inertia, as if by staying where he was he could stop time and the momentum of events. Canada had called him in to his office before lunch. It seemed that Reuther had made good on his promise to take his case over Dorman's head. Dorman doubted that Canada ever actually experienced glee, but the closest he came was when he was able to exercise his power against someone who didn't understand his capabilities, or the extent of his ruthlessness.

"He characterized," Canada said of Reuther, "his conversation with you. He told me that he thought I would be more reasonable."

Canada's mouth was contorted into something between a sneer and a smirk. Dorman waited patiently to hear the outcome.

"I slashed his neighborhood's take by half and the others' by a quarter."

Dorman nodded, though he didn't think this was a wise thing to do. It was better to let these things go—don't concede anything, but don't be punitive. It just courted trouble. Canada, of course, wasn't concerned about that kind of trouble. He would just crush that, too—or, in reality, get Dorman to do it for him.

Canada's mood had seemed so good that Dorman had broached the subject of Trochowski wearing a wire at the bar near St. Stanislaw's.

Canada's demeanor instantly changed. "How do you know he was wearing a wire?"

"I didn't like the way he was talking. It seemed like he was trying to lead me into saying something. So I ripped his shirt open."

"Have you run into this again—somebody wearing a wire?"

"No," Dorman said, then amended it to, "I don't know."

Canada thought for a moment before speaking again. "This is not something for you to worry about. I'll take care of this."

He'd found the words unsettling—almost threatening—though, looking back on it, it seemed as though he should have been reassured. But even now, at the Ares Club, the memory unnerved him.

HE RUBBED HIS PALMS AGAINST HIS EYES.

He thought about Anastasia, wondered where she was tonight, what she was doing. He needed some sleep to clear his head so he could think this through. He tapped gently on Fatima's shoulder to wake her up, and moved to slide out of the booth.

THE WIND HAD PICKED UP, BLOWING AN EARLY SNOW NEARLY HORIZONTAL, eddies formed by the skyscraper canyons whipping the snow into wild vortices under the street lights. Grip shook from the cold. His forehead hurt just above his eyes—an intense, precisely located pain. The streets were empty, and he left footprints in a quarter-inch of virgin snow. He saw Ben Linsky's building a block down. The promise of warmth had him picking up his pace.

He pushed the buzzer for the manager, waited. Despite the static on the intercom, the weariness in the voice was clear.

"What is it?"

"Detective Torsten Grip. Police."

"Yeah?"

"I need to have a look at the tape room."

"I didn't hear nothing about that."

Grip put some menace in his voice. "You think we need to clear this shit with you?"

"No, it's . . ."

"Unlock the fucking door. Bring a key so you can let me in the room."

"Yeah, okay."

This had been a guess on Grip's part, though not a blind one. There had to be a place where the bugs in Linsky's apartment were monitored, somewhere the wires led. They could have been transmitting to a truck on the street, but when he'd touched the bug the last time he was in Linsky's apartment, the cops had already been inside the building. So he was pretty sure there was a room, and there was nothing to lose by checking—even if he wasn't optimistic that he would find anything useful.

An older guy appeared in the hall, his hair sticking off to one side, his body thick above skinny, bowed legs. He walked to the door and stopped. Grip pressed his badge to the glass. The guy opened the door.

The heat came as a relief to Grip. His ears burned with the temperature change. He brushed the snow from his coat.

"Nasty out there," the old guy said.

"The fuck would you know about it?" Grip said, and the guy looked down. "Come on, I need you to open that door for me."

The old guy led Grip down a flight of stairs into an airless basement. The floor vibrated with the furnace's hum. It must have been close to ninety degrees down there.

"Keep waiting for you guys to come back, finish clearing the place out." The old guy unlocked a windowless door, reached inside to flip the light switch.

Grip stepped in. The place was small, clearly a utility room. A little table and two chairs were pushed against a wall under a chart of some sort. A small hole had been drilled in the wall above the table, and wires ran into the hole and presumably up to Ben Linsky's apartment. This was one of the problems with the fiefdoms—sloppy follow-up, a lack of accountability. He didn't think anyone would be coming back here soon, maybe ever.

Grip turned to the old guy. "Okay, you've done what you need to do. Piss off."

The guy slumped away, and Grip closed the door behind him. He took off his wet jacket, hung it over one of the chairs, then removed his shoes and his socks. The concrete floor was warm, and he felt the sting as sensation returned to his toes.

THE CHART ON THE WALL SEEMED TO BE A CALENDAR WITH THE NAMES of the cops on duty at specific times, along with a number that Grip knew from experience referred to the identification number of the tape recorded during that period. He thought that maybe he'd run across a name that he was familiar with and was rewarded when he saw the name Albertsson, Wayne's clean-cut young friend. He thought about this for a moment, trying to remember the conversation they'd had in Crippen's, how Albertsson had kept his mouth shut. His jaw tightened. He checked his watch, just after two in the morning. Crippen's would be empty by the time he made it over there.

He searched through the few folders that were left on the table. He found blank log sheets, blank expense forms, a couple of well-fingered smut magazines. He sat, stiff at first, but his body quickly relaxed. The warmth in the room and the hum of the lights seemed to suck the consciousness from him. In less than five minutes he was asleep, chin on chest.

69

WHEN HE'D AWOKEN, DISORIENTED IN THE BRIGHT, WARM ROOM IN THE
basement of Ben Linsky's building, it had crossed Grip's mind that he
could stay there for a while, use it as a sanctuary. It was tempting to
keep his head down, think things through, get some relief from the
moment-to-moment anxiety. But he'd checked his watch, found that
it was nearly ten in the morning, and faced an unpleasant reality: yes,
this place was probably safe, but he couldn't afford to let time pass.
He had a sense for these things, and that sense was telling him that
everything was about to start unfolding quickly. The longer he waited,
the more he risked falling behind.

Now he sat on a bed in a grim room in the White Rhino, drinking
a cup of stale coffee floating a healthy dose of whisky. Ed Wayne sat
in one of the ratty orange chairs, drinking his whisky straight. The
wig that he often wore was gone, replaced by the porkpie hat, his
head looking enormous over his narrow, sloping shoulders. The light
of the bare ceiling bulb seemed to highlight his grayish yellow teeth.
Grip couldn't keep his eyes off them, stealing glances. He again asked
himself what was wrong with Wayne.

"You've really stepped in it this time," Wayne slurred, his smirk
pissing off Grip. "I don't see you getting out of this one."

"Yeah, we'll see."

"I don't know where you have friends, 'cept for maybe me, and
you don't seem to be exactly nurturing that one as we speak."

"Fuck off."

Wayne laughed, drew in a wet breath. "See what I mean, Tor?"

Grip shook his head, bit down on his anger. He shifted his gun
around in his pocket, rubbed the safety with his thumb. He saw
Wayne watching the movement in his pocket and took his hand out.
Grip wondered if he was nervous. He didn't think so, but he sure as
hell wasn't sure what he was doing.

Wayne kicked back his whisky and stared across at Grip with
filmy eyes. Grip handed him the flask. Wayne poured himself another

drink. When they weren't talking, the sounds of the whores and their johns were audible. Grip felt the adrenaline rise with his annoyance. He would have kicked down every one of those doors, braced the johns, maybe taken their licenses, fucked with them in some way. The toilet ran ceaselessly in the bathroom. He shook his head.

"Troubled mind?"

Grip sneered, trying not to let Wayne wind him up. But he was on a knife's edge, and Wayne knew it.

The knock came out of nowhere. Wayne's eyes darted to the door, about as startled a reaction as Wayne was capable of. He walked over and put his hand on the knob.

"Albertsson?"

Grip could hear the voice from the other side. "Who the fuck do you think it is? Open up."

Wayne let Albertsson in and locked the door behind him. Albertsson stood motionless, trying to make sense of Grip's presence. Grip moved quickly, pulling the gun from his pocket, training it straight at Albertsson's forehead.

"Ah shit, Tor," Wayne said. "Why does everything have to be hard with you?"

Grip ignored him. "Pull out your gun with your left hand and put it on the floor."

Albertsson did as he was told, grinning uncertainly, and Grip nodded him to the bed. Grip took a step back, leaned against the wall, his gun still on Albertsson, but where he could also see Wayne.

Albertsson looked at Wayne, who shrugged: "I told you Tor was a little dim, but he makes up for it with unthinking aggression."

Albertsson turned back to Grip, his eyes moving from the gun to Grip's face and back again, unhurried, as if checking to make sure he understood the situation right.

"We're on the same side, Detective. You don't need the piece."

"That right? What side is that?"

Albertsson didn't say anything. Grip gave him credit for keeping his composure.

"You know where I was last night?"

Albertsson shrugged. How could he know?

"Ben Linsky's building, down in the basement."

Albertsson nodded.

"You guys had a decent set-up down there."

"It worked alright."

"Why were you guys running bugs on Linsky?"

"I don't know. I'm a soldier. I do what I'm told, Detective, you know that."

"Right. So who's the lead on this? Ving?"

"That's right," Albertsson said eagerly, "Ving."

The conversation stopped for a moment and the sound of a whore with her john was suddenly audible through the ceiling. Grip raised his gun to the ceiling, jaw clenched, and just stopped himself from firing. He brought the gun back to Albertsson.

Wayne chuckled. "You got to get a hold of yourself, Tor."

Grip glanced sideways at him, heart pounding. Back to Albertsson. "You do any other stakeouts for Ving?"

"Like Linsky? No. I do some pickups, though. Get reports passed to me by some of the other grasses."

"Like who?"

"Fucked if I know. I don't look at the stuff. I wouldn't know Linsky except I had to listen to him all the time. He'd bring men back to his apartment, and I'd have to listen to that, too. You think the shit upstairs gets aggravating, you should—"

"I get it. So where do you get these reports?"

"Different places. It's not as secret as you'd think. I just meet whoever it is in a park or on a corner or whatever and they give me a package and I walk away. Not a big deal. Either that or they put an envelope in the crook of a tree or a trash barrel, something like that. I pick it up. I do it all the time. I'm doing one tonight, if you want to come along."

Grip wasn't sure what to make of this. Albertsson certainly seemed sincere.

"Listen, Detective, I appreciate that you think you need to have the gun on me and all that. I've heard the rumors at the station. But you don't need it with me. I'm happy for somebody to take those motherfuckers down. I'm serious. You and me and Ed, here, we're all on the same side, man. You think I like dealing with these fucking heemies? You want to take them down, I'll help you out, long as you keep my name out of it, you know? Still got to pay the bills."

Jesus, this kid was stupid. Where the hell did Wayne find these guys? But there was a possibility here. Find a second snitch, maybe figure out what Kraatjes was up to, and why Zwieg thought it made him vulnerable.

70

THE BLOCK SEEMED STRANGELY BARREN. THE TREES HAD LOST ALL OF their leaves, standing now like scarecrows in neat intervals along the quiet street. An elderly woman walked a small dog wrapped in a red tartan sweater. Frings smiled at her as he walked by and received an elegant bend of the head in return.

The City was a fast place, and Frings was acclimated to that rhythm—hadn't, in fact, known any other. But at times like this it seemed uncontrollable. So many things going on, so many contingencies that he needed to navigate.

Sol's appearance had changed things. Frings had now done, technically, what Panos had asked. Sol was alive. Frings had made contact. He could report back to Panos and everything would be finished. But seeing the nervous, unstable kid the previous night had convinced Frings that there was more to all of this. Sol was involved in something.

FRINGS FOUND THE BROWNSTONE IN THE MIDDLE OF THE BLOCK, A PLACE he hadn't visited in more than a decade. He walked up the steps, pushed the doorbell, heard the clang inside, waited. He was about to ring the bell again when he heard the bolts slipping open, and the door opened in. An elderly man appeared, skin pale and thin, his face nearly hollow beneath his cheekbones.

The man smiled quietly. "Mr. Frings."

"Hello, Mr. Puskis." Puskis, Frings figured, must have been in his late eighties or even nighties, and had been living alone in this house for the past thirty years.

Puskis opened the door wider to let Frings in to the dim hallway. The air was stagnant, smelled of decaying leather and steeping tea. With short shuffling steps, Puskis led him down the carpeted hall and through a door to what had once been a living room, but was now a kind of study—elegant old tables neatly stacked with reams of paper and an improbable volume of newspapers. Puskis offered Frings a seat in an upholstered easy chair and sat down opposite him.

"Tell me the reason for my good fortune." Puskis's voice was faint but clear. Frings felt self-conscious as he thought how long it had been since he'd paid a visit. And just as last time, he was not here for social reasons—he needed information.

Puskis seemed to intuit these thoughts from Frings's hesitation. "I don't seek company, Mr. Frings, but it is a pleasure to see you when you do visit."

The wall behind Puskis was hung with masks—African, Chinese, American Indian. Through the windows, Frings could see to the backyard, where plants done in by a killing frost lay fading in a garden plot sited on a small mound.

Frings nodded. "I thought that maybe you could help me with something."

Puskis opened his hands as an invitation to explain. He had at one time been the archivist for the City's mammoth repository of criminal files. After the madness of 1935, he'd retreated to this house, where he kept on with his obsessive accrual and organization of information as best he could, given his current resources.

"Vilnius Street. In 1958 there was a disease scare. They quarantined the 5800 block for two days. Do you remember that?"

Puskis scratched at his temple with a yellowed talon of a fingernail. "I do. Interesting, that block."

Frings perched forward. "How so?"

Puskis pushed himself out of his chair, walked to a stack of papers. Frings noticed that they'd been arranged neatly, their edges carefully squared.

"I've been continuing my work"—Puskis said—"chronicling the

City's affairs, though I've found it necessary to change my methods. I have only the newspapers and other public records now, but this has still proven fruitful." As Frings watched, Puskis sifted through a pile of handwritten papers, flipping the pages face-down after he'd looked at them. "Vilnius Street. Curious the correlations." He found a sheet that he picked up to examine more closely. He replaced it on the stack, pulled it along with four or five other sheets and returned to his chair. Puskis read through the information on the sheets, his face grim.

"The correlations?" Frings prompted.

Puskis seemed distracted. "Mr. Frings, I fear my manners have atrophied during my hermetic existence. May I offer you a drink? My predecessor, Mr. Van Vossen, left me with a liquor that produces an interesting intoxication."

Frings shook his head. "Thank you, Mr. Puskis. But the correlations?"

"Yes," Puskis said, showing the slightest hint of disappointment. "I have collected and organized obituary notices, news stories, government reports. As you say, there was a two-day quarantine followed by a statistically anomalous series of events that I have documented in these pages."

"What kinds of events?"

"Suicides at five times the rate of the rest of the City. Six counts of spousal murder. I don't have official figures for consignment to mental hospitals, but the anecdotal evidence suggests that they, too, are at surprisingly high levels."

"It's like after the quarantine they all went mad."

Puskis shrugged. "While I wouldn't go so far as to say that they *all* went mad, I agree that, as a whole, something seems to have affected the psyches of those people."

Frings nodded, rubbed his face with his hands.

"Another thing"—Puskis said—"Andre LaValle, the man who murdered the chief of police in 1960? He was from that same block."

Frings nodded. "Yes. I've heard that."

"The City"—Puskis brushed his lips with a thumb—"the City is a composite of anomalies, Mr. Frings. Any generality that you make breaks down as you apply it to more specific populations. Suicide rates, incarceration rates, anything like that, you don't expect smaller samples to conform. But in this case, the deviation is highly pronounced and seems to apply to the full range of pathological behavior. And these anomalies begin with the brief quarantine."

"The quarantine is the key."

"That is, I think, a valid conclusion."

THERE WAS SOMETHING ELSE HE WANTED TO ASK PUSKIS, BUT, FEELING self-conscious, he'd waited until the pair had shared a pot of strong, smoky tea. Puskis had asked him about various conflicts within the City's government, many of which didn't make it into the papers. Frings was happy to help—the merger was now many years old, but he still felt affronted by the collapse of a newspaper that had once been so great, and so honest. Puskis, he knew, was savvy enough to know that he couldn't rely on what was on the page, so Frings filled in as many details as he could.

"Mr. Puskis," he said as he stood to leave. "I was wondering . . . I was wondering if you might know about something else."

"What would that be?"

"I was talking with a friend the other day, and he made a comment that Will Ebanks—you know who he is?"

"Oh, yes," Puskis said.

"My friend claimed that Ebanks is not as wealthy as, well, as I had figured. Do you know anything about that?"

Puskis frowned slightly, as if he was saddened by anybody's misfortune. "I don't have any real knowledge, though I remember that his father suffered heavy business losses toward the end. He had real estate throughout the Hollows, and those buildings dropped to almost nothing in value after the Great War. I don't know how that affected the family wealth, but it must have been damaging. I'm sorry I can't be more helpful."

"No, that's plenty helpful," Frings said.

71

NOT MUCH HAD CHANGED INSIDE THE PHARAOH'S CLUB IN THE DECADE and a half since Frings had last visited. The library lights were dim, covered in heavy shades, but you could still see the shabbiness of the old chairs—graying with smoke, fraying with age. Cigarette and pipe smoke mixed pungently in the warm room. The youngest person here, Frings thought, was well into his fifties. When Frings had first visited, some twenty years ago, the place had been alive, filled with the young, the wealthy, and the ambitious. Now, in a very real way, it was dying.

Frings watched a well-fed man with a fringe of gray hair wrapped around his skull labor in his direction. The man wore a corduroy jacket and old wool pants above leather slippers. Frings was used to seeing him with a pipe, but he didn't have it today. The man wove between tables, where men in sweaters played cards, and chairs in groups or alone, their occupants engrossed in books or just staring off into nothing.

Frings stood, shook the man's hand. "Good to see you, Silas."

Silas Birchall had owned Pharaoh's for the last two dozen years. He came from money and possessed the careless charm of someone who had never had to worry about his future.

"And you, Frank." They sat in chairs placed at angles to a low teak table. "Look at us," Birchall chuckled. "We can barely get in and out of our chairs."

Frings smiled, though he failed to see the humor.

"You know we're thinking of selling the building. Big offers on the table to make this place a nightclub or apartments."

"Would you buy another building someplace else?" It was hard to imagine the club inhabiting another building—this place had so much history.

Birchall gave a laugh. "Look around. How many years do you think this club has left? Ten? Twenty? Maybe we'll rent a place, a place for some of the members who don't have anywhere else to go, but . . ." He waved his hand around, noncommittally. "It's the Crosstown, Frank. We'll be right off it, a valuable location. Sell the property, pay off the Club's debts, offer some cash to the members." He lowered his voice. "Some of these men could really use it. A lot of these families, their wealth has evaporated over the years."

Frings nodded. "That might be what I'm here to talk to you about."

"What's that?"

"Evaporating wealth."

Birchall narrowed his eyes, not liking what he'd heard. "Okay," he said cautiously.

"Will Ebanks."

"Please, Frank."

Frings rubbed his nose, feeling weary. "You know how Will is, or was. You just said that there are a lot of people here who seem as though they have money but maybe don't."

Birchall sighed.

"I think that Ebanks might be in a situation like that," Frings pressed.

"You know these things are private."

"I know. But believe me: this is important. You know Will and I are friends." He realized, as he said it, that he was no longer convinced this was still true.

Birchall stroked his chin absently. Frings looked around the room, and wondered what the members would do if the club moved.

Birchall sighed and looked down. "I suppose I owe you."

"Don't look at it that way."

"Still . . ."

"It's important, Silas. I wouldn't be here if it wasn't."

"Will joined Pharaoh's because of his father," Birchall began, "who was president immediately before me. I don't need to tell you that Will was a bit out of step with many of the members, but he was not without his charms and was generally accepted as another of the eccentrics here. The reality, though, is that he has never paid dues in his life. He's been kept on as something of a legacy, you see. Too embarrassing to ask him to leave, in truth.

"The family wealth was tied to real estate in the Hollows and when that entire neighborhood fell apart, they lost the bulk of their money. They lived off some savings and then, little by little, they sold possessions. Did you ever go to the house Ebanks grew up in?"

Frings shook his head.

"I expect not. In the end, most of the rooms were bare. When his father died, Will was left with essentially nothing."

"That house that he lives in now—"

"The one by the Tech?"

"That one. Do you know how he acquired it?"

Birchall shook his head. "No."

"From talking to you, it seems like he probably couldn't afford to buy it. Is it lent to him?"

Birchall shrugged. "I honestly do not know. It's not really something that I've ever given much thought."

At this, Frings nodded slowly, things starting to clarify in his mind.

72

GRIP HAD RIPPED APART A BLANKET FROM THE WHITE RHINO AND SHOVED the ragged strips into the arms of his shirt. Despite this precaution, the wind cut through his overcoat, chilling him to the bone. He jiggled his knees and hunched his shoulders in a vain attempt to generate a little more warmth. Albertsson stood next to him, in the near-black shadow of a brick column holding up a pedestrian bridge. They were in L'Ouverture Park, several wooded acres cut into the neighborhoods of grim row houses that lay just south of the Tech campus. Christ, he was cold.

"The guy"—Albertsson said—"thinks that we use some kind of spy rules. He stashes his envelope in the hole in this tree down the way, and then he marks that sign that you see there before the bend." A sign listing the park prohibitions—alcohol consumption, unleashed dogs, motorized vehicles—was suspended maybe four feet off the ground by a metal pole. A magenta moon lit the area like a stage set.

The brightness made the shaded spots seem even darker, providing that much better concealment.

Albertsson kept talking out of the side of his mouth, keeping his voice at a confidential level, though Grip didn't think that anyone would be able to hear them over the noise of the wind. "It's all bullshit, though, the spy stuff. I just stand here and watch him go through the motions. He thinks he's being tricky, you know, keeping to the edge of the walk because he thinks the trees provide him cover, checking over his shoulder, moving quick when he makes the drop. I just stay here; let him do his thing if it makes him feel safer or whatnot. Then when he's gone, I go get the letter and wipe off the mark."

"Who is he?"

Albertsson shrugged. His coat had a fur collar. He looked warm. Grip considered punching him out and taking his coat.

"I've never met him, so far's I know. Never even got a close look. But it really doesn't matter, anyway. I just pass the note on. Never even looked at one."

Grip shook his head at Albertsson's lack of curiosity. They waited in silence, Grip hoping that it wouldn't take too long or, worse yet, "Your guy ever not show?"

"Nah, he always makes it. Guy gets a taste of the money? He'll be here on time."

Fifteen minutes passed. Grip had fought in World War II in Europe, where he'd developed the survival skill of spotting motion against a static background. He saw something now, up the hill to their right. He nudged Albertsson, nodded to the hill and what he could now see was a man picking his way along the heavily wooded slope.

"That your guy?"

Albertsson shook his head. "My guy just walks the path."

Grip watched the figure making his away along the slope, a dozen or so feet above a path that cut through the middle of the hill, a switchback connected to the path that they watched below them. The man stopped at a spot about a hundred yards off.

"Here he comes," Albertsson said. Grip followed Albertsson's eyes, saw a man walking on the path below.

Grip looked back up the slope to where his man leaned against a tree, invisible to the second man below them. Lit dark red, the scene seemed almost unreal to Grip, like a photo that hadn't been properly developed.

"So this is the way you always do it? You don't change it up?"

"Far's I know, this is the only way. Why?"

Grip didn't answer, thinking that Albertsson's superiors must not have been very concerned about security. This arrangement seemed more about making the snitch comfortable, or maybe making things exciting for him. Grip looked back up the hill, picked out the silhouette of the man leaning against the tree, waiting.

Grip's plan had been to follow Albertsson's source. He abandoned it. "You stay here."

"What?" Albertsson said, the rest of the sentence carried away on the wind as Grip made his way up the hill toward the switchback, legs stiff from standing in the cold. He stayed just off the path, where the trees gave him some cover as he headed for the figure in the woods.

He edged his way to the left, out of the man in the woods' sight line, so that he might be able to cross the exposed path unseen. He looked back down the hill, saw the snitch still walking along the lower path, a couple hundred yards from the drop spot. Grip looked to where he knew Albertsson was standing, but the darkness was impenetrable. Back up the hill, it seemed as if the man had also seen the snitch on the path and was slowly making his way down the hill.

Grip pulled his gun. No more time to wait. He jogged across the path and into the trees on the upper slope. He'd lost sight of the man as he'd crossed and now he scanned the woods before him, trying to pick him out. No success. It occurred to Grip that the man might now be hiding from *him*, might have seen him when he crossed the path. Grip realized he could wait the man out, let the snitch make the drop, figure out what to do from there. All of this would be much easier if he could hear above the wind.

Seconds passed. He saw movement in front of him. The man must have been getting antsy about the time. Grip ran forward, relying on the wind to cover the sound of his footsteps. But the man either heard

Grip or saw him coming because he stopped, and Grip saw the gun in his hand, reflecting the red moonlight.

A muzzle flash sent Grip sprawling to the ground, banging his left elbow on a rock. He fired two shots from the ground in return. The man turned, ran up the hill. Grip took off after him, the running difficult as he strode over roots, dodging trees and bushes.

His thighs burned from the uphill effort, breath thundered in his ears. The chase felt all wrong. The scene before him, lit by the red moon, came to him as if through tinted glasses. It was both too loud and too quiet, the wind drowning out the city sounds—sirens, car horns, pile drivers—but he could still hear his breath, the crunch of the ground under his feet.

Grip slowly closed on the man, who hadn't looked back since the chase began, and he was within twenty yards when the man crested the hill, turned, and fired twice in Grip's direction. Grip hit the ground again, watched the man disappear beyond the crest, then scrambled back to his feet and kept going. He reached the top, scanned the empty road, saw the man to his right, a gun in his extended hand. Four pops. How many shots had the guy fired, total? The guy wasn't a pro, couldn't shoot for shit. He was running again, toward the park entrance.

Grip's legs were heavy as he rejoined the pursuit. The skyline rose as a purple silhouette, tentacles of smoke reaching upward in a couple of spots. Sweat flowed, the blanket strips in his shirt now damp. He felt himself slowing, his legs refusing to move faster. He paused, trying to sight the man with his pistol, but his gasping breaths and pounding heart made it impossible to steady his hand. He forced himself to run again, having lost a dozen yards in the interim.

The man ran out the park entrance with Grip now fifty yards behind. He set his jaw against the burning in his legs, sure that this man was the key to whatever the fuck was going on. Traffic on de Gama was sparse. Grip paused, hands on knees, gulping air. The light to his right turned red. Grip saw the man run to the driver's door of a stopped car, gun pointed at the window. Grip ran for the car. He needed ten seconds. The door opened. The man pulled a woman from the car, pushed her away and climbed in himself. Twenty-five yards away. The car moved, blowing through the red light, no traffic to contend with. *Shit.*

Grip stopped in the middle of the street, holding his gun out with both hands. "Get down," he yelled at the woman who watched, dazed, as her car roared away, blocking Grip's shot.

"Get the fuck down." The woman finally dropped to the pavement, and Grip emptied his clip in the direction of the car. The car kept going. Grip heard honking as a car approached from behind. He turned, pointed his gun at the car. The driver accelerated around him. Grip tracked the car with his gun, caught a glimpse of the driver's startled face, thought that his best chance might have just slipped away.

73

FRINGS SMOKED A REEFER BY THE WINDOW IN HIS BEDROOM, BLOWING smoke through the narrow crack between frame and sill. From where he sat, the sun was just emerging orange over the buildings to the east. He'd gone to bed early the previous night, wanting to get a jump on the day. He didn't have a sense of Ebanks's current drug habits beyond the sheer volume he seemed to be ingesting, but figured that mid-morning was probably the best bet for finding him in some semblance of sobriety. So, he was up, drinking coffee, feeling the morning's edge leave him. He needed to be Ebanks's friend, not his adversary.

He took a cab, browsed the racing results and the obits as the hack accelerated and braked, feinted and dodged. They drove the perimeter of the Tech, the hack now distracted by the co-eds walking on the sidewalk, muttering back to Frings in an accent that Frings couldn't quite figure out. Frings got out at Ebanks's house.

He tried the door, but it was locked. He knocked. A kid answered, probably from the Tech—tousled brown hair, white button-down.

"Who're you?" the kid asked.

"I'm Frank Frings, I'm here—"

The kid stepped aside to let Frings in.

"It's an honor to meet you, Mr. Frings."

Frings had to shift his cane to his left hand to shake.

A collection of college-age kids hung out in the foyer, smoking any number of things. Frings noticed that unlike on his last visit, when they had seemed to fill the entire space, these kids had congregated off to the side, away from the stairs leading up to Ebanks's apartment.

"Will's upstairs," the kid said, glancing nervously at Blaine, who sat in an upholstered chair directly in front of the stairs, head lolling slightly to the side.

Frings walked over and found Blaine slumped over, heavy-lidded, his hand resting on a pistol balanced on his thigh. His hair fell lankly to his collar; the skin of his face was drawn tight with fatigue.

"What's your business?" Blaine muttered.

"I'm Frank Frings."

"I know who the fuck you are. I want to know what you want."

Frings didn't like the way he sounded or the look in his eyes. Mostly, though, he didn't like the gun. It was unnecessary and all the more menacing for it.

"I need to talk to Will."

"Nobody's talking to Will."

Frings nodded. "I need to talk to him anyway. This is important. For him."

Blaine wobbled the gun a little with his fingers.

"Listen," Frings said, "you know Will and I are friends, right? You *know* that. Let me just write him a message on a piece of paper. You bring it up to him, let him decide if he wants to see me."

Blaine had fully grasped the gun, but his demeanor seemed less aggressive—perhaps he'd decided that the gun's implied threat was enough. Blaine thought for a moment. Frings took advantage of his hesitation, opening his jacket.

"I've got a notebook and pen in here. I'm going to get them out."

Blaine raised his gun a little but nodded. Frings took out the pad and wrote: WE NEED TO TALK ABOUT ANDERS V. He folded the paper into quarters and handed it to Blaine.

"I'll wait here."

He watched the younger man lope up the stairs, taking them two at a time.

FRINGS HADN'T NOTICED CURTAINS THE FIRST TIME HE'D BEEN IN EBANKS'S sitting room, but they were drawn now. The shades had been removed from the lamps so that a harsh artificial light illuminated even the corners. Ebanks reclined in a plush chair wearing white linen pants and a white cotton shirt unbuttoned nearly to his navel. His hair was disheveled, his eyes lacked their usual shine.

Blaine hung around by the door, wanting to stay in the room, but Ebanks curtly dismissed him. Blaine gave Ebanks a long look.

"I've known Frank much longer than I've known you Blaine, now get the fuck out of here."

Blaine left, but Frings didn't relish running into him on the way out.

"Everyone's wearing white for Ben," Ebanks said, his whisper a contrast to the sharp tone he'd used with Blaine. "It's the color of Hindu mourning. They decided this was the best thing to do."

Frings sat down. "You read my note?"

Ebanks nodded. "We need to figure this out."

"When did you start taking money from Ving?"

He put this out there as if it were an established fact, though it was only a guess—a well-informed one. Ving had run Linsky. If he was trying to keep tabs on the radicals, Ebanks was another obvious soruce.

Ebanks grimaced. "No point in denying it, right?"

Frings shook his head.

"Okay"—Ebanks sat straighter, trying to project confidence where there was none—"1960, when I got run out of the Tech."

"Why?"

"Why'd I take it? I'm not going to pretend that taking his money is high-minded or principled, but what we are doing here is vital, maybe the most important endeavor since the invention of the wheel or the time of Jesus Christ. Does that sound crazy to you? Grandiose? Do I have delusions of grandeur for saying these things?"

Frings raised his eyebrows.

Ebanks laughed cynically. "I suppose I do. But have you taken the drug, Frank? You can't understand it until you've taken the drug. Earlier this year, Dr. Mowbray Alden came to visit me. You know that name?"

"British academic, expert in Buddhism and Eastern religions."

"Yes, that's the one. But also something more than a dabbler in mysticism. He's studied for decades, undertaken the most ambitious and advanced Eastern spiritual regimen that any Westerner has attempted with the possible exception of Sir Richard Burton. But he'd heard about the drug from a friend here at the Tech, and he came to see *me* to give it a try. Not Ledley, me. We took the drug together. He wanted to take quite a bit because he felt that his spiritual training had prepared him for the experience, and who knows, maybe it did.

"Frank, I can't even begin to explain to you what happened that night, but when we had breakfast two days later, the old man wept. Wept. He said that he'd spent his entire life searching for the experience that I'd handed to him in a sugar cube. You think I should give up this work because some small-minded assholes at the Tech don't want me around?" His voice had risen in volume. He wriggled up in his chair.

Frings showed Ebanks his palms. "I'm not criticizing you at all, Will. I'm just trying to figure out what's going on. They kicked you out of the Tech and then what? Anders Ving comes to you with a proposition?"

"You want a drink, Frank?"

Everyone was offering him drinks lately. "I'm alright."

Ebanks stood and walked behind a low bar. He still moved like a loose-limbed kid, part of his aura of youth. Frings waited while Ebanks played with ice and a couple of bottles. He came back with two highball glasses containing ice and a clear liquid. He put one of them on the end table by Frings's chair.

"I didn't want one."

"Maybe you'll change your mind."

"It's barely ten in the morning."

Ebanks smiled, a gesture that seemed almost a reflex. "I guess that's right."

Frings didn't want the conversation to get sidetracked. "You know that Ving works for Kraatjes, right? Since Kraatjes became chief?"

Ebanks nodded. "What's the point of this, Frank? Are you going to write an article?"

"Of course not, Will. Do you remember Panos, my editor back at the *Gazette*?"

Ebanks was sipping his drink. He nodded slightly.

"His grandson was missing and I was looking for him and all this came up—Ben Linsky, you, Ving, Kollectiv 61. I'm trying to figure out how it all fits together."

"Linsky?"

Frings nodded.

Ebanks closed his eyes in thought. "Who's Panos's grandson?"

"Sol Elia." He'd told him that before.

Ebanks nodded.

"You know him, don't you?"

Ebanks conceded that he did.

"You told me before that you didn't."

"Not well, Frank. Not well. And I want nothing to do with him or anything connected to him. Yes, he's been here a few times, to see friends of his. He's a radical, but he doesn't really fit in with the heemies. He's got a pretty violent vibe."

"Does he?"

"He does, Frank. Trust me."

"Is he in Kollectiv 61?"

"*That* is a complicated question. What the hell *is* Kollectiv 61 do you think, Frank? *I* don't know what it is. Is it something people spray-paint on walls when they go out and bust up a building site? Is it a secret society—terrorists blowing things up? Is it one guy? Five? Fifty? I don't know."

"I get your point," Frings said, thinking about what Sol had said—that Kollectiv 61 was just a slogan, an idea—and eager to calm Ebanks down, get him back to talking about Ving. "When Linsky was murdered, someone spray-painted *snitch* on his wall. Now that I find out that you have been taking money from Ving as well, I think this is something that we should talk about."

"What, so you can protect me?"

"Don't be an ass, Will. Something is going on here. Did you know that Linsky was one of Ving's snitches before he was killed?"

Ebanks shook his head.

"Do you know who else is on Ving's payroll?"

"No."

"Okay. So tell me how it happened. You got run out of the Tech. Then what?"

"Then what? Look, Frank, my research wasn't completed by any means, and you can't do research without money, so I was looking at the end of the whole thing unless I could scrounge up some cash. When you get kicked out of a university, there's not a whole lot of people looking to throw money your way, especially when nobody's heard of what you're doing. It's hard to go to the feds or to a foundation or even some rich biddy and say, 'Hi, my name is Will and the research I am doing is the most important spiritual work of the last two thousand years and, oh, by the way, my university kicked me out because of it.' You'd get laughed out of the room. But in my last few weeks there, Ving—he didn't identify himself as a cop at first—starting talking to me about a new source of funding. He was sketchy with the details—surprise, surprise—just trying to figure out how desperate I was for the money, I guess. We met maybe a half-dozen times, and he finally put his cards on the table: the cops would bankroll my research, give me a house, everything, and in return I'd keep them apprised of my research and I'd also fill them in on what was going on with the people in my orbit, mostly heemies, but some academics and others. They were still shook up about the LaValle murder, and I guess I don't blame them. But no one's ever been arrested from information I provided, Frank. No one."

No arrests? So then what was the point? Why not just let him focus on research? "Don't you wonder why they still have you reporting if they've never used your information?"

Ebanks bristled. "What are you saying? I'm mostly paid for my research. The reports, those are on the side. Why would they want that info?"

Frings nodded, thinking about Vilnius Street. "You ever wonder why the cops are so interested in your work? They don't seem like a particularly spiritual organization."

Ebanks didn't like this, but he thought about it.

Frings could think of a number of possible reasons, none of them consistent with Ebanks's apparent conception of his own work. Ebanks wasn't dumb. He must have thought about it in the past, had it linger on his psychic periphery. It may have even fueled the outsized claims that he made, as though this grand endeavor justified any negative consequences.

"Does it matter, Frank? Do you think about the uses to which your articles might be put—who suffers, who gains? Don't act like I'm the only one making moral compromises.

Frings didn't want to lose Ebanks to acrimony, so he switched tacks. "You didn't know Linsky was on Ving's payroll?"

"No. I wasn't sure until you just confirmed it."

"But you'd guessed."

"Sure I guessed."

"So who else would you *guess* is on the payroll?"

"I have no idea."

Frings paused to think.

Ebanks spoke quietly, his voice calmer. "The person who killed Linsky, I think he knows about me. I think he tried to kill me."

"What? What are you talking about?"

"I had a drop last night. I leave envelopes down in L'Ouverture Park. There were shots."

"Hold on. Someone tried to kill you *last night*?"

"Yes, Frank. I didn't see the guy. It came from up the hill. A bunch of shots. I got behind a tree, and they stopped, and there were a few more a little bit later, a little further away."

"Jesus, Will. But that doesn't sound like anyone was coming after *you*—not if the shots got further away."

"You don't think so? Because I see Ben Linsky dead, a snitch, and then a few days later I'm in a fucking empty park, dropping off my little report and suddenly the bullets are flying. What am I supposed to think?"

Frings nodded, conceding the point. "Okay. What are—"

"What am I going to do? I'm in a hard place here, Frank. I'm hoping that Ving is working Ben's murder, but I basically have to wait. What else can I do?"

Get out of the City, Frings thought. *Get the hell out of the City.*

• • •

EBANKS FADED AFTER A WHILE. FRINGS GOT UP TO LEAVE. THEY DIDN'T shake hands. Frings walked toward the door, anticipating another charge of hostility from Blaine, when a question occurred to him.

He turned back to Ebanks. "There's something else that's come up, I thought maybe you might have heard about it. You know back eight or nine years ago, they quarantined a block of Vilnius Street?"

"*Christ.* Look, you'll have to talk to Ledley about that. That's his thing. I really don't know anything about it."

74

GRIP CAUGHT SOME SLEEP IN A BY-THE-WEEK HOTEL IN THE HOLLOWS, IN the room of a prostitute he'd known both as a cop and a client for the better part of the last decade. It was a depressing place, bugs, mold, walls with gouges in the plaster. He'd given her a night's worth of trick money and he'd slept, fully clothed, next to her in the bed. For a few semi-conscious minutes he'd watched the reflection of the flashing red vacancy light on the ceiling, its glow sectioned by the shadow of the window frame. He'd glanced over to look at the woman, her cheeks slack with sleep, her red hair fanned across the pillow. Her face wasn't pretty, but there was an honesty to it, he thought, even after the life she'd led. He'd desperately wanted to tell her everything, thought it would be an almost physical unburdening. But—either because he didn't trust her or because these things were simply too private—he stayed silent until he was again engulfed by sleep.

Now, naked to the waist, he washed his face and hair in the oily water that ran from the tap in the shared bathroom at her end of the hall. For the first time in days he didn't feel the weight of fatigue. Instead, he was at a loss about what to do. His options seemed played out. He had vague ideas about getting together with Albertsson again, finding another way to use him, but he couldn't get past the feeling that his best opportunity with that moron had been blown the previous night.

He dressed again, noticed just how stale his clothes had become. He exchanged a long look with the woman, both of them silent, Grip unsure if the look conveyed some kind of mutual understanding or just the opposite. He walked down the stairs to find two uniforms waiting for him, guns drawn.

THEY TOOK HIM BY PROWL CAR TO THE RIVER AND WALKED HIM ACROSS a fallow field surrounded by abandoned buildings that had been obsolete since his grandfather's day, when the railroad had supplanted riverboats as the key to the City's commerce. The field was filled with debris—wood; sheets of tin; random artifacts—the landscape like an unruly archaeological site. Grip wondered if this was how it would end—shot and dumped in the river or maybe just dumped in the river, left to drown in the tricky currents. It seemed convoluted, though. Why not just shoot him in some alley, no witnesses, no mess? They'd taken his gun. They could make it look like a suicide. He'd clearly been isolated, acting strangely—even threatened a superior.

The uniforms weren't talkative, but they weren't unfriendly either—deferential, if anything. Grip figured that they'd either been told to treat him well or to ease him off his guard. Before they'd left the prowl car, one of them had notified someone through the radio that they'd arrived. At the riverbank now, Grip saw two men approach, recognizing, even from this distance, the size and swagger of Lieutenant Zwieg.

The wind off the river was chilly, but Grip didn't feel it, adrenaline coursing through him as if a tap had been opened.

Zwieg looked at Grip appraisingly. "I never figured you for a beard, Tor."

"I haven't had much of a chance to shave."

"You've had plenty of chances. You haven't taken them."

"No?"

"You've been running around like a fugitive, Tor. Why? We've been watching you the whole time, could have picked you up at any time. You think it's so easy to duck the police? You of all people should know better."

It was true, Grip thought. He'd been fooling himself, acting out some part in a strange theater. "Why am I here?"

"You're done. Assignment completed. Good work."

The words almost startled him. "I'm done?"

"You can go back to your old duties, work the sites. Take the rest of the day off, show up tomorrow, good to go."

"But I never found Kollectiv 61."

Zwieg smiled, probably trying to look reassuring, but failing. "You did better, Tor, trust me."

Grip stood quietly, disoriented, aware of the four men around him, that he had no control over anything that happened right now. He heard the roar of the river, its noise somehow playing with his perceptions; Zwieg seeming too big, too vivid before him.

"I knew you'd find this confusing, but you have to trust me." Zwieg laughed at this, the absurdity of asking for Grip's trust. "As I promised you, here are the photos." He reached into his pocket, handed Grip an envelope. Grip opened the flap, saw the burnt orange strip of negatives.

"You have any more copies?"

"I don't, and I didn't have to give you the negatives. But I'm a man of my word. You have nothing to worry about."

Grip blinked a few times, trying to normalize his vision. "I don't know what to think about this."

"Of course you don't know, Tor. You have no idea what's going on. But give it a couple of weeks, and you'll see. Two weeks and you will see it all for yourself. We won't forget what you've done for us." Zwieg extended his hand. Without thinking, Grip shook it. "But one thing—do not talk to Ving or Kraatjes. They are already finished, but they don't know it yet. Don't undo all the good will you've earned. If I get word that you've talked to them, I will fix you good when they go down. You're on the winning team, Tor, don't fuck that up."

Zwieg nodded to the other three cops and, as a group, they left Grip by the riverbank. Grip followed their progress from a seat on a tree trunk deposited by the current, their figures blurring as they receded. He was exhausted and bewildered, but, mostly, he was angry. He rubbed the negatives against a rock until they were scratched beyond any hope of repair. Then he tossed them into the roiling water.

75

FRINGS SPENT THE DAY IN HIS OFFICE, DOOR CLOSED TO THE SILENT HALL, putting in his most concerted effort since the *News-Gazette* merger, working on a story he didn't intend to find its way into print. It was, in fact, meant for only three pairs of eyes, none of them in this building.

It was very rare for anyone to visit his office, but in the afternoon word had apparently gotten around—maybe the mail delivery ginks—and Littbarski arrived unannounced in his doorway.

"The scuttlebutt is that you've got the proverbial bit between the teeth." He had a lopsided grin that Frings found hard to read. Was he gratified that Frings was working on something that he had every right to imagine was big, or was he merely mocking Frings?

"We'll see what it comes to."

"That's enigmatic, Frank. Close to the vest. I like that. Keep the brass guessing right? Once a rebel, always a rebel and all that?"

"It might be a while, getting everything sorted out. I think you'll like the finished product."

"Front-page material?" There was that smile again.

"Special-edition material."

Littbarski barked out a laugh, clapped his hands once. "That's the Frank Frings of legend, not the impostor who's been haunting these corridors for the past five years. Blood in the water."

Frings returned to his typing, and after a few moments, Littbarski left without a word.

FRINGS WENT TO PANOS'S APARTMENT LATE THAT NIGHT. TO FRINGS'S surprise, Panos answered the door freshly shaved and wearing a suit. There was a moment's pause, a flash of awkwardness between the old friends. Frings had called Panos the day before to tell him of Sol's visit. He'd anticipated Panos's reaction: relief that Sol was alive; anger the Frings hadn't found a way to call him at the time, at least given him a chance to speak with his grandson on the phone; and hurt that Sol wouldn't seek out the man who had provided so much for him—his only living relative.

"I know I asked you to find him," Panos had said. "And you have. But now that I know he's okay, I am wanting more. I want to see him myself."

Frings wasn't sure that he'd describe Sol as "okay," but didn't mention that fact. "I'll try, Panos. But I don't know if I can find him again. I didn't, really, this time. He found out I was looking for him and came to me. And even if I *do* find him, I have no influence over what he does."

They had hung up with Panos unhappy, and Frings unable to offer honest solace.

Now, Panos poured them each a glass of port from a crystal decanter, one of the few remaining signs of wealth left in his home. He'd shed most of the rest of it—couches, paintings, carpets, china—not because he couldn't afford them, but because they put him in mind of his late wife. He'd loved the spoils of wealth because she had. Now that she was gone, they held only the memory of *her*.

Frings passed Panos a folder containing the article, which now stretched to sixteen typewritten pages. The old man was pale, somehow withered beneath his suit. Frings wondered about the emotional toll learning about Sol had exacted on Panos. If he was right, though, the information in the folder would rouse the old man, however briefly, from his lethargy.

"What is this?" Panos asked, opening the folder.

Frings reached across the table, gently folding it shut again. "Read this when I leave. I've set up a meeting with President Milledge at the Tech for tomorrow morning."

Panos raised his eyebrows. Frings saw some of the spark, a Pavlovian reaction to an unspecified promise of the hunt.

"Panos, this could be our last story; our most important story."

"Explain this."

Frings shook his head. "Read the article cold, let me know how it'll play with Milledge."

• • •

FROM THE KOLLECTIV 61 MANIFESTO, *Prometheus*, FALL 1961

12. a. The Mass Communication of Lies: The second operating principal is the firmly held belief that representative democracy (a method of governing that, in theory, comes closest to manifesting a "will of the majority") is the most morally defensible form of government. This judgment is predicated upon the principle that people are able to make rational decisions about their own governance. This may or may not be true, but what is inarguable is that a people's will is formed by their reaction to "facts" about the political, economic, and social climate in which they live. IT IS CLEAR THAT, WITH THE ACQUIESCENCE OF TELEVISION, RADIO, AND NEWSPAPERS, THE PEOPLE ARE CONSTANTLY AND CONSISTENTLY MISLED BY THE GOVERNMENT AND BIG BUSINESS ABOUT THE BASIC FACTS OF THEIR (AND SOCIETY'S) SITUATION. WHEN THE ASSUMPTIONS ON WHICH DECISIONS ARE MADE IN A DEMOCRATIC SOCIETY ARE FALSE, POPULAR WILL HAS NO MEANING IN ANY REAL SENSE. THE ELECTED GOVERNMENT, THEREFORE, IS ILLEGITIMATE, AS ITS ELECTION WAS FACILITATED BY LIES CRAFTED TO ENABLE ITS ASCENSION TO OR MAINTAINANCE OF POWER. IN THIS WAY, WE HEAD BY INCREMENTS TO TOTALITARIANISM.

76

DORMAN STOOD UNDER AN AWNING WITH FACHE—WHO WAS OFF DUTY and out of uniform—sheltered from the gray rain that kept the sidewalks largely clear of traffic. The smell of booze radiated off the cop, but Dorman didn't care. Fache didn't have to do much, just point a finger. In truth, that was all he was willing to do, point a finger as he saw Ed Wayne coming and then get the hell inside the diner behind them.

Dorman had planned on hitting Crippen's, to talk to him there, but a detective he knew had talked him out of it. Wayne was volatile, and Dorman would have no friends inside. Better to talk to him somewhere neutral, which was why he was here with Fache, waiting.

"Yeah, there," Fache said, indicating a man shambling toward them, head down, umbrella angled against the rain.

"You sure?"

"You don't get Wayne mixed up with anyone. Trust me." With that, Fache retreated into the diner, leaving Dorman alone on the street.

Dorman watched Wayne shamble toward him on the sidewalk. Even under an overcoat, it was clear that his shoulders sloped, that his body was soft. His gait was almost comical, his toes pointing out and his feet spread wide with each step.

Wayne had just about passed by when he surprised Dorman by turning to him. Dorman felt a chill in the stare of Wayne's too-small eyes.

"Phil Dorman," Wayne growled.

Dorman could feel his face flush. He'd been caught completely off guard. "Mr. Wayne."

"I was in the process of trying to hunt you down." Wayne let the statement stand, as if no further explanation were necessary.

"I wanted to speak to you, as well." Dorman stayed under the awning.

Wayne pressed his lips together in a smile. "That is a truly fortuitous coincidence."

"Maybe we should go inside to talk."

"I don't believe that suits me."

Dorman wasn't sure what to say to that, so he waited. Water dripped off the brim of Wayne's battered hat. His overcoat was soaked, though he seemed not to notice.

"Not now. Not here. I like to choose the place and time of my business meetings. I do *not* like to be waylaid on the street. I do *not* like pukes like Fache pointing me out from among the masses."

Wayne looked past Dorman, through the plate glass and into the restaurant, with a rage and intensity that made clear to Dorman why he was so widely feared.

With a quickness that Dorman wouldn't have credited him with, Wayne shot his left hand in between Dorman's jacket and shirt. Dorman reflexively pushed the hand away. His shirt was damp where Wayne had touched it.

Wayne smirked. "You wearing a wire, Phil?"

Dorman shook his head.

"Say it."

"I'm not wearing a wire."

Wayne stared at him. "I believe you. I really do. I am confident that I would be able to see though any attempt at deception on your part, but I see nothing. I need to speak with you about a business proposition proposed by a mutual associate of some means. I believe you know who I'm referring to."

"Yes." *Gerald Svinblad.*

"And you have indicated that you wish to discuss something with me. Would this be a different matter?"

"Yes, I—"

Wayne raised his hand to silence Dorman. "Not now. Let me see." He closed his eyes, rocking his head slightly. "Tomorrow night. Midnight." He laughed again. "Midnight, I like the sound of that." His voice changed, more menacing. "Idaho Avenue building site. Alone. No guns. No wire. Comprende, amigo?"

Dorman wanted to put his fist through the guy's face. He figured he wasn't the first one to have had that thought.

HE WALKED BACK TO CITY HALL WITH HIS UMBRELLA UP AGAINST THE rain. He couldn't shake the unpleasant sensation of being in Wayne's presence, the way he seemed to exude ill health—both physical and mental. Interacting with Wayne seemed sordid, left an impression that something immoral had taken place.

Dorman barely noticed the other pedestrians, gray in the rain, heads down, intent on getting to their destinations. A street preacher stood at a corner, an Old Testament figure under an umbrella, his grievances against the world drowned out by the sound of the rain. Dorman had the uneasy sense that the man was watching him as he walked away, but he didn't turn around to see.

The steps leading up to City Hall were empty. Dorman had ascended the first few when he saw a man, without umbrella or hat, coming down toward him. The effect of the man's sheer disregard for the elements put Dorman on his guard, even though he didn't recognize Reuther until they were barely ten feet apart. At that distance, Dorman could see the rage and pain on Reuther's face. Dorman stopped.

"You goddamn bastard," Reuther howled, and Dorman saw that he had a knife, holding it inexpertly, like a tennis racquet.

Dorman took a step back. "I tried to warn you."

Reuther took a wild swipe. Dorman barely had to move to avoid it. He threw his umbrella down the steps. Reuther took a step closer and swung the knife as hard as he could, but he wasn't even close to being cut out for this type of thing and succeeded only in throwing himself off balance. Dorman stepped forward and punched Reuther hard below the eye, knocking him down the steps so that he landed with his feet higher than his head. The knife had slid out of his hand and down to the sidewalk.

Dorman walked to where Reuther lay, his body shaking with sobs. Dorman knelt down next to him.

"You're ruining lives for no reason but spite," Reuther managed. "It was bad enough, but now people are going to be on the street."

Dorman stared at him, the rain now penetrating his clothes. He wanted to say something reassuring, but knew that it would be bullshit. Nothing was going to change Canada's decision. He looked up and saw guards hustling down the steps toward them. He stood.

"Bastard," Reuther spat.

Dorman started up the steps, moving aside to let the guards pass him as they went to arrest Stanley Reuther for violently threatening a government official.

77

GRIP RETURNED TO THE STATION TO FIND THAT HE HAD BEEN ASSIGNED A partner, a detective named De Flandre. Grip assumed that De Flandre had been told to keep an eye on him, though what anyone expected Grip to do was a puzzle. He himself didn't know what he was going to do—he couldn't even piece together what it was he'd done to convince Zwieg to let him off the hook. He knew it must have something to do with Ving and Kraatjes—he had exposed their relationship with Linsky and with whoever had made the drop at L'Ouverture Park. Albertsson was the connection. Kraatjes/Ving to Albertsson to the snitches. Still, it just didn't feel like anything had been settled—everything was tenuous and uncertain.

The detectives in his squad knew that something had happened, but did him the favor of pretending that they hadn't noticed. As far as Grip could tell, though, it seemed that most of the cops knew that he had been involved in something either important or at least out of the ordinary. He caught looks from cops he didn't know, cryptic comments as he passed by them in the hall. Did they know something he didn't? Or was this just the old paranoia?

Despite being on guard with De Flandre, Grip found that he liked the guy well enough. He was younger, but not green, and he seemed to share Grip's politics. De Flandre had been working the cases that Grip had abandoned while working for Zwieg—clearing some, letting others languish.

That night he went to Crippen's—mostly to drink but also hoping to run into Albertsson. Instead, he found Wayne reading the newspaper, three whisky shots lined up before him. Grip took the chair opposite.

"You cleaned yourself up," Wayne said, dropping the newspaper on an empty seat.

Grip shrugged. Wayne was bare-headed, and his skull was not pleasant to look at, somehow slightly lopsided, the pale skin mottled with pink patches.

"Nervous times among the brass." Wayne tipped back a shot, then pushed one to Grip.

"Is that right?" Grip hadn't sensed anything like that at headquarters, but of course he'd only been focused on people's reactions to *him*.

"Keep your head low's what I hear."

"From who?" For an unrepentant asshole, Wayne seemed to have an inordinate number of people who fed him information, even if a lot of it was far-fetched.

This time it was Wayne who shrugged, smiling.

Grip drank the shot. He wondered about the meeting with Albertsson's snitch, and the potential killer on the hillside. How could this not be connected to the anxiety that Wayne claimed was afflicting the upper reaches of the Force? How could it not be related to Zwieg's plans to make a move on Kraatjes? He couldn't quite figure out Zwieg's game—he didn't have enough information or wasn't understanding that which he had. But he was in no doubt that Zwieg did have a game going and that he'd played a part in it. He was in a precarious position.

"This got anything to do with Zwieg?"

Wayne raised the nubs where his eyebrows would have been. "That's an unexpected question, Tor. I haven't heard as such, though I will certainly keep an ear out."

78

PRESIDENT MILLEDGE'S OFFICE AT THE TECH SEEMED TO GLEAM IN THE light that slanted in from four tall windows set in the corner walls. Frings sat in a wood and leather chair, apparently designed for discomfort, the Tech's seal etched into the top of the back. Panos slouched in his wheelchair, grim, making little humming sounds. They didn't speak. Waiting, Frings scanned the titles of the books lined neatly in the glassed-in bookshelves covering the wall to the left of Milledge's immaculate desk—law books, books with Latin titles, a row of very old Bibles.

Milledge had wandered out to his secretary's office, sitting in her chair to read the manuscript that Frings had given him. Milledge hadn't wanted to read it with Frings and Panos watching, and not wanting to inconvenience the frail Panos, had sent his secretary to an early lunch.

Frings had prepared himself for the conversation that was to follow. He didn't necessarily relish these kinds of situations, but he didn't avoid them either, existing as he did in a complicated world of debts and pressure. He preferred giving favors—the quid pro quo that made his and so many other people's jobs work, and which were, in fact, the City's real currency. Today, though, he would have to apply pressure. Milledge didn't owe him anything, and anyway, what he was after was beyond the scope of the normal debt relationship.

The chatter from the hallway echoed in to them, the secretarial staff exchanging news about children, minor gossip: all subjects alien to Frings.

He'd brought Panos along out of respect rather than need. The old man didn't have a role to play, except that his mere presence as a friend of Milledge's could help things along. Milledge was grim when he returned, avoiding eye contact with Frings. He looked to Panos when he'd taken the seat behind his desk.

"You've read this?"

Panos nodded wearily.

Milledge turned to Frings. "Are you going to press?"

"That's what we're here to talk about."

"Has Littbarski seen it?"

"Not yet."

"Thank Christ." Some of the tension seemed to leave Milledge's shoulders. Frings read this as a willingness to negotiate.

Milledge said, "You realize I had no idea about the details of this research. I knew he was working with this kind of drug, but the methods. . ." He let it trail off, but when Frings didn't speak he started again. "It's impossible to know the—"

"Damn it, Estes," Panos snapped. "My grandson was one of the subjects."

Milledge seemed startled by the outburst, looked in the direction of Panos's knees. "I'm sorry, Panos. I understand that I failed all of those boys."

It was silent for a moment as Frings let this comment hang, giving Milledge a chance to absorb his culpability.

"We need to figure this out," Frings said.

Milledge brightened a bit. "I would be interested in your thoughts."

"I'll get straight to the point. In 1958, Simon Ledley conducted an experiment that may have involved some unwitting members of the public. I want to see the files."

Milledge sank back in his seat, looking, if it were possible, worse than he had after reading the manuscript. "1958."

"Vilnius Street."

"How much do you know?"

"Does it matter? I know enough that I need to see those files. This is the deal that I'm offering you: show me the files, and I'll kill the story about the 1959 study with the boys."

"What will you do with the information about 1958?"

"I won't know until I see it."

"I need a guarantee."

Frings kept his voice low, calm. "I guarantee that if you don't show me, the Tech is going to be all over the news for allowing its students to be used in dangerous drug experiments. That's a guarantee. If you show me the Vilnius Street files, I guarantee you that I will kill that 1959 story. What I can't guarantee is what happens after I see the Vilnius Street files."

Milledge looked to Panos, but Frings saw that the old man's eyes were closed. It wasn't clear whether he was asleep or just thinking.

"You're asking quite a bit. Is there no other way?"

For the first time in this conversation Frings felt some anger. Milledge knew something about the Vilnius Street study. At a minimum he knew that he wanted it kept hidden.

"I'm going to give you two minutes to think about what you want to do. After two minutes, I take back my offer. I take the manuscript to a judge along with everything I have on the Vilnius Street project, and he'll issue a ruling to release those files. Then the story hits hits the newsstand tomorrow, maybe the next day. Two minutes." Frings made a show of looking at his watch, though he knew it wouldn't take thirty seconds.

"Okay," Milledge said, deflated. "Okay, let me arrange it for the earliest chance, say tomorrow afternoon."

Christ, he was pushing it. "I'm sorry if I was unclear. I want to see them now."

Frings watched Milledge closely. Just an hour before, the man's life had been moving along as normal. Now Frings had shown up, destroyed whatever stability Milledge had had. Still, he couldn't muster up much sympathy for him. The more he heard, the more he was convinced that even if Milledge hadn't known about the specifics of these projects, he'd known that the Tech was on—to be charitable—treacherous ethical footing and had allowed them to continue. He had created an environment where that kind of research could be conducted.

"I don't know if I can arrange it this quickly."

"You're the goddamn president. You can arrange anything any time you want. Do you need more motivation?"

Milledge sighed, looked at his hands clasped on his desk. Frings thought that he could almost feel the president's desire to will all this away.

79

GRIP HEARD SOMEONE CALLING HIM AS HE WALKED FROM THE ELEVATOR to his squad room, and he felt his day go to shit.

"Drop your coat and hat off at your desk. We need to go upstairs."

Grip nodded at Deputy Chief Ving, walked into the squad room and found it empty. He draped his coat over the back of his chair. He sighed, placed his hat on the desk, walked back out into the hall to find Ving leaning against the wall, listening with half an ear to a uniform who talked with staccato hand gestures. Ving caught Grip's eye and excused himself from the cop.

"Come on." Ving led him up the stairs, moving in that effortless way he had. It was almost a relief to be doing this, Grip thought— the dread anticipation would finally end. They walked past Ving's door to the meeting room where Grip knew Kraatjes would be waiting. Kraatjes didn't have meetings in his office, which was unusual and provoked a lot of rumors among the ranks. What, exactly, did he do in there?

Ving opened the door and stood aside for Grip to enter. Kraatjes was leaning, almost sitting, on the back of a chair, smoking a cigarette—languid. He was thin, his narrow face showing a day's worth of beard, his short hair more gray than white. He wasn't wearing a jacket, but his pants and shirt were expensive.

He stood and flashed Grip a pro forma smile. "Detective, have a seat."

Grip sat, forearms on the table. Ving closed the door, and Grip was vaguely aware that he'd taken up a spot against the wall behind him.

"Cigarette?" Kraatjes asked.

Grip accepted, more to be agreeable than because he wanted one. Kraatjes slid the pack across the table. Grip took one, slid the pack back, and inhaled as Ving, from behind, provided him with a light.

"You know why you're here, correct?" Kraatjes's tone was soft, not exactly friendly, not adversarial—just calm.

"I think so."

"Why don't you tell me?"

Grip hesitated. This was dangerous ground. He had a guess about what was going on, but he wasn't sure, which made discussing Zwieg a tricky prospect.

"Detective," Kraatjes prompted.

"Lieutenant Zwieg. He had me investigating Kollectiv 61."

Kraatjes nodded. "Did you make any headway on Kollectiv 61, develop any leads, make any arrests?"

Grip shook his head.

"Instead, what?"

"I found Ben Linsky, sir. I found out that he was a snitch. My assumption was that he was connected with you and Deputy Chief Ving." Grip paused, but Ving didn't say anything. "And then Linsky was murdered."

"Do you have any idea by who?"

Grip shook his head.

"Neither do we. Go on." Kraatjes was very still, two fingers resting against his left temple, his cigarette cupped just off the table.

"I met a cop who does bag work for Ving."

"Name?"

Grip sighed. Best just to get it out there. "Albertsson."

"Albertsson." Kraatjes absently ground out his cigarette in an ashtray, pulled another from his pack, lit it. "He took you to the drop in L'Ouverture Park."

Grip nodded.

"There was someone with a gun there. Was that you?"

"I had a gun, sir. But I think you're talking about a man that I saw on the hill. He had a gun as well."

Kraatjes didn't say anything.

"I saw him and gave chase, but he had a good head start."

"I'm sure he did, detective. Do you know who it was? Did you get a good look at him?"

Grip shrugged. "Not really. Caucasian. Dark hair. That's about it."

"Do you think it might have been Zwieg or someone who Zwieg put up to it?"

Grip had thought about this himself, but if it was, he didn't see how it fit in with the rest. "No, I don't think so. I don't see how that plays."

Kraatjes looked surprised. "Plays into what?"

Grip felt the heat in his face. He had no idea what to answer.

Kraatjes nodded quickly, seemed to switch to a new speed. "How did you get involved in this, detective? You aren't under Zwieg."

Grip told him about Nicky Patridis's story—his lie—and the work that Grip had been coerced into by Zwieg. He told him about Ben Linsky and the memo that he'd left on the table. He told him about Zwieg's protection of Patridis.

"When you found out that . . ." Kraatjes looked to Ving.

"Nicky Patridis."

"When you found that Nicky Patridis had lied about the theft, why did you continue with this line of investigation?"

"I owed Lieutenant Zwieg a favor."

"You owed him a favor."

"Yes, sir."

Kraatjes stared at him for a moment. "That doesn't strike me as an adequate explanation."

"I'm sorry, sir."

Kraatjes took this in. He sighed. "Okay. What do you think Zwieg is up to?"

"I think he's trying to get at you, but I don't know how. He seems to think that it's too late to stop him."

"Good. Thank you, detective." Grip watched as Kraatjes looked past him to Ving, who must have given some sign because Kraatjes nodded. "Detective, you have put in three decades of good police work. Your tactics aren't always . . . sound, but you are loyal to the Force. Because of this, I am going to ask you to forget this meeting and forget these past few weeks that you have been working with Zwieg. Go back to your job, do what you've always done. If I hear that you have told anyone about this or that you were in fact a more willing participant in Zwieg's project than you have said, we will have another meeting. Is that clear?"

Grip nodded.

"Zwieg has always looked at his hand and seen a flush, even if he held a pair of deuces. It's not a trait that serves him well."

The guy had a way of intimidating without raising his voice, crowding space, any of the usual tricks. Grip just wanted to get out of there.

"Another thing: I may ask for your peripheral involvement in what could prove to be a tricky arrest. I would like you to participate without revealing any of what we've just discussed. I think seeing you at the scene might clarify a few things for Lieutenant Zwieg."

Grip nodded, though he didn't like the sound of it.

"I'm going to hang Zwieg's balls from the flagpole in front of this headquarters." He exhaled smoke through his nose. "Nobody makes a move on me, detective. I'm frankly surprised that Lieutenant Zwieg lost sight of that." Kraatjes ground his cigarette into the ashtray and, with a subtle nod to Ving, stood and walked out of the room.

80

PANOS HADN'T ACCOMPANIED FRINGS TO LEDLEY'S BASEMENT STORAGE room. Once Milledge had acquiesced, he had gone home, where he now slumped in his chair, engulfed in a kimono he'd bought when he was a hundred pounds heavier.

Frings fought his fatigue, telling Panos about his trip to the locked hallway just past Ledley's office. Panos listened with great concentration, his face drawn with the strain of it.

"Milledge stuck it out for a little while, but he begged off eventually, said he had obligations."

Panos snorted in disgust.

"I think he really did. Anyway, it was better to have him out of there, not looking over my shoulder. He was so disconcerted that he left these." Frings shifted in his chair so that he could pull out a ring with five keys.

"Are those Milledge's?"

"They're the ones he needed to get to Ledley's hallway."

Panos nodded.

"It was incredibly quiet in there after he left. The place is practically soundproof."

The sound of papers being shifted had seemed to echo off the close walls, and the overhead light had barely held off the encroaching darkness.

"So I started with the financials. He had two file cabinets basically full of ledgers, invoices, check stubs, bank statements, all that. I found the files for the incoming funds for the project, and they were drawn off City government accounts—prefix 610—the force."

Panos took this in. "Black budget?"

Frings shrugged. "That'd be my guess. You'll see. I think if this had shown up in a budget, there'd have been some questions. But I'm getting a little ahead of myself. I found a drawer filled with memos on City letterhead. Most of it was pretty tedious—requests for payments, notices for meetings, administrative stuff. But there was a folder with about a half dozen memos that had been partially redacted—names blacked out, routing initials—but the rest of it was there. I had to spend some time with them because there were a lot of identification numbers, and it wasn't exactly clear what they referred to. But eventually I figured out that they seemed to be arranging to shut down a section of the water system. One block, I think."

"Vilnius Street?"

Frings nodded. Traffic noise drifted up from outside. A siren howled somewhere in the distance.

"The last interesting piece of the logistics was something I found buried in the middle of a stack of invoices and receipts—again, most of it pretty mundane: office supplies, receipts for take-out dinners. But with all that was an invoice from Consolidated Industries for"— he pulled a notebook from his jacket pocket, consulted his notes— "five thousand gallons of lysergic acid distillate."

Panos said, "That's the drug, right? Ebanks's drug?"

"Yeah. Ledley was interested in it, too, and at least one other guy at the Tech. But, yeah, that's the one."

Despite his ill health and exhaustion, Panos spoke with a re-strained excitement that Frings remembered from the days when they were working big stories at the *Gazette*. "Let me be sure that I'm straight with this one. The City police were funding this project by Ledley where he somehow pumped this drug—lysergic acid—into the water supply for this one block of Vilnius Street.

"That's how it looks to me. They quarantined the block for that period."

"What is it that happened when they did that?"

Frings delayed his answer, wondering if other words would be more accurate, but knowing they wouldn't. "According to the files, the people in the 5800 block of Vilnius Street went crazy."

81

THE ARES CLUB WAS BACK TO NORMAL, THOUGH THIS IN ITSELF FELT somehow suspicious. Dorman paused at the maître d's table, waited for his vision to adjust and peered into the shadows of the booths. He felt the maître d's nervous eyes on him, turned, gave him a long look before nodding.

"Usual table," Dorman said and walked off.

"Mr. Dorman," the maître d' called from behind him.

Dorman was already slowing, a mixture of outrage and fear. "Yes?"

"There is someone at your table tonight." The maître d' had his hands clasped before him, trying to placate.

Dorman saw the couple in his booth—*his booth*. Their features were hidden, but the man was broad and the girl next to him was thin as a sylph. She wasn't Anastasia, though.

"Who is it?"

The maître d' opened his hands. Dorman knew he couldn't betray their anonymity.

"Why my table?"

"I do not make the decisions, Mr. Dorman. This comes down from upstairs."

"It's Gerald Svinblad, isn't it?"

"Mr. Dorman," the maître d' said, soothingly.

"It's Svinblad," Dorman said. He made a move toward the table.

The maître d' put a light hand on his arm—somehow, its calmness stopped him. The moment of irrationality passed.

"Please, Mr. Dorman, Anastasia is waiting for you."

He indicated a table to the side of the room.

Dorman looked that way, saw Anastasia's silhouette. "Okay." The initial outburst had been defused, but the nervous adrenaline still raged inside him.

Anastasia smiled as he approached, the maître d' trailing behind him. She wore a black, strapless dress and a thin necklace that hung just below her collarbone. Her hair was up, mascara making her eyes look long and thin.

Dorman picked the vase of flowers off the table, looked under the base, handed it to the startled maître d'. He took the wine bottle off the table, placed it on the floor. Anastasia picked up on what he was doing and grabbed the two wineglasses. Dorman tipped the table back.

"Mr. Dorman," the maître d' said, troubled. Dorman became aware of a change in the music. Some of the musicians had stopped playing and were watching him, as was most of the clientele. There was never a flap in the Ares Club. It was what made the Ares Club what it was. He found nothing attached to the bottom of the table, flipped it back up. He took the wine from the maître d', held his eye for a moment, but saw only confusion.

"Okay," he said again and slid into the booth next to Anastasia.

ANASTASIA TRIED TO SOOTHE HIM, RUBBING HIS ARM, KEEPING HIS GLASS full, listening, asking perfectly weighted questions. No, she didn't know who had his table; no, she didn't think he was strange for wondering. *Let me help you.*

"With what?"

She frowned. "I don't know, Phil. But something. You need help with something."

The band was playing a new number now, very slow.

Could he talk here? Could he explain his isolation—that everyone he knew in this goddamn city had knowingly or, mostly, unknowingly betrayed him in some way? Everyone except her. That, like quicksand, the more he attempted to sort through the complications—the Crosstown, Svinblad, the Ukrainians, the City Center, the Kaiser Street heist—the more hopelessly entangled he became.

So he said nothing. They drank in silence for a while, the music flowing, Anastasia apparently able to watch him endlessly in silence, a worried twist to her mouth.

Finally, she said, "Take me home."

• • •

LATER, DORMAN SLUMPED, BACK AGAINST THE BEDFRAME WHILE ANAS-
tasia slept silently next to him. He looked out over his room, the light
from the street angling up through the blinds, brightening things just
enough that he could see the shapes of his furniture, like shadows.
He'd barely changed a thing since the day that he'd moved in. He felt
no connection here, no permanence.

He looked down at her tiny frame and thought, *Is this how it
worked? Did she wait until you had reached your limit and then, for
just a few moments, she took the pain away?*

82

"I BROUGHT A BLANKET FOR YOU, FRANK."

Frings needed it. Up on the roof of this tenement, there was no
shelter from the freezing wind. Sol wore a heavy coat, a wool hat
pulled low over his ears, his hands in his pockets.

"Why are we here?" Frings sat on the cornice, sharp, hot pain
needling through his knee, first from the effort of ascending the access stairs, and then from the cold. The moon was setting, the scattered night clouds lit purple from beneath. Frings's phone had rung
just after midnight—Sol calling from a payphone with an address.
Meet me there as soon as possible. Frings had pulled himself out of
bed, dressed, called a cab. The address hadn't registered with him
while he was still groggy with sleep, but in the cab he triangulated
in his mind, realized that it was near the Municipal Tower where he
and Nathan Canada had stood just days ago. This was confirmed
as they approached the building, the silhouette of the Tower black
against the crowded, urban sky. Sol had been waiting for him in the
empty lobby. The elevator stank of urine as they rode it to the top
floor. They'd then taken the access stairs up to the roof, where they
now stood.

"Look at it, Frank."

Frings didn't need to ask what to look at. A river of illuminated
destruction—rubbled buildings, empty expanses, motionless construction vehicles; all brilliantly lit by security lights—slashed rudely

through the City's manmade topography. The Crosstown path. Frings felt the dismay in his chest.

"You ever been over here at night, Frank? Have you ever seen this?"

Frings shook his head. The wind was brutal; his nose was becoming numb. He pulled the blanket up over his head to shield his ears. The view was stark, shocking.

"We need to stop this."

"We?" Frings asked. "Who are we?"

"Me. You. Everyone who understands the importance."

"The importance of what, Sol?"

"This." He gestured broadly to the panorama before them. "Goddammit, you of all people know what I'm talking about. We are ceding our humanity to this—commerce, machines. Every advance we make alienates us more from our nature, Frank. You *know* this. Our kind of progress is inherently destructive, it's inevitable, and it's accelerating. If you learn nothing else at the Tech, Frank, you learn that."

Frings nodded. He did understand. He'd written about it, probably been one of the sources of Sol's inspiration.

"It's too late, Sol."

"Bullshit."

"I wish it wasn't."

"Maybe the Crosstown will be finished. Maybe. But we need to make the point that we *understand* what is happening. We need to inform others. People are apathetic because of their ignorance."

"What is Kollectiv 61, Sol?"

Sol laughed. "Details, right? That's your reporter's mind, isn't it? Kollectiv 61 is whatever you think it is."

"But you're part of it."

"Sure, but *anyone* could be part of it. Everyone. It's just an idea, an idea that is available to anyone."

"To oppose the New City Project?"

"To oppose *progress*," Sol snarled. "There's no list, no clubhouse. Radicals in the City are *so passive*. Art. Protest. But what has that achieved? Nothing. Kollectiv 61 is about action. Kollectiv 61 *is* action."

"Who's in charge? You?"

"Nobody's in charge."

Frings was getting frustrated. "Who started it? Who leads by example? I think it's you."

Sol nodded. "Sure."

"You and Andy Macheda."

Sol narrowed his eyes. "You're good, Frank. My grandfather always said that *you* got it. That's why I wanted you to come here. That's why I trust you. You *understand*. You appreciate that I, we, are doing your work."

"Killing Ben Linsky is my work?"

"What, you're accusing me of that?"

"Am I wrong?"

Sol stared at him, eyes blank.

"Did you kill him Sol?"

Sol was silent, staring.

Frings thought about Ebanks claiming that someone had shot at him. "If you did it, if someone else did it, it's counterproductive. It doesn't achieve anything."

"That's enough, Frank. Shit. I don't get you. You can see it, maybe better than anyone, but you've given up or don't care or something. What is that? You're just willing to let this happen? I didn't kill Linsky, but if he was a snitch, he was a traitor. And traitors are executed."

Frings stared at him. While he and Sol were in agreement on some very basic political level, they were terribly far apart on just about everything else. There was no common understanding from which he could reason with Sol.

Sol was pacing the roof. Frings saw his breath come out as clouds of steam.

"I'm just not sure that killing people is the answer," Frings said, lamely. He knew how this would sound to Sol.

Sol gave an exaggerated, frustrated sigh. His shoulders slumped. "Okay, I see this is going nowhere." The anger had suddenly left his voice, replaced by resignation. "But I need you to do something for me."

Frings was shaking from the cold now.

"Come on," Sol said, taking Frings gently by the shoulders, guiding him toward the access door. "We need to get you inside."

Frings limped badly to the stairs, then descended one painful step at a time. Three stairs from the top-floor landing Sol stopped him and helped him sit on the step, blanket still around his shoulders.

"Listen, I'm sorry to have to get you out here in the middle of the night. I heard you were at the Tech yesterday, that you got behind Ledley's door."

Frings nodded. How did he know that?

"I need you to go back there, get my file for me." His voice echoed off the close, cold walls.

"Why do you need it, Sol? What can it do for you?"

"You don't need to know that. I just need the file." He was nearly yelling.

Frings sighed. "I don't know—"

"Damn it, I'm owed this." Sol's yell was almost deafening in the confined space.

Frings thought about this, about what he'd read on Ledley's study, what he'd heard from Finch and Sol. Sol had been tortured in a way that Frings could not even begin to understand. If there was one thing that people kept telling him about the hallucinogens it was that, having never experienced them, he had no idea about them.

"*I* don't owe you them."

"It doesn't matter who owes me them. I'm *owed*. I will get them any way I can. I trust you, Frank. You might think that I killed Linsky, but I trust you. If I can't get them from you, I will try something else, fuck the consequences."

Frings was fatigued. His knee burned. He held up his hands. "Okay, Sol. I'll try to get your records."

83

GRIP HAD THE DOOR TO THE DETECTIVES' ROOM CLOSED TO NO EFFECT against the noise from the booking area, filled with angry prostitutes rousted in some kind of sweep. Grip figured that there was something at work here—someone not paying their protection money—or maybe a councilor or even the mayor had sent a note that they wanted something done. Regardless, the din of dozens of whores yelling at equally pissed-off cops drove Grip upstairs to the cafeteria, where he worked on some overdue reports and drank stale coffee.

It was here that a Negro lieutenant named Dominguez told him that Ving wanted him to ride along for an arrest run that Dominguez was going to lead. Grip left his cup on the cafeteria table and carried his paperwork downstairs to the detectives' room, where he locked them in a desk drawer.

"What's this about?" Grip asked as they took the elevator down to the garage.

"Buddy of yours," Dominguez said, "Lieutenant Zwieg."

He rode shotgun in a cruiser that followed just behind Dominguez's lead car. He thought he counted six cars in all, which seemed like a lot. But arresting a lieutenant with Zwieg's clout wasn't something to take lightly. They didn't use lights or sirens as they wound through the streets. The wind had shifted, and people on the sidewalks seemed in a hurry to get where they were going. Others, who'd read the forecast, carried closed umbrellas.

Grip didn't make small talk with the uniform who was driving, another Negro whose name he didn't get. As he watched the blocks slip by, Grip, with his chest tightening, began to understand where they were heading. He'd been surprised that Kraatjes had seemed so quick to absolve him of any responsibility. Even though he'd come clean, it was hard to understand why the chief had barely even bothered to admonish him. But now he saw that Kraatjes had been waiting; he would punish Grip by isolating him even further.

They turned on to the block that Grip knew they'd eventually arrive at, and watched the pervs on the street hustle away as the police cars pulled to the curb. It happened fast once they'd parked, since there was no way to conceal their presence, and they didn't want to give too much forewarning. They assembled on the sidewalk, twenty officers in uniform in addition to Grip. More than half of the cops were Negroes. Grip shook his head—sending Negro cops to arrest a racist like Zwieg was a masterstroke of humiliation.

He saw Art Deyna and a photographer loitering a few doors down from Crippen's, watching the police assemble.

Dominguez waved Grip over before they went in.

"Why are we doing it here?" Grip asked, though he already knew the answer. It would have been much easier to arrest Zwieg when he arrived at work, or even at his home, but ease wasn't the issue.

"Ving said he wanted to send a message," Dominguez said.

Grip understood that *he* was supposed to be getting a message too.

"Some of my guys," Dominguez continued, "were real enthusiastic when they heard where we were headed. Ving wanted you inside, but once you're in, you can just sit back and enjoy."

Grip nodded. Then, without further delay, the cops pushed through the door and flooded into Crippen's.

BY THE TIME GRIP GOT INSIDE, THE COPS WERE ALREADY PUSHING PEOPLE up against the wall. Tables were overturned, drinks spilled on the floor; a couple of younger men who Grip thought might be off-duty cops were yelling back at the uniforms who were moving them toward a wall. One of the Negro cops cracked the bigger of the two across the knees with a nightstick, and the guy went down, curling up with his knees to his chest.

A number of the patrons, guys who Grip had known for years, now noticed his presence and kept their eyes on him—some with surprise, some with anger. Wayne was leaning against a wall, smiling crookedly, holding in his hand a blond toupee that had apparently been knocked off during the commotion. He gave Grip a half-lidded glare.

Flashes of light added to the chaos. Grip turned toward the source and saw the press photographer standing on a chair, shooting the bust. Deyna sidled up to Grip. He seemed uncertain.

"What are you doing here?" Grip asked.

"I got a tip."

"From who?"

"I don't know."

Grip thought about this for a moment. Then he laughed.

"What's funny?" Deyna asked, his usual arrogance entirely missing.

"You work with Zwieg, don't you? That's why you always know where to find me. He's your big source."

Deyna didn't bother to deny it. "So?"

Grip shook his head. "Do you know what's going on here? That tip was from Kraatjes. *He knows*. He knows that you were helping Zwieg make a move on him, and he's letting you know that he knows. And it doesn't matter if Zwieg used you or what, you were involved."

The blood drained from Deyna's face.

"Get the fuck out of here, Art. I can't afford the trouble I'd get into for kicking your face in."

Deyna looked uncertain, and Grip walked away from him, toward Zwieg.

Zwieg had not been moved to the wall, like the rest of the patrons. Instead he sat, isolated, in a chair flanked by uniforms. Dominguez walked over to him and it seemed to Grip that the rest of the noise in the room ceased.

"Lieutenant," Dominguez said, formally.

"The fuck is going on?"

"You're being arrested."

"For what?" Zwieg sneered.

"Why don't we start with theft of the Kaiser Street explosives," Dominguez said, evenly.

"Fuck you. You've got no idea what you're fucking talking about."

"No?" Dominguez snapped a punch to Zwieg's face, knocking him backward. Both Zwieg and the chair flipped hard onto the tiled floor. With his foot, Dominguez pushed Zwieg's head so that one cheek was on the linoleum, and then he put his foot on the other cheek, holding Zwieg's head in place. "I think that before we go back to the station, you need to bring me to wherever you have those explosives stashed."

Zwieg managed to say, "Go fuck yourself."

Grip could see Dominguez lean some of his weight onto Zwieg's head. Zwieg's legs squirmed, but he stayed silent.

"Tell you what. Why don't we get into my car, and I'll get the pliers from the trunk, and we'll see if you can give me some directions, okay?"

AS THEY WALKED OUT, GRIP STOLE A LOOK AT WAYNE, WHO WAS STILL leaned up against the wall, his shoulders shaking with silent laughter. Deyna and the photographer were gone, and when Grip emerged onto the street, they weren't there either.

84

THE SIX PROWL CARS ROLLED WITH THEIR LIGHTS OFF THROUGH THE narrow blocks of the City's South End. The neighborhoods here were small, low, cramped, the script on the signs constantly changing from Cyrillic to Arabic to Roman to any of a number of Asian alphabets. Rain had begun to fall steadily.

The lead car carried Zwieg, cuffed, in the back. Grip was in the second car, riding in the back next to Deputy Chief Ving. Two uniforms sat in front. Grip was relieved that Zwieg had finally been arrested and that he still seemed to be in the clear. But he still didn't understand what had happened, the details of the plot he'd been dragooned into.

"You seem anxious, Detective," Ving said, looking straight ahead.

"Sir?"

"I would have thought you'd be relieved that this is almost over."

"I think I'd feel better about it if I knew the full story."

"We're still trying to get a handle on that ourselves."

Grip didn't say anything to that.

Ving waited a moment—maybe calculating how much he was willing to share—before continuing. "The way the Chief sees it, is something like this. Zwieg wanted to make a move, get rid of the Chief, probably put himself in line as the successor. He thinks Zwieg figured out that there was some kind of link between headquarters and the radical community—and he probably thought, or maybe just hoped, that it led to Kollectiv 61. In any case, he thought he might be able to use it to undermine the Chief. So—and this is still unconfirmed—he, and he obviously has help here, he pulls the Kaiser Street heist. He plans to spray-paint one of those sayings that Kollectiv 61 leaves, but is interrupted by something—probably an after-hours delivery. Kaiser Street is on his turf, so he figures he'll be able to keep it relatively quiet. Canada's people won't want to make it a big deal because it'll make people nervous. He lets his pet reporter know it happened and tells him to sit on the story, that he'll get the real scoop later, meaning when he makes his final move on the Chief. He gives the guy a hint, though, tells him that the spray-painted message was there, even though it wasn't.

"So, they need someone to do the investigating—someone who they have some control over, who they don't think can hurt them. They choose you, because, quite frankly, you don't have many allies. They get Nicky Patridis to provide the connection between the explosives and Kollectiv 61. From there, they hope that you can turn up the connection between Kollectiv 61 and the Chief. You found it, but it wasn't with Kollectiv 61, it was with Ben Linsky. Zwieg thought that this, along with the connection between Linsky and Kollectiv 61, would probably be enough once it hit the newspapers. But it won't be. Linsky was an informant."

Grip sighed. "So Zwieg is history?"

Ving looked over at Grip. "He's history."

THE LEAD CAR TOOK A LEFT ONTO A STREET BARELY WIDER THAN AN ALLEY, each side dotted with makeshift awnings above doors and windows with signs in Chinese characters. The car hit its lights, and the driver of Grip's car did the same, then tapped on the siren and performed half a k-turn so that they blocked the entrance. The other cars stopped in the middle of the block. Cops emerged slowly into the rain. Grip slid out of his car, pulled the hood of his gray rain jacket up. He counted about a dozen cops.

There were groups of men huddled under most of the awnings, drinking from teacups or eating from bowls. Rainwater, thick as curtains, poured off the low roofs.

Three police cars—lights going, sirens off—pulled into the far end of the block. Six uniforms emerged and walked toward Grip's group, aggressive, hands on their holstered guns.

"This ain't your turf," said a uniform with painful-looking cauliflower ears. "What the fuck business you got here?"

Grip scowled at him beneath half-lids. "See him?" Grip nodded at the handcuffed Zwieg. "You think this is something you want to screw with?"

The uniform tensed, his hand tightening on the pistol grip. Ving, who had been watching, stepped forward.

"You know who I am, officer?" Ving's voice was calm, almost quiet.

The uniform stopped, looked from Ving to Zwieg.

"Turn around and go, before I read your badge number," Ving said.

"Yeah, okay," the officer said and retreated with his crew.

"I thought so," Grip taunted.

The uniform turned back to him. "We ain't done."

Grip waved.

Ving was calling the shots. Grip walked down the block to where he stood with Zwieg.

"That one." Ving indicated an unmarked door between what appeared to be two teahouses. "Down in the basement, he says."

Zwieg stared at Grip from behind swollen eyes. His right cheekbone had turned purple and yellow. His lips were ragged, misshapen. He looked resigned. He'd lost, and somehow Grip had come out okay.

"He got a key?" Grip asked.

"No." Ving nodded toward two uniforms pulling a battering ram from the trunk of a squad car.

Grip led the two men to the door. It was steel, four locks. It took eight blows from the ram before the hinges finally gave way and the door hung useless from two bolts. One of the uniforms held it out of the way, and Grip led the men into the darkness. He felt against the wall, found the light switch.

He was on a service landing. In front of him, narrow steps led steeply down to a tiny room, barely touched by the light. A cop handed Grip a flashlight from behind and he led the men down, the stairs squeaking under their feet. At the bottom, the tiny room was empty, except for a door and the smell of must. Grip held his hand up, pressed his ear to the door. Silence. Still, they'd made a racket on the stairs coming down, and anyone inside would have been alerted.

"Police," Grip yelled. "Anyone in there?"

Still silence. He tried the knob. Locked.

He yelled up the stairs. "Bring the ram."

The battering ram team eased past the cops waiting on the narrow stairs.

"Guns out," Grip said. He held his gun in his right hand and his flashlight, trained on the door, in his left. The guys with the battering ram looked to him, waiting for the go-ahead. Grip nodded.

The door came down with the first blow. The cops next to him tensed. The flashlight lit the room—no one home.

It was a storage room—eight by twelve, he guessed—boxes of stick dynamite stacked against the far wall. There was a lot there, but not enough. Not even close.

Grip nodded one of the uniforms in. "This look like enough dynamite to fill a trailer?"

"No way. A quarter, maybe. Probably less than that."

Grip shook his head, climbed the stairs two at a time, shouldering aside startled uniforms. He stepped out onto the street, felt the cold rain on his face. He found Zwieg, grabbed him by the coat with both hands, slammed him into a wall. Zwieg barked in pain as his hands and arms, cuffed behind his back, took the impact.

"The trailer, how full was it when you cleaned it out?"

Zwieg looked at him, weary and condescending. Grip tapped Zwieg's forehead with the heel of his hand, bouncing his head off the wall.

"You'll regret that." Zwieg said.

"How full?"

"Nearly full. Four-fifths."

"'Cause there's less than a quarter trailer's worth in there."

Zwieg didn't smile, but his eyes were amused. He shrugged.

Grip walked away, paced in the street, hair soaked, shoes soaked. He felt the eyes of the assembled cops, most of whom could not have heard his conversation with Zwieg over the rain and urban noise. Anger, frustration, the feelings of powerlessness and humiliation that had tormented him these last few days—all of it built up within him as he paced.

"Fuck," he muttered to himself, turned, and advanced with speed on a startled Zwieg. Four uniforms intercepted him, held him back, prevented him from getting himself into trouble again.

* * *

EXCERPT FROM TRANSCRIPT OF DYADIC INTERVIEW WITH SUBJECT 8

3/8/60

because then I would . . .

Interviewer: You would what? What do you think you would do, because you say that you value the equality of men, isn't that right? The equality of men: those are the words you used.

Subject 8: Yes, I think that . . . equality . . . I'm . . .

Interviewer: You say it, you use those words, but I know that you don't really mean them. Look at you. Look at where you are. You're at the Tech. You think that's a place where you can find equality? You think that there is anything equal about people who are at the Tech?

Subject 8: I guess, I think that it's hard to say what's equal because when I look at you now and I think that you're like another human and just the same as someone else like maybe a farmer or something in Peru.

Interviewer: Peru? You think that some impoverished Peruvian farmer is equal to me, much less you, who are at the Tech? You don't believe that. You are lying to me. You lie to the world when you say that you believe things like that. You say them because it makes you feel better about the fact that you take every explicit opportunity, equality be damned. So stop it with this bullshit. Stop lying to me. Stop putting forward a false image to the world—it rots the soul. I look at you and I think that your soul must be rotting because you are incapable of being honest even when you write your own personal fucking philosophy, which will not be shared with anyone. You are so rotted and degraded that you will tell lies to no one, you will try to deceive yourself about the truth of your own corrupted nature.

Subject 8: <Does not respond>

Interviewer: That's it? You have nothing to say for yourself—no defense, no admission?

Subject 8: I . . .

Interviewer: You are as diseased a subject as I have had the misfortune to come across. Based on what I've read and heard, I don't think I can trust you about anything—I don't think that you can trust yourself . . .

85

FRINGS KNOCKED ON THE DOOR TO EBANKS'S HOUSE, BUT NO ONE ANswered. He knocked again and waited, but again there was nothing, just a stillness that made him think that the place was empty. The previous day's rain had passed through and the sky was brilliant, the air clear and cold. Frings limped away from the house, leaning on his cane, his knee throbbing.

He walked slowly to the Tech campus and then along a brick pathway toward Bristol Hall—the psychology building. He had the keys that Milledge had left behind, and thought he'd have another look at Ledley's files. If nothing else, he could retrieve the files that Sol wanted. He saw no reason to deny Sol that small favor. Classes were in session, so the paths were mostly empty. Frings thought that final exams must be coming up. The usual protestors were nowhere to be seen.

He was startled to see, approaching him on the path but oblivious of his presence, Will Ebanks. Ebanks seemed to be lost in thought, staring at the pavement ahead of him as he walked.

"Will?"

Ebanks started at the sound of his name and looked at Frings with wide eyes. His irises were nearly entirely black. "Frank," he said, vaguely. "What are you doing here?"

"I'm going to take another look at Ledley's files."

"I don't know if that's a great idea."

Frings noticed now that Ebanks's hands were trembling; in fact, his entire body was shaking slightly.

"What's going on?" Frings asked, cautiously.

"Frank." Ebanks was clearly trying hard to figure out what to say. Frings wondered if he was on LSD.

"I need to hear something, Will, or I'm going to Ledley's."

"Sol Elia came to see me this morning. He came to kill me. He was going to end my life. It's hard to fathom that my body might very well not have made it until now. Do you know? The thing, though, the thing that I needed to make Sol understand was that ending my life didn't accomplish anything for his soul. If his act was truly to get some redemption for his life, my death would be of no use."

Frings wasn't sure that Sol would see it that way—but here was Ebanks, alive.

"Where is Sol right now?"

"Where is he? He's with Si." Ebanks gave a strange laugh. "The thing with Sol is that he . . . he was part of those experiments that Si did, the ones that he conducted in the hall behind the door. Sol—the way he is—it goes back to that time with Si and that weird little assistant he had. The experiments. He came out a different person. That's what he needs to exorcise."

"Is that what you told him?" Frings asked, incredulous.

"I was faced with my own mortality. It was unjust. It's not my time."

"Is Sol in that building with Ledley?"

"Yes. Sol and Si and Andy Macheda."

Ebanks was dazed.

Frings wanted to say a number of things to Ebanks, but there wasn't time, and he could confront Ebanks later. Instead he fixed Ebanks with a quick, furious glare, and limped off as fast as he could toward Bristol Hall.

Classes were letting out as he entered the building against a tide of students. All of these kids were oblivious to what Frings suspected was happening just below them. He took the steps down to the basement as fast as he could. The lights in the hallway were on, bathing everything in greenish illumination. Ledley's door was closed. He tried it, found it locked. He knocked, the sound echoing back to him. No answer. Satisfied that Ledley wasn't around, he walked to the door that divided the hallway. He unlocked it with Milledge's keys.

The first thing he noticed as he opened the door was a patch of light coming from a room down the hall. He was immediately on his guard. He took a step in, heard talking—Ledley's voice, strangely pitched. He left the door dividing the hall open behind him, just in case. He moved slowly, not using his cane because he didn't want anyone to hear the tapping. He paused just outside of the light. He hadn't yet heard another voice, couldn't make out what Ledley was saying, but Ebanks had said that Sol and Macheda were in there with him.

He peered around the corner, saw Ledley sitting in a chair under bright lights, reading from a sheaf of papers in his hand. To his side, Sol half-sat against a table, papers in one hand, gun in the other, watching through slitted eyes. In front of Ledley, with his back to Frings, Andy Macheda peered through the eyepiece of a movie camera aimed at Ledley. They were in a big room, one door down from the storeroom where Frings had gone through Ledley's files. The area around them was dark, except for the wall behind Ledley where the men's black shadows were carved out of the brilliant light.

Without thinking, Frings stepped into the doorway, distracting Ledley from his reading. Sol turned toward him, smiled. Macheda turned around as well, not seeming too surprised to see Frings.

"Sorry, Frank"—Sol said—"I went to see Ebanks to have a talk, and he made a pretty good case that my anger toward him was misguided. It's really Dr. Ledley and people like him who are the problem, he says. They are the ones using the instruments of revolution against the revolutionary. I came here with Ebanks to have a talk with Dr. Ledley and thought I'd bring Andy with me. Do you know Andy, Frank?"

Frings nodded.

"Frank, call security. End this madness." Ledley was pale, his eyes shone with desperation.

Sol slowly shook his head. "We're being nice to you, Dr. Ledley. Don't push it."

"Frank," Ledley implored.

"What exactly is going on here?" Frings looked to Sol.

Sol nodded toward Ledley. "Ask him."

Ledley made to stand, but Sol held his gun up.

"Will came with these two. They forced me to take LSD and brought me back here. Will left."

Frings looked from Sol to Macheda.

"We're filming," Macheda said. "This is the crucial piece, the most important piece."

"Jesus Christ," Ledley screamed, "aren't you going to do something."

Sol laughed. "Did you shut the door behind you when you came in? The one at the end of the hall?"

Frings shook his head.

"You mind getting that, Andy? I can say from experience that with that door closed, it doesn't matter what you do, no one will hear."

Macheda left the room to close the hallway door. Ledley slumped in his chair, his brief moment of hope gone. Its passing seemed to have drained him of the fight. Frings couldn't summon any sympathy for the man, but he was troubled by what Sol might do. How was this going to end? Down the hall they heard the steel door closing.

Sol was up now. "Tell him what you're reading into the camera."

"They're making me read transcripts from the study."

"You can do better than that."

"Transcripts from the dyadic interviews where—"

"Where you gave us LSD and tried to destroy our minds."

Ledley shuddered.

Macheda returned. "It's funny how we were living in the middle of it and we totally missed it, you know what I mean?"

Frings didn't.

"I was making this movie, you know, and the Films, they were kind of like the sketch pad, trying things out. The whole time, I didn't get it, man. I thought it was all about the New City Project, how they were going to rearrange the City and people were going to lose out, you know, to capitalism, business. But that's just a part of it—a big part of it, but just a part."

"A part of what, Andy?"

"A part of what?" Sol said. "I thought you would have figured this out by now. You were on the right track. You showed a lot of us where to start. But we made the mistake of thinking that there were all these different problems—the New City Project, the people they let in and don't let in at the Tech, the Vilnius Street experiment, this project. All these things, Frank, all these bad things. But something dropped in our laps and we thought about it a little."

"Do you—" Ledley started.

"Shut up," Sol yelled.

Frings held up a hand to Ledley, trying to both quiet and reassure him.

Macheda said, "Looking back on it, I think Andre LaValle must have figured it out, which is why they keep him drugged at City. That's why he must have killed the chief, because he figured it out."

"What fell into your laps?"

"One of Ben Linsky's roommates gave me a letter that Ben had written about his friends and meetings and who was where when."

Frings felt the dread rise up in him.

Sol returned to his perch against the table. "It was a snitch report, Frank. Ben Linsky was a snitch, though I guess that's not exactly a secret now. But it got us thinking about Ben, you know? What does he do? What does he think?"

"What effect does he have?" Macheda said.

"Effect?"

Sol was up and walking again. "Ben Linsky, the champion of abstraction, of muddling the message."

"Art can't be straightforward or it isn't art," Macheda said, quoting Linsky. "Everything needs to be obscure."

"Ben wasn't being paid for his information," Sol continued. "He was being paid for his beliefs, to keep him influential. Did you know that the police fund *Prometheus*? It's their baby, their way of making sure that Ben's message gets out—to keep radicals at bay."

"I'm not sure—" Frings began, though he saw that they were right.

Sounding frustrated, Sol interrupted him. "His purpose was to obscure the message. Make it hard to understand, only accessible to a small group of people. It's how they control the radicals."

"One of the ways," Macheda said.

"It seems crazy," Frings said.

"Does it?" Sol said. "How about this—how about your friend Will Ebanks. What do you think about him?"

"What about him?"

"He's on the payroll, too, right? Why do you think? You think it might be that the mayor, the police, whoever it is that's calling the shots—that they don't mind people looking for revolution inside their own heads? Think about it. Look at it from another point of view: that this is all about controlling people. Tell me it doesn't make sense."

It did make sense, but only after making some big assumptions that Frings wasn't sure he could make.

"Did you kill Ben Linsky, Sol?" Frings asked.

Sol's face darkened. "And what if I did?"

SOL HAD GROWN MORE AGITATED, PACING AROUND THE ROOM. LEDLEY looked terrible, and Frings had to remind himself of the students who'd been subjected to far worse. Macheda leaned against the wall, staying out of Sol's way. They seemed reluctant to resume filming with Frings in the room. This concerned Frings, though he wasn't scared for himself. He didn't believe that Sol would harm him. But the question hung in the air: what would he—Frings—do when he walked out of the room? Would he call the police? It left Sol, he knew, in a difficult position.

"Look around you, Frank. This is where it all happened, where *this bastard*"—he turned ferociously to Ledley—"conducted his study. This is where they tried to break down my psyche, leave my mind in rubble. And I can't forgive that. I really can't.

"But what I want you to realize before you leave here is that the enormity of this is not what happened to me or to any of the other guys who were involved. No, this was just one part of a bigger effort, a consuming effort to control people in this city.

"So, when you ask me if I killed Ben Linsky, my response is—if I did, I had every right to do it. He was part of this, Frank. At least Dr. Ledley doesn't pretend he's something that he isn't. Linsky took money to keep artists from using their art to communicate with the people. He was a malevolent presence in the radical community. He was a part of the effort to control us. He was one of the people responsible for what happened to me."

Frings could follow the logic, but again couldn't quite endorse the assumptions. "Even if that were true, it's still murder. His not being who he said he was, even being a *malevolent presence*, doesn't change that fact."

"You know what I'm interested in, Frank? I'm interested in your moral arithmetic. I think we agree on most things, am I right? What's happening in our City is destructive to the vast majority of people who live here. That people who see this are morally bound to oppose the New City Project, the Crosstown, the way the Tech keeps the rich rich and the poor poor, all these things. How many people are negatively affected by these things? Hundreds of thousands? Millions? And then we have people working within the community of resistors, people who have assured us that they are working for the same things that we are, and it turns out they are undermining our efforts, that they're on the payroll of our enemies. How can we *not* respond to that? How are drastic measures not called for? One man, Frank. One treacherous man versus the well-being of the City. You think I'm wrong?"

Sol was becoming more and more agitated. Frings snuck a look at Macheda and saw that he didn't seem overly concerned, which he took as a good sign. Sol had always oscillated between amiability and anger.

"I don't"—Frings said cautiously—"think that killing Linsky, or anyone, is the best choice, the moral choice, for dealing with this kind of issue. Expose him, use the outrage when the public catches wind of it to your advantage." As he said this, he was thinking of Ledley, catatonic in his chair, as much as Linsky. "Get the people on your side; don't force them away from you with violence."

"That's always your answer, isn't it? Expose the truth and things will right themselves. How did that work with your book? Did that stop anything? You wrote it and left the action to others. What does that get you? I don't see anything."

"And yet—"

"We're making the movie. Yes. We'll try it because that's the best we've got right now. Your book, visionary as it was, was a tract. You don't get huge numbers of people to read tracts. This is art. Maybe it will inspire people. If it wasn't dangerous, why would they be so concerned about it, pay Ben Linsky to undermine it?"

Why indeed, Frings thought. "I'm going to leave now. But I need to know that you're not going to harm the professor."

"Not to worry. As long as he cooperates, we'll leave the bastard at his desk with a cup of coffee."

Frings nodded.

Sol looked to Macheda, back to Frings. "The question is, what are you going to do? You going to turn us in?"

They stared at each other.

"Because, Frank, this is the test, right? Are you an armchair radical, or are you willing to let your people do what they need to do?"

Frings shook his head. "I don't know." He turned to leave.

Ledley suddenly snapped back to the present. "My god, Frings, don't leave."

Frings looked to Sol, who gave him a reassuring smile. Frings took a last look at Ledley and walked out of the room.

• • •

FRINGS SAT IN LEDLEY'S OFFICE WITH HIS FEET ON THE DESK, SMOKING A reefer. He looked at the pictures of Ada Hauptman staring back at him, wondered what it said about Simon Ledley that this was his lover.

After a while he used Ledley's phone, got passed around head-quarters, until he was patched through to Grip, the sound distant, fading in and out, occasionally interrupted by a burst of static. Frings pictured an operator holding the phone receiver to a police radio, get-ting Grip on the street somewhere..

"Detective Grip, I'm at Simon Ledley's office at the Tech. Sol Elia's here, too. You were right about Sol. You were right all along."

"What is this, Frank?"

"It's Sol. He's here for you. Come get him."

87

GRIP PULLED HIS GUN AT THE TOP OF THE STAIRS AND DESCENDED SLOWLY, trying to work out what to expect. He didn't like Frings, but he trusted him. The man was in many ways an adversary, but one who confined his actions to his columns and politics, not violence—at least as far as Grip knew. He didn't think this was a setup.

But still, it was hard to figure what was going on. At the bottom of the stairs, he pushed the door open and led with his gun. The hall-way was empty. Light came from an open door to his right.

"Detective Grip."

Grip recognized Frings's voice. "You alone?"

Frings emerged from the room. "They're in there." Frings nodded toward a closed door at the end of the hall.

"Is that right? What are they doing?"

"They've got a professor in there—Simon Ledley. He's drugged. I don't think they're going to hurt him physically, but I'm not sure. Sol's got a gun."

"How do you know this?"

"I was in there."

"And they let you go?"

Frings nodded.

"You know why?"

"They didn't think that I would call the police."

Grip thought about this. "Why wouldn't you?"

"Sol thinks we're on the same side. He doesn't think I'd turn him in."

Grip shook his head. "That's a crazy risk."

Frings shrugged.

"You say he confessed to killing his parents?"

"No, he confessed to killing Ben Linsky. I'm pretty sure he also tried to kill Will Ebanks. He didn't say anything about his parents— but I don't doubt that he did it, not anymore."

Grip barely registered the second part of what Frings said. Sol Elia had killed Linsky. He—Grip—had planted the letter in Linsky's apartment, it had ended up in Sol's hands, and Sol had killed Linsky. He realized that he was grinding his teeth. Frings had seen his agitation as well.

"You said he has someone else in there?"

"Yeah, Andy Macheda."

Grip nodded. It made sense. "Door locked?"

Frings shook his head.

GRIP OPENED THE DOOR SLOWLY, SAW THE DARKNESS THAT LAY BEHIND it. A splash of light came from a room about halfway down on the left. He heard voices, sensed the agitation. He forced himself to move slowly, trying to contain his anger, be sure that the adrenaline wouldn't cause him to make a mistake. Morphy had moved too quickly down in the tunnel.

At the doorway, he glanced in. Sol Elia stood with his back to the door, reading from a piece of paper, a gun in his other hand. In a chair, facing him, was Simon Ledley, also with a clutch of papers, looking terrified. Ledley looked toward him and Grip thought that they'd made eye contact, but the professor's eyes didn't seem to register his presence. He couldn't see Macheda, but guessed that he was to the left, because both Ledley and Sol were angled in that direction. He took three quick, deep breaths and followed his gun into the room.

"Drop the fucking gun, Sol."

He took a quick glance at Macheda to see if he was armed, but the guy had turned his camera Grip's way and it was clear he was intent on capturing this on film.

Sol turned. "I'm not dropping the gun, Torsten." He said Grip's name mockingly. Grip tried not to let it get him more worked up.

Grip took a step closer, but Sol raised the gun and he stopped.

"What's it going to be, detective? Are you going to wait and let me kill you or are you going to pull the trigger?"

Grip was still, his hand steady. He wasn't sure what Sol was trying to do—get himself killed? People did that, committed suicide by provoking cops into shooting them. But this didn't feel like that kind of situation.

"I was right about you, Sol."

"Were you? I guess you could look at it that way, but you never really *got* it."

"Got what? You killed your parents. Now you've killed at least one other person and from what I've heard today, looks like you tried to kill Will Ebanks, but you fucked it up."

Sol seemed mildly disappointed by this news. "So shoot me then, Torsten. I'm armed and dangerous, right? You have every reason."

"You don't get to make that decision."

"Maybe I do." Sol seemed to lean forward, about to make a move.

A voice came from behind Grip. "Sol—"

Sol's eyes shifted. Grip pulled the trigger, hitting Sol in the shoulder, knocking him on his back. The gun skittered to the corner.

Sol curled up into the fetal position, moaning, blood soaking his shirt. Frings moved around Grip to kneel beside Sol, put a hand on his undamaged shoulder. Macheda kept the camera rolling.

"You want to turn that fucking thing off?"

Macheda shook his head. Grip walked over to Sol's gun and picked it up. He popped the clip.

Frings looked up at Macheda. "I think you can turn that off, Andy."

Macheda put the camera down, looked uncertainly at Grip.

"Sit down," Grip said, waving his gun toward a chair.

Ledley sat silently with his head in his hands, trembling. Sol pulled himself to a sitting position with his back to the wall. His skin was waxy, his shirt saturated with blood.

Grip watched Frings try to squat next to him, wince, and sit on the ground with him.

Frings said, "Sol, we need to get you an ambulance."

Sol nodded. Macheda took Ledley with him to make the call. Grip leaned against the wall and watched Frings help Sol into a chair.

"I knew you'd betray me, Frank," Sol said, his voice strained with pain.

"Sol—"

"I knew when I let you go that you'd call the police. You're not a revolutionary, you don't have the conviction that it takes to make things happen."

Grip resisted the urge to pistol-whip him. "Shut up."

Sol turned to Grip, then back to Frings.

"We talked about it after you left, thought maybe we'd get something good on camera, cops busting in."

"You wanted to get shot," Frings said.

Sol tried to shrug, winced, and stopped. "I *got* shot, damnit. Get the fuck out of here, Frank. You . . . I can't stand to look at your face."

Grip watched Frings nod, use the wall to lift himself painfully to his feet, and, leaning his hand on his cane, retreat from the room.

"You're a fraud," Sol called after him, his voice barely more than a stage whisper. "You're a scared old man."

Grip had heard enough. He walked over to Sol and with a flick of his wrist tapped Sol hard on the head with his pistol butt. Sol's eyes shifted out of focus and then back in.

Grip leaned over, putting his face right into Sol's. "Shut the hell up." Then he walked over, took a seat in Ledley's chair, waited for the medics to arrive.

88

SPARSELY LIT IN THE NIGHT, THE CONSTRUCTION SITE RESEMBLED A NO-man's land—gravel, dirt, and in a far corner, their shapes difficult to make out, feral dogs, or maybe coyotes. Dorman wore a scarf under his pea coat, a wool cap pulled over his ears. His back was hunched against the cold wind that blew through the chain-link fence, scattering leaves. Above, the finished part of the building rose thirty stories above Idaho Avenue, before giving way to the steel skeleton, which rose another twenty-eight. Red lights flashed at the corners of the top floor, almost impossibly high. A searchlight perched at the top of the Municipal Tower, ten blocks in the distance, swept the sky, illuminating the scaffolding twice a minute or so.

Dorman walked toward the partially finished building and saw a man waiting by the construction lift. It wasn't Wayne. Dorman hesitated.

"Mr. Dorman." The man yelled to be heard over the wind.

Dorman walked again, but the nerves that he'd arrived with now lashed through him like venom. Why was there a second man?

When he was within fifteen feet, the other man stepped forward.

"Mr. Dorman, are you carrying a weapon?"

"No."

"Wearing a wire?"

"No."

"Mind if I pat you down?"

Dorman held out his arms, let the guy give him an efficient search. Professional.

"You a cop?" Dorman asked.

"Sure."

"Name?"

The man hesitated.

"You've got mine."

The man shrugged, laughed a little. "Albertsson."

The name didn't mean anything to Dorman. "Where's Wayne?"

Albertsson looked up.

Dorman nodded. "Okay."

They ascended in the lift. With each passing floor the City revealed more of itself, glittering and monstrous. The wind was getting stronger as the shelter of the surrounding buildings gave way. Dorman looked at Albertsson, caught his eye, received a smile and a wink. Dorman wondered if this should worry him.

They passed the top of the finished section. Dorman could see through the steel skeleton to the east side of the City now, the darkness of the Crosstown route a glorious, violent river of light. From up here, at night, the Municipal Tower seemed menacing, looming over the smaller buildings. The searchlight hit them, momentarily blinding Dorman.

They were approaching the level of the landing. Dorman noticed that the safety lights were on. Maybe Albertsson or Wayne had turned them on from below, before they'd come up. He covered his eyes against the searchlight on its next sweep.

They crested the landing. Wayne waited for them in the dim illumination, tall and pear-shaped.

Albertsson stepped aside to let Dorman off. Dorman hesitated.

Wayne spoke. "Come aboard, Mr. Dorman. We need to talk." He spread his arms wide as if to indicate that he had nothing to hide. The searchlight lit him briefly in silhouette.

Dorman stepped on to the platform and saw that he had a gun, holding it loosely at his side.

"Why are we doing this up here?"

"Away from prying ears, Mr. Dorman. Besides, we thought maybe you'd want a good seat, watch it with us."

"Watch what?"

Lit in the pale glow of the security lights, Wayne was even more grotesque, like a wax figure partially melted. He wore a huge fur hat and a trench coat that flapped in the wind. When he smiled, his teeth were small and gray.

"You'll see. The surprise will be half the fun."

• • •

THE SEARCHLIGHT LIT WAYNE FROM BEHIND AGAIN.

"Why don't I explain why I asked you here. It may turn out to render your conversation moot."

Dorman looked from Wayne to Albertsson, who had moved to the far edge of the small platform. Dorman didn't like the feeling he was getting about this meeting. Wayne was an unnerving presence—he cast off malice like spores.

"Our mutual acquaintance—and please let me know if you are unclear who I am referring to—asked me to talk to you, see if you'd be amenable to taking home a little extra monthly pay for representing his interests with Nathan Canada. He said he broached the subject with you, but couldn't get a read on whether you'd accept such a proposition. So I made inquiries. No one seems to know you very well. You are an unknown quantity. So I thought I might meet you in person, see what my instincts told me."

Beyond Wayne, the Municipal Tower seemed too big and too close, giving him a slight feeling of vertigo.

"Do you have anything to say about this?" Wayne asked.

Dorman shook his head. It seemed the safest thing to do.

"That won't work," Wayne growled. "You must give me an answer, one way or the other. Let me make this clearer. My understanding is that you had some interest in the three murdered Bulgarian security guards—the ones from the Kaiser Street site. Is that right?"

Wayne waited until Dorman nodded.

"Good. They pinned it on some poor saps who work muscle for Smed Nanyan down in the Hollows. But they didn't do it. I did. Or, I did one of them—credit where it's due. So you see, I've got too much to lose to let you off this building without an answer. And there's only one answer. You understand that."

"Why wouldn't I bullshit you to get down?" He said, with all the bravado he could muster.

Wayne smiled. "You can't bullshit me, son. Let me explain something to you about how power works in the City, because I think you may be under some . . . misapprehensions. There is power like Canada and Kraatjes and the mayor have—the power to muster the City's official forces; there's the power that men like Svinblad have—the power to buy anything that has a price; and then there's the power *I* have—because I'm smart, because I know things, because I keep my hand in everything, because I am not afraid to wield my power. Do you understand? I have my hand in everything, but I always have an angle. That's something that you need to learn to do. Zwieg, Svinblad, whoever—they think they use me; but I use them. I am the only one with the big picture, and that is power."

Dorman looked to Albertsson, who seemed to be enjoying this, getting excited.

"Okay. What's the big picture? Where do I fit?"

Wayne laughed. "Where do you fit? An arrangement. Svinblad wants to pay you to look out for his interests and you will do that, but you will also work for me—pass me information. You see, I have my hand in *this*, too. I make the payments—I'm the bagman. Svinblad pays you, and you work for both of us. Your assistance is about to be of even greater value."

Dorman was sweating hard. He believed Wayne when he said that he couldn't be bullshitted. The power dynamic here was not in his favor, and at this moment he did not see how he was going to be able to talk himself off this building alive.

The searchlight swept again, and while they were momentarily blinded, Dorman jumped off the platform onto a girder, jogging away in a crouch as fast as he dared. He heard shots fired behind him and kept moving in the dark, the frame of the building discernable as black lines against the background of the City's lights. He heard more pops behind him as he came to a point where girders intersected with a beam coming down from above. He edged around as the searchlight swept across again. A bullet pinged off steel somewhere very near. He looked back toward where the two men still stood on the platform. They seemed to be talking, the wind carrying their words toward him, but too faint to make out.

He looked out over the City, the lights brilliant and clear and almost all below him. *Searchlight*. Wayne and Albertsson were still on the platform. They were in a difficult situation, Dorman knew. They couldn't afford to wait him out. In seven hours or so the first workmen would begin to show up on site. Then it would be over. But he doubted that they were eager to venture out on the girders. Not many people would do it in the best of conditions—but in the dark, the wind, it would take some nerve. Or desperation.

"Mr. Dorman," Wayne yelled from the platform. "I expect that your leaving us is your answer to our offer of employment."

Dorman kept quiet. He waited for the searchlight. It would be helpful if he could find a way either down or up a floor. Then he would most likely be able to hide. He got a moment of illumination, but saw nothing. This building was big. He probably couldn't see everything from where he stood.

He turned back to the platform. Albertsson seemed to be edging out onto the girder that led in his direction. He moved with awful slowness. He must have been terrified.

Wayne was still shouting at him. "You asked why we brought you up here, and I alluded to a surprise best witnessed from this vantage. It'll be quite a show, Mr. Dorman, regardless of whether or not you choose to accept our invitation."

89

THIS IS THE WAY THEY HAD TO PLAY IT, DORMAN THOUGHT. LEAVE ONE man on the platform to prevent him from doubling back, and take the lift down. Wayne's friend would get faster, he thought, either because he'd get used to walking the girder, or he'd realize that his only chance was to get Dorman, at which point he might be willing to risk the fall.

Searchlight.

Wayne continued to taunt from the platform. "You've done an admirable job in many ways. From everything that I've heard, you've stayed disciplined, not allowed your many disputes to become personal, never sought individual recognition. That's why we would welcome you to our cause. You are discreet. Are you listening to me, Mr. Dorman?"

The searchlight again swung across the steel skeleton. Dorman stayed quiet, watched Albertsson make his slow progress.

"Mr. Dorman?" Wayne repeated.

Dorman walked quickly down a girder parallel to the platform, getting some more distance between him and Albertsson. The searchlight hit him, he ducked, didn't hear a gunshot. The brief moment of illumination might have allowed Wayne to locate him. The next sweep and he'd shoot. Dorman moved quickly to the next intersection and stepped around the vertical girder for cover. The searchlight flashed by, but he was shielded from the platform.

When it had passed, he stole a look around the girder to find Albertsson approaching the first intersection. Dorman leaned back against the vertical support, taking a moment to calm himself and listen to Wayne rant.

"Do you ever doubt what you're doing, Mr. Dorman? Are you so convinced of your own righteousness that you could not be swayed otherwise?"

Wayne seemed to wait for a response as the searchlight swept through.

"Nothing to say?"

Dorman saw Albertsson's silhouette moving across the beam toward him, steadier now and faster. Dorman jogged across a girder leading away from the platform, the vertical girder shielding him from Wayne. He was less concerned with Albertsson out on the beams. Between the trouble with balance and the brief intervals of light, Albertsson would need time to ready himself, and be close to have a chance to hit him.

He no longer heard Wayne, and though he was further away, he would surely hear *something* if the guy was still yelling. He looked back to the platform and saw lights descending then stopping. The lift. Wayne was one floor below. The lift was inaccessible now unless he could find a ladder down. He paused for a moment, thinking this over.

Searchlight. A bullet pinged off the bottom of his girder. Wayne had an angle now. How many rounds would he have? Would he have another clip? It didn't make sense to doubt it. Dorman needed to move further away from the platform and from where Wayne was perched below it. He walked quickly along the girder. Another search-

light, another ping off the steel underside. He was putting some distance between himself and Albertsson but needed more distance to
make Wayne's angle more difficult. He couldn't imagine Wayne walking out on the beams.

Two searchlights passed without the sound of a gunshot or a ricocheting bullet. Maybe he was conserving ammunition. Dorman kept
moving until he reached the far edge of the building. He'd lost track
of Albertsson, somewhere back behind him. He sat with his back to
a vertical girder, looked for a silhouette. He scanned systematically,
left to right. The searchlight swung through when he was halfway
across. He didn't see Albertsson. He might be resting. He might have
fallen. Dorman's chest tightened with the uncertainty.

Dorman let the searchlight illuminate the scene a couple more
times, trying to locate a ladder up or down. There must be a way to
get between floors other than the lift. It was impossible to see, though.
The light was too quick. He thought it would be safer to keep moving,
so he walked along the outermost girder, heading toward the corner.
The Municipal Tower was to his immediate right—nothing between
him and it at this height. The Tower seemed to pull him slightly in its
direction, as if through gravity. He felt his balance become less steady,
and shortened his steps.

Still no sign of Albertsson.

He stopped again, one intersection from the corner. The corner
seemed dangerous, as if it would pen him in too much. He walked in
the opposite direction. The searchlight swung around again, and Dorman felt himself tense. He'd caught something in the periphery. He
froze, not sure where to look. Above, it was nearly pitch black, just
the blinking of the red warning lights. The searchlight swung through
again, and he saw someone—it must have been Albertsson—on the
next level up, getting closer, about a hundred feet away. The light
swept past and Dorman could see nothing. He knew, though, that he
was visible to Albertsson, silhouetted against the city lights.

Dorman moved as fast as he dared toward Albertsson. He needed
to get under his girder, to avoid giving him an angle for a shot.

Searchlight. Two shots from close range. He ducked reflexively,
almost lost his balance. He scrambled forward, heard the ping of a

bullet ricocheting off the girder behind him. Then he heard a loud noise coming from below in the near distance, and turned to see a red ball of fire bursting skyward from the base of the Municipal Tower. The building structure shook. Dorman saw the searchlight jerk so that it shone straight up, and then it went out. So, he thought vaguely, that's where the Kaiser Street explosives ended up. After the explosion, the City seemed unnaturally quiet—only the sound of rubble falling in the distance, and, seconds later, sirens from all directions. The Tower remained standing, but smoke was billowing from a gaping hole in its side.

He kept moving to get under the girder, but he felt a punch in his arm, knocking him backward, his sleeve suddenly wet with blood. The next one found his leg above the knee. He took a step back to steady himself, found nothing but air.

EPILOGUE

90

FRINGS STOOD OFF TO THE SIDE OF THE CROWD AT THE OPENING OF AN exhibit held to memorialize Ben Linsky, which had been created by a cadre of young artists. The younger faction of the crowd—which was the vast majority of the hundred or so attendees—wore white. Frings wore a houndstooth jacket and brown pants.

The exhibition, he thought, was actually pretty dire. The idea had been to ask young artists to respond to different poems that Linsky had written, but the connections between the poems and the work—displayed side by side—were forced and unenlightening. Both the poems and the art suffered.

Ironically, Wendy Otis, whom Linsky had so harshly criticized, had created the most interesting piece of work. She had enlarged and combined a half-dozen photographs of a section of the City dominated by tall office buildings, and transformed the image through collage and paint. The sky was made of dollar bills; tiny, identical men in gray suits and hats had been painted entering and leaving office buildings in a seemingly endless single file, like lemmings. The colors of the buildings were muted and somehow flattened, exaggerating the sense of sharp angles and rigid lines. In the top right corner were pasted three typewritten strips of paper, each with a line from one of Linsky's poems:

> *You can be employed in any system*
> *If you are convinced*
> *That it doesn't exist*

Rappaport, the old art critic, was there, and he wandered over to Frings.

"Frank, you must have the inside scoop, why have they not arrested anyone yet in the Tower bombing? Surely they won't get away with it?"

Frings smiled weakly. "They're closing in, from what I hear at the paper."

"But they would say that, wouldn't they? They can hardly say, 'we're flummoxed.'"

"No, I guess they can't." But Frings knew that Zwieg would eventually name names to save his own skin. It was just a matter of time.

"And the Tower still stands—a triumph of modern engineering. I was thinking that I might—"

Frings was saved from having to respond by the flickering of the lights, announcing the imminent start of the main event. Rappaport went off to find Wendy Otis, and Frings followed the crowd through a large white-walled room that held only one work: a huge enlargement of a film still showing Simon Ledley, sitting in a chair, his face blank. You could, Frings thought, project any emotion that you wanted onto that expression, but knowing what he knew of that night, he felt certain that behind Ledley's opaque stare was a feeling of profound dread.

The crowd filtered through a second door into a long, narrow hall where folding chairs had been set up in rows facing the far wall. Frings sat toward the middle of the room. He saw Joss Eastgate take a seat next to a young man with artfully tousled hair. At the front of the room he saw Andy Macheda speaking with two men wearing white button-downs and heavy-framed glasses. Macheda, a drink in one hand, a cigarette in the other, gestured broadly, laughing, smiling, a different man than the one Frings had seen in the Kesh and in Ledley's basement lab.

Announcements were made, the gallery owner thanking all manner of people, then giving a breathless introduction that Macheda had the grace to find embarrassing. When his turn came, Macheda spoke quickly, reading prepared remarks, slurring his words a little, his eyes tearing, talking about what an influence Ben Linsky had been on his art, and so on and so on. At the end he set down his piece of paper.

"This film is dedicated to Andre LaValle and Paul DeBerg, and to all the others who have sacrificed in the battle to preserve some semblance of humanity in our society. But, mostly, this film is dedicated to my friend Sol Elia, who is in prison now, awaiting trial for crimes that he has committed. I hope that this film helps in some way explain his actions."

He stepped aside, the lights dimmed, the projector rolled. On the screen, Simon Ledley sat in a chair, a stack of papers on his lap. His speech was stilted, strained.

"My name is Dr. Simon Ledley. In 1959 and 1960, I conducted an experiment at the Tech using young men selected from our student body. What follows are excerpts from transcripts of interviews conducted during the course of this experiment. During the interviews the subjects were under the influence of lysergic acid diethylamide. Interview number one. . ."

91

THE STATION WAS NEVER REALLY EMPTY, BUT IT WAS LATE, NEARING TWO in the morning, and the cops who were there were occupied with drunks, whores, and the other upstanding citizens that had come to the attention of the law that night. Grip sat at his desk in the empty detectives' room, trying to clear out paperwork, abandoning hopeless cases with a signature. The room was dim, most lights off. His lamp was on, illuminating his desk like a stage prop.

Grip heard the door open but kept his head down. He wanted to finish his work, get the hell out of there. He had no interest in talking with whoever had just come in. Someone dragged a chair across the floor toward him, deliberately making noise. Grip reluctantly looked up. Albertsson, wearing his uniform, sat on the other side of the desk.

"Detective"—Albertsson said—"you've been scarce, people are worried."

"Yeah? What about?"

"You."

Grip, in truth, had been waiting for this. He'd been avoiding Crippen's, hadn't seen Wayne in the two weeks since the Municipal Tower had been bombed. It was the kind of thing that *would* make Wayne nervous. "I'm fine."

"Yeah, well, I don't think that's what they're worried about."

Grip knew that. "I can't help you, then."

Albertsson gave him a long, hard stare. "You sure?"

Grip nodded.

THE NEXT MORNING, GRIP LOOKED OUT THE WINDOW OF HIS APARTMENT and saw Ed Wayne across the street, wearing a military-issue winter coat, a fur hat pulled low over his ears. Wayne stood in the doorway of a German bar—not yet open for the day—staying out of the wind. It was cold outside—frost had formed along the edges of Grip's window.

Grip was happy to make him wait, taking a long shower, frying an egg for breakfast. He glanced out every few minutes to see if Wayne was still there; but he knew the stubborn bastard wouldn't leave. The guy wouldn't be driven away by the cold or by boredom. He wondered if Wayne was carrying a gun, decided that he probably was.

He took the stairs down two floors to the lobby, thinking about the next few minutes. He had spent years with Wayne, doing the dirty work in the struggle with the City's communists. Others had come and gone or shown that they didn't have the stomach for the unpleasant side of things. But Wayne had been a constant—the unpleasant side seemed to be his only side. Things had changed, though, with the bombing of the Municipal Tower and Phil Dorman's death. Neither of these had been in the service of anticommunism. That had been the result of wild, imagined conspiracies, and Grip didn't like it, both for the senseless destruction and for the way it made the cause—his cause—seem less serious, promoted by lunatics. Wayne had taken everything much too far.

Grip left his building, saw Wayne spot him. Wayne walked across the street, not paying attention to the traffic, forcing a car to brake hard to avoid hitting him.

"Tor."

Grip waited until Wayne had made it across the street.

"Tor, we've missed you," Wayne said with mock sincerity. "I've been lonely."

Grip walked, forcing Wayne to speed up a little to catch him.

"What's going on in your head?" Wayne said. "I'm sensing that you've drifted from the fold, that you are not the contented sheep that you once were."

Grip shrugged. "I'm keeping some distance for a while."

"I'm not sure that we're comfortable with that."

"We?"

"Me. Is there a problem? Because I'm trying to figure out where your mind is at right now. Burning Zwieg, sure, I get it. You fucked up our plans a little, but you couldn't have known. It would have been perfect for Kollectiv 61 to be blamed for the Tower, but not crucial. Zwieg thought he could take down Kraatjes if people thought that Kraatjes had been secretly supporting the people who bombed the Tower. But that was a fucking pipe dream. Too much at once."

Grip stopped, forcing Wayne to stop as well. He looked up into the taller man's small, mean eyes. "You've gone over the edge, Ed. The Tower. Phil Dorman's dead, and your fingerprints are all over it. That little puke Fache couldn't find me fast enough to let me know that he'd pointed you out to Dorman. The noose is tightening; you must know that. What do you think you have? Another day? Maybe two? Zwieg's not going to take the fall alone if there's anything in it for him. So, is there a problem? Yeah, I'd say so. You've lost it."

Wayne laughed. "You've gone soft, have you? The Municipal Tower was a goddamn triumph, Tor."

"A triumph? It's still standing, Ed. You put a hole in it, but you sure as hell didn't knock it down."

Wayne reddened. "You think too small. Your mind is not capable of seeing the bigger picture, the larger dangers. You think the New City Project will ever seem safe again?"

"And Dorman?"

"He had a choice. He made the wrong one."

"Yeah, well, I'm choosing to step away."

"That's a problem, then, Tor."

Grip started walking again. "Not for me, Ed."

Wayne wheeled on Grip. "You don't understand," he growled. "You have a big fucking problem."

Grip had his gun out, pushed the barrel against Wayne's forehead.

Wayne laughed. "You going to shoot me, Tor? Right here?"

Grip reached into Wayne's pocket, pulled out his gun, stuck it in his own pocket. He took a step back. "You know what this is?" He opened his jacket, unbuttoned the top of his shirt, revealing the wire sneaking down toward his pants. This was another task he was performing to placate Kraatjes, prove his loyalty.

"You son of a bitch," Wayne said, shaking his head, half-smiling. "You. . ."

Grip turned to watch two squad cars ease down the street, flashers on, sirens off.

"You know, Tor, that you're dead. There's nowhere you can hide. I've got guys on the Force, on the street, everywhere. *You're fucking dead.*"

Grip pursed his lips, cocked his head, looked at Wayne through narrow eyes. He was, Grip thought, probably right.

92

KRAATJES LEANED CASUALLY AGAINST THE GLASS WALL OF THE RESTAURANT of the Hotel Leopold II smoking a thin cigarette, the lights of the City spread out below him. Frings sipped a gin and tonic where he sat at a window-side table. The place was empty, save for a waiter who stood at a distance, attentive but discreet. The lights had been dimmed, the chairs tipped up against the tables. It was well past midnight, but Kraatjes seemed able to look fresh no matter the hour. He wore a fashionable suit, dark-framed glasses. His body was relaxed, but Frings saw the tightness in his jaw. He had struggled to bring Kraatjes here, eventually resorting to the only type of threat that seemed to bother him—exposure.

"You going to tell me what you want, Frank?"

"I don't know. An explanation, maybe, go from there?"

Kraatjes thought about this. "You're calling the shots."

"Why the experiments?"

"Which ones?"

"Vilnius Street. Ledley's studies with the kids."

Frings followed Kraatjes's gaze out the window. The City looked impossibly vast from here, a galaxy of lights, beautiful and distant. For a fleeting moment Frings thought about how far he would have to travel to escape this place, the neighborhoods he would need to traverse. That, in a way, was what the Crosstown was all about. Escape.

"Take a look at the size of this place," Kraatjes said, exhaling smoke against the glass. "I'm in charge of keeping the City under control, Frank. They say the cop's job is to protect, but it's to control, at least here. You can't protect everybody. It doesn't work. A stupid, infeasible goal. We've tried so many things over the years, different chiefs, but in the end all our efforts are overwhelmed by the sheer size—the *numbers*, numbers I can recite, but which are impossible to hold in your head. Too big.

"So when I was assistant chief, we started looking into ways we could control the City. Not the whole City, of course, but certain places, certain elements. Where do you have the least control, and how can this be remedied?

"The chief before me, he was adventurous, he'd take a look at anything. Simon Ledley, I've come to realize, has a nose for opportunity. He came to us, said he had this new drug that he thought might be useful for influencing behavior, controlling crowds, whatever—we jumped. Ledley had no idea, of course, what the hell it would do— these were early days—but he wanted money, and what he hinted at, it seemed like it was potentially the grail, the answer. We give him money, resources, tell him what we want, and he'll work an experiment. So we did Vilnius Street."

"Surely it didn't turn out the way you wanted."

Kraatjes exhaled through his teeth. "Of course not. It was a disaster. But we knew all along that it could hit or miss."

Frings saw a helicopter hovering at an altitude below them, training a spotlight where the west leg of the Municipal Tower was gashed open, revealing a cross section of floors and rubble. "Andre LaValle."

Kraatjes dragged on his cigarette, held the smoke while he thought. "Nothing connected with Vilnius Street went well. We could never figure out how LaValle found out about the experiment, our involvement, any of it. But he did. The way we treated—still treat—him is not consistent with what I value as an officer of the law. But I had no choice."

Kraatjes's tone was dispassionate, as if he were talking about a moderately bad day at the track.

"But you kept up with the experiments."

Kraatjes nodded. "Sure. Using the drug on a population didn't seem effective, or at least we didn't know how to do it correctly, so we turned to individuals, to see if it would be helpful in reorienting deviants, keeping them from further trouble."

"Another disaster."

Kraatjes conceded this wordlessly.

"So why were you paying Ben Linsky? Why are you paying Will Ebanks? Is this the same program?"

"Same idea. Look, drugs, coercion—nothing controls people like money and fear. When the chief was murdered, I realized that we had to do something about the radical scene. You couldn't just round them up, but you needed to keep them under wraps. We contacted Ebanks and Linsky because a lot of the radical kids looked up to them, and we figured out what combination of money and threats we could use to coerce each of them. We put them on the payroll, told them they didn't really have to change much, just keep things tamped down. Ebanks needed the money, and he didn't have to do anything different, just keep the kids taking the drugs, looking into themselves—keep them from from being too active in the real world. Linsky—we told him, don't let things get too belligerent; keep it obscure, aesthetic. He was a little harder. We had to threaten him with morals charges in addition to the cash. Once he started getting the cash, though, he decided he liked it. We had them reporting back to us about the goings on, but that was just to keep them involved, feel some pressure. It wasn't the point."

"Are there others?"

"In the radical scene? No."

Frings sighed. He'd subconsciously held out some hope that he hadn't fully understood Kraatjes's operation or misapprehended its goals. But now, hearing it from a man he'd respected, he felt a sudden bleakness.

"What now?"

Kraatjes seemed mildly surprised by the question. "Nothing's changed. The New City Project will get back on track. We'll remain vigilant with the radical scene."

"What about Canada?"

"What about him?"

"Weren't you running something on him, trying to get bribes on tape?"

Kraatjes shrugged. "It's nothing. Look, I'm not here to upset the applecart. Nathan Canada is ambitious and he's got the scruples of a cobra. I need to have something on him to protect myself if he goes after me the way he's gone after others. He needs to know that I have ammunition I can use against him. That's all it is."

"So the corruption . . ."

"Have you been listening, Frank?"

Frings nodded. Kraatjes wasn't worried about the corruption in the New City Project, the weight brought to bear on neighborhood bosses, the pervasive theft, the resale of stolen goods. These weren't threats to order—they were just crimes, and thus beneath Kraatjes's concern.

Frings set his drink on the table and walked to the elevators.

93

TWO NIGHTS LATER, FRINGS WAS BACK AT THE HOTEL LEOPOLD II. THE occasion was a reception to unveil and celebrate the additions to the New City Project that were being proposed to the City Council, in what seemed a fait accompli in the wake of the Municipal Tower bombing. The dining tables had mostly been removed, creating space for people to mingle and, in the center of the floor, for a scale model of the City. A jazz band played off to the side, the music a little louder and rowdier than what was generally played during the dinner service.

There was press here, but that was not why Frings had been invited. Nathan Canada had personally called to make sure that he'd be there. It was an opportunity, Frings thought, for Canada to gloat.

He was barely through the door when Canada walked over to him, cigarette clasped between two fingers. Canada was in a rare good mood and they exchanged small talk for a few moments. He wanted to show Frings the model, with the proposed additions. But Frings wanted to broach something first, while he had Canada's ear.

"I noticed there was no memorial or anything for Phil Dorman."

"We sent him home to be buried by his family."

"But no acknowledgment here?"

Canada seemed genuinely confused. "Why would we do something like that? He was a worker. It's a tragedy, of course." That seemed to be as much as he was going to say.

"Do you know what he was doing up on that building in the night?"

"We've looked into that—believe me—but we haven't made any headway. We may never know."

"Maybe," Frings said, and he saw that Canada heard something in his voice that put him on edge.

IT SEEMED TO FRINGS THAT CANADA WAS RELIEVED TO FIND A SMALL group of businessmen examining the City model. Frings could see his confidence return. The model was big, about ten feet square—little houses and roads with tiny cars placed on them, green parks with trees not much taller than a thumbnail, the river rendered in blue paint. The Riverside Expressway, Canada explained to the assembled group, was going to be lengthened, following the river further south and east to a new bridge that would connect the City to what was now a fairly rural agricultural zone. Canada gestured to this area on the model, which was colored, Frings noticed, a shade of green very similar to that of dollar bills.

These tiny, historic towns would be bought up quickly, and bedroom communities would pop up in their stead. One of the things that would happen at this party, Frings knew, was that various businessmen would approach Canada with whatever bribes—or contributions—they were willing to make in order to have the chance to buy some of that land. And so the New City Project would roll on.

He recognized many of the faces in the room. If you had any doubts that the City was a plutocracy, Frings thought, an hour in this room would dispel them. Wealthy men with their beautiful, aloof wives talked in small groups. Frings saw the mayor sitting at one of the tables at the side of the room with a few of the older men. People stopped by to greet him, pay their respects. But the dynamic personality in the room was Canada, who moved through the crowd like a shark, people eager to talk with him but also wary. Nobody was here to do business with the mayor.

Frings saw Milledge, the Tech's president, speaking with Rolf Westermann, the lawyer. He saw councilors talking with the men who'd financed their elections. Panos had been invited, he knew, but his health was not great, nor was his desire to attend. Without Panos, in this room full of the people who constituted the Establishment, he had no real allies.

Eva Wise approached him, carrying two glasses of wine. Frings thanked her, kissed her on the cheek, and took one.

"I didn't expect to see you here, Frank." She wore a conservative dress and a matching felt hat, which made it look as if she'd walked into the wrong party, but the outfit lent her a gravitas that the more glamorous women in their cocktail dresses lacked.

"Nathan called me himself."

She pursed her lips. "Is he still trying to win you over?"

"I don't think so. He doesn't think he needs to."

"Maybe it's time to pick a new battle. You realize you could even take a break—travel, enjoy yourself. The City will be here when you get back."

Frings smiled weakly.

She nodded. "I guess not." She seemed to regard him with real affection. "It would be so nice to be on the same side again."

"I'd like that as well," he said, wondering whether there was anyone left on his side—what that side even was.

Past Eva's shoulder, he saw Canada and Gerald Svinblad walking

together in his direction. He nodded his head toward them, and Eva
sighed.

"Frank."

"It's okay. I'll talk to you soon."

"IT'S IRONIC," CANADA SAID, "THAT, FAR FROM CAUSING AN OBSTRUCTION
to the New City Project, this bombing has actually increased our support and allowed us to expand our goals."

Svinblad was listening with a smirk, sipping a gin and tonic.
Frings could see that he'd been drinking heavily, his eyes watery and
a little unfocused.

"People in this City," Canada continued, "don't like being fucked
with. You try to keep something from happening, they'll try ten times
as hard to make sure it happens."

Frings nodded. Canada was right, of course, though the Project's increased popularity had done nothing to lessen Frings's objections. In fact, the expansion of the project just made those
objections more urgent.

"Nothing to say to that?" Svinblad slurred.

Frings turned to Svinblad. If Svinblad hadn't been drunk, he might
have seen something in the calmness of Frings's eyes that would have
given him pause. But he *was* drunk, and he was cocky, and the
prospect of celebrating his good fortune in the face of someone who
stood for everything he hated made him drunker still. He didn't register anything.

"You didn't say anything when I saw you here the other night, either. You don't say a fucking word unless you're sitting behind your
typewriter. Am I right?"

In his peripheral vision, Frings could see that Canada was uncomfortable with Svinblad's demeanor.

"I'm glad that we ran into each other," Frings said. "I had a conversation with the chief of police today—do you know him?—and he
let me in on some information that I think you'd be interested in."

Svinblad looked back at him in inebriated confusion.

Frings looked to Canada—who wore an expression somewhere

between interest and concern—and then back to Svinblad.

"I'm sure that you've heard that they arrested a man named Ed Wayne in connection with the Tower bombing."

"Sure."

Frings could see that Canada was intently watching Svinblad now.

"You know Ed Wayne, right?" Frings asked.

"I don't believe that I do," Svinblad said, slowly. Frings could almost see Svinblad trying to will himself to sobriety.

"I think that you might. You see, Wayne has refused to talk about the bombing. But, he's not stupid. He knows that he needs some leverage, or he'll never see the outside of a prison again. And it turns out that there was another crime he was involved in on that very night. Are you following me?"

Svinblad stared at him, dully.

"I can't foresee the future, Gerry, but my sense is that people aren't going to be too pleased to hear that Ed Wayne, the gink behind the Tower bombing, did work for you. At the very least, I think it will prompt a look into your connection to the New City Project. Worst case, I think, is probably accessory to murder and then also corruption. What do you think? You must know that Wayne doesn't like the Project. That's why he bombed the Tower. If he knows that he can help himself and at the same time take down the Project . . . it doesn't get much better for him."

Svinblad had gone very pale. "I don't have anything to do with the bombs."

Frings shook his head. "I wouldn't think so. It would make no sense. If the Tower had come down, things would not have worked out this well. The rest of it, though . . . that's where you have a problem."

Canada looked at Frings. "What is this?"

"This," said Frings, "is what trouble looks like."

Canada laughed ruefully and shook his head. "Frank Frings. You don't know when to goddamn quit."

ACKNOWLEDGMENTS

Many thanks to my agent and friend Rob McQuilkin, who worked with me on early drafts of this book and then went out and found it the right home. Mark Krotov at Overlook Press provided great insight in matters large and small and was invaluable in helping me shape and focus the manuscript.

Thanks also to Jack Lamplough, Kait Heacock, Anthony Morais, Molly O'Laughlin, and Bernie Schleifer at Overlook Press and Derek Parsons at Lippincott Massie McQuilkin.

Thank you, as always, to my parents for their enthusiasm and support, and to my mom for her help with the late stages of the manuscript.

Finally, love and thanks to Sadie, Jake, and Deborah.